ORDINARY ANGELS

A Novel of Love and Loss
after World War Two

JOAN LA BLANC

Northampton House Press

Cover image is adapted from a painting by Tom Lovell originally published in Ladies' Home Journal © February 1944. The Meredith Corporation has no objection to the use of the material. With thanks.
ORDINARY ANGELS Copyright 2013 by J. H. La Blanc. All rights reserved. Fourth in a series of novels about Anna Donovan. Published by Northampton House Press. Ebook edition 2013, ISBN 978-1-937997-21-2. First trade paper edition, 2014, ISBN 978-1-937997-52-6.
Library of Congress control number, 2014947053.
9 8 7 6 5 4 3 2

ORDINARY ANGELS

PROLOGUE
December 16, 1945

The day after she came home from the war, Anna Donovan huddled in a front pew in St. Stephen's Episcopal Church in Portsmouth, New Hampshire, and tried to focus on her father's Advent sermon. Despite plenty of sleep the previous night, she was still rocking from endless hours on the trains that had brought her across the frozen continent. Even now, with her fiancé's hand wrapped around hers and her mother's ample girth radiating heat, she felt those miles in weary bones, in icy fingertips and toes. And most of all, in recollections of Mark on the platform at Oakland as the first train had pulled out. Four days now, she thought. Dear God, when would that image stop tormenting her?

Maybe when her body, accustomed to South Pacific heat, acclimated again to a New England winter? When she'd caught up on the rest she'd missed sitting up in packed day coaches? When she felt like a civilian again? Or when her heart, accustomed to Mark's presence, learned to enfold Jim's again?

She was barely aware the sermon had ended until the Reverend Thomas Cranmer Moss stepped down from the pulpit to make the announcements. His gaze shifted to her

and a smile lit his well-worn face. "In case anyone hasn't
noticed, we have a Navy nurse with us this morning." He
pointed. "Most of you know her. My daughter, Mrs. Anna
Donovan." His voice broke; he cleared his throat and went
on. "She's been on a hospital ship since last year. Just got
home yesterday."

Her mother's nudge brought her reluctantly to her feet.
With a tight smile, she turned so the congregation could
better appreciate her newly-pressed dress blue uniform.

"The chap with her is Doctor Jim Millett, her fiancé," her
father added. "They're going to be married. Right here. Next
Saturday. Four in the afternoon. And you're all invited."

Leaning on his cane, Jim also stood. A smattering of
applause rippled through the packed church. They both sat
again as Rev. Moss recognized an Army corporal newly
arrived from a war zone. He concluded with a prayer of
thanks for all military who'd returned safely. It was
extemporaneous, not a collect from the prayer book, so it
dragged on, almost as long as the mournful sixteenth-century
recessional. Even after the benediction, they were engulfed
in well-wishers for fully fifteen minutes.

When they finally came outside, Jim asked if she wanted
to walk down to her child's grave. Her heart clutched, but she
nodded and led him down the brick path to the cemetery. By
now most of the previous day's snow had turned to slush;
she brushed a chilly layer from atop the small cube with
Baby Boy Donovan—4 August 1943 chiseled into the marble.
For her, the gesture felt merely symbolic, though Jim seemed
more emotional than usual, squeezing her hand as they stood
there.

But it was lunch time, and her mother hated to be kept
waiting, so they straggled back to the rectory. And ate fried
Spam, Welsh rarebit and Waldorf salad in the sort of silence
that often follows a high-pitched family drama. Afterward,
she walked Jim to his car and told him not to worry about the
wedding details: she'd take care of everything; all he had to
do was show up. He said, "Easiest thing I'll ever do," leaned

toward her for a last kiss, then got in and started the engine.

Hugging herself in the cold wind, she watched him drive away until he turned the corner toward Route One. Suddenly deflated, she came back into the house and followed her parents' voices to the kitchen where her mother was washing and her father drying the lunch dishes. Yawning, she asked if anyone minded if she went up for a nap.

Of course they didn't. Not with her looking so peaked, so washed out, so thin. "We've got to get the roses back in your cheeks by Saturday," her mother said in her most serious tone.

Then, one arm over her shoulder, her father walked Anna to the foot of the stairs and told her if she ever wanted to talk about the war, he'd be delighted to listen. "And it'll just be between the two of us."

She promised she would, but not just yet. Then, as he'd done for as long as she could remember, he closed her against the clerical shirt with the silver pectoral cross and the jacket with his pipe in the chest pocket, patted her head and told her loved her better than anyone in the world.

She brushed her lips against his whiskery cheek, turned and plodded up the stairs. Even after she closed her door, she knew he was still standing there, gazing after her in a way that said more than words ever could. Her eyes stung, but no tears came, so she hung her uniform away, shrugged into her old pink chenille robe and stretched out on the bed.

She'd barely closed her eyes before she drifted off. Almost immediately, however, she jolted awake again. As if someone had called her name. Or a PA system had blasted out, Now hear this! Now hear this!

But it hadn't, and wouldn't ever again. Perhaps what had woken her, then, was this very absence of sound: the stillness of her childhood room, and downstairs, the muffled hush of her parents congratulating themselves on having a daughter who'd been to war, then come home safe and made them proud in front of the whole church. A fine girl, who'd survived losing a husband and a baby without so much as a whimper, then gone off to serve her country in a strange and dangerous part of the world. And was now about to marry an outstanding doctor with whom she'd soon be working to alleviate more suffering. What more could any parents want?

Subsumed in irony, she lay a few minutes longer. Until restlessness urged her from the bed to the one small suitcase still unpacked on the floor. Inside, she found her writing kit with the dog-eared notebook listing the addresses of all her friends on the ship. Including Mark's, at his family home in Charleston.

She had no idea what to write, but compelled by an urge to say something, she sat at her old desk, tested the pen on the blotter a moment, then wrote the date:

Dear Mark,

Well, here I am, still trying to believe I'm home again even after 24 hours! Jim met me in Boston, in the snow. Like homecoming in a movie. Anyway, I want you to know we're going to be married next Saturday. I expect Luke will be here, so I'm concerned he'll tell Jim about you and me. If he does I can only trust that Jim loves me enough to understand something I don't quite understand myself.

Maybe the war brought out weaknesses I didn't know I had, like needing comfort so much I ignored my commitment to Jim and my innate belief in morality. Now I feel haunted by what we jokingly referred to as our "debauchery". Of course we can take pride in having done our duty and been faithful to our mission. But that other part of ourselves...well, someday I'll tell Jim, because married people shouldn't have ugly secrets from each other. But not just yet. Not till I make my own peace with it.

I wish I could talk to you again, but maybe we can write now and then. You were such an important part of my life this past year, I hope we can stay in touch. Meanwhile, I'm trying to picture you back home, and wondering if you feel as disconnected from our shipboard experiences as I do. Funny, I never expected it to be this way. Jim says when I catch up on rest, I'll be as good as new. I hope that's what it is.

Guess that's all for now. I hope you're well, safe and happy with your family. I look forward to hearing from you, and wish you my very best always.
With love,
Anna.

Satisfied she'd expressed herself as well as possible in the situation, she folded the sheet into an envelope, wrote Ensign A. M. Donovan, USS *Compassion* AH-4, c/o FPO, San Francisco, Calif, and almost added FREE where the stamp would go. One more aspect of the life she'd completed. Like a thousand other small details that had no bearing on the present, this habit was still imbedded in her consciousness. Not quite as noticeable as shrapnel in the flesh, but enough to remind her she'd been part of a major something that had now ended.

When she replaced the pen in the writing kit, she noticed the menu from *Compassion*'s Christmas dinner, 1944. Almost a year since she'd stuck it there. Now in the low red light of a winter afternoon, with shadows stretching purple across the snow outside, she studied the cover picture of the ship and on the back, a group shot of officers. Touching each face with her fingertips, she named them all, even those she hadn't known except anecdotally and distantly, as well as those whose lives had intersected hers– in the wardroom and Nurses' Country and Receiving, on the wards and on liberty, at meetings and movies. And funerals on the fantail. Lots of funerals, more than she wanted to remember.

Like hers, their recollections would be newsreels of these routines, as well as more dramatic events. Like the Kamikaze attacks, the kissing mutiny, the Marine's suicide, Roosevelt's death, the loss of Indy, the VJ-day celebration, the foul air at Nagasaki, and the hesitant, disbelieving joy of returning war prisoners. And in the final frame, the glimpse of the ship at Oakland when they'd filed down the gangway for the last time.

So it wasn't only Mark's absence she grieved now, but that of a whole family of others, all of them part of that same something the past fourteen months. A multitude of brothers and sisters, including a few to whom she felt an even deeper bond, like Willi and Floyd. And one closer yet than any of these.

For a while longer, she sat on the edge of the bed holding the menu with all those faces staring back at her. Most, including her own, were smiling, though standing off at the edge of the group, Mark and Luke were merely solemn. As if they'd seen too much pain, too many devastated young bodies, too many tortured minds. And their faith had begun to waver. At least Mark's had.

Sighing, she returned the menu to the folder and lay back on the bed, all those black and white images whirling in her mind when she closed her eyes. Remnants of the sorrow they stirred soon coalesced into an awareness of loss, heavy as a boulder in her chest. The tears that followed stung like acid, but she was incapable of resisting them.

When they'd run their course, she felt drained and ready to sleep. Yet even as she drifted into it, another absence, insignificant in the larger scheme of things, began to gnaw at her. It kept on nagging until she flung herself from the bed again and dumped her sea bag on the braided rug. The shoes, hose and underwear, khaki shirts and slacks and nurses' whites that tumbled out were as disordered as her memories of wearing them. Digging deeper, her fingers finally touched the old Westclox alarm. Somewhere in the thousands of miles since she'd last wound it, it had stopped at ten after seven. She twisted the key in the back until it started ticking again, set the hands to 3:35, then placed it on the nightstand where it had stood before she'd taken it to Hope Island in 1943, and the next year, to the South Pacific, where, as the war wound down, it had lulled her to sleep in Cabin C-14. Several times during those months at sea it had crashed to the deck in rough weather, but, undaunted, had maintained its gentle, reassuring rhythm.

She'd long since stopped trusting the time it kept. But time was not what she wanted it for now. Rather, the full-circle sense that the hours it measured had returned her to her starting point. And would continue to do so– on her honeymoon, then in Jim's old Victorian in East Point, Maine, and wherever else the future led her.

Back in bed, eyes closed against the dimming day, she saw Mark's face again, and was hit by another lightning flash of pain. It soon faded, replaced by the more immediate memory of Jim at South Station, snow melting on his hat, smiling, holding out his hands as he closed the last space toward her. Welcoming her back into his life, with no idea of the changes he'd eventually discover in her. Ready to love her forever.

Or at least, as long as she let him.

CHAPTER ONE

Just after eight on the morning of her wedding day, Anna
was contemplating the mountain of French toast on her
plate when her father rushed in from his study. His wild-
eyed breathlessness suggested he'd just learned someone had
died. Yet she hadn't even heard the phone ring.

His voice was high-pitched and urgent. "On the wire,
Anna. Person-to-person from a Reverend Whitmore in
Charleston, South Carolina. Say, isn't he one of the
chaplains from your ship?"

Her heart thumped so loudly she was afraid he'd realize
the news had knocked her virtually senseless. "Oh, my," she
stammered. "I guess…well, he must want to offer good
wishes. I mean…I wrote him about the wedding. That must
be it."

Afraid the unsolicited explanation sounded defensive, she
was relieved her father didn't follow her to the study. Her
hands trembled as she grabbed the receiver, but the caller
was only an operator making sure she was Anna Donovan,
then, "Go ahead, please; your party's on the line."

At first there was only the crackle of static. Until the
familiar voice spoke through it: "Is…is that you, Anna?"

Her mouth was almost too dry to speak. "Mark?"

"Yep. Surprised?"

"Oh my goodness, of course. Especially today. But
why…?"

"Well, when I got your letter I took a chance you'd be up
this early. Couldn't let you get married without my blessing,

could I?"

"Oh?" Shock kept her stupefied. "Oh. That's so kind." He didn't answer, so she blathered on. "Uh…How are you?"

"Fine. Just fine." He cleared his throat. "Nice to see my kids again. And my parents—well, the war aged them a lot."

"Mine too. Guess they worried about us." Wondering what to say next, she glanced around the book-lined walls and inhaled the dry fragrance of old paper. "Uh…and what about your wife? Have you… have you seen her?"

"Couple of times. She's…well, she wants to get back together. Maybe things didn't work out with that other guy. Don't know. She won't talk about it."

"Are you going to? I mean…you know…reconcile?"

"Probably. Be best for the children."

She faked enthusiasm. "Oh, I'm glad to hear it. And what about the ministry? I mean, you're not going to quit, are you?"

"No. The bishop says doubt's only natural after our war experiences. Thinks it's probably temporary. So I'm going to stay in the Navy awhile. At least till I get my bearings."

She hesitated, wrapping her fingers in the phone wire. "If I weren't getting married, I might stay in too." From the mantel, the brassy tinkle of the carriage clock striking the quarter hour returned her briefly to her father's study, the white-globed lamp on the desk, the crystal winter light at the window. And the momentous remainder of the day. "Will you let me know how things work out?"

"Sure. If you send me your new name and address."

"I will. Oh, by the way, Luke's here. At the base BOQ. We picked him up at the train yesterday. His mother's coming down for the wedding, so they'll finally meet. I can hardly wait."

"Hmm. You worried he'll say something to Jim about, uh…you know…us?"

"Oh, no! He wouldn't. Not today of all days. Unless…" She paused to let the horrifying notion subside. "Unless he speaks up when they ask: if any man can show just cause…"

"If he does, just call him a Sodomite. Tit for tat." Mark chuckled, pulling her back to his distant reality. "Meantime, I'll pray nothing spoils your day. Even though you're not marrying me."

In the mirror above the fireplace, her face was sour, more like that of a dried-up spinster than a bride. "Mark, that part of our lives is over. You need to put it behind you. I certainly have." Even her tone was that of a finger-shaking Puritan.

"Oh Anna, Anna," he sighed in a forlorn way she'd come to know so well on the ship.

"What?"

"Don't tell me you've forgotten. Only been ten days."

"No. Of course not. But today, well, I have so much else on my mind."

"Sorry. Shouldn't have brought it up. Anyway, promise you'll stay in touch."

Would she? If she was serious about forgetting him, should she? Still she said, "Certainly."

They rattled on another minute, exchanging the vague pleasantries of people who might say more if circumstances hadn't recently forced them into a state of belated virtue. Finally she said, "Mark, I have to go now. I have a hundred things to do before four o'clock. Anyway, thanks for calling. And…God bless you."

"You too, dear. Now, don't forget I love you. Okay?"

She inhaled deeply to calm herself, then said only, "Goodbye, Mark," and hung up, though her fingertips lingered on the phone.

After a few such steadying breaths, she felt composed enough to return to the kitchen. Her mother was folding laundry on the table; her father was watching the coffee pot on the range as if to hasten percolation. His gaze followed her as she sat again. "Well? Was that your friend from the ship?"

She made herself speak primly. "Yes, the Protestant chaplain. He wanted to tell me he's staying in the Navy. And wish me well. I mean Jim and me, of course."

"Oh, how lovely," her mother crooned.

"Well, he's a Methodist." Disgusted by the soggy breakfast remains, she pushed them around with her fork and wished she could dump them without incurring a waste-not, want-not lecture. "You know how they are."

"But person-to-person from South Carolina! He must think a lot of you."

Trying to appear nonchalant, she cut off a triangle of French toast, dragged it through congealed syrup and popped it into her mouth. So sickeningly sweet, she had to swig cold coffee to wash it down. She shoved the plate away. "Sorry. Too excited to eat."

Her mother scowled. "You'd better, though. If you don't, your stomach will growl through the whole ceremony."

"And if I do eat, I'll throw up. Don't worry, Mother. I'll have a sandwich later." She forced her mind back to wedding events; the prospect made her giddy, but didn't override the greater giddiness generated by Mark's voice. And the knowledge she was still in his heart.

God, what kind of sleazy bride-to-be entertained such notions?

In the background, her parents were squabbling about what time Luke wanted to be picked up. With her mother distracted, she scraped the plate into the colander, set it in the sink and listened to her complain about having more to do than any one person could possibly get done. Still, she went on folding underwear, socks, and Anna's Navy shirts, stiff from the hot air in the basement.

Impatience sharpened her tone. "Really, Mother. You don't need to bother with my wash. I'll take care of it later."

"You'll have enough to do without that." Mrs. Moss sighed and shook her head just enough to set her newly-permed silver curls trembling. A gesture Anna knew well; more articulate than words, it proclaimed the weary helplessness of the professional martyr.

* * *

Just after nine, she rode with her father to the base. Luke was waiting outside the old brick BOQ. Even huddled into a Navy topcoat in full sunlight, he was shivering in a blustery northwesterly that had scoured the sky clean overnight. As they pulled up, she climbed into the back seat so he could ride up front.

"Well, Father Salaunas," her father said in his hearty, greeting-parishioners voice. "Did you sleep well?"

"Like the dead, thanks. I can sleep anywhere."

"Guess you must mind the cold after so long in the tropics."

Luke slammed the door as they lurched away from the curb. "Don't know if it's the cold. Or nerves about meeting my mother."

Anna's mind flashed to the series of shipboard events that had convinced her he was the son Lorraine Cropper had given out for adoption as a newborn. His reluctance to believe this astonishing coincidence had eventually crumbled; and now, ten thousand miles and a year later, mother and son were about to be reunited.

Anna said, "They were leaving East Point at eight, so they'll probably be here by eleven. Maybe earlier. Alex Cropper's a speed demon."

"Alex. Remind me again who he is."

"Lorraine's husband's nephew. He was a B-17 pilot. Now he's home with his English war bride. They're getting ready to open the hotel on the island."

He shook his head with a dazed expression. "Take me a while to figure out who everybody is. Like the baby Lorraine's raising."

"You mean Johann. Okay. His mother was Alex's sister, Jean. She died right after he was born."

"That's right. His father was a German sailor. Shot trying to escape from prison camp, wasn't he?"

"Salt of the earth folks, every one of them," her father said as he steered the quivering Packard along the base's quiet streets. As if he could personally vouch for them all, even the deceased Wilhelm Himmelreich, who'd arrived in Maine on a U-boat to serve Hitler as a Nazi spy.

"Anyway, this year you'll be with your mother on your birthday," Anna piped up cheerfully. "Dad, did I tell you Luke was born on Christmas?"

He nodded. "Kind of a miracle, Anna's running into you so far from home. Wouldn't you say, Father?"

"Yes, sir, it really was." Luke lit a cigarette and slipped the match out the air vent as they approached the gate, then leaned over with his ID and saluted the Marine sentry who waved them through. "Seems odd being on a base again. Can't wait to get back to civilian life."

When her father said, "That reminds me," she tensed, intuiting his news. "Anna had a call from that other chaplain this morning. He's staying in the service, isn't he, dear?"

Luke turned quickly with the judgmental expression she knew well—lowered brows, darkening eyes, tightened lips. "Mark called you? Today, of all days?"

She smiled, resolved nothing he said would add to her guilt. "Sure. I wrote him about the wedding. Same as I did you and Willi and Floyd and Audrey. He wanted to send his good wishes."

With a disbelieving shake of the head, Luke pulled on his cigarette. And returned his stern gaze to the gray Maine landscape and the rusting iron bridge back to Portsmouth.

Her father slid him a quick glance. "Sure glad Anna had you two chaplains for company out there."

"Well, we certainly enjoyed her, I can tell you that." But even if he'd added, "Whitmore enjoyed her a hell of lot more than I did," she knew her high-minded, virtue-seeking father would hear nothing but the implicit good will of another clergyman. Luke's attitude, however, would probably not fly over Jim's head quite so easily.

Oh Jesus, she prayed. Please don't let him ruin this day.

Back at the rectory, her mother was in a dither because the cake was still in the oven, the florist was delivering the flowers, Ladies' Guild women were bringing covered dishes for the reception, and soon the folks from Maine would show up, all expecting coffee. "At least we won't have that orphaned toddler underfoot," she murmured.

Anna said, "Don't worry, Mother. I'll meet the florist at the church, and check on the food. Luke's volunteered to help."

The small, plump body sagged with relief. "When do you expect Jim?"

"Just before the ceremony. But don't worry; we won't see each other beforehand."

"Oh, dear, I hope not. I'd hate for anything to spoil your big day."

With more certainty than she felt, Anna said, "Nothing will, Mother."

Then, trailed by Luke, she hurried across the snow-patched lawn to the parish house. A gaggle of coifed, corseted ladies were bustling around setting tables and packing the refrigerator with Cut-Rite-covered plates of deviled eggs, chicken salad sandwiches, three-bean salad and tomato aspic. One woman took Luke for the groom and blushed furiously when he explained that no, he was just a friend, and a Roman priest...not really marriage material. Another was upset that the cake wasn't ready yet. And every single one asked if Anna was nervous.

Each time she laughed, and said, "I went through so much in the war, I'll never be nervous about anything ever again."

The depth of that lie quivered within her as she led Luke into the church. Yet except for this inner turbulence, all was serene: the hanging lights glowed gold; the sexton was vacuuming the red-carpeted aisles, and two graying ladies were setting up communion on the white brocade altar hangings.

Luke glanced around at stone arches and pillars, stained glass windows, newly-polished altar brass, communion rail, kneelers at the pews. "Anna, would you believe I've never been in a Protestant church before? Except Navy chapels.

This is as grand as a cathedral."

"Some Episcopal churches are so high you can't tell them from Catholic. With statues and crucifixes and holy water and incense and stations of the cross, and all that." Still vibrating with nerves, she slid into a front pew. When he eased in beside her, picked up a prayer book and began leafing through it, she tensed, sure he was about to mention Mark. The specter of his potential threat clutched her like a heart attack waiting to strike.

Yet when he said, "Tell me something, Anna. On the phone this morning, did Whitmore try to talk you out of marrying Jim and running off with him?" she felt a strange sense of relief.

Nonetheless, she forced herself to glare. "Don't be silly. That part of our lives is over. He's reconciling with his wife."

He sniffed. "Told Jim about him yet?"

"Not yet. But I will. Husbands and wives can't have secrets."

His smile was sardonic. "You know, Lorraine thinks that man hung the moon. Hate to think you wouldn't be honest with him."

She huffed, "Oh, for goodness sake, Luke, you needn't worry about us, today of all days. Or are you just trying to keep your mind off meeting your mother?"

The slow grin softened both his face and her fear. "Well, maybe. I mean, what if she doesn't like me? Or her husband doesn't? Tomorrow, I'm going back to Maine with them and check out an idea I got when she told me there's no Catholic church on the island. See, I could get a parish in Baltimore, but if this diocese can support a mission, I'd rather be here. But first I'd better find out if she and her husband would want me around."

What if, she wondered, he ended up living on Hope Island, seeing her and Jim every week, and insidiously but incessantly hinting at the nasty secret he might divulge? Suddenly the day's golden promise seemed to dull to tarnished brass. Before anxiety could darken it further, she spotted the florist with buckets of calla lilies and baby's breath. Motioning Luke to follow, she carried vases to the parish house, then hurried back to the rectory.

Out front, a salt-streaked Oldsmobile with Maine plates was parked behind her father's Packard. The courthouse clock had just struck eleven when they came into the kitchen, sweet now with the scent of browning pound cake. Her mother wasn't in sight, though her apron was tossed on a chair. When Anna heard her perky greeting blending with visitors' voices in the parlor, she realized Mrs. Rector was welcoming the Hope Island visitors. Including Luke's mother.

"Okay, Luke," Anna whispered. "Ready?"

He blinked, tightened his lips. "Guess so."

"Come on, then. I'll introduce you."

The parlor was just a few steps up the hall. There, perched on the burgundy mohair chairs and sofa with crocheted antimacassars were both her parents as well as Lorraine, Cleve, Alex Cropper and a delicate blonde with a complexion so pale, so perfect she could have posed for a Yardley's Old English Lavender Soap ad. Everyone was smiling stiffly and sitting bolt upright. Anna was about to introduce Luke when Lorraine jumped up and engulfed her in a perfumed embrace. Behind her, Cleve's gap-toothed smile beamed his own greetings.

Turned loose, Anna took Lorraine's hand and led her to the priest in naval officer's dress blues. Though she'd rehearsed this moment a hundred times, emotion made her voice unsteady: "Lorraine, this is Luke Salaunas. Father Luke, that is."

For a split second, the older woman stared up with brimming eyes and trembling lips. Then she opened her arms and whispered, "Come here, son. So's I can finally give you a good big hug. Been waiting forever to do that."

He seemed reserved and cautious as she embraced him, but kept smiling through a bedlam of other hugs, handshakes and introductions. At some point Anna met Alex's wife Pamela, the nurse he'd met in an English hospital after his second bomber had been shot down. A joyous moment, this intersection of chance meetings in different parts of the world. Its details were so subsumed in confusion, if anyone said anything even remotely embarrassing, Anna never noticed.

Finally Cleve suggested they check in at the inn in town, get some lunch, and give Lorraine and Luke time alone. Reverend Moss volunteered to lead them, because, "It's one of those historic places you'll drive right by if you miss the sign. Coffee shop's not bad, though, if you want a bite of lunch."

After the others had finally straggled out to the cars, Anna followed her mother back to the kitchen. Sniffing, Mrs. Moss observed that the cake smelled too brown. "Well, it'll just have to do." Grim-faced, she removed the tube pan from the oven and inverted it on a wire rack. "Too bad I didn't have time to make a proper one. One we could put a bride and groom on. Now, dear. Would you open that can of Crisco in the pantry? Hate to use common shortening, but it's the only way to get a really white icing. Unless you use oleo. That seems so cheap, though. Even worse than lard."

While her mother creamed Crisco in the Mixmaster, Anna washed up a sink full of baking pans and bowls, then made a ham sandwich heavy with mustard, washed it down with milk, and tried to remember what she still needed to do before the wedding. But when her mother began talking about what a sweet young man Luke was, her mind slid to the secrets she and he cosseted about each other. Would they be unique among those at the wedding? Or were secrets a component of everyone's life? If so, what did Jim have to balance hers? Once she'd suspected he'd fallen for the nurse he'd hired while she was away. Today that notion seemed as ridiculous as expecting Santa and Mrs. Claus to show up at the wedding.

* * *

Just as Mrs. Moss was urging Anna to leave for the beauty parlor, Margie Halvorsen drove up in a little blue Morris Minor borrowed from her current boyfriend, a Mass General Neuro-Psych resident. "Just as well he couldn't come today," she said. "He's a regular Clark Gable, but he drinks like a fish."

"Good. Then you can drive her to the beauty parlor," Mrs. Moss said. "Make sure she doesn't let Sallye do anything extreme to her hair. Sometimes her ideas are just…well, cheap."

Driving downtown, Margie expressed her own notions. "Someday I'm going to talk you into going really blonde"— she patted her own Jean Harlow coiffure—"but there's no time today. We'll just have to settle for a gold rinse."

When Sallye had followed Margie's instructions about the cut and the rinse and the soft waves, she settled Anna under the dryer with a *Silver Screen* from the previous July. Photos of uniformed stars at USO canteens swept her back to the war, to a reality far grittier than anything Hollywood would ever portray. To Guam, and the doomed *Indianapolis,* and Nagasaki and Pearl Harbor. And of course, Mark. Her own private conflict. Her personal nemesis.

When they came back to the rectory, Mrs. Moss was in the kitchen squeezing a border of white icing roses around the snowy-frosted cake. She gasped when Anna pulled the bandana from her head. "My stars, child. What in the world have you done to your hair?"

She rolled her eyes. "Oh Mother, it's just a rinse."

"I think it's perfect, Mrs. Moss," Margie purred. "Adds nice highlights. She looks swell."

The older woman didn't say it looked cheap, but her pursed-lip expression did. "Well, go up and get your bath now so I can use the bathroom." Her nervous glance went to the wall clock. "Good Lord, two-thirty already. If I'm not at the church in an hour, who's going to light the candles and make sure the flowers are done right?"

"I'll take charge of everything here," Margie assured her. "Don't you worry about a thing."

The older woman sighed deeply. "I'll only stop worrying when they've left on the honeymoon."

When Anna came back to her room after the bath, Margie had laid out underwear, hose and the winter-white jersey dress, and was pawing through the vanity. "Good Lord, Anna? Is this all the makeup you have? Just Pond's and powder and rouge and two old lipsticks?"

"What else do I need?"

She shook her head and sank to the bed. "Well, at least your hair's glamorous. But from everything you've told me about Jim, he won't even notice."

"He'll notice." She slid a new lace-topped satin slip over her head.

"Hmm. And tonight you'll find out if I was right. If he's impotent, I mean."

"Oh that," she said airily. "Don't worry. I found out before I went into the Navy. And he's not. Not at all."

"Well, thank God for small favors! Oh, I know what you said. But it's one thing to say it doesn't matter, but it's something else to live without proper loving. By the way, where's that priest from the ship? Isn't he here to meet his mother?"

"They're down at the Colonial Inn. You'll see him at the wedding. Remember though, he's Catholic, so no flirting."

She giggled. "He's still a man, isn't he?"

Anna decided she didn't need to know he was homosexual, then wriggled and squeezed her hips into the rubber girdle her mother wanted her to wear, to avoid jiggling, which, of course, would be cheap. It cut into her flesh like some medieval instrument of torture, so she yanked it off and substituted an old garter belt. Pulling on the new nylons, however, despite Margie's constant chatter, she was captured by the recollection of Mark's hands unfastening her white nurse's hose on the bunk in his stateroom. Horrified, she closed her eyes and silently prayed *Jesus, Jesus...Take away this cross. Or carry it for me till another day. Please?*

By the time Mrs. Moss made an appearance in her gray silk tea dress, Margie had zipped Anna into the white jersey and fastened Jim's pearls at the neck. With pearl earrings and a white satin pillbox perched atop her new blondness, she turned for inspection. Her mother pronounced her appearance "sweet", much more so than when she'd married Dan.

"This whole wedding's going to be more bridal," Margie said. "Except...except the other was so romantic, what with Dan in uniform, and the war just about to start. Of course, none of us knew it'd be the very next day."

Mrs. Moss wrinkled her nose. "I had nothing against Dan, rest his soul, but thank God, Jim's Episcopalian." Then, with a covert smile at her own mirrored image, she announced she was off to the church. "Now, you girls wait another fifteen minutes, then come in the back way so you don't run into Jim." Her sensible low-heeled pumps clattered down the steps.

From the window Anna watched cars parking in front of the big stone church, well-dressed people hurrying toward it in the pale pink late afternoon before the sky darkens to purple and the street lights come on. Winter twilight in New England had always felt lonely, even when her life was full. Perhaps it seemed less so in warmer climes, like Charleston. Or would Mark's solitude be more acute today than when they'd parted at the train in Oakland? She wanted this to be so; wanted him to feel scraped raw by the knowledge she was now finally beyond his grasp. To ache in every cell of his being.

Mainly she wanted him to feel what she had when she'd learned she wasn't the only nurse he'd enjoyed out there in the Pacific.

Swallowing old bitterness, she smiled at Margie in her rose wool suit, frothy white blouse and neat little cap wreathed in satin ribbons. "Ready?"

"Sure. But aren't we supposed to carry bouquets?"

Anna stared in horror. "Oh my goodness. I never thought of that. What'll we do?"

She gave a *what's-it-matter?* shrug. "Just grab some flowers from the parish house. Don't worry, Anna. No one'll know the difference." She grinned, deepening her dimples. "Not even your mother."

Downstairs, the carriage clock pinged quarter to four as they shrugged into coats and left the house. The wind had dropped off and the sky was still pastel overhead, parish house lights yellow in the dusk, stained glass windows glowing from the church like a Christmas card scene. No one was in the parish hall, so they plucked strands of baby's breath from the table arrangements, then raced across the frozen lawn to the church.

A side door opened into a storage room where the muffled tones of the sanctuary organ were barely audible. Anna had left the music up to the organist, an elderly spinster who claimed this would be the two-hundred-and-seventy-seventh wedding in her long career. When Anna told Margie, they both began giggling. Contagious, it spread between them like wildfire in the wind. Even in high school, they'd had a reputation for inappropriate laughter. Anna had no idea what triggered Margie's now, but she suspected her own arose in that narrow territory between extreme joy and unspeakable sorrow.

Convulsed, they threw their coats over some folding chairs, then, hands clapped over their mouths, tiptoed to the vestibule. A few guests were still arriving, her father pacing in small circles, white brocade stole around his shoulders.

He hurried over, a sudden smile warming his face. "Time to go in, sweetheart. Jim and the best man are already up front." His voice shook as he offered his arm.

Gulping back a final giggle, Anna curled her hand into the crook of his elbow. The three of them waited at the entrance to the sanctuary until the last latecomers had been seated.

Then the organist struck the first familiar notes of the wedding march and everyone turned to look; Anna nudged Margie into motion and gripped her father's arm tighter. When the other girl was halfway up the aisle, they stepped out to the slow cadence of the music.

In front of the altar, Jim was standing with hands folded over his cane, and on his face, an expression of joyous solemnity. He wore a new blue suit and his hair was slicked down, and as Anna stepped toward him, a slow smile lit his eyes. Beside him stood a stooped and gangly fellow in the ill-fitting dress blues of a Navy lieutenant-commander. She hadn't met Tom Mullen yet, but Jim had known him since medical school and contracted with him to join the practice. He looked kindly but weary, as if he'd just run all the way from Providence.

When Jim's smile widened, the innocence on his face touched her. There was very little innocence left in her, but his eyes shone with it, with the absolute purity of his soul. In a way she wished he'd slept with his nurse while she'd been gone, but today she knew with total certainty that his commitment to her had been irreversible from the start. A stone wall of defense that shielded him from even recognizing temptation, let alone yielding to it.

His shining gaze sent tears into her eyes, hot and sudden. Nothing turned them off, neither a glimpse of Luke's faint scowl nor the miniscule fear that he might interrupt the ceremony.

By the time she reached the front, her throat ached, her nose was running and tears streaked her cheeks. All she could do was sniffle and maintain the smile so everyone would recognize them as tears of joy.

Then they were at the altar. Her father kissed her cheek, whispered, "I love you, sweetheart," tucked her hand into Jim's, and stepped up to assume his official duties. Her tears continued undiminished. Behind his glasses, Jim's eyes were full too, but his smile was incandescent.

As the familiar ceremony began, she felt the past slide

from her shoulders like a heavy cloak she no longer needed. Despite the lingering connection to Mark, she felt certain that though Jim wasn't her first love, he was the love of her life. And would be as long as that life endured, whether with him, or–God forbid–without him.

CHAPTER TWO

Two hours later, with only the makeshift bridal bouquet to toss before they could leave the reception, Anna went into the ladies' room to comb her wilting golden locks. Lorraine was already at the mirror, swiping on fuchsia lipstick the exact shade of her satin dress. A smile crinkled her mascara-ringed eyes. "Oh Anna," she crooned, "I know I told you before, but this is the best day of my life."

Studying the other woman's reflection, Anna noticed new white strands in the obsidian swirl of her pompadour. And for once, her perfume wasn't overpowering. Maybe being officially the mother of a priest had toned her down a bit. "I bet it is for Luke too."

Lorraine's face softened under a heavy layer of powder. "That sweet boy... any woman'd be proud to call him her son. Having him here now makes up for all the years I didn't know if he was alive or dead."

"Makes you think of that verse in the Old Testament, doesn't it? You know. The one about the Lord restoring the years the locusts have eaten?"

Her look was blank. "What?"

She'd forgotten Catholics didn't study the Bible as avidly as Protestants, if at all. "Ask Luke to explain."

"Oh? Well, sure. Because I want to know everything about him. Like, what he went through on the ship. What he's going to do now. Stay in the Navy? Or go back to Baltimore? Or what? But it's funny; he only wants to talk about my life, not his."

"Has he asked about his father yet?"

She nodded, well-plucked brows gathering in a frown. "But I'm scared to tell him, being you thought it might upset him his daddy was a priest too. What'll I do, Anna?"

"Well, even if he's upset, sooner or later he needs to know. Maybe not right now, but soon as you know each other better." Look who was talking—she who turned to stone at the mere idea of sharing her recent past with her new husband.

"But what if he hates me for it?"

Anna patted her hand. "Listen, Lorraine. The Lord wouldn't have led me to him way out there in the Pacific if he didn't want you to be together. No matter what."

"Oh Anna. I don't know. Some secrets are best taken to the grave."

"Nonsense," she said, as if she believed it.

When she left the ladies' room, Jim and Luke were deep in conversation at the head table. Fear buzzed past her like a wandering hornet. Until she reminded herself Luke was a man of God, anointed as surely as her father was. A thousand times more judgmental, sure, but not vindictive. Besides, she'd never sinned against him, only smashed his illusions of her purity. Perhaps he only considered her more fallen than other nurses in shipboard liaisons because she'd corrupted a clergyman, even one who'd long since been corrupted before she came into his life. If that was how Luke judged sin, what did it portend for his own mother?

Lorraine grabbed Anna's arm in the doorway; her eyes were soft as she gazed across the room. "Look at him, Anna. So handsome I can hardly stand it. Spit and image of his daddy. Pity he can't marry and give me grandbabies just like him."

The irony of her comment recalled what Mark had said about how Lorraine might react to learning this sainted son was a pederast. Except she wouldn't use that word. "Isn't it enough she's found him after so long?" he'd asked. "Does he have to be perfect too?"

As they approached the table, Luke jumped to his feet, slid one arm around Lorraine. "Anna, I was just telling Jim about the day you told me you knew this lady. Remember?"

"I think it shocked you as much as the stabbing. Gosh, that was scary." She turned to Lorraine. "See, I was right there when the patient attacked him, but I never saw it coming. Then I was afraid he might not live to hear my news. But the wounds weren't as bad as they looked at first. Thank God."

Lorraine's eyes shone with tears. "After I found out, I kept my fingers crossed the whole time. Till this morning, when we finally met. Yes, I'll thank God every day the rest of my life."

Luke bent down to kiss the top of her head. Then, arms linked, they wandered back to the Hope Island table, the personification of happily ever after. At least, Anna thought, as long as their mutual illusions remained intact.

Jim stared after them a moment, then leaned over and nuzzled her cheek. "How soon can we decently leave, dear? We've been married two hours now, and I've waited so damned long...."

She patted his hand and gave him a wifely smile. "Only a few more minutes."

Around them, aproned parish women were passing out wedding cake and collecting plates with traces of deviled egg and aspic mingled like melted sunset. At the next table, Tom Mullen huddled with Margie, while in the background, Anna's parents drifted around chatting with friends, smiling, occasionally even holding hands. They seemed happier than she'd ever seen them. Perhaps they'd finally stopped worrying about her. At least for the moment.

When Margie slipped into the chair beside her, Anna knew what she wanted even before she asked, "Going to throw the bouquet any time soon?"

"What's your hurry?"

"Oh, Tom wants to take me out to dinner after you leave." She smiled prettily, eyes full of the stars Anna had noticed whenever she set her sights on some new boyfriend, a long series of them, starting in ninth grade. If her latest was the best man, God help him. Of all the mismatched pairings she'd ever known, these two might be the worst.

"Tom? Really, Margie. He's hardly your type. After all, he's Jim's age, and a widower. And a Catholic!"

She nodded. "Oh, I know all that. But there's something about him...maybe his eyes. You can tell he's suffered when you look into them." Her sigh was deep, rich with drama. "Then there's Luke. Wow, what a dreamboat! Way too handsome to be a priest. You sure he's celibate?"

Anna's laugh was nervous. "How would I know?"

"Well, did he have a girlfriend on the ship?"

"Two of them. The head nurse and a man-hating Red Cross worker."

Margie's eyes narrowed. "Gee. I hope he's not queer."

Anna fluttered her fingers. "Does it matter if he is? Anyway, we need to leave. So I'll throw the bouquet right away. Get ready."

After she hurried away, Anna banged a spoon on her coffee cup. "Listen, girls," she called. "If you want to find a sweetheart, line up to catch the bouquet." Then, turning her back, she heaved the pathetic little wad of baby's breath over one shoulder. Someone squealed, and when she turned around, there was Margie clutching it like a holy relic. Two other high school friends rolled their eyes and stalked away.

"Okay, now we can go," she told Jim.

Slipping through the chattering crowd, they got their coats from the rack in the vestibule. Her father brought her suitcase and her mother tugged up her coat collar, then smoothed it down, as if to prove Anna still needed maternal attention. Outside, well-wishers tossed grains of rice into the icy wind, then scurried back into the warm parish house.

Jim's car was parked halfway down the block; by the time he got it started, they were shivering in the cold night. But after he'd pulled into the street, Anna slid across the seat and rested her head on his shoulder. "Alone at last," she murmured. "You've been very patient."

He chuckled. "Funny. The whole time you were gone, patience came easy. I guess because I had no choice. But this past week's been an eternity."

"Sorry, dear. If I hadn't been dead on my feet after I got home, I'd have come to your room that night. Like I did before I left last year. Remember?"

Stopping for a red light at Route One, he twisted his face to hers and managed a small, sideways kiss. "Anna, I remember everything about you. From the first moment we met."

The light turned green and he accelerated through the intersection in a burst of speed totally foreign to his usual staid and cautious driving style.

Built in 1874, the Wentworth was a weathered four-story shake-and-clapboard Victorian hotel at the mouth of the Piscataqua River outside Portsmouth. Its gingerbreaded porches, dormers and turrets gave it the wedding cake look so revered by nineteenth-century architects. Dan had taken her to dinner there during their courtship, which had made its long porch the perfect place to watch his sub leave the Navy Yard three days after Pearl Harbor. That afternoon, as the gray hull had merged with the even grayer Atlantic, she'd been chilled by more than winter wind. And gripped by a premonition that this cruise would lead to others of greater peril, and eventually the last, doomed one into the Sea of Japan.

Now the lobby seemed less grand than she remembered, cloaked in the genteel shabbiness of much of the country after four years of wartime neglect. Self-conscious in her bridal finery, she stood aside while Jim picked up the room key.

"Lucky you reserved early, Dr. Millett," said the clerk. "We're full up for Christmas this year, what with so many servicemen coming home."

Jim nodded toward her. "My wife got back from the South Pacific just last week. Nurse on a hospital ship."

"Oh my. If that's not something! Bet you could tell some stories, couldn't you, Mrs. Millett?"

She smiled, but her fingernails bit into her palms through the leather gloves.

Their room was on the second floor, reached by a shuddering elevator operated by the pimple-faced bellboy who'd carried her bag from the lobby. He gave her a furtive once-over, then asked, "Say, you two newlyweds?"

Jim's Down-East accent was dry as hardtack. "What makes you think that?"

"Well, this afternoon you checked in alone, and now, here you are with a missus. And she's got rice on her hat. Lots of honeymooners here these days. I know the signs." His face was smug. Reading *I know what you'll be doing later* in his shifting eyes, Anna averted her gaze.

Jim had already unpacked, but the boy hung around, turning on lights, closing curtains, explaining how the radio worked and reciting times of meals in the dining room. Jim let him run on a few minutes before he pulled a dollar bill from his wallet and nudged him toward the door. Leaning it closed, he said, "Good Lord, I thought he was going to move in with us."

She laughed, unaccountably nervous now that they were alone, then opened her suitcase and withdrew the lacy white nightgown her mother had bought, perhaps the better to pretend Jim and she were virgins. At least to each other. "Now," she said in a shaky voice. "Unless you want to use the bathroom first, I'll slip into something more comfortable. As they say in the movies."

"And I'll get out of the damned brace."

Instead, she tossed the gown to the desk chair. "Here. Let me help you."

"Thanks, dear, but you don't need to."

"And I don't need a white nightie either."

"Really, Anna. Helping a cripple with a brace isn't something a bride should do on her wedding night."

"Then pretend I'm just another nurse. Okay?"

He chuckled and shrugged out of his suit jacket. "All right. But close your eyes while I take off my trousers."

She rolled her eyes. "As if I haven't seen it all before."

"I know, but tonight's supposed to be special. Like our first time ever."

"Well, it'll be the first time I ever helped with your brace. That'll be special."

He draped the trousers over the chair back, then limped over to sit on the side of the bed. "Come here, then. I'll show you what to do."

She took off her dress and hung it away before she knelt in front of him. She'd seen the straps and steel rods that encased his leg before, but not at such close range. As she unbuckled and lifted the contraption from the withered flesh, her heart twisted in pity for the pain he'd endured as a child. And still did at the end of a busy day.

Tentatively, lightly, she ran her fingers over the shrunken thigh and calf muscles. Certainly not her first experience with a polio victim; in nursing school, pediatric wards were full of them. "Has anyone ever tried massage to help circulation in these muscles?"

He set his glasses on the night stand. "In the beginning, they tried everything. Hot packs, warm oil massages, hydrotherapy, electro-stimulation. But nothing did much good." He smiled grimly at his leg. "See, I'm still crippled."

Kneading the flaccid flesh, she said, "Maybe it'd be worth trying again. Might prevent those spasms you've mentioned."

"Couldn't hurt, I guess." His tone was laconic.

For a while, she focused solely on the damaged parts of his leg. But after a few minutes, feeling a certain devilishness rising, she let her fingertips wander under the hem of his shorts.

Sure enough, in no time at all, he gave her a wicked grin.

"Well, I must say. That really does help circulation. And not just in the leg."

She glanced up with wide, innocent eyes. "Oh, really?"

"Don't act so surprised. What'd you expect, half-dressed like that?"

With a come-hither smile, she moved closer so he could slide down the straps of her bra and slip, and kiss her with growing ardor. Finally, she pushed him back on the bed and climbed on, the way she'd invented the first night they'd been lovers, right before she'd left for the Navy.

He didn't protest. In fact, he didn't say an intelligible word for the minute or so they rocked the room.

But afterward, breathless, he murmured, "Well, that was nice, but not what I had in mind."

"Oh? What did you have in mind?"

"Something a little more reserved. You know. Fumbling around like proper newlyweds." His eyes crinkled in a smile. "As if we don't know what the hell we're doing."

"You mean, pretend it's all new?"

"Can you remember when it was?"

Lying beside him, she traced the lines of his face with her fingertips. "But Jim, it's new now. After all, it's been fifteen months since the last time."

"I mean before. When you married Dan."

Reluctant to revisit that old landscape, she said, "Well, it wasn't exactly new then either. See, after we got engaged, we tried it in my apartment a couple times. Hope that doesn't shock you."

"No, but I am surprised. Aren't preacher's daughters above reproach?"

" Oh, you mean, like doctors?"

"Huh! Doctors are wilder than anyone. Except me, of course. I've always been too dull."

Closing her eyes, she said quietly, "But didn't you tell me with your first wife it was all heat and no light? That doesn't sound dull."

He sighed, pulled her closer. "Please. Not tonight, dear.

Tonight's just you and me. The first lovers ever. So why don't you put on your new nightie, and then we'll pretend neither of us ever knew anyone else."

Since he'd invited Dan into their conversation earlier, she wondered why that pretense mattered now. But she didn't ask; tonight she wanted him to be pleased beyond the capacity to question anything about her, past or present. So she went into the bathroom, slid into the silky white gown and meticulously brushed her teeth, then her hair. She returned to the bed aware that the wall of her pretenses would have to be higher and stronger than his. Unless, of course, his secrets were as insidious as her own. With as much potential for torpedoing their life.

She doubted that if he had any, they even came close.

Snuggling into his arms again, she told herself such speculation had no place on the first night of a new marriage. He and she, here and now, were their only realities. Sanctified by the Episcopal Church and the State of New Hampshire, this passion nullified all previous ones. And restored them to a state of innocence like Adam and Eve's. At least before the apple episode.

CHAPTER THREE

It was still dark when, on the verge of wetting the bed, she crawled out of a miasma of sleep and staggered to the bathroom. Unable to find the light switch, she didn't notice the toilet seat was raised. The porcelain bowl might have been a cake of ice. Shaking with cold, she hurried back under the covers. Though she smelled steam and heard the radiator pinging, the warmth of the room didn't begin to thaw the Arctic chill gripping her.

She had no idea what time it was; the sky was inky, but a red glow smeared the horizon. For a moment she wondered if a torpedoed ship was burning out there. Until it came to her that the war had been over for four months. Still, the muffled thud of breakers slamming the rocks below the hotel recalled the bombardment of Iwo Jima before the invasion.

Seeking heat, she cuddled against Jim, face in the curve of his neck, one arm around his waist, legs entwined. A gale rattled the window panes; the old hotel trembled in the gusts. Much as the ship had whenever they'd run into rough weather. Once in a squall off Guam, she'd barely made it down the passageway to Mark's cabin. Intent on confronting him about his other love affairs, she hadn't given a thought to the possibility of capsizing. Oh damn; Mark again, even in her marriage bed with Jim.

She pulled the blankets higher; he stirred, breathing accelerating. When he reached under her nightgown, his hands were so cold she flinched. Between that and the remembered chill of the toilet seat, sex was the last thing on her mind. She let it happen anyway for its warming effect.

Afterward he said, "Is it my imagination, dear, or are you feverish?"

She barely managed to say, "Only with love," through a constriction in her throat that felt like steel wool.

He laid a cool palm on her forehead. "No, darling, it's more than that. Feel okay?"

"Jim, I'm fine. Just too much screwing, not enough sleep."

He laughed, swung his legs to the floor. "Still, wouldn't hurt to look you over, in case you're coming down with something." He reached for the phone on the nightstand, jiggled the hook, and asked for a bellboy.

"What're you going to do with a bellboy?"

"Send him to the car for my medical bag." Grabbing his cane, he limped into the bathroom. She stared at the blushing sky, and wondered if he was right. The last time she'd been even mildly ill had been in OCS, a cold so trivial she hadn't even gone to Sick Call. Nor had she had a sniffle the whole time on the ship, just a few bouts of seasickness and the occasional hangover. Nothing like this nasty whole-body sense of impending disease. Damn. Sick was no way to start married life.

Jim came out of the bathroom in scuffed slippers and a moth-eaten blue wool robe. "Don't get up, dear. Wouldn't want the lad to see you in that nightie."

When the knock came, he handed out his keys, told him where to find the bag. "And on the way back, would you bring a pot of tea? And some toast, please."

Perching on the edge of the bed, he touched her neck in a manner more professional than loving. She winced when he pressed tender lymph glands, almost gagged when he told her to stick out my tongue and say "Ah". His expression was grave, not the mask of reassurance he usually assumed for patients. Startled, she realized she hadn't seen him this concerned since Jean was dying, and he'd known only a miracle could save her.

She kissed his fingertips. "Don't worry, dear. I'm just a little under the weather."

"Some weather to be under." He glanced toward the window; the red glow had spread, like fire in the sky. Or fire on the water from torpedoed ships offshore. She shuddered, unable to keep from reverting to the Indy; had there been flames, or just flares of light when she took the torpedoes? "Blowing a gale. Waves are really slamming the beach," he added. "Reminds me of a storm when I was eight. On a liner, going to England with my parents. Only a year after the *Titanic* went down, so I was scared shitless." He smiled, smoothing hair back from her face. "Wondered about that while you were away. Were you ever scared?"

When she blinked, her eyeballs ached, along with her head and neck. "Once, in a squall. We usually went around the worst weather." She swallowed with difficulty. "The other—when the Kamikaze buzzed us— that was worse than anything. But it was over in an instant."

His gaze was fond, pensive. "I hated that we couldn't share those things while they were happening. Of course, you had plenty of friends to talk to, didn't you?"

Even smiling hurt. "Sure. We were all in the same boat."

He nodded, studying her with the perplexed intensity of a medical professional trying to diagnose with incomplete information. "Once we get settled, let's go through your letters so you can fill in the blanks. Not just where the censor cut things out, but the stories you didn't have time to write. You know, about the people you worked with. Like the chaplains. And that Australian nurse you were so fond of. And the dentist who knew something about everything."

"Oh. Floyd Einhorn." She had to smile again; now that she hadn't seen him for ten days, Floyd seemed even more comic than he had in real life. "Funny. They're all a million miles away today. Last week I missed them so much. But now...." Her throat closed and she couldn't go on.

That speculative medical look again. "Does it hurt to swallow?"

She nodded, turning her gaze toward the window again. The portentous red layers were turning ashen, wind blustering, radiators ticking and groaning against the nor'easterly pounding the coast. The very thought of such weather sent icy spasms through her.

Jim said, "Your teeth are chattering," then went to the closet for another blanket, powder blue with a satin binding. When he tucked it around her, the trace of some other woman's cloying perfume turned her stomach. "Damn. Where's that boy? You need a hot drink. Should've asked for a hot water bottle too." He was reaching for the phone again when the knock finally came.

"Sorry I couldn't get back quicker, Dr. Millett." This bellboy was older than the other, clean-cut and serious, with a fading tan; perhaps he'd been in the South Pacific too. "Kitchen's real busy, what with folks wanting to get home before the storm hits. You leaving today too?"

"Hadn't planned to." Jim took his keys and medical bag, instructed him to set the tea tray on the desk, and tipped him as he left. "What do you think, darling? Should we go back to your parents' today instead of tomorrow?"

All she could think of was, if she was sick, her mother would dither and fuss and slap a mustard plaster on her chest. "No. Tomorrow's soon enough. If it wasn't Christmas Eve, I'd wait even longer."

Opening the black bag on the chair, he pulled out a stethoscope, tongue depressors and scopes for inspecting, eyes, ears and throat. Last came the thermometer; after wedging it under her tongue, he poured tea, adding sugar and lemon with the easy grace of a woman. While he was otherwise occupied, she sneaked a look and saw her temp was over 102. In sickness and health, she thought wryly. A hell of a thing to have to test such a vow before it was twenty-four hours old.

After he read it, he finished looking her over, then reloaded the bag. His frown was too noticeable to ignore. "My goodness, Jim. You're so grim. What do I have, bubonic plague?"

The chuckle sounded forced. "No, dear. From the look of your tonsils, more likely strep throat. Now, I'll give you aspirin with the tea, and you'll feel some better. But you need penicillin. See, even if you threw it off now, there could be complications later. Remember Beth, on the island? That's what caused her rheumatic fever. Nephritis'd be just as dangerous for a lady who wants to be pregnant."

"Can you get penicillin yet?"

"Could if we were home. But here, well, probably be best if I took you to the base so you'll get enough to knock out the bug." His eyes clouded. "Hate to take you out in this weather, but the sooner you start the drug, the better. Okay?"

It hurt to nod, so she smiled. "You're the doctor. Whatever you say."

She didn't feel like eating or drinking, but made herself sip hot tea. Her throat was so swollen the aspirin tablets disintegrated when she tried to swallow. The bitter particles made her gag again, but eventually went down. Jim helped her bundle up in slacks and a bulky cabled sweater, then dug into his suitcase for the six-foot scarf she'd knitted him for Christmas, 1943. "Here. This'll keep you warmer than that silk thing you wore last night."

The multicolored muffler was a foot shorter than it had been, and the wool was matted, as if someone had washed it in hot water. The smell of mothballs was overpowering, but she managed to wrap it once around her neck and twice over her head before they went to the elevator. Still, as they left the hotel, wind-driven cold penetrated layers of wool and set her shivering again, so Jim tucked the car blanket around her before they set out.

Sleet ticked against the windshield as they headed toward

Portsmouth. On the far side of the leaden river, buildings on the base and the ominous bulk of the naval prison were swathed in white gauze. Few other cars were out; only die-hard churchgoers, she concluded when she remembered it was the Sabbath.

The base hospital was a massive brick structure dating from the Navy Yard's World War One glory days. On the ground floor, Emergency was a cheerless, overheated place crowded with sniffling sailors, puffy pregnant women and whining, snot-nosed children. It smelled of steam, Lysol, chlorine, damp wool, Vicks Vapo-Rub, and the musky tang of unwashed humanity. Anna shuddered even harder and went to the desk to log in.

The duty corpsman only half-listened to her symptoms. "Bring your records, ma'am?"

"Records? No. I'm on my honeymoon. I didn't think I'd need them."

His raised-eyebrows glance shifted to Jim, then back to her ID card. His expression suggested he doubted she was actually the person in the blurry picture. "Well, now, I don't know. Better let the charge nurse figure it out." He took off down a hallway and disappeared into the murky bowels of the old building.

From the moment she laid eyes on her, Anna knew the charge nurse was not happy. A plump jaygee, her stringy hair was longer than regulation, and her breath smelled of cigarettes. Her hard gaze never softened as Anna explained why she didn't have her records.

"Ensign Donovan, don't you know you're supposed to hand-carry them whenever you change duty stations? Now I'll have to stop my work just to make you a new chart." She gestured toward the crowded waiting room. "And on a Sunday when every sailor on base and half the dependents in Maternity Village are sick too."

Anna took a deep breath and stood straighter than her aching body wanted to. "Sorry to put you to that bother, ma'am. When I was on the hospital ship, the wounded boys we picked up didn't have their records either, so we had to make charts for every last one. Even the ones who couldn't talk. They needed help, but we still had to chart them before we did anything else."

The older woman's face reddened. "Well, that was different. That was war. Next time, be sure and bring yours." She waved them toward seats. "Wait out there, please. Be a while till a doctor can see you."

After they'd sunk into the closest chairs, Jim said. "Good for you, telling her off like that."

"I didn't tell her we triaged them first, and the worst cases went to surgery even without charts."

He patted her hand. "Doesn't matter, dear. You got your point across."

Waiting, Jim paged through some ragged magazines while Anna tried vainly to get comfortable. By now her muscles ached in places she couldn't attribute to sex, and swallowing was so painful she wanted to cry. Beside her, a bleary-eyed woman coughed and snorted into a man's handkerchief, but never wiped the runny nose of the squirming toddler in her lap.

Closing her eyes in self-defense, she managed to nod off. When the corpsman finally called her, Madonna and child were gone. Leading her to an examining room, however, the nurse turned to Jim and snapped, "Sorry, sir. You got to wait out here."

"The hell I will." His gaze fell to her name badge. "Listen, Nurse Pierce, I'm this lady's husband, and a licensed physician too. If you don't let me come in with her, I'll find someone who will."

Her look warned them not to expect more concessions as she motioned him to follow. But when Anna had seated herself on the examining table, the nurse ordered her to remove the sweater and tossed her a cold sheet. Brusque and tight-lipped, she took her vitals, scribbled on the pristine chart, then stomped out.

Scowling, Jim draped his topcoat over Anna's shoulders. "If this is the kind of care the Navy gives their people when they get back from the war...." He shook his head, glanced toward the small window, where snowflakes straggled by. "Rudeness like that's inexcusable."

"Oh, it's probably just because it's Sunday and they're understaffed. Sometimes on the ship, we felt overwhelmed too."

"But I bet you were never rude." He laid his fingertips on her forehead again. "How're you feeling now?"

"Awful. But not terminal. Don't worry. I'll be fine."

"I do worry, though. Because I can't do anything for you." He took off his glasses, rubbed his eyes. "Think I probably told you, I never expected to marry again after the divorce. Life was fine the way it was. Don't know that I was happy, or too busy to feel anything." He shrugged, replaced the glasses. "Then you came along."

Though he was close enough to touch, the fever in her body made him appear distant and unreal. Like a wavering mirage. "You've told me before. But why now?"

He blinked a couple of times. "Oh, just remembering how sterile that life was. With nobody to worry about but patients. Now...well, here you are. And if we have kids, I'll really find out about worry. Least that's what people say."

Momentarily speechless, eventually it came to her to apologize and add, "Honeymoons are supposed to be happy."

"Don't be sorry." The grin came slowly, as usual. "Hell, now I want everything a man and woman can have." He glanced around the dismal, institutional closet of a room: mesh-screened window, asbestos-covered pipes along the ceiling, battleship-gray steel furniture and floor tiles. "Even this."

Overwhelmed with emotion, she couldn't speak, was about to lie back on the table, when the Medical Officer of the Day came in. Wearing a rumpled lab coat over a wrinkled shirt and food-spotted tie, he looked about fifteen. He peered into her throat, inspected her ears, palpated lymph nodes and listened to her heart, his halitosis undisguised even by some minty gum he was chewing. He did, however, pay attention when Jim explained his own diagnosis. And concurred immediately that she needed penicillin.

"I'll do a culture, but even without the results, I'll give her a shot, and pills for the next ten days. But if she doesn't respond in, say, seventy-two hours, I want to see her again. Understood?"

"Of course. Thanks, doctor," Jim said.

After he swabbed her throat and injected her hip, the MOD dispatched a corpsman to the pharmacy for the pills, shook Jim's hand and shuffled from the examining room. Jim helped her back into her clothes and wound the scarf around her neck again. By then all she could think of was curling up under a dozen blankets, but still she had to walk out to the car through the storm and huddle under the lap robe while he navigated streets half-covered by blowing snow and pellets of ice.

Tiny scurrying flakes fought the windshield wipers as they crossed the river, gusting in clouds across the exposed causeway back to New Castle Island, where the Wentworth was a ghostly Alpine castle in a wild white wilderness. By the time they pulled up out front, she felt trapped in a bad dream, unable to awaken to a better reality. Hauling herself up the steps to the entrance reaffirmed that this frigid landscape was real. Like climbing Mount Washington during the storm of the century.

In their room, the light was silver with reflected snowfall. She'd packed only romantic silky nightgowns, so she crawled into bed in her clothes. The pillowcase felt icy against her cheek, but wrapping up in Jim's scarf again helped. He gave her two more aspirins, but even with water, she couldn't get them down. After that he had room service bring a club sandwich for his lunch and chicken broth for her. Before he took a bite, however, he slowly fed her spoonfuls of the hot salty liquid. Until her stomach clenched and refused to take more.

"Can I get you anything else?" he asked, this hovering and anxious angel of mercy. "Ginger ale? More tea?"

"No, thanks. Just let me sleep. Please."

His lips brushed her cheek. "Okay, dear. Probably the best thing now. I'll be right here if you need anything."

Closing her eyes, she drifted on a febrile tide, not a proper sleep, but a limbo of discomfort in which time was trackless and external sensations warped. She was only dimly aware when the short winter day turned dark, when Jim made a couple of phone calls, speaking in low, muffled tones, then finally stretched out atop the covers beside her. Sometimes he read the *Boston Globe*; sometimes he slept, snoring lightly. Once, seeing she was awake, he took her temperature again, but wouldn't tell her what it was. No matter; she didn't need to see the numbers to know she'd crossed into the delirium zone.

Between patches of semi-consciousness, she dreamed, fragments of distorted images connected by flashes of color and muted, unintelligible sounds. Once she was sure she was back on the ship, in bed with Mark. Then she was on a train racing through whirling white cascades. After that she lay in her childhood bed under a strange patchwork quilt shaped like a map of New Hampshire. Finally she was wandering empty rooms in the Hope Island hotel, calling for Jean as a banshee wind howled outside.

Finally there was nothing except the haunted darkness around her.

When she opened her eyes again, she had no idea where she was, or who was with her in the dim grayness that precedes first light. Drenched with sweat, she tried to get up, but her legs went limp. Whimpering, she fell back on the bed.

Jim was instantly awake. He switched on the lamp and, lurching on the cane, came around to help her stagger to the bathroom. He even held her as she huddled on the toilet, then changed her damp clothes for a pair of his flannel pajamas.

The effort left her exhausted, but aware the fever had dropped. She was no longer burning, could swallow more normally and move without sharp pinpricks of pain everywhere.

After he covered her again, he laid his cheek against hers, then drew back. His face brightened like the coming of dawn. "Well, dear. Fever seems to have broken. Feeling any better?"

"Mmm. I think so."

"Thought you would after the shot and a good night's sleep. Now. How about some water?"

"Yes, please." Watching him hobble toward the bathroom, tenderness surged through her system like a healing drug. Despite his own permanent disability, he'd responded automatically to her infirmity without regard for his personal inconvenience. With devotion surpassing that of physician, husband, friend or even parents. In that moment, she realized she could never disclose her infidelity with Mark until such time as she'd proved her fidelity to this man in as many ways as a wife could. Until she'd atoned for that brief carnal faithlessness by her loving constancy in all the time since. Until their marriage was a granite-solid reality, and Mark a mere flickering shadow in her past. Like an unnamed character in a half-remembered movie.

She gulped the water Jim brought as if she'd just wandered in from Death Valley. By then the sky was bright; the wind had dropped off, and the snowfall had stopped. After he came back to bed, she curled up alongside him, remembering almost absently that this was the morning of

Christmas Eve. She hoped he hadn't bought her a gift; in just the few hours they'd been married, his presence had already given her more than she'd ever expected.

Or, perhaps, deserved.

CHAPTER FOUR

The clunk of tire chains was muffled by packed snow as they rolled away from the rectory on December 27. With the sense of rounding a metaphorical corner into a wonderful new life, Anna waved at her parents until Jim turned onto Court Street. Morning light gilded vast expanses of white and contrasted with the long blue shadow of the courthouse, so dazzling she rummaged through her purse for sunglasses. Until she remembered they were in her seabag, still unpacked in her room in the rectory. During a year in the Pacific, she'd forgotten sun dazzle on snow could be as blinding as equatorial light on a tropical sea.

She squinted over at Jim as he steered them along rutted streets toward Route One. "You know, last Christmas we were steaming between Guam and the Philippines, and it was hotter than hell. So I prayed for a white Christmas this year. I just didn't mean this white."

He smiled, nodded. "Be a slow trip back to East Point. But there's no hurry. The housekeeper'll have supper whenever we get there."

"Oh, she cooks?"

"Yep. Has her own tin lizzy, too, so she can go for groceries. I figure if Tom lives with us and you work in the practice, you'll have your hands full without KP."

"That'll be good when I'm pregnant."

"Thought of that too." His tone was Down-East flat and dry.

She waited for more, but he kept staring straight ahead till they came to a Stop sign. He looked both ways and pulled onto the deserted highway. It appeared to have been plowed but hard-packed snow covered both lanes.

She said, "I like Tom. He's a lot like you. I mean, kindly, and quiet. And humble. Easy to see why you're friends."

"Speaking of friends, did you notice Margie batting her eyes at him at the reception?"

"Did you notice he was enjoying it?"

The frown was only a passing shadow. "Well, she's certainly glamorous. And...what's the word? Vivacious. That's it. Nothing like his wife. She was a plain girl. Worked in her family's Italian restaurant in downtown Providence."

"Oh? What'd she die of, food poisoning?"

The frown deepened, indicating this wasn't a facetious matter. "No. TB. One of those fulminant cases that doesn't respond to any therapy. Still haunts him that he couldn't help her. Glad you asked him to bunk with us for a while. I was going to, but didn't think you'd want someone else around so soon after we were married."

"Well, it'll cramp our style. I mean, we won't be able to rush into the examining room and get a little every time the urge strikes, will we?"

His shocked laughter filled the car. "Well, there is that. I'd planned to give him the room across the hall. But maybe my sister's would be better. Less worry about the bed squeaking. Or you yelling."

"Oh, Jim. I don't yell."

He squeezed her knee. "Don't you?"

"No, I'm too dignified."

"That's one of the things I love about you," Mark had once said. "You're such a lady, except in the sack." She squeezed her eyes closed to suffocate a memory as unwelcome as the serpent in the Garden of Eden.

Jim laughed again. "Whatever you are, dear, I enjoy it."

North of Kittery, the highway hugged the coast; the snow

was patchy and the roadway clear. Still, the air had an Arctic shimmer and every stream they crossed was iced over. Outside Biddeford, he pulled into an Atlantic station and had the attendant fill the tank and remove the chains. It took so long, the car began to feel like an igloo. After they headed north again, even with the heater turned up full, the lap robe over her legs and sunlight on the windows, she couldn't get warm. Probably a leftover effect of the infection. Or maybe the old wives' tale was true: living in the tropics really did thin your blood.

When she'd left the ship, she'd expected homecoming to require only a geographical leap across the continent. Now it felt more like a continuing series of small adjustments, not just to a harsh New England winter, but to people she hadn't seen in over a year. And most of all, to the absence of a large cause in which to immerse herself. Even if she conceived right away, an uncomplicated pregnancy required neither conscious thought, determination nor hard work. At least until after delivery.

Of course, there was always Jim's house to fix up and make her home. Presently it was an echoing Victorian barn filled with his grandparents' worn furniture, somber rugs and ancient gilt-framed paintings. The only cheerful spot was one front bedroom which his first wife had redone in sunny yellows during her brief tenure. But she hadn't touched Jim's bedroom, the patients' waiting room, or the sunless kitchen, a dismal cave inhabited by archaic appliances and cabinets crammed with chipped crockery, glasses from Old English cheese spreads, and figurines of winsome shepherd girls. The range was new enough to be streamlined, but the refrigerator was probably the first electric model ever sold, condenser perched atop it like a mechanical troll.

She waited till he'd navigated them through Portland traffic before she said, "You know, Jim. I was just thinking. Were you serious when you said I could redecorate your house?"

His gaze connected with hers for the half-second it took a red light to go green. "Certainly. Can't imagine you'd be happy the way it is. Especially the kitchen. My mother hardly ever cooked, and my first wife never did, so it's still like it was when I was a kid. Grandma didn't mind; she always had hired help."

"Well, we will too. But it's so gloomy. And your room…I'd like to spruce it up a bit too. Nothing expensive, just paint and paper, and new drapes. And a nice bedspread. You know. So it looks less like a bachelor's den."

"Fine with me. Or we could move across the hall. It's already fixed up."

"Oh no. It'd always remind me of Ellen."

He clasped her hand on the seat between them, fingered her rings, sighed. "Oh, Anna, that's silly. She was nothing but a social butterfly. All she thought about was looking pretty, and wearing expensive clothes, and giving big parties. And visiting her friends. She never did a thing she didn't want to."

Like the bed thing? she wondered. "What didn't she want to do?"

"Cook. Clean. Discuss my work." He paused, squinting in sunlight glittering off the hood. "Or have children. That was the big one. Said if she ever conceived, she'd have an abortion."

She gasped. "My goodness. I can't imagine you so infatuated you'd ever marry someone like that."

He shrugged. "Back then, I didn't know what I know now. See, she was the first woman who ever paid me any attention. Cripples don't have a lot of choices, you know."

"Well, I hope I never disappoint you. You know. When our heat fades."

He laughed too quickly, too heartily. "Sweetheart, the day we met, I knew you were different. Working together only proved it. Now I know you so well, you could never disappoint me."

Forcing her lips into a tight smile, she averted her gaze and didn't answer. To her relief, he said no more about it. For the next few miles they rode without speaking of anything other than traffic and snow conditions. Until beyond Portland, they pulled up to a line of cars at lowered crossing gates. The ground trembled as a train approached, putting on speed as it left for Brunswick and eventually Augusta. Only two red Boston and Maine coaches and a baggage car were in the string of others from the Pennsy and the New York Central. Then came a Burlington Lines Pullman so grimy she could hardly make out the name.

"Did I tell you Luke and Willi and Floyd and I were in a B and M coach from Oakland to Chicago?" she asked. "I was surprised it was out there, but Floyd said the railroads can't find enough cars for all the troops coming back, so they're shuffling them all over the country."

"Notice the number of the one you rode?"

All she'd noticed that day was Mark, walking alongside as they'd rumbled out of the huge train shed. And all she'd felt was a convulsive ache when they'd left him behind. "Mm, no. I was too anxious to find a seat."

A black plume rose from the locomotive as the last car clattered across the highway. Like the smoke pouring from *Compassion*'s stack as they'd left the Golden Gate on the last cruise. A speed run, so a final load of convalescents could be home for Christmas. And the rest of their lives.

How long, she wondered, would it take to dissolve these leftover memories, or at least water them down? Or would she forever flash to scenes too trivial to remember in detail, except that Mark had been in them?

The crossing gates came up and they began to move again. She closed her eyes against the sun glare, but the last image of Mark lingered as if burned on her retinas. Damn, she didn't want him floating on the surface of her mind; if Jim ever read her like a newspaper, Mark would be a bold, black headline.

Jim shifted into high gear. "How old did you say Luke is?"

"Luke? He turned twenty-seven Christmas Day. Why?"

"Just curious." He tapped the steering wheel a moment. "From your letters, I take it you were closer to the other chaplain."

A warning tingled through her like a mild electric shock. "Actually, I got along with both of them. But Luke has this dogmatic, judgmental strain. Anytime we disagreed, he got huffy. Don't know how he'll react when Lorraine tells him his father was a priest."

"From the little I saw of him at the wedding, I think he may be a homosexual. What do you think?"

"Well, that was the consensus on the ship." She quoted her conversation with Mark about Lorraine's reaction to that news, adding, "I hope it works out."

"I'm sure it will. Anyway, that was perceptive of him. Mark, I mean." He paused, a minor frown gathering his brows. "He was older, wasn't he?"

She gulped a deep breath. "Some. Maybe thirty-five. By the way, did Dad mention he called the morning of the wedding? To wish us well?"

"No. Luke told me."

Luke told him? Why? To sabotage her? Not with some big destructive salvo, but small random shots--one word, one vague implication, one subtle hint after another--until her pretense of virtue was riddled with holes. Was that how it was going to be?

She said, "I thought I told you too."

"Guess I forgot." His tone was as bland as hers. Covering up too?

She coughed to dissipate escalating tension. "Anyway, he's staying in the Navy till he decides if he should go on being a minister. See, by the end of the war, he'd started to doubt his faith. He did a beautiful service for the Indianapolis victims, but he said it was all just words.

Because he wasn't sure the Lord gave a damn about us anymore. It got worse after we picked up the prisoners and found out how the Japs had treated them." She sighed as if her regrets were all about his apostasy. "But I told him, even if his own faith was wavering, he was still helping the boys keep theirs."

"I can't imagine it, Anna." Jim's voice was soft-edged with the compassion that seemed his second nature. "I mean, what it was like. Even if you told me every last detail, I still wouldn't know." He released her hand to downshift as the line ahead slowed for another light. "Mark was lucky having you to talk to. And vice-versa."

Panic clenched her fingers. "But when I was upset, you were the only one I wanted to tell."

He gave her a quick, fond glance as they stopped moving. "And now you have me. In case things ever get bad again."

If things ever get bad again? The implication ignited so much fear she didn't ask what he meant. God, how much had Luke told him anyway?

"Don't worry, dear," he added. "Worst thing I can imagine is being away from you. Had enough of that to last a lifetime."

She patted his hand. The light changed; as they jolted forward, she closed her eyes in hopes of falling asleep long enough to develop a specific amnesia, one that erased all Mark's traces from memory's album. But she was so tense and nervous, it was another hour before the hum of the engine and the rhythm of the wheels lulled her to the edge of a comfortable doze. She was just sinking into it when Jim's shout—"Jesus Christ!"—brought her abruptly awake.

Braking hard, he swerved onto the unpaved shoulder. Tail lights flashed as cars ahead narrowly missed an overturned sedan skidding on its roof in the center lane. Friction ignited sparks where metal scraped paving. When it finally came to rest against piled snow, the wheels were still spinning.

"Dear God, what happened?" she gasped.

Jim's voice was shaky. "Guy's been passing everything on the road. Must've hit ice when he tried to get back in line."

They shuddered to a stop, front bumper just missing the car in front. He set the hand brake, wrenched open his door. "Hand me my bag, will you, Anna? I'll see if there's anything I can do."

She lifted it from the back seat. "Maybe I can help too."

He grabbed his cane and the bag, and eased his legs outside. Frigid air poured in. "No, stay here. No sense taking a chill now." He slammed the door and began limping toward the accident as other drivers emerged from the line of vehicles.

By the time he reached the wreck, a small crowd had gathered. Even from a hundred feet away, she realized he'd taken charge. Unable to bend his bad leg, he directed another man to stoop and look in the windows. Someone else tried to wrestle the driver's door open, but failed, so Jim organized three others to rock the coupe onto its side, then upright. As soon as it was resting on its wheels, the men managed to open the door. Jim peered inside, then leaned in as if examining a victim.

Twitching with curiosity, she wrapped up in the long scarf, pulled on gloves and buttoned her coat. Outside, the cold shocked her convalescent lungs, but if it was therapeutic for tuberculosis patients, it shouldn't hurt her.

By the time she got to the accident, another vehicle had made a U-turn and sped off in the southbound lane. Jim was still leaning into the wreck. When she called him, his face was pinched and bleak. "Go back to the car, Anna. Nothing you can do here."

"Oh. Does that mean...you know?"

He nodded, drawing one hand across his neck in such a way she concluded the victim had been decapitated.

She swallowed back nausea. "How long do you have to

stay here?"

"Till the police come. Somebody's gone to call them. Meanwhile, close the doors and stay warm. And take my bag, if you will."

Avoiding looking into the sedan—a black '39 or '40 Nash with a smashed windshield—she whipped off the scarf. "At least put this on."

She waited till he'd wrapped up, then hustled back to the Buick. Other cars had begun to leave, so she got behind the wheel and pulled up whenever there was space. Jim continued talking with onlookers, breath steaming in the cold. During the year they'd worked together, she'd formed a clear sense of his dedication, but the depths of it during her recent illness had surprised even her. When she'd first seen his wife's picture, she'd been awed by her glamour. Now her contempt bordered on disgust. And not solely because she didn't cook or want kids, but because this fine man hadn't been enough for her.

Her eyes filled as she pictured the myriad ways Ellen might have rejected him. Not hard to imagine she'd been unfaithful too. Righteous indignation rose like a storm tide, until she felt bloated with it. Then a thunderclap of truth knocked it out of her: she and Ellen weren't really so different. Except he'd been only her fiancé when he hadn't been enough. At least not enough to keep her pure. Had that been due solely to the ten thousand miles between them? Or an ugly strain of faithlessness in her?

Sirens were approaching; a red light flashed in the distance. A state patrol car screeched to a stop and a trooper hurried over to the wreck. Jim pointed into the interior. The trooper looked inside, then returned to his vehicle and talked into a microphone. Jim spoke with him a minute longer, shook hands and limped toward their car. His ears were red under his hat, and after he took off his gloves, he breathed on his hands before he released the brake and shifted into low. "Sorry it took so long, dear. At least I didn't have to wait for the ambulance."

"Was the victim decapitated?" She didn't want to know but was incapable of ignoring her own curiosity.

He threw her a quick, shocked glance. "Holy God, why'd you ask that?"

She repeated the beheading pantomime.

He laughed aloud, but instantly sobered. "No, thank God. Looked like a broken neck, though, so he didn't suffer. Poor devil. A sailor, with orders to Brunswick. Wonder if he'd been overseas. Hell of an irony if he'd lived through combat only to die like this."

She shook her head. "War's full of ironies like that."

"So's life. Now. You didn't get chilled, did you?"

"No. But you must be frozen."

He nodded. "Diner a couple miles up the road. We'll stop and get some soup. Hungry?"

"Starved. Should've asked Mother to pack turkey sandwiches. We could eat them with the soup. Or tonight, at your house."

"But Kate O'Neill's making supper. She might take umbrage if we brought food with us."

She hoped he was joking; the last thing a new wife needed was an umbrage-taking housekeeper: a Mrs. Danforth to her Rebecca? She didn't ask; he was obviously too shaken by the DOA to deal with the trivial issue of Kate O'Neill's temperament.

The eatery was a retired dining car from the Grand Trunk Railway, painted caboose- red and set on pilings in a pot-holed parking lot. Inside, the heat was heavy with the universal restaurant smells of hot grease, cigarette smoke and coffee, plus oily whiffs of old train. Jim ordered his favorite New England clam chowder, she went for beef-barley. "And coffee now, please," he added.

Waiting, they wrapped their fingers around thick porcelain mugs and sipped cautiously of the steaming brew. When she noticed he was still shivering, she said, "Listen

Jim, after we eat, I'll drive the rest of the way. Okay?"

He shrugged. "If you're up to it."

"Of course I am. I didn't stand out in the cold for half an hour."

"Better me than you, dear. Could cause a relapse, what with your low resistance. Should've known it'd be low after such a big change in climate."

"I'm fine now. Look how fast I got over the strep."

"Thanks to penicillin. But no wonder drug's going to help you recover from the past year." He smoothed his napkin, then impressed lines into it with the fork tines. His eyes were so serious, she braced herself for heavy words. "Anna, listen. I know you want a baby, stat, but I'd rather we held off awhile. Not long. Just till you've got your strength back."

Shock kept her speechless a moment. "But why, Jim? Why would it be risky now?"

"No big reason. Still, if you were one of my patients, I'd recommend you wait till you're in better shape. Say till Spring."

His smile was the gentle, fond one that had attracted her long before admiration had morphed into love. Still, she felt so slapped down, she pouted.

"Now, dear," he coaxed. "What difference will a few months make?"

She stared through the grimy window at low sunlight winking off passing cars. "If I hadn't already lost a baby, it wouldn't matter. But you know I want another. And if I hadn't gone into the Navy, we'd have one by now." She shrugged. "I've postponed the maternal instinct so long, it must be working overtime."

"I understand. It's just that I want our child to have the best chance to thrive. You too, since you'll have to deliver by section again. That make sense?"

She nodded with reluctance, until he reached across the red checked oilcloth. But even as she clasped his hand, she knew her urgency was only partly generated by the previous loss. Another part had to do with building a bridge between them strong enough to withstand the Mark bombshell, whenever she dropped it. Or Luke forced her hand. "Okay, Jim," she said, trying not to sound petulant. "If you think we should—well, okay. We'll wait."

The soup arrived, with oyster crackers and coffee refills. By then she was glad for something to do besides disguising disappointment with idle banter. At the same time she felt a loving imperative to honor his wishes as Ellen never had. So she ate silently, praying their frequent couplings the past five days might just have rendered this discussion academic. And superfluous.

If that turned out to be the case, she'd claim the Lord had other plans for them. Surely Jim wouldn't argue with the will of God.

CHAPTER FIVE

When Anna had told Kate O'Neill that Tom Mullen's first meal with them didn't have to be a banquet, her large pink face took on the lugubrious expression of some Celtic martyr. "Now, Anna. The poor soul's been through so much, 'tis the least we can do to welcome him. Especially on New Year's Day night." Delivered in that lilting brogue, the argument sounded like a line from *Danny Boy*.

Averse to arguing this or any other point with the housekeeper, Anna told her to do whatever she wanted. Which turned out to be dinner in the formal dining room.

"But not before it's had a proper cleaning," Kate had added.

Proper indeed. When she'd finished, every mirror, every piece of silver and every prism on the chandelier sparkled as they hadn't in probably twenty years. Moreover, the lace curtains and tablecloth were fresh from a drying rack on which they'd been pinned and stretched like medieval heretics. Gone was the smell of antiquity and dust, replaced by lemon furniture polish and the wax of burning candles in triple candelabra at both ends of the long table, set now with Jim's grandmother's crystal goblets, sterling flatware, Limoges china, and linen napkins starched stiff enough to scratch skin.

Jim was at one end, Anna at the other, closest to the kitchen. Midway between, Tom, in wrinkled brown tweeds, perched anxiously on the edge of the chair, as if he'd never dined in such splendor before. Anna certainly never had, at least not with a serving girl in a frilly apron over moth-eaten woolen slacks and Aran sweater.

The elegant setting seemed more appropriate for Beef Wellington than a shepherd's pie made with lamb that was obviously verging on mutton. Anna wasn't surprised; Kate prided herself on patronizing a butcher who sold the thriftier cuts. When Anna had told her not to worry about economizing, Kate had given her a look of wide-eyed dismay. "Ah, but you never know when the wolf'll be at the door. Mind you, one day the doctor'll be thanking you for your thrifty ways."

That afternoon, Anna had watched her chop carrots, celery, onions and turnips with a lethal-looking chef's knife she'd brought from Ireland. "I know your mother needs you," Anna had said in her most solicitous tone, "So don't feel you have to stay past five tonight. We can serve ourselves just fine."

And she'd come back with, "Ah, but Mither's not such an invalid she can't fend for herself another hour or two."

Earlier, Anna had asked how old Mither was, but Kate was vague, as she was about all personal details. When Jim had hired her, she'd said she'd come from County Wicklow in 1933 to keep house for a Back Bay family, whom she'd left only for patriotic reasons–a wartime job in the Bath shipyard. Satisfied with her references, he'd never asked marital history, age or other personal details about which Anna was inordinately curious. She reckoned Kate was something beyond forty, a broad-hipped, large-breasted woman a head taller than her and Jim, but eye-to-eye with lanky Tom. Her hair, a faded ginger, was fastened behind her head with tortoise shell combs in a haphazard knot from which wild wisps constantly escaped. And in the four days since Anna had met her, she'd shown only two emotions, both in the extreme–mirth and mournfulness, with occasional quick stops at incredulity. She'd observed the second during a conversation about Jim's lameness. And again, when she'd told her both she and Tom had been widowed. Her over-the-top lugubrious reaction prompted Anna to withhold the fact she'd also lost a child.

After she'd doled out portions of shepherd's pie, Kate reappeared with cole slaw congealed in lemon Jell-O and a basket of thick-cut Irish soda bread. Surveying the table, she moved the salt cellar closer to Jim and topped off Tom's ice water before she untied her apron. "Now, then. If nobody's needing anything more, I'll just be taking meself home. Mind you, Anna, the baked apples are in the oven and the coffee's all made. Just leave the dishes for morning."

Anna thanked her and said everything smelled wonderful. They all dug in. Kate's heavy footsteps retreated, the back door closed and her Model T sputtered out the drive.

Observing rivulets of liquid grease trickling from under the pie's mashed potato crust, Anna was about to ask if anyone wanted her to open a can of Spam. Until Tom gulped a huge mouthful and rolled his eyes. "Gosh, that lady can sure cook." Then, with another forkful halfway to his mouth, said, "Jim, how long did you grandfather practice medicine here?"

"Fifty-three years. He'd only been gone ten when I took over in '41." This answer instantly kicked off a long, earnest discussion about the evolution of medicine in their lifetimes.

Anna listened in silence as long as she could stand it before she interrupted. "Jim, could you two please discuss that another time? Right now I want to hear from Tom. So far, all I know is, you met at Tufts because you were seated alphabetically. And you interned together at Mass General. Then what'd you do, Tom?"

He turned with the eager look of a child finally allowed to speak. "Went back to Providence. See, my wife and I grew up there, so we were real happy when St. Agnes's offered a residency."

"Oh? A residency in what?"

"Surgery." He smiled at Jim. "Don't you tell this lady anything?"

Jim shrugged and gnawed on a chunk of soda bread. The raisins in it were so hard she suspected they'd been left from his grandmother's supply.

"Only finished the first year, though," Tom went on. "Midway through the second, my wife died. And all the steam went out of me." Bleakness crossed his face like a cloud shadow. "After that, I couldn't wait to get out of Providence. So I joined the Navy."

"Jim did tell me you were at Pensacola the whole time. Flight surgeon?"

"Once in a while, when they were short-handed. Mostly though, I worked with dependents. Pretty dull compared to what you did." He pushed his chair back. "Mind if I help myself to more of everything?"

Jim grinned. "Take it all, if you like."

At the sideboard, Tom heaped his plate even higher than before. When he'd sat again, he said, "Oh, by the way, Anna. Margie says to tell you hello."

Shock made her gasp. "Margie? Margie Halvorsen?"

He nodded with unusual enthusiasm. "Yep. Stopped off in Boston last night to see her. Being it was New Year's Eve and all." A blush crept up his neck into his thinning gray hair.

"Oh my. Did she take you to a party?"

He picked up his fork again. "Why no, we went out to dinner. Place was so packed we didn't get done till eleven, so she said we might as well go back to her flat and drink champagne. And we did." The blush deepened.

Jim cleared his throat and glanced at his watch. "Excuse me, dear. Need to make a few calls. Won't be long." He pushed his plate away, rose on the cane and retreated up the hall.

Intent on discovering what Tom and Margie had done

after the champagne, she was momentarily speechless. Before she recovered, Tom said, "Now, Anna, tell me what you did in the war. On a hospital ship, in the South Pacific, right? Where all did you go?"

"Oh, all over. Pelelieu and Leyte and Luzon, then Iwo Jima and Okinawa. But I didn't join the ship till October, '44, so the worst of it was over. I mean, the early days when there was nowhere to take casualties except Australia and New Zealand." She nibbled at the lumpy mashed potatoes. "The most impressive part was, after the Japs surrendered we picked up six hundred former prisoners of war at Nagasaki and took them to San Francisco."

His eyes widened. "Nagasaki? Where they dropped the second A-Bomb?"

She nodded.

"Gosh, that must've been a sight."

"We couldn't see the ruined area where we tied up, but some of our people went out to look at it up close. Said it was just rubble everywhere. Even the cathedral. Maybe you saw the picture in *Life* a few months back? With the head of Christ in the ruins?"

He rolled his eyes. "Gee. Wish I could've been in on all that. Once I asked for a transfer to a carrier, but they said I was too old. Maybe if I'd been a surgeon, they'd have sent me anyway. But that's all water under the bridge now, isn't it? Someday, though, I want to hear more about your work. If you don't mind talking about it."

"No, be glad to. Except a lot of it was downright boring. You know Navy routines."

"You bet I do! Anyways, Margie really admires you for signing up. Says she wishes she had too."

"Oh?" She was sorting through ways she might learn more about their night together when Jim came to the doorway.

"Sorry, dear. Hate to run off, but Peggy Lowell's membranes ruptured and her contractions are five minutes apart, so I'm heading to the hospital. Looks like it'll be a fast labor, but with a primip, you never know."

Tom shot to his feet. "Mind if I tag along, Jim? In the Navy catching babies was my strong suit."

"Well, it's never been mine, so I might let you take over." Looking apologetic, he came over, kissed her cheek. "I'll try not to wake you if I get home late. Be sure and set the alarm for six, so we have time for Kate's breakfast. Think I told you, Tom, we work on the island every Wednesday. Boat leaves at eight. Hope you're not prone to seasickness."

The two of them bustled out before she heard Tom's answer. No matter; the trip took less than an hour, even in rough seas. But she was sure if she even mentioned the possibility to Kate, she'd come up with some mythical Irish tea that miraculously cured motion sickness. None of them needed a mother hen, but faith and begorrah, if they hadn't found one anyway.

After the men left, she mused in front of the remains on her plate awhile, then blew out the candles, cleared the table, rinsed the dishes and set leftovers in the refrigerator. Finally she slid the baked apples from the oven. Shrunken and shriveled, they looked the way she'd begun to feel since she'd moved into Jim's house. And it had begun to feel more like Kate's.

Upstairs, she got ready for bed, then withdrew her journal from a dresser drawer Jim had cleaned out for her lingerie. This copybook was new; the one she'd filled on the ship was stashed in a suitcase along with one from Hope Island and the first, which she'd begun when the romance with Dan Donovan had turned serious in 1941.

As customary, she began with the date, but forgot it was a new year till she'd written 1945. She made the 5 into a 6, then scribbled everything that had happened that day. After those dull domestic details, she added, *Maybe the honeymoon isn't REALLY over, but tonight I FEEL like it is. Maybe that's normal after ten days. Still, it makes me sad.*

There was so much more she might have added, but she never wrote anything she wouldn't want someone else to read. It had been a challenge on the ship when things were going on with Mark, so she'd developed a code—a heart symbol followed by some variation of *I sure miss Jim right now*. Even without chapter and verse, though, she didn't need the little Valentine to remind her how often she'd been to bed with Mark.

Or that the mention of Jim wasn't so much about missing him as feeling shitty, because at the time she'd written it, she didn't miss him at all.

CHAPTER SIX

Wanting to miss no detail of the crossing to Hope Island the next morning, Anna braced herself on the deck beside Fletcher Hood as he steered *Molly B* across the Sound. The sky was rippled pewter, the seas gunmetal, high enough to give them a rough ride. In one of the chairs in the pilothouse Tom was holding on against the trawler's pitching and yawing, but so far he hadn't gone green. Maybe he'd been distracted by Fletch's non-stop chatter since they'd cast off at East Point.

"Jim ever tell you about the sub hit a mine out here?" Cigarette dangling from his lip, Fletch pointed ahead in the channel. "Went down just there. Navy couldn't raise her 'cause she broke up too bad. Plenty of U-boats in these waters, but the guv'ment kept it secret so civilians didn't panic. Even torpedoed a training ship off Portland last spring. First they claimed her boiler exploded, but after they sunk a U-boat near Newport, Navy owned up." He wagged his head, furrows on his face deepening into a frown. "This weren't no war zone, but plenty went on right under our noses."

"Gosh," Tom murmured. "You saw the one here blow up, didn't you, Anna?"

She nodded, bringing Jean into focus, and the moonlight bike ride that had taken them to the right spot at the right time. And the ensuing net of circumstances in which Jean had been caught as inextricably as any hapless creature of the deep. "Guess Jim's told you that story."

"Mighty sad. And ironic. You folks up here saw more of the war than I did the whole five years at Pensacola."

As they neared the island, Anna made out the hotel's red mansard roof, the church spire, the haphazard buildings along the wharf, and what looked like an LST standing out of the harbor. Fletch jabbed his index finger toward it. "Look. New car ferry. War surplus. Big doors on both ends. Had to build a special loading ramp here on account of the tides. Only runs three days a week, but they say she'll bring plenty more tourists come summer. Pshaw. Next thing you know, they'll be building bridges to every damned island south of Bar Harbor."

Inside the breakwater, the harbor was frozen along the shore, slabs of pack ice floating in the sheltered water. Visions flashed of other ports, some lush and tropical, others gray and dismal with wrecked ships; how long, she wondered, would she feel these backward tugs to other times and other places? And worst of all, to the man who'd shared them with her?

Blinking hard, she focused on the post card scene ahead. Except for the new ferry pier, it was unchanged from her first trip on *Molly B*—town hall and Lunch Box, firehouse and Civil War monument and a smattering of lesser shops down the slope from the general store, where Lorraine had been postmistress. And on the hill behind them, the boxy shake-and-clapboard houses of the village and the white-spired church. Closer, on the old wharf, Cleve Cropper waited beside his blue wagon and black horse, and Chester Philbrick's old red pickup, even the hotel station wagon. Her throat tightened as she recalled Jean's scolding that first day when she'd offered to carry Jim's medical bag onto the boat: "Never treat him like a cripple. He hates that." Poor Jean; so full of anger she missed almost all the joy life offered in her few years.

After the oily warmth of the pilothouse, the wind on deck

bit with cold teeth. "Another damned storm making up," Fletch muttered as they came down the gangway to the pier. "Remember, Doc, if it starts snowing, we need to head back before it turns thick."

"Then we'd best make house calls before we see clinic patients." Jim walked with one hand on the cane, the other hefting his medical bag.

Waving them over, Alex Cropper popped out of the station wagon. His grin was toothy and confident, as always. She wondered if marriage had toned him down from the brash young pilot home on leave that Christmas of 1943. Or had the loss of two bombers imbued him with a new strain of humility?

When Alex offered a ride to the clinic, the three of them crowded into the old station wagon for the short trip across the square and just up the hill. Normally an easy walk, even for Jim, but not on such a bitter day. Inside, the clinic still smelled of antiseptic and tobacco smoke; the same Red Cross posters hung in the waiting room, and most of the patients had cigarettes going. Grace and Beth came out from behind the check-in counter with welcoming hugs, but aware this was their busy day, Anna promised to have a proper visit another time. Brushing a kiss on her cheek, Jim led Tom toward his office. And Anna went back to the station wagon to resume her reunion with the island.

Alex wrestled the car into gear, his smile now warm and intimate. "Hey Annie. You're looking good. Marriage agrees with you."

"Thanks. Except it's only been ten days."

"I know. I was at the wedding, remember?"

"Of course. But what about you? Does it agree with you too?"

"Yeah, sure. Except Pam's knocked up already." His face turned sour. "I wanted to wait a while but...oh well. At least she's happy. And if it's a girl, we'll call her Jean."

"Oh, that's nice. Must seem strange though, being home

with her gone."

His face went dark. "I'll say. So maybe it's good there's a baby on the way." Then a grin lit it again. "Say, you're not on the nest yet, are you?"

She smiled despite cramps from the period that had started that morning. "No, we're going to wait a few months. Jim thinks I need to get over the war."

"But you weren't in actual combat. What do you need to get over?"

She shrugged, hiding irritation at the way he'd minimized her wartime duty. "Mainly being in the tropics so long. Anyway, he's the doctor."

He frowned out the windshield as the engine strained up the steep hill. "Tell me something, Annie. Were you sweet on him when I was home the other year?"

"Well, I liked him, yes. But I didn't have strong feelings till later. After I got word my husband was killed in action. Why?"

"Cause I sure could've fallen for you. Except you never gave me a chance. So I wondered if there was somebody else. Never thought it'd be crippled old Jim, though."

She felt the same flare of disgust she'd often felt with Jean. This sort of talk had been typical of her, and now her brother. No surprise there; the brief time she known him before, he'd always been full of himself, always larger than life. No, he hadn't mellowed. She bit her lip and looked away.

Since Alex and Cleve were refurbishing the hotel, she'd expected to see major changes, but the only difference was that the lobby no longer smelled of ancient wood but of fresh paint and varnish. "Cleve and Matt already finished the guest rooms," he said. "Except your old room, and Jeannie's, they're the owners' suite now. Including the hall bath." She didn't ask if he'd discarded Jean's yellow toothbrush. Of course he had; what was it to him? "Right now we're just doing cosmetic stuff, but once the weather warms up we'll start the new pavilion. Can't wait. Now. Come on back to the kitchen and say hello to Mrs. Leech."

The smile on the old woman's corrugated face was a pleasant surprise. After a stiff hug, she looked Anna over with a critical glance. "Oh, nurse," she said with a shake of her head, "you've lost so much weight, the war must've been terrible."

"No, we just didn't have cooks on the ship as good as you."

She chortled. "Oh, go on with you."

Alex leaned close to the old woman's ear. "Pam up yet?"

"Hour ago. Had tea, then took a sinking spell." She nodded toward the parlor door. "In there. Lying down again. Miss Jean was never that sick, was she, nurse?"

"If she was, she never let us see." Of course not; she'd been too ashamed.

Pam was stretched out on a sofa near the coal stove, her delicate features white and drawn, the pale blonde hair disheveled. But as Anna approached, she smiled, sat up and held out her hands. "Sorry to be such a drag, Anna. Thought I was going to give morning sickness a miss. Then they started painting. With all the fumes, I can't keep a thing down. Not even tea."

Anna pulled up a carved side chair. "Then try bites of dry Saltines as soon as you wake up. And a baked potato for breakfast. And instead of tea, little sips of Coca-Cola or ginger ale."

"Very well, I'll try. At least I wasn't sick at your wedding. It was so beautiful."

"Thanks. Now. How far along are you?"

"Haven't seen a doctor yet, so I'm not sure. Two months or so."

"Jim and his new associate are in the clinic today. Tom's had a lot of obstetric experience. Maybe he could give you something for the nausea."

"No need. Next week I have an appointment with the

specialist in Rockhampton. What's his name, Simon? Don't want to take any chances after what happened to Alex's sister."

She winced; Jean's needless death still rankled. "If only Jim could've gotten more sulfonamide...but, well, in '44 there still wasn't enough for civilians." She didn't mention their suspicion that her care in the hospital had been compromised, perhaps by someone who couldn't forgive her for having given such tangible aid and comfort to an enemy combatant that she'd gotten pregnant.

"I think it bothers Alex more than he lets on," Pam went on. "He hasn't taken to the little boy, almost as if he blames him for what happened." She shook her head wistfully, then pressed her fingers to her mouth and suddenly bolted toward the ladies' room in the lobby.

Anna had hoped to ask about her life in England, but by now Alex was pacing and scowling at his watch. "Sorry to rush you, but I need to help Cleve with the coal, so I'll take you down to Lorraine's now." They came out into the damp, bone-chilling cold. "Don't know how Cleve ever kept this place going while I was gone."

"He didn't. That's why he closed it after Jean died."

Alex chuckled. "Starting to think it'd be smarter to burn it down and start over."

"Oh don't say that. It's a wonderful old place. Almost as fine as the Wentworth."

The grin again. "Don't worry, Anna. Only kidding."

Was he? He braked in front of Lorraine's; Anna left the car and he sped off even before the other woman answered the door. Behind her, Jean's little boy stared up at her with blue-eyed suspicion. Johann was eighteen months old, tow-headed and so robust the floor shook when his sturdy legs pounded across it. A calico cat jumped to the mantel to escape. Watching its easy leap, Anna noticed a photograph of Luke in uniform propped against the mirror there. A familiar filigreed frame surrounded it like a halo. She walked over and picked it up. "Say. Isn't this the frame you had on the priest's picture in the guest room? I mean, the one of Luke's father?"

"Shh, Anna. Don't even mention it." Lorraine glanced nervously at the child, as if he was old enough to carry tales. "Yes, it's the same frame, but I hid that picture in the bottom of my cedar chest. So Luke wouldn't start wondering. " She led the way into the overheated kitchen, walls and cabinets and floor painted the joyous hues of pomegranates, limes and grapes. "Don't want him asking questions." She poured coffee into white china cups on the lemon-yellow table, gave Johann a graham cracker, a stack of pans and a wooden spoon, then set him on a rag rug by the big coal range where an iron pot wafted steam fragrant of cinnamon, cloves and tomatoes.

"So you haven't told him about his father yet, I guess." Anna sipped the strong, bitter brew, added canned milk and three teaspoons of sugar.

"Well, yes, I told him, just not the truth. See, I couldn't stand it if he turned on me. So I said he was the town banker. Even made up a name. And when Luke asked if he could meet him, I said he'd died. And that was the end of that."

"Oh, Lorraine. Suppose he learns the truth. He'll never trust you again."

"But how could he find out? Only you and Cleve and Jim know, and y'all'd never say anything. Besides, maybe he won't even come back here."

"I thought he was interested in starting a mission church."

"Well, yes." She lit a Lucky, waved the match out, inhaled deeply. "But it depends if he can get the diocese to support it. See, he wants a boat, some sort of floating chapel he could take to other islands too. He's back in Baltimore now, looking into it."

"Would he live here, with you and Cleve?"

She nodded vigorously. "Oh I hope so. He and Cleve get along just fine. And he loves Johann like a little brother. And he and I...well, we couldn't be closer if I'd raised him. Would you believe he calls me Mom?"

"That's nice. But I still wish you'd tell him about his real father."

"Oh Anna. Don't worry. He'll never find out."

She studied the older woman's face, pale now and blotchy without the heavy makeup she'd previously worn, and wanted to add that secrets had a way of emerging from even dark, locked places. You might hide a corpse in a closet, but before long, it would announce its presence anyway. Of course she said nothing of the sort; who was she to give such advice anyway?

"But enough of that. Now let's talk about you." Lorraine's dark eyes narrowed. "You look tired. Married life treating you okay?"

"It's fine," she said quickly. "Except Jim's so busy. And Tom's staying with us. And we have a housekeeper that doesn't let me do much of anything. I wanted a baby right away, but Jim thinks we should wait. And then, this morning I got my period..." She shrugged, chagrinned when her voice broke and her eyes filled.

Lorraine's expression shifted to pity. "Oh, Annie, that's awful. Don't he know how bad you want a family?"

"Certainly. But if he wants to wait, what can I do?"

Her voice was firmer than usual. "Trick him. Like Alex's wife did. See, he felt that way too. About waiting, I mean. So she got a safety pin and poked holes in all his rubbers, and sure enough, now she's in the family way."

Anna's mouth gaped. "That proper English lady did that?"

She nodded. "Listen, if you want a thing bad enough, sometimes you got to take matters in your own hands."

Something in her rebelled at the idea of such reproductive chicanery. "I'm surprised she told you."

"After a couple drinks, she'll tell you anything. Just wait and see."

She laughed as if the suggestion was a joke. "I could never do that to Jim." The self-righteousness in her tone rebuked her even as she spoke.

Lorraine shrugged and bent with a ragged diaper to wipe graham cracker mush from Johann's chin. Anna couldn't tell what he babbled, but the older woman said, "Hear that, Anna? He said 'More, mama,' clear as day. Cleve can't make it out, but I understand every word he says."

New cracker in hand, the child suddenly noticed Anna and toddled over, holding it out. "Bite," he said, so she did, but only a corner. He stuck the rest in his own mouth and went back to the pots and pans. Even peripherally, she felt Lorraine's scrutiny.

"Tell me something, Anna. How old would your little fellow be now?"

The question was so startling, she gulped coffee to loosen her throat. "Uh, two and a half. Why?"

Lorraine studied her another moment before she got up to refill her cup. "That's plenty long enough to wait for another. So just remember Pam's little trick."

They dawdled so long over lunch—a delicious Cajun chicken and rice dish Anna wished she could teach Kate O'Neill—and the kitchen was so quiet with Johann down for his nap, she didn't notice fine snowflakes straggling by the windows. Until Jim called from the clinic. "Time to get back now, dear. We'll meet you at the boat."

She hung up. "Sorry I can't stay longer, but we don't want to be stranded over here."

Lorraine brought her coat from a hook in the front room, helped her into it. "Can't say as I blame you." She kissed her cheek. "Will you be back next week?"

"Depends on what else I have to do. I'd like to, though. Your cooking's a lot better than the housekeeper's."

"Wait a minute. I'll send some chicken for y'all's supper."

She almost told her not to because of Kate's potential umbrage. But what the hell? "That'd be wonderful. We're probably only having leftovers." She watched Lorraine scoop heaping spoonsful into a Pyrex bowl, pop a shirred cover over it, and stow it in string bag. Then she headed out into the first wave of another snowfall. Still sparse, but at the pier, the trawler's engine was already thrumming when Anna hurried down the hill.

In the pilothouse, Jim met her with a casual kiss, then resumed his conversation with Tom. The mate cast them off and Fletch backed the boat around, crunching through ice that had thickened during the sunless day. Even at not quite three, dusk was closing in. They'd barely cleared the breakwater when the island disappeared in the whiteness, only a few lower lights shimmering along the harbor, fog horns bleating in the murk. Anna shivered with sudden nostalgia.

It didn't take long for her to realize the two doctors were discussing the day's patients. Of course they were; what else would concern them on Tom's first day on the island?

Feeling excluded, she sank into a seat, absorbing their conversation and stifling the urge to comment. After all, she was no longer the clinic insider she'd once been. Ironic that while she'd been working there, she'd been the one left behind on the pier when the boat left. Sometimes she'd watched until it disappeared in the distance, suffering pangs of separation from Jim even before her feelings had turned romantic. Today all that had changed: not only was he was close enough to touch, but she was going home with him to sleep in his bed and share the concerns of a married couple. Yet strangely enough, their lives still felt separate. Almost more so than when she'd been in the Pacific.

Maybe she'd expected too much. Had expected marriage to fill all her empty places, satisfy every need of her soul, and keep her glowing with the light of love. Silly; she'd lived with Dan Donovan only four months, but it had been long enough to teach her that marriage was as full as ups and downs as any other human enterprise.

Back at the house, Jim and Tom were in and out quickly, checking with Kate about patient phone messages and restocking their bags before they headed out again on house calls and hospital rounds.

Following Kate back to the kitchen, Anna sneaked Lorraine's leftovers into the fridge while the older woman stirred a huge enameled pot on the range. Judging by the smell, she was boiling laundry. Anna was wise to ask only, "Is that tonight's supper?"

"Well, there was scarcely enough shepherd's pie for me own lunch, so I got a nice corned beef brisket and a cabbage and carrots, and some fine potatoes for a proper boiled dinner. So we'll have plenty of leftovers for hash tomorrow."

"Oh, good. I love corned beef hash. Meantime, I'll set the table in the breakfast room."

"All taken care of, dearie. Now." She squinted down at Anna. "Why don't you get off your feet a while? You're looking a mite peaked, I guess from your monthly."

Anna's mouth dropped open. "Why is that any of your concern?"

"Oh, don't look so put out. I just noticed the Kotex in your bathroom when I cleaned earlier. I only meant a nice lie-down might perk you up before the men get back."

She didn't mean to snap, but her "Yes, it might, mightn't it?" sounded as irritated as she felt. Leaving the housekeeper sighing in the kitchen, she banged up the front steps. And wondered if she should complain to Jim about Kate's disregard of personal boundaries. No, of course not. He'd made romantic honeymoon speeches about his house now being hers too. But the fact was, he was proud of having found Kate, and if Anna had problems with her, he'd expect her to resolve them on her own.

So once again, she felt the need to live up to his mental image. As she would again tomorrow when, in nurse's whites, she'd work in the office with him and Tom. And when they went on house calls and she began to organize the mishmash of files and answer the phone. And listen to Kate s ideas about ripping up the old kitchen linoleum, then painting the floor and everything else in the room, and making a skirt for the sink, with matching curtains at the window. She'd already assured Anna she'd do all the work; she needn't worry about anything except picking colors and fabrics.

No, she thought, she wouldn't worry about anything except being what Jim needed. Two years before, as Hope Island's resident nurse, she'd handled emergencies with only a Merck manual and his telephoned advice. Once she'd even discovered a dead man among the housebound patients. One day a week she'd worked with Jim in the clinic and gone with him on house calls. But the other six days she'd been alone. In the meantime, she and Jean had watched a German sub blow up offshore, then nursed a survivor back to health. Nine months later, she'd stood by helplessly as Jean died of childbed fever.

Then she'd gone to the South Pacific, and cared for war wounded and visited exotic places she'd never expected to see. But in the end, she'd returned home with the satisfaction of seeing a long, tedious job through till thousands of casualties had been returned to the States.

In contrast, now she was no more than a day person on the island, a tourist whose life was elsewhere. Yet where? In this house, where her husband shared his profession with Tom? And Kate did all the things a wife did, except sleep with him? Would helping in his office qualify as a life of her own?

Maybe. If she were pregnant, if she had that to look forward to. Right now it was still only a vague promise. Even if she conceived immediately after Jim's recommended

three months, the earliest she could have a baby would be a
year from now.

A year like this? Talk about world without end.

In the bedroom, she turned on lamps, pulled her 1945
journal from the suitcase, then sat on the bed reading the
entry for January 2.

*Off Leyte again; worked the 7 to 3 shift on G-11, then
went to a funeral on the fantail for the scalded sailors we
picked up on Christmas. Taps as they slide the flag-wrapped
bodies over the side always makes me blubber. "Eternal
Father" does too, reminds me of Dan and the service I never
had for him. At least somebody cared for these boys while
they were dying. Luke showed no emotion, but Mark made a
point of finding me after the service, even lending me his
handkerchief to wipe my tears away. He's not an
Episcopalian, but he's a really good chaplain.*

It had taken four more months for this professional
admiration to swell into personal attraction, but even without
it, she'd worked with a sense of purpose she hadn't felt
before, nor could she imagine any situation that might evoke
it now. Sighing, she closed the notebook on her tiny, precise
writing and lay back on the pillow. She ached with more
than cramps now, so she closed her eyes and yielded to
fatigue, sliding in and out of sleep until Kate called up the
stairs that she was leaving. "And everything's ready as soon
as the men want to eat." Of course—as soon as the men want
to eat.

Dutifully, Anna thanked her; the back door slammed and
the flivver sputtered away. In the basement the oil burner
was churning, and from the Sound came the deep-throated
moan of foghorns in the snowfall. Desolate and distant, like
the night she'd left the ship, all those bleating horns in San
Francisco Bay enhancing her sense of nevermore.

None of that now, though; nothing so heroic and

dramatic–just impatience and frustration and a restless strain she couldn't account for.

When she heard Jim's car pull into the drive, she stuffed the notebook into a drawer and clattered down the back stairs just as he and Tom came in, stomping snow onto the green and black swirls of the kitchen linoleum. Jim's face was cold when she kissed him, and the end-of-the-day lines were deep, but his smile illumined the dismal room and sharpened her appetite for the boiled dinner she'd serve–whenever they were ready.

As she bustled back and forth from kitchen to breakfast room, she resolved to stop looking back, stop waiting for life to fulfill her dreams. Instead, she'd endure the next three months with the saintly patience of the virtuous wife she aimed to become.

Virtuous wife? Or a domestic martyr, like her mother?

No, never a martyr. More like a woman withholding a dark personal secret from a loved one. More like Lorraine.

CHAPTER SEVEN

On the afternoon of Wednesday, April 17, Anna was waiting at the East Point pier when *Molly B* materialized from a blur of offshore mist. As the trawler chugged into the little harbor, she got out of the car, polished a smudge on the hood with her jacket sleeve, and leaned against it in a proprietary slouch. The 1940 Cadillac coupe was hardly new, though its chrome trim and pearl gray finish gleamed as if fresh off the assembly line. And even with 18,000 miles on the odometer, the interior still smelled of good leather, overlaid by a ladylike tinge of lavender eau-de-cologne.

When the trawler had tied up, she walked toward the gangway. Preceding Jim, Tom gave her a quick hug and a "Welcome home," as he stepped off the boat. Since she'd been away the past week, she expected Jim's kiss to be more amorous, but by then he'd already spotted the car and begun edging up the hill toward it. Finally he smiled at her. "Well, I see the new car made it back. Nice birthday present. How'd she handle on the trip?"

"I'm glad to see you too, darling," she said snidely. "Anyway, she handled fine. The way a Caddy should."

Taking the slope to the parking area faster than usual at the end of a long day, Jim circled the vehicle with an appraising gaze, doing everything but kicking the tires. Tom stood back and chuckled. "Classy buggy, Anna. When Margie sees it, bet she'll pester me to trade in my old Chevy for something better."

Jim stroked the hood ornament with the reverence usually reserved for holy relics. "Damned fine of your dad to get it for you. Now. When can I test-drive it?"

She handed over the keys. "Right this minute, if you promise not to speed."

Inside, she pointed out the low mileage. "See, the previous owner never drove it anywhere but church. And once a year, to Lake Winnepesaukee."

He switched on the ignition, stepped on the starter, than cocked his head to assess the engine's smooth purr. "Did she happen to be a little old lady?"

"How'd you know?"

He laughed. "That's what car dealers always say."

"But this one really was. She was one of Dad's parishioners; he did her funeral service last winter."

"Well, I'll be damned." He caressed the steering wheel as if making love to it. "How much trade-in did he get on Dan's old Plymouth?"

"Don't know. He only said it was generous."

Gently, he shifted into reverse and backed around, waiting for Tom to leave first in the Buick. "Were you sad to see it go?"

She nodded, remembering she'd left Dan's cigarettes in the glove compartment, where they'd been since the boat had first left for the war. "A little. It was worse when we took his gold star out of the window. Actually, everything about cleaning out the rectory's been sad. Especially for my father. You know, he's been at St. Stephen's since I was five. And now he's retiring, he won't even have a new parish to occupy him. I'm glad I went down though. Otherwise, they wouldn't have started packing till the movers were at the door."

Apparently assessing the whine of second gear, he nodded absently and drove up the long hill and onto the steeper slope of Holden Avenue. Turning into their street, he finally shifted into high, then coasted to a stop in front of the house. Sunlight radiated off its white clapboards and blue gingerbread trim, dazzled in the long narrow windows and twinkled in the gold-green umbrellas of budding trees overhead. He edged closer to Kate's Ford, set the hand brake and switched off the ignition. "Fine car, dear. Your father knows a good deal when he sees one."

"Can we drive it to the restaurant tonight and unload some boxes at their new place? Trunk's full of them."

Another casual nod. "Hope you don't mind, but I told Tom I'd make rounds while he takes the house calls. Gave him the night off too so he can call Margie and talk as long as he wants. Never seen him as excited as he is about her visit this weekend. Wants to set a date for the wedding."

Anna sniffed. "I only hope she doesn't change her mind when she sees the way we live up here. She might've been raised on a farm, but now she's got Boston in her blood."

Jim shook his head morosely. "Hate to think he'd leave the practice for her, but he'd probably move to the city if she changed her mind about living here." He sighed, pocketed the car keys as if he'd assumed ownership, then gave her a bright smile. "But I'll worry about that later. This is your birthday and tonight we're going to celebrate."

The hall clock was bonging five when they came into the house. In the vestibule, Anna caught the sweet aroma of roasting meat. Before she could even set down her purse, there was Kate, enveloping her in a massive, onion-smelling hug and the faintly mildewed scent that always clung to her clothing. "Oh, Anna, welcome home! And happy birthday. Hope the trip's whet your appetite. Because I'm making the finest dinner you'd ever want—a lovely leg of spring lamb, with new potatoes and fresh peas. And mint jelly, of course. Yeast rolls too, and a cake with 28 candles. Chocolate. Jim said it's your favorite."

Overwhelmed by this spate of unexpected news, Anna backed away. "Oh? Well, it all sounds wonderful. But you shouldn't have. See, Jim and I – "

He shot her a warning glance. "Kate, I told you this morning, I'm taking Anna to La Grande Chartreuse tonight. Remember?"

Her eyes widened, one hand flew to her mouth. "This morning? Oh no, you never did. I swear. But I bet being gone so long, she'd much rather eat right here in her own fine home than some fancy foreign place. Wouldn't you, Anna?"

She glanced at him for guidance, but his gaze had dropped to the frayed Oriental carpet under their feet. "Uh...up to you, dear. We can always go another time."

"Or have the lamb tomorrow," she suggested.

Kate wrung her hands. "Oh no, 'tis never anywhere near as good the next day!"

Feeling trapped, Anna began to twitch. Until Tom came to the office doorway. "What's this I hear about a lamb roast?"

She gave Jim an uneasy glance as Kate launched into the tale. In her best martyred tone, of course. When she finished, Tom had clearly fallen into the trap. "Now don't you fret, Kate, it'll all work out fine. See, I love leg of lamb more than anything except Margie, and with Jim and Anna at the restaurant, I can have all I want." He smiled at her puckered, mournful face. "Even better, why don't you eat with me? Afterwards, you can take a nice big plate to your mother."

"Oh, Doctor Tom, I couldn't." Still, her eyes had begun to glow with the clear light of undisguised adoration, as if she were addressing one of the marble saints in Our Lady Star of the Sea Catholic Church in Rockhampton.

"Sure, you could. Now call and tell her you'll be late."

When they left for town, Tom was on house calls, and Kate was humming in the kitchen. This time Jim got behind the wheel of the Cadillac without even asking Anna if it was okay. Resolved to try to get pregnant later, she wanted romance to sweeten the evening, so didn't remind him whose car it was. Romance, she'd long since realized, was not one of Jim's natural moods. Rather, it was a tenuous, fragile state that would always take a back seat to medical concerns, as it did now when he parked behind the hospital.

"Won't be long, dear," he called as he got out.

She waved him on, watched him limp up the marble steps. At the top he turned and blew her an afterthought kiss, which caused her spirits to rise a bit. Nothing like a week away, she thought, to sharpen lust, even in a man as devoted to his patients as Jim.

Waiting in the long, low light of late afternoon, she fingered her rings and watched the power plant smokestack smudge up the spring sky. Then Dr. Simon exited the medical office building and hurried across the parking lot, still in lab coat, stethoscope dangling from his neck. He walked hunched over, perhaps a consequence of doing so many pelvic exams. One day soon she hoped to provide him with another. He'd probably spend more time with her than he did the average multipara, because she'd have to deliver by C-section. The scar from the first was now a thin pink line across her belly; would the next be vertical? And would he make her wear a damned maternity corset for support?

But biggest question of all–what were the chances of another placental abruption? She and Jim had discussed it, but clinically, as if it hadn't already happened to her. On the other hand, Dr. Simon would quiz her for every small detail that had led to up to it. Then, weighing all the factors, he'd assure her it wouldn't happen again. He would, wouldn't he? Surely an abruption was like lightning–it never struck twice, did it?

Shortly after the OB man went into the hospital, Jim came out, walking as jauntily as a man could on a cane. Her heart lightened as he approached. The next stop was the house she'd rented for her parents to move to after Easter: a cedar-sided Cape Cod two blocks down the hill from All Saint's Church, with a sliver of Penobscot Bay visible from the front porch.

As they set the packing boxes in the front hall, the closed-up stillness felt smothering, heavy with a pall of all the meals ever cooked in that tiny dark kitchen. Her parents hadn't seen it yet, but her mother was sure it'd do till they found something grander where she could entertain all the new friends she intended to make at the church here.

They were on time at the restaurant, but it was busy, service slower than it had been even during the war. Impatience gnawed her, though the *Mittelschmerz* she'd felt that morning meant she had a good two days to conceive. Nonetheless, she wanted to get to it tonight, implanting that new promise in her heart as soon as possible. None of which she spoke aloud, of course, chattering instead about the awful job she'd had cleaning out the rectory while her father had wandered around with a bereft cast to his face.

"I understand it, though," she added." It's what you do when time's running out and everything you look at it makes you sad because you're not going to see it again."

His eyes narrowed. "Is that how it was when you left the ship?"

She nodded and blinked rapidly to keep nostalgia at bay. "Poor Dad. Don't know what he's going to do after thirty-two years as a priest. I'm not worried about Mother, of course. She'll move right into All Saints' and take over all the ladies' guilds. She won't be Mrs. Rector any more, but she'll still act like it."

He laughed, swiped a glance at his watch. Almost eight, and the harried waiter still hadn't removed their soiled plates. "Want dessert, dear? Their crème brulee's outstanding."

"Do you have time?"

"Nothing else to do tonight." He leaned closer. "Except take you to bed."

"Good. That's on my agenda too." She was trying to come up with a more seductive addendum when the waiter appeared, scooping the soiled plates onto a tray before he asked about dessert. His tone was weary, as if he hoped they didn't want any.

"Yes, two crème brulees, please," Jim told him. "And coffee too."

The young man sighed as he lugged off the heavy tray.

"You know, Jim. Maybe we should wait and have birthday cake back at the house. So Kate's not upset."

"Too bad if she is. Damn, that was awkward earlier. Tom confirmed I did tell her about our plans tonight. Don't know why she didn't remember."

"Well, it worked out well for her. You know, sometimes I think she has designs on him."

His eyes went wide. "If she does, she'll have to get over it before Margie comes Saturday. And moves into his bed."

"No, they're going to stay at the Mansion House. So they don't intrude on us, he says. Meaning, make a lot of racket in bed."

His grin was wide and happy. "God, I've missed that kind of talk this week."

Even as the promise of the night began to blossom, she noticed the tuxedoed maître-de advancing toward them; in his hand, a phone trailed a long cord. His little mustachioed face was so anxious, Anna's heart clutched with apprehension.

But there he was, bending over the table with the phone. "So sorry to intrude, Dr. Millett. But the party on the line says it's an emergency."

"Thanks, Henri." Jim picked up the receiver. Henri shrank back, hands folded, eyes lowered while Jim listened with the gathering frown she recognized as professional concern. As she waited to learn how seriously Fate had interrupted their evening, he asked into the receiver, "Anything I can do that you can't?" More listening. "Well, okay, if you think I should. Half an hour, then." He replaced the receiver; Henri swooped in to take it away. When Jim's gaze met Anna's it was troubled and apologetic.

"Okay, what was that all about?"

"Bad news, dear. Kate found her mother unconscious when she got home this evening. Tom's at the hospital with her now. Looks like a stroke. Not much either of us can do, but he thinks Kate'll feel better if I come too. Hate to on your birthday, though."

Ah, the revenge of the spurned cook, she thought. She patted his hand and forced sweetness into her tone. "But you have to, dear. After all, we've had dinner. We can have dessert later."

"No, there's time now. Then you can leave me at the hospital; Tom'll bring me home."

They ate the crème brulees too fast to savor them. Then with the rich taste still lingering on her taste buds, she drove the few blocks back to the hospital. She came inside with him, through the deserted lobby and down the same dismal corridor she'd once walked to see Jean on her deathbed. The place was hushed, lights dimmed, only the occasional nurse dispensing meds visible. The combined pungency of antiseptic and body wastes was barely noticeable.

They found Kate slumped on a bench at the far end. As they approached, she rose unsteadily and reached for Jim's hands. Her voice was a wail. "Oh, Jim, Jim. Me poor Mither. Quick, go see her, and tell me what you think."

He extricated himself. "Of course, right away."

When he'd gone into the room, Anna slid her arm around Kate's broad shoulder. "Oh Kate, I'm so sorry," she crooned, the perfect combination of priest's daughter and doctor's wife. "When did it happen?"

Kate sniffled, daubed at her eyes with a man's handkerchief. "Found her like that when I got home from your place. Laid out like the dead on the davenport, she was." She shivered and crossed herself. "Oh, I knew she was upset I stayed late, but I never thought...."

"No, of course not. Well, you probably found her in time.

And between Jim and Tom, she'll get the best possible care."
Her large, gray-green eyes filled. "Oh, I pray so, Anna. I couldn't go on without her."

"Well, I'll pray too, as hard as I can." Something warned her not to ask, "Or do you think Protestant prayers will work against her?"

She sat with Kate until the men emerged from the room ten minutes later. She hoped the housekeeper couldn't read Jim's nothing-more-I-can-do expression, or hear him whisper, "Go on home dear. And don't wait up. Might be a while."

"Stay as long as Kate needs you." She kissed his cheek, patted her hand. "Now don't you worry. They'll take good care of her."

Feeling guilty about her own disappointment, she drove the winding road out of Rockhampton, across the inlet where berthed boats glistened in the light of a rising moon, full and golden in the sky, a shimmering path on the water. The scene reminded of the amber moon low above the Philippine Sea after the Kamikazes had sunk a destroyer, buzzed the hospital ship, then attacked a nearby oiler. They'd picked up hundreds of casualties in the water, then worked till nightfall stabilizing them. With no appetite for supper, she and Mark had watched the moon rise, swigged bourbon in his cabin, then spent the night together in his narrow bunk, supposedly so neither would have to be alone with these fresh, horrifying memories. They hadn't undressed, or kissed or done anything improper; just slept spoon-fashion, with nothing between them but tenderness and comfort. Until close to dawn, when he'd woken her with purely carnal intentions. Filled with righteous indignation, she'd fled to her own cabin like a raped nun. Hard to believe now that she, who in the four years before had already slept with two men and worked around enough others to know the relentlessness of lust, she'd been horrified. As if she was totally innocent of stirring Mark's.

Still touched with the memory, she came into the darkened house, turning on lights as she headed toward the stairs. The fatty residue of roast lamb followed her to the bedroom until she opened the window to a fragrant spring breeze. She wasn't hopeful that Jim would get home in time to notice, but she slid into a new pink nylon nightie, admiring her image in the mirror over the bureau when she retrieved her old diary from the underwear drawer. Then, getting into bed, she read the entry from the year before.

At sea en route to Pearl today, my 27th birthday; the only thing special about it was the cake in the wardroom and that silly song from everybody. With 65 officers on board, there's at least one birthday a week, so it's never a surprise. Afterward we all resumed griping about our slow progress–barely making ten knots because of engineering problems. Seems worse because we're desperate for our first overnight liberty in six months. Audrey, Willi and I are bunking in nurses' quarters at the hospital; then we're going to the beach at Waikiki, and shop, and have our hair done, and eat in restaurants in Honolulu, and Sunday night before we sail, go to a luau at the Officers' Club. Oh, I can't wait to get off this tub!

She was surprised to see no mention of Mark; obviously at that time, she wasn't yet hooked. In spite of their night together, flirting with him had still seemed merely innocuous. Because her will was still free, her body still Jim's.

She paged through the diary a while before she turned off the light and listened to the old Westclox ticking off the last two hours of this birthday. The breeze was faintly scented with spring blossoms, the sky bright with moonlight. Letting herself dwell on Mark as compensation for Jim's absence, she closed her eyes and wondered if he was at this very moment in bed with his wife. Or staring at the moon over

Portsmouth, Virginia, and thinking of her. Did he still? Having never answered his letter with the news he'd been assigned to the Naval Hospital there, she had no idea. Something had always stayed her hand; maybe the rectitude she'd sworn to uphold when she'd embarked on the good wife stint, her penance before she conceived another child.

She didn't realize she'd fallen asleep till she felt him beside her, moonlight behind him, his face too shadowed to discern his features. But she knew instinctively it was Mark whose fingers pressed into her arms, whose breath was hot on her cheek, whose murmurs filled her ears. And whose body met hers in a familiar rhythm. Oh God, Mark, fresh and real as ever, unblurred even by the months without him.

But abruptly he was gone, evaporated in a few heartbeats. Instead, on the far side of the bed, Jim was unstrapping the brace. Her heart was still thudding and desire oozed from every pore, warm and sweet as honey. Surely he'd notice if he touched her. Or had the demanding day sapped him of even this primordial instinct?

Downstairs, the clock chimed half-past the hour as he shifted under the covers, turning onto his side away from her. She slid over, wrapped one arm about his waist, and kissed the side of his face. The late-day beard was rough against her lips, skin bitter with Bay Rum residue.

"Sorry, darling. Didn't mean to wake you," he murmured.

"You didn't. I've been waiting." Ignoring the good-girl urge to ask for Kate's mother, she licked his lips and flicked her tongue into the toothpaste freshness of his mouth.

His breath quickened. "Hoped you would, but it's so damned late. Eleven-thirty."

"That's okay. It's still my birthday."

He laughed. "Made it in time then. Wouldn't want your present to be late." He kissed her again, then made the familiar move toward the night stand.

She stayed his arm. "No, Jim, no condom tonight. Let's not wait any longer."

He hesitated. "You mean…?"

"Sure. It's been three months now."

"Well, then."

Though it was her husband with her now, the interrupted dream with Mark resumed. At the end it was all she could do not to gasp out his name. Right after God's.

CHAPTER EIGHT

The Saturday morning train from Boston was ten minutes late when it thundered into Brunswick station, moving so fast it overshot the platform and had to back up. When it finally screeched to a reversed stop, Margie was ready to descend the steps of the last coach. In a tailored red suit, a white straw cloche pulled over her platinum curls, she could've been a model. Or a movie starlet. Tossing Anna a wave first, she let the conductor take her hand, help her down, then carry her suitcase to the platform. From his silly grin, he considered it a rare privilege.

Anna rushed over, hugged her carefully to avoid creasing the linen jacket, then grabbed the bag. "Is this all the luggage you brought… for a week?"

"Well, I planned to stay a week. But then they offered me private duty starting Tuesday." Her patent leather heels clicked on the macadam as they crossed the parking area. "The pay's so good, I couldn't turn it down. Don't worry. Tom understands."

"I thought he wanted to look for an apartment while you're here."

She slipped on white-framed sunglasses from her purse. "We still can. I'm not leaving Monday till the four o'clock train. That's why I asked you to pick me up today. So we can catch up. Seems like a year since your wedding."

"Good. We don't have to meet Jim and Tom for lunch till

one. An hour and a half." She dropped the suitcase into the back seat and they climbed into the car.

Ooh-ing and ah-ing, Margie caressed the leather upholstery. "Gosh, Anna. If your father can afford a Caddy, priests must make more than I thought." Her bright red lips pursed in the suggestion of a pout. "But I bet if I asked, Tom'd get me one too."

Anna started the engine and backed into the street. "Probably. He's so crazy about you, I believe he'd do anything you ask."

Margie's shrug was exquisitely nonchalant. Well, of course. Men were always crazy about her. Anna had suspected Tom was as soon as he'd mentioned their New Year's Eve date. Since then, she'd only become more certain. Whenever the weather was reasonable, he'd drive the two hundred miles to Boston Friday afternoons, and come dragging back Sunday nights with the sappy look of a man who's been laid more in two days than the whole rest of his life. Anna hadn't been surprised when he'd bought an engagement ring, just shocked that Margie'd accepted it. But now that she'd finally come up to see how they lived in coastal Maine, she feared it wouldn't be long till she gave it back. Or broke the engagement and kept it anyway, as she had once or twice before with other hapless men.

Margie sighed as Anna turned north on Route One. "Oh, I don't know if he'll do anything for me. See, I want us to live in Boston, but he says he can't let Jim down. So, if the mountain won't come to Mohammed...well, you know the rest."

"Really? Even if you don't like it here?"

"How bad can it be? I mean, you put up with it."

"Well, sure. But I never went in for city life. You took to Boston the first week of nursing school."

"You would've too, if you'd ever given it a chance. Now, though...golly. You look like you've been married forever. At least longer than four months."

She felt the pin-prick of her friend's insult. "You mean I've turned into a frump?"

"No, of course not." She patted Anna's arm. "Just... oh, so contented. Uh-oh. You're not *un peu enceinte*, are you?"

Anna tried to smile mysteriously. "Could be. Too soon to tell."

"Well, if that's what you want... Tom's desperate for kids too, because he's almost forty. But I've told him not before I'm thirty-five. Myself though, I don't care if I never have any."

Anna wasn't surprised. Since high school, she and Margie had wanted different things from life. Sometimes she'd wondered how they'd ever become chums in the first place. Her part of the equation was obvious: her friend was an exciting, even daring presence in her own staid, conservative existence. Eventually she concluded that "the blonde bombshell" tolerated her mainly because boys rarely gave her a second look. Her heart skittered, imagining her friend's shock if she confessed about Mark. She was tempted; what use was being colorful if no one knew?

On the drive north, she pointed out the few spots of interest, like the Brunswick Air Station, and the Bath shipyard, but Margie'd already heard about them from a Coast Guard officer she'd met on the train. "Just the sweetest man. I think he could've gone for me. In spite of the ring." She waggled her left hand so the diamond flashed in the sunlight.

Anna rolled her eyes. "No doubt."

Beyond Bath, she searched in vain for some scintillating commentary about the farms and tidal inlets that comprised the roadside scenery. Instead, she shifted to Luke; any girl who appreciated men would find him infinitely more interesting. "Say, Margie. Remember the Roman priest at my wedding?"

"I'll say! Best-looking guy there. His mother lives on that island, doesn't she?"

"He does too, now. In fact, the bishop's coming today to consecrate a trawler he's converted into a church boat. He'll take it to islands that don't have a Catholic church. Starting with Easter services."

"That's nice." Margie stifled a yawn. "Will we see him while I'm here?"

"Sure. This afternoon, if you come to the consecration. Tom said he'll be there, but only if you want to go too. Gosh, you haven't asked him to turn Protestant, have you?"

"Not yet. But he probably would."

"Hmm." If he wouldn't move to the city, maybe he wouldn't change his faith either. The more they talked, the more she realized that crazy though this pair might be about each other, they'd likely never marry. Or if they did, not for eternity. Her feelings about that swung from relief that Tom wouldn't leave Jim's practice, to disappointment that Margie wouldn't be close enough to resume their friendship.

With time to spare before they met the men, Anna drove around Rockhampton, pointing out the town square so Margie she could admire its iconic white Congregational church, Benjamin's department store, the hospital, the Roxy Theater, and down at the harbor, the new car ferry terminal. Just beyond it, Luke's church boat was tied to a finger pier. Except for the brass cross atop the mast, her white-painted hull and long, windowed deck house gave *Evangel* the appearance of a tour boat rather than a floating chapel. Workmen were lugging folding chairs aboard, but there was no sign of the priest or the sweet-faced young man who'd come from Baltimore to work with him, so she continued on to the Clam Bake. The tide was out and the black muck around its skinny pilings reeked of dead sea creatures; Margie shuddered and pressed a hanky to her nose.

They came back into town past All Saints' and the house Anna's parents had rented so Margie could see what was available for fifty a month. But her friend only yawned and looked away from the potholed street to the shabby old homes lining it. To Anna it had all seemed beautiful, but shifting to a citified vision, she saw a backwater town that had barely scraped through the depression and war years, about as far from sophisticated Boston as you could get.

As a last desperate measure, she cruised past La Grande Chartreuse where they were booked for dinner that evening. In the harsh noon sunlight the ginger-breaded pink Victorian mansion looked as faded as a retired chorus girl.

Margie sniffed. "A French restaurant, here? Really, Anna, how good could it be?"

She shrugged. "We're not used to Boston cuisine, so we think it's fine."

Back at the square, she parked just down from the hotel. As they emerged from the car, Tom bolted from the canopied entrance; a wide grin transformed him to John Garfield, only taller and gray-haired. Margie picked up her heels and actually ran into his arms. Their embrace was so lengthy, passersby began to stare and snicker. The lovers came out of it only when the Camden bus tooted as it slowed for the stop at the Rexall.

"Were we ever that bad?" Jim whispered.

"I would've been, but you were too stodgy."

He chuckled. "Always thought Tom was too. But Lord, look at him now."

Anna looked, knowing what she'd see—Margie's bright, perky face gazing up as if he were the last man on earth. The same adoration she'd turned on every boy or man she'd fancied since seventh grade. The only problem was, Tom thought he was the first.

"She seems crazy about him now," Anna said." But that doesn't mean she won't break his heart."

Jim squeezed her hand. "Thank God you're not that sort of woman."

Remorse clutched her; it always did when he credited her with greater virtue than she deserved. Then a whiff of stale coffee and cigarette smoke wafted from the nearby coffee shop. When her stomach turned, she told herself it couldn't be pregnancy nausea. Not yet, not after only four days. But even this slight possibility lit the smile she gave him.

That evening, the four of them had parted at La Grande Chartreuse after coffee and éclairs, but Anna and Jim saw nothing of the other couple till the next afternoon. And then they were half an hour late for Easter dinner. It was Kate's first day back on the job since Mither's stroke, so she'd concocted an over-the-top feast–a gigantic ham studded with cloves and pineapple slices, about twenty side dishes, and a tall white cake topped by a coconut nest of yellow marshmallow chicks trying to hatch a rainbow of jelly beans.

All this food was ready to serve on the dot of two, except that the guests hadn't arrived yet. As the clock ticked off the minutes, Kate's frenzy of hand-wringing and nervous pacing grew ever worse. "Oh, me lovely dinner's going to be ruined! And I'll be late feeding poor Mither. By the saints, where could they be?"

"Still in bed, I'll wager." Jim pulled aside the dining room curtains to scan the street. "But don't worry, Kate. The nurse'll feed your mother if you're not there." Since the old lady was now miraculously on the mend, he'd arranged private duty care so Kate could resume her household duties here.

"Margie's always been late for everything," Anna said. "First school, then work. Sometimes I think the only thing that keeps her from being fired is how cute she is."

He shook his head, backed away from the window. "Sounds a little like my first wife. She was never on time either, not even for our wedding. She got away with it because she was pretty too."

She pondered the disturbing implications of this news. "If their romance turns out like yours did, will Tom ever get over it?"

"We get over what we have to, dear. He will too."

His answer was one of those innocent ambiguities that often prickled her with guilt. It dissipated only when Tom's old black Chevy rolled into the drive. Kate instantly bustled back to the kitchen, all smiles now and humming *In Dublin's Fair City.*

Hands linked, the lovers came in the back door. Margie's cheeks were pink with beard-burn.

And Tom looked sheepish, hair wild, as if uncombed since the night before. Anna shook her head and went to help Kate bring the meal to the table.

When Kate had announced she'd make Easter dinner, Jim in his great compassion had invited her to share it, but as guest, not hired help. This meant passing endless dishes of food , which reminded her of childhood meals on the Auld Sod. "Except there were so many of us, we couldn't all sit at one time. Once I even heard me Da say, 'By God, I've screwed meself out of a place at the table.'"

Anna stared in disbelief. Jim continued loading his plate without a change of expression. Margie shot Anna a horrified glance. Tom blushed.

Reaching for the platter, Kate speared a slab of ham. Then another, and a third. "And now, poor Mither, so far from home and kin. Thank the good Lord, at least I'm here for her." She wiped a tear on her blouse sleeve, and lunged for the mashed potato bowl.

In his flattest tone, Jim said, "And for us too. It's certainly good to have you back."

"Amen to that," said Tom. "This is a swell dinner."

"And 'twas a joy making it for such dear ones. You're me family now." She finished helping herself, then began eating with a speed Anna had observed before only in ex-war prisoners the ship had brought home from Japan.

"Ah, and Father Luke too," she went on. "'T'was so wonderful having the Easter Vigil yesterday on his fine new boat. It has an angelic glow, it does. Like that sweet young priest he brought from Baltimore."

Anna stifled a malicious snicker. "He's not a priest, Kate. Just a friend from the orphanage. More like an...an acolyte. And the boat's mate." She'd already heard Lorraine's explanation of why Luke and Tim were sharing her guest room: "He's training him to be a deacon," she'd said with great maternal pride.

"And did you ever see anything as precious as that little Johann in his tiny sailor suit?" Kate asked. "Poor wee tyke, with nary mother nor father to raise him."

"But Lorraine's doing a fine job of it," Jim said.

"Oh, that one," Kate spat out. "Painted hussy. No wonder she got herself in trouble all those years ago. Now you'd think there's nary a sin on her conscience, running around like the Blessed Mother herself with the Baby Jesus in her arms."

Tom cleared his throat and helped himself to seconds of everything. "Mm, Margie, want to ride with me on house calls later? Just a few, so it won't take long."

"Thanks, but I promised Anna I'd help clean up. Since Kate has to leave."

"Ah sure, and glad you reminded me. This is all so grand, I near forgot Mither." She pushed her chair back. "Anna, I'm just going to take her a wee slice of cake. You can serve the rest, can't you?"

"Of course." Relieved, she almost promised to wash the dishes.

"I'll stop by to see her after rounds later," Jim called as she retreated.

They finished eating in a stunned silence broken only by the inevitable medical dialogue between the men. By now, Margie was looking wilted. Or forlorn. Or perhaps just horribly bored.

After Tom and Jim had left to tend the sick, Anna brought cake and coffee to the table. "Well, now," she said with patent irony. "Wasn't dinner fun?"

"Oh Anna," Margie wailed. "How do you stand living like this?"

"It's not so bad. You're just not used to it yet. If only you could stay longer."

For a moment, Margie glared at her cake, then began fork-stabbing it so viciously it was soon reduced to a pile of crumbs. "Actually, it's probably good I'm leaving earlier. Honestly, Anna. I'd go mad here. It's so backward. So small town. Even worse than Portsmouth. What would I do anyway–work in some doctor's office? Or that prehistoric hospital?" She tossed her platinum coif. "I couldn't take it."

Disappointed but in no way surprised, Anna said, "I hope you're not going to break the engagement."

"Oh, I don't know. I really don't. I mean, I love Tom more than any man I've ever known. But this life…well, maybe he'll change his mind if I refuse to move up here. Sorry, Anna, but Jim'd just have to find someone else."

Anna plucked the marshmallow chicken from her cake and bit the head off. "Don't count on it. Changing his mind, I mean. If Tom can't have you, well, there's plenty other fish in the sea."

She sat taller, arching her eyebrows. "Not fish like me."

Anna made her shrug casual. "Sure there are. My cabin mate on the ship was one. Pretty and vivacious. The patients loved her. So did some of the docs. And the Protestant chaplain. When she got pregnant, she didn't know who the father was because she'd slept with so many men. Said she was having too much fun to be tied to anybody."

Margie sniffed. "Listen, that'd never happen to me. I'm too careful. Besides, I'm faithful to Tom. Sure, I go out with other guys--he knows that--but I don't sleep with them. She must've been a tramp, just a tramp." She sipped coffee. "What ever happened to her?"

"Had an AB in one of our ORs. When it went sour, the chief surgeon did an emergency hyssie. They transferred the whole guilty trinity off when we got to Guam–Patty, the doc who botched it, and the sinful chaplain. I never heard anything after that."

"Was there much of that on your ship? Promiscuity, I mean."

"Oh, a few romances, but I didn't know anyone else who slept around like that. Could've been, though. Plenty of temptation. And we all wanted to forget the non-stop casualties. I guess screwing helped."

Her gaze bored into Anna. "But you...you were never tempted, were you?"

The truth within her goaded her into saying, "Sure. But not enough to make me forget Jim."

"Really?" Margie's eyes widened. "Who was it, some cute surgeon? Or Father Luke? Now there's a man who could turn my head."

"Well, he is handsome. And when I first met him, he reminded me of Dan. Then I found out he's queer. But the other chaplain, the replacement for the one who slept with Patty...." Heat rose to her face at even this vague reference to Mark.

Her eyes went wide. "What about him?"

Anna regarded the mutilated chick, the gaudy jelly beans, the lard-based icing, the unnaturally yellow cake crumbs. "He tempted me." She pushed the plate away. "Until I...until I found out he'd had affairs with other nurses. And was married."

Her face relaxed into a smile. "That's funny, Anna. I've always thought you were such a goody-two-shoes. But tell me more. Was he a dreamboat?"

"No, not really. Just a nice man. And a good chaplain." Her mind drifted a moment. "For instance, last Easter was early, the first of April. The same day we invaded Okinawa, so we were offshore, waiting for casualties." She squeezed her eyes closed. "There were none all day, which made it worse. The waiting, I mean." She drew a deep breath.

"Anyway, that evening he had a prayer service that touched everybody. See, no matter what happened, he helped us remember the Lord was still with us."

Margie regarded her solemnly. "Is that when you were tempted?"

"No. Just filled with admiration."

"Gee. Does Jim know? About the temptation, I mean?"

"He knows we were friends. Besides, anybody can be tempted." She got to her feet and began collecting dirty plates. "So don't say anything to Tom, okay? I wouldn't want him to mention it to Jim. He'd be hurt." Then, having lied her way out of the corner she'd painted herself into, she strode righteously to the kitchen with an armload of soiled dishes.

Margie followed through the swinging door. "Okay. My lips are sealed. But getting back to that…that awful woman. You know. Typhoid Mary? How do you put up with her?"

"She's not awful. Just coarse, and overbearing. But a really hard worker." Anna gestured at the newly-enameled white cabinets, table and chairs, yellow walls, blue-checked curtains, glossy blue linoleum. "It was dark as a cave in here till she painted everything. And made those curtains." She ran hot water and began rinsing plates. "So if you break it off with Tom, I bet she'll set her cap for him. If she hasn't already."

Margie dropped a handful of cutlery into the sink. "Oh Anna, that's crazy. She's so…so shanty Irish. So servile. She's cut out to be a domestic, not a doctor's wife."

Anna shrugged; beyond the potted red geranium on the windowsill, neighborhood kids in Easter finery were pawing through the shrubbery in search of dyed eggs. "Well, he could do worse. For one thing, they're both Catholic. She's about his age, too, and a lot smarter than she lets on. Would you believe she reads Tolstoy to her mother?"

Margie shook her head firmly. "Do you honestly think after me, he'd settle for an immigrant housekeeper, no matter how bright she is?"

"If he was class-conscious, no. But his wife worked in her parents' Italian restaurant. Tom's father was a millworker and his mother took in laundry. So what do you think?"

"Oh no. He'd never." But her brows were lowered, her mouth down-turned at the corners.

"Maybe not. But they're already friends. She confides in him, and he tells her how to deal with her mother's condition. Sure, he'd rather have you. And he'd take it really hard if you broke things off. But he'd get over it, Margie. Because he wants to be married. To belong to somebody." She shook suds from her hands. "So don't let his feelings stop you from doing what you want."

Margie sagged against the kitchen table, oblivious to scraps of ham and crumbs of cake that might besmirch her pleated navy dress with the white sailor's collar. "You can't mean that, Anna. I know how Tom feels. Even if she was good enough for him…well, I don't want to sound vain, but you have to admit I'm a lot more attractive."

"Hell, Margie, you're 'a lot more attractive than ninety percent of the rest of us. Just remember, though, all cats are gray in the dark."

She didn't answer, scowling and rubbing the toe of one black patent pump against the floor until the old pattern began to show through the new paint.

Anna added, "Look, maybe you're right. I'm just saying, if you leave him, he probably won't be alone very long. If it's not Kate, he'll find someone else. There's a few cute war widows in town." She draped the dishrag over the faucet and waited for her friend to speak. When she didn't, she said, "Now. Why don't I show you the rest of the house before the men come back."

Her face was troubled, a rare expression for Margie. Good. Anna hoped she'd given her something to chew on. Though the scenario was unlikely; she was fairly certain Tom would never settle for Kate O'Neill, even for one night.

Upstairs, she was telling Margie about Jim's sister's tragic death when they heard Tom come in. He bounded up the steps and embraced her as if they'd been separated a month, not just an hour. Cuddling, she said, "Sweetie, Anna tells me there's some nice little villages around here. Maybe we could find a cottage out this way before we start looking in Rockhampton. Or would you rather be near the hospital?"

He shrugged. "Darling, it's up to you. Just thought that coming from the city, you'd like town better. Me, I'll be happy anywhere you say."

"And we need to set a date too. What do you think about June?"

His eyes took on a new glow, while hers reflected a new humility, a grudging acceptance of compromise in the name of love. Anna still wasn't convinced they'd ever go down the aisle, let alone live out their lives together. But now Margie had realized even she might be expendable. Or at least replaceable.

Anna followed them down the stairs, then waved from the front porch as they drove off toward the winding road that looped around the small peninsula where they hoped to find a rose-covered cottage with a picket fence, a view of Hope Sound, and the promise of happily-ever-after.

When their car rounded the corner, she breathed a prayer of thanksgiving, then went back to the kitchen. The sight of the half-eaten cake produced a sudden irresistible craving to stuff all the marshmallow chicks into her mouth. Yielding to it, she bit into one sugary little body after another; and wondered if some Easter, years from now, she'd tell her son or daughter about this weird appetite that had developed when she'd first suspected she was pregnant.

Half an hour later, she barely made it to the toilet off the examining room to vomit up the sweet mass. As she flushed it, Jim's tires crunched in the drive, so she rinsed her mouth and ran to the back door. Without giving him a chance to report on poor Mither's condition, she said, "Guess what, darling? Tom and Margie are out looking for a place to rent. And they've decided to be married in June. And...and I'll bet you five dollars I'm pregnant!"

His eyes widened. The smile lit his whole face. Nonetheless she suspected his logical physician's brain was telling him, Wishful thinking. So, while he took his black bag to the office, she heated the coffee and cut him a huge piece of cake. And made a bargain with the Lord—if Jim threw up too, okay, it was wishful thinking. Or food poisoning. But if he kept it down, she really was pregnant.

She'd always been fond of signs. She gave no credence to the negative ones. But the good ones, those that pointed toward the answer she wanted, those she trusted with her whole heart. Which was not to say she wouldn't also offer up a few ardent prayers. Adding, as she always did, "If it be thy will, of course. Only if it be thy will."

CHAPTER NINE

O n Memorial Day morning, it took her so long to fasten the brass buttons on her dress blues Jim had already started the car by the time she hurried out the back door. She'd begun dressing early, but hadn't reckoned on how tight the jacket would be. Bad enough she hadn't been able to zip up the skirt and had to close it with a safety pin. Then her fingers turned to thumbs as she attached the service ribbons and knotted the necktie. Hard to believe that a year before, these routines had come as naturally as breathing.

Tom was in the front with Jim, so she slid into the back seat and Jim reversed out the drive. "Sorry to keep you waiting," she said. "Took me longer to get into uniform than it used to."

Tom laughed and patted his belly. "Mine's tighter than it was last winter too. Kate's cooking's sure fattening me up."

"I've put on a few pounds lately too, but this is…you know. My condition. Funny. Haven't even had morning sickness, but I'm already showing."

Jim sent her a fond smile in the rear view mirror.

She hadn't seen Dr. Simon for confirmation yet, but all the signs were favorable. Though it had been three years since her first pregnancy, she hadn't forgotten one detail. "Sure hope I fit into my dress for your wedding. Another two weeks, though, I might not."

"Don't worry, dear," Jim said. "I'll be the only person

looking at you, not the bride."

Tom sighed one of his morose missing-Margie exhalations. "It's really gonna be a long two weeks."

"You'll live." Jim's tone was as Down East dry as she'd ever heard.

The two-lane blacktop to town was crawling with traffic, as if everyone in East Point was headed for the parade. Just outside the village, they caught up with a slow-moving four-door touring car, so old she couldn't tell if it was a Pierce-Arrow or a Cord. The top was folded back; inside were five middle-aged men in the faded uniforms of World War One doughboys, including Cleve Cropper, Matt Foye and Chester Philbrick. From what Anna could see, their uniforms were tighter than her own.

Someone roared up behind then and began an impatient beep-beeping. Through the rear window she saw Alex Cropper grinning at the wheel of the '42 Olds he kept at East Point. He was in Air Force pinks, Luke besides him in Navy dress blues; Grace Foye and Lorraine waved from the back seat. Alex tooted again, gave them a thumbs-up and roared into the other lane.

Jim frowned as the Olds raced past a line of cars ahead. "Pam must not be with him today. Man drives like a maniac unless she's right there. Guess she's staying off her feet, what with her EDC next week."

"Can't blame her," Tom said. "Besides, it's an American holiday, not English."

All along the road, Old Glory fluttered from porches and poles, even the masts of sailboats moored near the inlet bridge. Inside the town limits, flags were affixed to utility poles as well. Against a backdrop of enamel blue skies, vivid sunlight, and crisp shadows, Rockhampton was a living portrait of small town America the first year after the war. Anna's eyes misted as she remembered the past year, when their ship was still receiving casualties from Okinawa. Maybe then the Plan of the Day had mentioned the holiday,

but if there were any official observances, she'd been too
busy to notice.

When they reached the big post office, the parade was
already forming up in the parking lot. Leading off was a
color guard of sailors from Brunswick Naval Air Station,
followed by six fire trucks draped with red, white and blue
bunting. There followed the high school marching band, and
a squad of baton-twirling cheerleaders. When she arrived,
the chief of police, in an Uncle Sam costume, pointed her to
a milling assemblage of veterans being directed into neat
rows. They were to march six abreast, but there were only
five nurses, so Tom filled out their line. Luke was behind
them, next to All Saints' new rector in an Army chaplain's
uniform.

She couldn't count how many people were marching, but
finally in formation, they filled the whole block along the
town square. Behind them were open cars with elderly
veterans waving tiny flags, three troops of Boy Scouts, about
a thousand kids on crape-paper decorated bikes, the VFW
drum and bugle corps, and a team of dancing horses ridden
by young women in tight, star-spangled bathing suits that
glittered and twinkled in the sunlight.

As Anna regarded this colorful organized confusion, the
clock in the Congregational church steeple bonged ten.
Police whistles shrilled and the parade moved out with a roar
of fire truck engines and the beat of *Stars and Stripes
Forever* from the leading band. The one in the rear
immediately went into *The Battle Hymn of the Republic* but
there was enough separation of the two to keep the
cacophony minimal. By the time Anna's group was directed
forward, she couldn't hear the last band at all.

The route took them once around the square, where
observers stood in the dappled shade of ancient oaks and
maples, then out past the hospital on the road to the town
cemetery and Penobscot Bay. Just beyond the hospital, Jim
and her parents squinted in the sunlight, waving and cheering

with a line of townspeople. Trying to look dignified, she only beamed them a small smile, then snapped into "eyes front" again, as she'd learned early on at OCS.

In hat and gloves and uniform, with service ribbons on her chest, as she stepped along smartly with the other nurses, Anna felt herself part of that enormous company who'd left their homes and traveled to unknown parts of the world to confront an intransigent enemy, and horrors beyond description. Yet even on the ship, she hadn't felt this sense of belonging and camaraderie quite so acutely. Since she'd come home, she'd worn the uniform only when she'd gone to the base to be officially switched from active to reserve status, a perfunctory, inglorious little ceremony that spoke to none of these feelings of pride and accomplishment. But this straggling small-town parade took her right back to the essence of her wartime service.

By the time they'd marched up the hill to the cemetery, she was winded and light-headed in the intensifying heat. At the black granite obelisk commemorating the victory of Joshua Chamberlain's Maine regiment at Gettysburg, they stood at parade rest until the others caught up. Then the mayor read a resolution commending them for heroic service. Everyone pledged allegiance to the flag, and both bands broke into *The Star Spangled Banner* but at slightly different tempos, so it was hard to know which to sing with. Finally, while the veterans maintained rigid attention, seven sailors lined up and fired their rifles three times above the cedar trees separating the burying ground from the cliffs overlooking the bay.

As gunfire shattered the quiet, her throat clutched in sudden remembrance of her first loss, the one that had united her with millions of women the world over. Now, holding Dan Donovan in her heart, she blinked away tears as the bugler stepped up to the monument. At the familiar opening notes of Taps, they all saluted. The dirge took her back to *Compassion*'s fantail and the countless funerals for those whose bodies had been slid over the side, while those who'd tried to save them stood by in respect and regret.

She might just have sniffled a bit at this recollection. But as she visualized the nine hundred men on *Indianapolis* who'd died in the water without ceremony of any kind, the sorrow in her swelled into a wave that threatened to pull her under. Her throat hurt and her lips trembled as she pictured Bobby McWherter, jaunty in immaculate whites with cap squared on his forehead, saluting her as he boarded the jitney to the doomed cruiser. Sudden heat flooded; the bugled notes faded into an amorphous, distorted shriek. And a cold mist rose within her, a dark and quiet refuge that engulfed her as consciousness faded.

She came to when someone loosened her tie, unbuttoned the jacket and fanned her with a hat. "Mrs. Millett, are you all right?" a woman's husky voice asked.

She opened her eyes and looked into the bespectacled blue gaze of another Navy nurse, a gray-haired full commander who'd been in her line in the parade. Behind her, Tom hovered anxiously. Anna mumbled, "Mmm. Yes. Think so."

"Can you get up and walk over to the shade?"

She nodded, got to her knees and rose unsteadily as the nurse and Tom took her arms and helped her across the uneven lawn. By the time they reached the shade of the cedars, a Boy Scout was ready with a tin cup of icy, rust-tasting water. Sinking to the grass again, she sipped and took deep breaths until strength began trickling back.

"Sorry," she told the older woman, "I'm six weeks pregnant. Guess I'm not as tough as I thought."

"It's such an emotional day. Too much for you in that condition, I'd say." Her gaze shifted to the crowd, now dispersing after the ceremony. "Oh, good, here comes your husband. He'll probably take you home and put you to bed."

Trailing Jim, her parents hurried toward her with expressions of such anxiety Anna immediately said, "Now don't worry. I'm fine. Just..." she started to say pregnant, but that was one of several dozen medical terms words that caused her mother to flinch with distaste. So she said "Expecting", instead. She hadn't intended to tell them till she'd had Dr. Simon's assurance everything was fine, but decided they needed to know now.

They both gaped. Anna couldn't tell if her mother's reaction was one of pleasure or concern. With her father, that it was pure pleasure was immediately obvious.

She napped all afternoon, came downstairs about five. Jim and Tom were in the kitchen dithering over a supper of scrambled eggs and bacon. Kate had the day off, so they'd planned to go to the island for a picnic, but Jim had since vetoed it on the basis of Anna's fainting spell. Now, to prove she'd been restored, she volunteered to make toast, but when the phone rang, he sent her to answer instead.

A vaguely familiar voice said, "Mrs. Millett, this is Kathryn Visser. The nurse at the cemetery this morning? Hope I'm not interrupting. Just wanted to make sure you're all right."

"Oh, yes. Thanks. And I'm fine. As you predicted, Jim made me take a nap."

She laughed. "Did he tell you I was in his high school class all those years ago? Of course, he probably doesn't remember me. I was never much of a looker, so men tended to forget me. But by golly, I remember him. In my book, the nicest boy in the class. Always a gentleman, never gave anyone a bit of trouble. And so shy."

I laughed. "Shy. Yes, that's Jim, all right. He always considered himself a cripple, so he didn't let himself notice girls. He thought nobody'd ever go out with him."

"Oh my goodness! Well, I certainly would have. If he'd asked, of course. And I knew two or three others felt that way too. I'd heard he'd married a few years back, but they said it didn't last. Just as well. Now he has you. With a family on the way. Things are working out for him after all."

"I like to think so. Now, tell me about your service. Where were you stationed?"

She laughed. "Everywhere. Including the Philippines, back before the war. Good duty till then, but when those yellow bastards took over...."

Something in her tone prompted Anna to ask, "Say, you weren't one of the Navy nurses they took prisoner, were you?"

"Thank God, no. Damned near, though. We were at Corregidor right before it fell. Got out by the skin of our teeth. On a sub to Perth."

"Oh my goodness. My husband was on a sub that took some nurses to Perth. *Wolf Fish* . Was that the one you were on?"

"No. It was *Gudgeon.*" When she paused, Anna suspected she was tempted to ask more. Until she resumed, "After that I worked at a Navy hospital in Brisbane. SeaBees built it to handle all those casualties nobody expected we'd have." She chuckled.

"Brisbane! I joined my ship there in October, '44. By then I heard they'd moved that hospital to one of the secured islands."

"Which ship were you on?"

"*Compassion.* AH-4."

"*Compassion*! By golly, I knew another gal served on her. Came to her from *Solace*, right after *Compassion* joined the fleet. Think she was head nurse."

"Oh..." She was about to say Old Horseface when she remembered her real name. "Would that've been Norma Welch?"

"The same. You mean she was still aboard in '44?"

"Till the end of the war. Now I believe she's at Oak Knoll."

"You don't say! I'd love to get in touch, if you have her address. No, don't bother now. Didn't mean to keep you. Just wanted to make sure you got over your syncopal episode. Next parade, I'll make sure I've got aromatic spirits in my purse."

"Even without them, you did everything right. By the way, are you retired now?"

"From the Navy, yes. But I'm working at Rolling Hill. A private hospital outside Belfast. A sanitarium, actually. Maybe you've heard of it."

"Can't say I have." Anna wanted to ask if they were seeing any battle fatigue victims, but the older woman seemed to have said as much as she intended for the time being. Like Old Horseface, she could talk a blue streak, but when she'd had her say, she was quick to move on.

Back in the kitchen she said, "Jim, you'd never guess who that was."

He looked blank.

"An admirer of yours. From high school. Kathryn Visser, remember? "

"Who?" He was working on the toast now, buttering it as it emerged from the toaster, stacking a soggy pile on a plate.

"The Navy nurse who helped this morning when I fainted."

He looked puzzled. "High school? Name doesn't ring a bell."

"Well, she remembers you, all right. Sounds like she had a crush on you. Gosh, Jim. If you had noticed her, you and she might have married years and years ago. Might even have grown children now. And grandkids."

He stared at her for a long, pensive moment. "No," he said quietly. "That would never have happened. Because the Lord meant me for you."

Heaping scrambled eggs onto a Blue Willow platter, Tom smiled wistfully. "Funny. That's exactly how I feel about Margie."

Her first inclination was to let emotional tears flow. Until she quipped, "Then you're both the luckiest men alive. Because we fell for you too."

Before either could respond, she grabbed the plate of toast and carried it to the breakfast room where they would share a meal that was about as far as you could get from a traditional Memorial Day picnic. The only nod to the holiday was a tumbler holding a small, bedraggled flag she'd found in the grass at the cemetery. From the looks of it, it had been trampled by almost everyone hurrying home after the parade, eager to forget it…and every other reminder that less than a year before, the war had been a relentless machine devouring the country's national treasure. As well as the lives of those they remembered today.

Well, that was how the world went. All the coincidental connections she'd learned of today would soon pale into insignificance. By next Memorial Day she'd have a baby; four months old, if her reckoning was right. She wouldn't march in that parade, just watch from the sidelines behind a perambulator. Likely she wouldn't even go. Today was the time to look back in honored remembrance. Next year, with her focus on a new generation, the war would have faded and dwindled, its dead joining the ghostly procession listed on honor rolls from a long string of wars the world over.

Like Bobby McWherter's and Dan Donovan's. Just names and faces retreating into the dark silence of history.

CHAPTER TEN

Late afternoon on the day before Easter, 1947, Anna was nursing the baby while Kate welcomed the last of the christening guests at the front door. Most were Hope Islanders who'd come over on Luke's church boat, then been bused up from the pier by Fletcher Hood in his new Ford Estate Wagon. Since the house was already crowded with those from the church, Anna was sequestered in Jim's office for this private ritual. Even muffled by the closed doors, the hum of familiar voices surrounded her with the tender knowledge that so many people she loved were in one place for one reason: to celebrate parenthood with her and Jim.

Her eyes filled and a tear dropped on the infant's tiny fist, clenched against her breast. She'd expected maternity to be fulfilling, but even the pregnancy had been softened by a serenity she hadn't expected, a peace and contentment beyond any she'd previously experienced. And since his birth in mid-January, James Edward Millett, Jr., had delighted her beyond all reason. To be his mother had become her main raison d'etre. No longer was she satisfied merely to be her parents' good daughter, Jim's office nurse, his helpmate, or even his lover; her new goal in life was to excel at being this happy child's source of care, nourishment, and the sense he was loved beyond all children in the history of the world.

Someone tapped on the door, startling him from a semi-doze. The dark blue gaze turned to hers, until she smiled and he went back to suckling.

Margie slid open the pocket door and squeezed through the narrow gap." Okay if I come in?" Ten months of marriage had changed her in ways Anna hadn't foreseen. Most obvious—she'd stopped bleaching her hair and let it revert to its former mousy state. Even more shocking, she'd started collecting cookbooks. And from the tender looks she gave Little Jamie, what was next? A change of heart about motherhood?

"Is he almost finished?" she said. "The island folks are dying to get their hands on him."

"They've seen him before. They can wait till he has his nap."

Margie nodded approval like the baby nurse she'd become since she'd been hired by the new pediatrician in Rockhampton. She extended her arms. "Okay. Now. I'll burp him while you go up and put on some lipstick. You have absolutely no color these days. And that dress … honestly, Anna. Pink doesn't do a thing for you."

Reluctant to give up her cherished offspring for any reason, she blotted his chin with a diaper, then handed him over and reassembled her clothes. "It's the only thing in the closet that doesn't hang on me."

Margie deftly hoisted him to her shoulder and began patting. "Then maybe it's time you weaned him and started eating for yourself."

During ten weeks of convalescence from the C-section, Anna had done little besides catering to the infant's needs and writing detailed progress notes in a blue taffeta baby book a patient had given her. Beyond these minimal exertions, she'd eaten and slept as much as she wanted; nonetheless, she'd lost all the pre-natal weight, plus another ten pounds she couldn't spare.

"Soon," she said. "But there's no hurry. The new office nurse loves the job. I might not go back to work till the baby starts school."

She shrugged. "Whatever you say, Anna. Now, go comb your hair too."

She'd left him before, briefly with Jim or Kate, and that morning with her parents when she'd gone to be spruced up at the Cut 'n' Curl. But part of her still didn't quite trust his endurance, or his ability to thrive without her. He was sturdy and healthy in all measurable ways, but Kate constantly warned that even the most robust infants sometimes died suddenly, choked on their own puke or fell prey to fearful and mysterious diseases. "Why, me own baby brother, a big strapping fellow already six months old, didn't he come down with a fever one bitter night, and even with the doctor there, poor wee tyke didn't last till sun-up. Mither's last child. She was never the same after that." Kate's stock of horror tales was as long as the list of Irish *Titanic* victims.

Upstairs, Anna dabbed at her lips and combed her lifeless hair; nothing made her look perky. She wished she had time for a quick nap, but still hadn't greeted the latest guests or spoken with those who'd been at the church, including the young rector who'd replaced Father Danner. All she knew about Ted Bigelow was, he'd been in the Army overseas. Yet during church services, she sometimes glimpsed what looked like the blank, distant stare of battle fatigue in his eyes. A gaze that penetrated here-and-now realities to memories too relentlessly horrific to ignore. After all those shifts on *Compassion*'s nut ward, of course she wanted to know more.

She was just leaving the bedroom when Kate came bounding up the steps. "Oh Anna, you all right? When Margie said you were up here, I worried you might be poorly."

Annoyed with this incessant doom and gloom, she said, "Now why would you think that?"

"Oh, you just look so peaked today. So pale." Her dark eyes narrowed in one of her limitless speculations. "Say, you wouldn't be in the family way again, would you?"

"For God's sake, of course not! Now let's start serving the food."

Following Kate down the steps, she was relieved the woman wasn't keeping track of her sex life. If she had been, she'd have realized there was no way she could be on the nest.

"Well, thank the saints for that. That's what wore poor Mither down so bad. One little one after another, near every year for fifteen years."

"Poor Mither," Anna whispered under her breath.

Downstairs, she checked on the baby in his bassinet in the office; even with the doors open and visitor's voices drifting in, he was sleeping soundly under a lacy blue blanket Grace Foye had crocheted. Now she found the older nurse with a cluster of women in the breakfast room—Mrs. Leech and Pam Cropper and Lorraine and Maude Hood and Elaine Bigelow and Margie and Anna's mother, and even Mither in her wheelchair, balancing little Jean. Pam and Alex's little girl was a pallid, listless child who, even at eight months, could still barely sit unsupported. Now there was a baby to worry about. In contrast, the floor trembled every time Johann clambered past, usually with a half-chewed cookie in hand.

Grace watched him roar by with a shake of her head. "Lorraine, that child's not going to eat a bite of food if you give him a cookie every time he wants one."

Lorraine stubbed out a lipstick-smeared Lucky Strike in an ashtray that needed emptying. "But this is a party, Grace. I never give him sweets at home."

Anna caught her mother's skeptical glance as she went to the kitchen to help Kate bring food to the dining room. "Nothing fancy," she'd told the housekeeper when they'd planned this party. "Just boiled ham and chicken salad sandwiches and potato salad. And maybe one of your Easter cakes."

All of which Kate had obediently produced, along with platters of deviled eggs and yeast rolls and three-bean salad and a fluffy lime-green molded concoction she identified as a shamrock salad. There were also two identical cakes adorned with the traditional marshmallow chicks and coconut nests of what she called "Jelly Bird Eggs."

By the time this abundance was on the table, the men in the front room had lined up to load their plates. Luke and Ted Bigelow and her father were in clericals, so Anna asked all three to offer a short blessing. The other two priests' were cut and dried, but her father's was rich with gratitude for every blessing he could list, starting with the baby, of course, and Anna's safe return from the war, and the company of so many friends, old and new, and this beautiful day, and mainly the Resurrection of the Lord himself. It was only when her mother began coughing that he finally wound down.

Anna waited till everyone else had helped themselves before she filled a plate and took it to the front room. As she entered, Luke and Timmie made a place for her between them on one of the sofas. Nearby, Johann stood beside a card table, picking up food with his fingers, tasting, then setting the rejected remains back on the plate.

With the widest smile she could muster, she squeezed between the two churchmen. "Golly, Luke. Can you believe it's been a year now since the church boat went into service? I understand it's going great guns."

He chuckled. "Great guns? Sounds more like a warship, Anna. Actually, though, I've been real pleased with the reception we get wherever we put in. We've already had thirty baptisms, and even more weddings. Some funerals, too, of course, though not nearly as many as we had on *Compassion.*"

She nibbled on a deviled egg so spicy hot she immediately identified it as one of Lorraine's. "Must make it a lot easier not to have to commit the bodies to the sea afterward."

He blinked, swallowed half a sandwich at one gulp and swigged coffee. "Anyway, we're holding confirmation classes on three of the islands. And drawing up plans for chapels too, 'cause we're outgrowing the boat. All in all, it's a most rewarding ministry."

"Better than you expected?"

"Actually, I had no expectations. Just faith, and trust that the Lord would send us where we're needed. As indeed he has." He smiled past her at Timmie with his cropped red hair, earnest green eyes and face full of freckles. Like Luke, he was in a black suit with the dog collar, having been recently ordained to the diaconate. "Right, Deacon?"

"Oh yes, Father. Yes, indeed."

She bolted a mouthful of tasteless potato salad. "Well, I'm happy for you. When I sent birth announcements to people from the ship, I told everybody about your work here. Old Horseface said to give you her best. She's still at Oak Knoll, but Young Horseface left the service to marry an enlisted man. " She smiled at Timmie. "Luke was great friends with the Horseface sisters, actually the head nurse and her assistant on the ship. Nobody called them that to their faces, of course."

"I'll write her myself, if you'll give me the address." Luke said.

"Remind me later. Oh, and Nell and Ed are married. Floyd and Willi are too. He's opened a dental practice in Philadelphia. And they're almost finished their book about the war prisoners' experiences."

"Good for them." He disposed of another triangular sandwich in two swift bites. "I suppose you heard from Whitmore too?"

She nodded, careful not to let her expression change. "Had a nice card from him and his wife. They're at a Navy hospital in Virginia."

Luke's snicker was almost inaudible. "One big happy

family again, eh?"

Smarting with his thinly-veiled sarcasm, she was relieved to hear the baby whimper. Excusing herself, she was halfway across the room when she saw Jim in the hall. "I'll get him, dear," he said. "Enjoy our guests a while longer."

Since she wasn't particularly enjoying those she'd just been talking to, she took her plate to the kitchen, then headed for the breakfast room where Kate was spoon-feeding Mither in the wheelchair. The old woman was paralyzed on the left side, half her face drooping, one eye closed. But with the part of her mouth that worked, she was able to chew and smile and try to talk, though only Kate could decipher her gibberish. This was her first outing from the rest home where Jim's largesse now insured her care. Anna had no idea what it cost. Then again, she had no idea how much the practice made. He'd often invited her to look over the books the accountant kept, but all she needed to know was, he never worried about money. At least enough to talk about it.

Around the table now were Margie and Tom, Pam, Lorraine with little Jean, and Ted and Elaine Bigelow. Mrs. Moss hadn't yet sat anywhere but was charging around removing dirty plates and taking orders for coffee and tea. "Go talk to the new rector," she whispered as she whisked by with a tray of cups. "He wants to hear what you did in the Navy."

In his few months at All Saints', Anna had spoken to him only as she had the former rector—in reverential platitudes at the close of services. Even planning the baptism, she'd had no chance to get to know him personally. Now, she slid into a chair beside Ted Bigelow and waited for him and Tom to finish talking about the Easter service. By fair means or foul, Margie had almost convinced her husband the Episcopal Church was close enough to the Catholic to assure his salvation. This discussion, Anna realized, was not one to be interrupted.

While she waited, Jim came to the doorway, leaning on his cane with his right hand and cuddling the baby in the crook of his left arm. The glow of contentment and pride on his face made him look ten years younger. A sudden warmth suffused her, stronger than the tenderness she usually felt whenever she observed his paternal instincts. Mildly shocked, she recognized these as the first womanly feelings in months not related to motherhood. Well, not directly.

Jim's gaze touched hers. They both smiled and nodded, as if in some tacit mutual agreement, perhaps to meet later. Then he wandered off to parade their son through another room full of admiring guests.

Suddenly aware the priest seemed to be waiting for her to speak, she snapped back to the moment. "Uh, Father Bigelow," she said brightly, "I understand you're interested in my Navy service. What would you like to know?"

He was a slight man, balding, with large dark eyes that gave him a faintly mournful expression even when he smiled. "Ah, yes, Mrs. Millett. Your mother tells me you were a nurse on a hospital ship. In the Pacific?"

"Only the final year of the war. When things were winding down. Now. What about you? I mean, where were you posted with the Army?"

"Europe. France and Germany, mainly. From D-day till last June. Two years." His slow blink put her in mind of a shade being lowered against an unwanted sight.

Tempted to poke and prod to see what he was hiding, she asked only, "Did you know Father Luke and I were on the same ship?"

"No, I didn't. Sorry to say, I haven't had a chance to get to know him yet. Whenever our paths cross, we're both rushing somewhere else. Was he the only chaplain on board?"

"No, there was a Protestant too. I knew him somewhat better. In fact, toward the end of the war, he confided that he'd begun to have doubts. I mean about...well, his faith.

Because of what we saw out there."

Their eyes held a moment. "I'd like to hear more about that. Maybe we could compare notes some time. Unless you'd rather not talk about it, of course."

"Oh no. Talking's the only way to make sense of what happened. I mean, if there is any sense."

"I keep wondering that myself." He cleared his throat. "Is he still in the ministry, do you know?"

"Last I heard, he was. And still in the Navy, but trying to get his bearings, faith-wise."

"Interesting." His gaze shifted to his pretty brunette wife, chatting with Margie across the table. "Well, I promised Elaine we wouldn't stay long, so I guess we'd better start for home. Big day tomorrow, you know."

After the Bigelows left, other friends began moving toward the doors too. Filtering back to their lives one by one, except for the mass exodus when Cleve rounded up the island people so they could cross the sound before nightfall. Then Kate bundled Mither and the wheel chair into her flivver; accompanied by Margie, Tom headed out on house calls and hospital rounds so Jim wouldn't have to leave the party. Anna was about to take the baby from him, when her father volunteered. "So you and Mother can clean up. You know her. Won't go home till she does."

Back in the kitchen, Mrs. Moss had already filled the dishpan with Chipso suds. Anna told her to leave everything; she'd clean up in the morning."

"Nonsense. Tomorrow's Easter. You don't want to face a mess like this. We'll just wash everything right now. If you dry, we'll be done in three shakes of a lamb's tail. Now, get me an apron, please."

As they worked, her mother's commentary on Kate's shortcomings left no stone unturned. Beginning with the fact that the potato salad was too dry. "I told her to use plenty of Miracle Whip, but she always acts like there's going to be another famine tomorrow."

"She's just thrifty," Anna said.

"Well, I am too for that matter. But when one entertains, one has to spare no expense. That's why I made the chicken sandwiches myself."

"People liked her cake well enough."

Mrs. Moss's glance was incredulous, "Well, maybe some did, but I found it dreadful. Just dreadful. You have to use butter in pound cake, not oleo. And the icing—you could taste the lard, and that artificial vanilla. Oh, she's a hard worker, I'll give her that. But she doesn't realize there's no substitute for quality. "She sniffed. "Talk about silk purses and sow's ears."

As she dried endless piles of plates, Anna found herself mentally defending Kate. As if she wasn't aware of the woman's faults; as if Kate's invasions of her privacy never made her want to scream. What was that all about? Could she never side with her mother about anything? Now that her parents were only thirty minutes away, the closeness to her father warmed her heart, whereas she tolerated her mother best in increments of an hour or less. Today's visit, which had begun with the 2 PM baptism at All Saints', was already hours over the limit.

By the time they finished in the kitchen, her father was napping on the sofa, the baby sprawled like some antipodean marsupial atop his chest while Jim pored over paperwork in his office. Anxious to see them off, she woke her father, returned the sleeping infant to his bassinet and packed a basket with all the things her mother had brought for the party. Nonetheless, her parents' leave-taking was prolonged and tedious, full of sentimental clichés. No doubt about it: her father needed another parish. Retirement offered too much empty time for a man who'd shepherded four hundred anxious parishioners through not only The Great Depression but World War Two as well.

As the Packard's tail lights finally disappeared around the corner, Jim slipped one arm over her shoulder and shoved the front door closed with his good foot. "Well, dear, what now?"

Relaxing, she leaned into the familiar smell of his shirt, a residue of laundry soap and starch mingled with the day's faint perspiration. She smiled and pulled him closer. "Now I just want to be alone with you."

He pulled back and regarded her with a faint grin. "Must've read my mind."

"Any idea how long it's been since we... since we've been alone? I mean, like this?"

"Oh a couple of months. Since before you delivered."

She nodded emphatically. "Four months, Jim. That's not right."

"Hey, I'm not arguing."

"Well, then, why don't I feed the baby and put him down for the night, then come back downstairs and...."

"And?" he prompted.

"Maybe we can drink the champagne the Bigelows brought. And sit and talk and... well, have a romantic evening."

"The Bigelows brought champagne? To a christening party?"

She nodded. "Elaine told me they always do. To help the new mother and father remember the other side of themselves. Guess that means, the husband and wife side."

His gaze held with hers. "How very wise of them."

"Must be a lot of couples like us."

"Must be," he said, with a small, knowing smile.

"Anyway, we can still have romance. And champagne. All I have to do is give Jamie his Pablum and get him ready for bed. Busy as the day's been, I bet he'll sleep through the night."

"Sounds good, dear," Jim said in his matter-of-fact Down East voice, the one with which he responded to almost every situation life presented.

It was after eight by the time she took care of all the

details she'd so easily listed, had stuffed the gooey cereal
into the baby's eager mouth, then nursed him and wrestled
him into his double diaper and nightgown with the string tie
at the bottom so his feet didn't get cold, After she laid him in
the bassinet near the bed, she brushed her teeth and
freshened her lipstick. She was combing her hair when she
realized she was still wearing the pink dress she'd had on all
day. And remembered Margie's comment that it did nothing
for her. Fortuitously, Margie had given her a black
nightgown and peignoir for Christmas. Nylon, invented to
replace silk in parachutes, was said to be perfect for slinky
lingerie too.

"But save it till after you have the baby," she'd said with
a salacious wink. "For a special night." Trust Margie to
know a way to a man's heart besides the traditional stomach
route.

Slightly self-conscious in the seductive outfit, she found
Jim in the kitchen wrestling the cork from the champagne
bottle. Two delicate Waterford flutes stood on the table.
She'd seen them before in the dining room cabinet with his
grandmother's imported crystal and china.

Intent on removing the stubborn cork, he didn't glance at
her till it erupted with a bang like gunfire, then slammed into
the window over the sink. As she went to check the pane, he
looked her up and down with a surprised, pleased smile.
"Hey, sweetie. Haven't seen you in that before. Where'd you
get it?"

"Margie. Told me to save it for a special night. Guess this
is it."

He nodded. "Maybe that's what the Bigelows had in mind
too. I like that. About remembering the other side of
ourselves."

The other side of ourselves. The phrase played in her
mind as she watched him trickle the bubbly into the flutes.
"You haven't told him...I mean, you didn't tell him how
long it's been since we...since we remembered the other side

of ourselves, would you?"

His face turned serious. "Darling, of course not. You know me better than that." He handed her both slender glasses. "Here. If you carry these to the front room, I'll bring the bottle."

Balancing them, she returned to the shabby waiting room and set them on the card table, still littered with crumbs from Johann's lunch.

Jim patted the cushion beside him on the sagging sofa where earlier, she'd sat between Luke and Timmie and made stilted social conversation. "Wish we had some music. Maybe *Deep Purple*. Or the one you like so much. *All the Things You Are,* I think it is. Something to make tonight more special." He handed her a flute, took the other for himself.

"Feeling romantic, are you?"

The grin was wry. "Guess it's hard to tell with me. So if I make a toast, it'll probably sound corny."

"Nothing you've ever said has sounded corny."

"Well, then." He raised his glass, then went on in the serious, official voice he used to address patients and professional associates. "Now, dear, here's to our life together. And our baby boy." They touched glasses with a crystalline musical clink. "And the happiest year of my life."

As she sipped, the sweet, sharp effervescence stung the roof of her mouth, ascended her nose, made her eyes water. "Mine too. Today most of all." Blinking quickly, she averted her gaze so he wouldn't notice the tears. "I thought of that this afternoon, when you were walking around with him. I mean, how you've given me everything I ever wanted. How much you've blessed me. How lucky I am."

He drank again, gaze drifting around the well-used utilitarian room to the decrepit old sofas and chairs, the dog-eared copies of *Ladies' Home Journal, Popular Mechanics, Life, Look, Colliers* and *New England Farmer* that Kate stacked into neat piles every day after office hours. "Funny.

This kind of life... well, other men take might take it for granted. But I never expected anything like it myself." His shrug was casual, but she sensed his emotions were at flood tide. "So I didn't let myself want it."

"Oh Jim. You could've had it. You probably just never noticed how many women had eyes for you. Like that nurse who knew you in high school. Why, you missed me, even when I threw myself at you."

He laughed. "Couldn't risk getting burned again, I guess. Oh well, all water under the bridge now, thank God." He drained his glass, poured more for both of them.

"Amen to that. Thank God indeed."

They sipped again, more lengthily. Then he leaned toward her, touched his mouth to hers. Hesitantly, as if uncertain the black nightie meant what he hoped it did. When she returned the kiss, she made sure he understood. That tonight was special, that these kisses weren't the same sort that they exchanged first thing in the morning, last thing at night and occasionally in between–affectionate and sweet, but without passion or even the promise of it. This was different, like old times. Before they'd turned into parents.

Before long, he asked, "Want to go upstairs?"

She got to her feet. "No. But I will turn off the lights. And lock the front door."

"Okay. Then while you're up, get one of those things out of my desk, will you? Second drawer on the left."

But she didn't. Instead, she twisted the door latch and turned out every light except the floor lamp in the hallway. "Actually, we don't need those anymore. Remember, Ben Simon fitted me for a diaphragm?"

She didn't mention, however, that it was still in her nightstand. She'd never used it and didn't want to disrupt the mood by trying it now for the first time. Besides, she was still lactating, and even Dr. Simon agreed it inhibited ovulation. This had been the best, the most complete day of her life, and she wanted no distractions from the rediscovery of the other side of themselves.

In the shadowed parlor, it was easy to ignore the squeaking, lumpy sofa or the fact they were in the dismal room where patients waited to tell Jim or Tom about their rheumatism, or constipation, skin rashes or hemorrhoids. On this lovely evening, the ordinary problems of ordinary people seemed as trifling as rumors of border skirmishes on the far side of the planet. Like memories of the ship. Even of Mark.

She heard the phone ringing only when Jim jumped up and hurried toward the office. In the glow of the hall light, she was shocked to see he was wearing just his undershirt. Swallowing an ugly, sour taste, she sat up, setting off a throbbing at the base of her skull. Then she realized her lovely new lingerie was in a rude heap on the dusty old Axminster rug, the uncorked champagne bottle next to it. And both flutes stood empty on the card table.

Pulling on the nightgown, she heard Jim tell the caller to go to the hospital; Dr. Mullen would meet them there. Then he asked the operator to ring Tom so he could tell him about a patient with a heart attack. Anna twisted her wrist to see her watch, surprised it was ten-thirty. The last thing she remembered was the hall clock chiming nine, and Jim wondering aloud if Jamie would be all right upstairs alone. She'd assured him she had mother's radar and would hear no matter what she was doing.

But she hadn't. Lord God, she'd been unconscious for almost two hours.

Bolting to her feet, she took the steps two at a time, burst into the bedroom and switched on the bedside lamp. Panic set her heart to galloping as she inspected the baby, making sure he was only deeply asleep and hadn't gone lifeless while she'd been subsumed in carnal pursuits.

Sure enough, the blanket rose and fell with his every

breath and his mouth twitched with small sucking motions, as if he was dreaming of his next meal.

Weak with relief, she stroked the pale fuzz on his head, tucked the blanket around him and inhaled his sweet milk-and-Johnson's-Baby-Powder fragrance. In the bathroom she brushed away the sour champagne taste in her mouth, washed the sticky residue of lovemaking from her body and changed into chaste rosebud-print flannel pajamas.

Back in the bedroom, Jim was seated on the far side of the bed removing his brace, one of the new lighter, more comfortable plastic ones developed in the war. Anna slid under the covers. "Do you realize what time it is?" Even as the words came out, they sounded sharp and accusing.

He glanced at her alarm clock. "Close to eleven. Why?"

"Why? My God, Jim. If the phone hadn't rung, we might've slept down there all night. What if the baby'd needed me? I wouldn't have heard him."

He turned with a surprising half- grin. "But I would have, dear. Champagne didn't hit me as hard, maybe because I wasn't as tired." He chuckled. "Remind me tomorrow to thank the good rector for our evening of debauchery."

She pressed her fingers to her lips to stifle a gasp. "Oh, don't call it that."

"Probably as close as we'll ever come, dear."

Damn. There was Mark again, walking back to the ship with her on that final night in Guam. Full of booze, he'd suggested a conjugal shower in her cabin. And when she'd commented, "That sounds like the ultimate debauchery," he'd said, "Take it while you can get it, sweetie. Cause you'll have damned little of it after you marry that Puritan doctor of yours."

A year and a half later, she knew well what to do with such shards of unwelcome memory—inhale deeply, blink hard and will them away until they faded like curling photos in an old album. This one, however, wouldn't diminish. Because she'd given in to Mark that night. And so many others. And though she was with her husband tonight, what they'd done seemed just as sordid and wanton, not the manifestation of a loving spiritual connection between husband and wife.

She said, "But I never gave a thought to the baby. I left him alone all that time. Anything could've happened. What kind of mother does that?"

He leaned over on one elbow. "Darling, you're a wonderful mother. God knows, I love that about you. But I love the other side of you too." He stroked her cheek with gentle fingertips. "Any idea how it makes me feel?"

Unable to bear the sweetness of his expression, she pressed her eyes closed. "Probably like you're with a whore."

He stiffened and pulled away, looking slapped. "My God, Anna, how can you say that? Nothing could be farther from the truth. This is special. We're connected in so many ways. Yet when you say that I feel as if something's wrong. Something I don't know about. As if we weren't really together tonight. Just tipsy."

When she glanced at him again, the misery on his face stung her with remorse. She said, "I'm sorry, Jim," because it was the only explanation she knew to make. Let him think the apology was for her words, then, not the weight of guilt sitting on her like an elephant she kept trying to ignore. Yet here it was again—the wanton streak that had drawn her to Mark. And made her forget the war, and her principles, and even her fiancé. Yet now it was worse. Tonight it had so blinded her, she'd forgotten her own baby.

Jim patted her shoulder, grabbed his crutch and pulled himself to his feet. "It's okay, dear. I'm sure you didn't mean it the way I took it." Before she could answer, he thumped out of the room and up the hall.

After another look to make sure Jamie was still fine, she turned off the light, pulled the covers around her shoulders and turned on her side. And tried to pray with gratitude for such a fine day, such a fine life. But she kept coming back to that guilt, and the need to beg for forgiveness instead.

A few minutes later, when Jim climbed into bed and murmured, "Good night, dear," she pretended she was already asleep. But it was several hours before she stopped wrestling with the re-awakened specter of the other side of herself.

CHAPTER ELEVEN

A rt Simon didn't seem surprised to see her that warm June afternoon. Maybe he knew human nature too well to be surprised at anything his patients did. As she sat facing him across his desk, his first question was the standard, "Well, Anna. What brings you here today?"

"Nothing serious. Just…uh, fatigue and nausea the last few weeks. And my milk's dried up. And I haven't had a period since the baby was born." She hoped her shrug was nonchalant. "I almost feel…oh, pregnant again."

His brows arched above the horned-rimmed glasses. "Didn't I give you a scrip for a diaphragm?"

"You did," she said evenly. "But…but I guess maybe I didn't use it soon enough. I thought you said lactating inhibited ovulation."

His mouth twitched in the suggestion of a smile. "Yeah. But it's not foolproof. Anyway, go on in the other room and we'll have a look. Nurse'll be right in."

Leaving the house earlier, she'd told Kate this trip to town was to visit her parents and cruise through Benjamin's new summer fashions. Leaving Jamie with them, she'd told her parents the same lie. As for Jim, she'd purposely waited till his day on the island so she didn't have to explain the trip. Not that he was suspicious; she was quite sure he didn't keep track of how often they had intercourse or the intervals between her periods. She loved that he was so trusting. But hated that she felt unworthy of it.

She couldn't read Art's expression when he examined her, but as soon as he stepped back and stripped off the gloves, she had to know: "Well, am I right? Am I pregnant?"

He chuckled. "We'll talk after you get dressed." He picked up the chart and ambled back to his office.

Calming herself with a few deep breaths, she raised herself to a sitting position. The nurse, a bouncy little redhead, handed over her clothes, then began folding the sheet Anna had been covered with. "That'd be good news, wouldn't it, Mrs. Millett?"

She fastened her bra. "It's so soon, though. My little boy's only five months old."

"Oh, but it's nice for kids to be close. My sister and I are eleven months apart. We're just like twins."

"Yes, that is nice," she said, editing the sarcasm from her tone. When she went into the office, Art was at his desk scribbling on her chart, his expression too dour to ignore. With mounting apprehension, she sat in the facing chair and rearranged the skirt over her knees to maintain at least part of the illusion that she was a lady.

After a few minutes, impatience forced her confront him. "Okay, Art. Tell me. Am I pregnant? Or is something wrong?"

He dashed off another line, closed the chart. "No, you are. Six to eight weeks, by the look of things. As for fine, well, if you hadn't just had a section in January, I'd say everything was. But with sections, the medical consensus is, you need at least two years between pregnancies to let the uterine scar strengthen. This soon, well, it's going to put a strain on it. Could even be looking at the possibility of a rupture as things progress."

She swallowed a ballooning lump of fear, all too aware of what he was leaving unsaid—that a rupture was life-threatening. That she could die. She took a deep breath. "Well, then. Suppose I wear one of those special maternity corsets. And stay off my feet. Wouldn't that help?"

"Might." He cleared his throat. The glasses gave him an owlish look, while a monk-like black fringe encircled an otherwise shiny bald pate. "Then again, might not. Tell me. Does Jim know?"

She shrugged. "If he does, he hasn't said anything. I wanted to be sure before I told him."

"He'll be upset. Might even want to talk about a therapeutic AB."

New shock kept her speechless a moment. "AB! Why? I mean, surely there's a chance of carrying to term without a problem."

He nodded, but with troubling gravity. "Listen, Anna. We don't have to decide anything today. You still have, oh, four weeks before the second trimester. After that you'd need a procedure other than a routine D &C. So…go home and talk it over with Jim. Meanwhile, want anything for nausea?"

But she didn't go home, not until she'd drifted through all three floors of Benjamin's Department store, with particular emphasis on the Mother-to-Be section—twice as much choice as they'd offered the year before. But with a closet full of smocks, dresses with elastic waists, and slacks with stretch panels in the belly, she bought nothing now. If she followed Art Simon's advice, she wouldn't need them. At least this year. Would she ever again?

She drove to her parents' in a fog of dread. Not for what they'd say; in her mother's case, there'd be judgment enough even without the risks. Just the past week, she'd commented that this postwar population explosion was just so common. "People are breeding like rabbits!" God forbid her own daughter should fall into that category. She decided to say nothing.

Carrying Jamie outside and wrestling him into his car seat, she felt mild cramps, as she had for weeks. Good; maybe she'd miscarry and put the question to rest. Or maybe she was already feeling the effects of the strained scar.

On the way back to East Point, she tried to pray about it,

but had no idea what to ask. Maybe just, please let Jim not be upset.

It was almost five and his car wasn't yet in the drive when she parked. A rancid odor assaulted her as she lugged the baby in through the kitchen. Kate was at the sink, peeling potatoes while a skillet of bacon sputtered on the range. Anna took a nursing bottle from the fridge and set it in a pan on the stove for warming. When she turned on the gas, water brash rose to her mouth. "Kate, that bacon doesn't smell right. How long have we had it?"

"Not that long. But don't worry. You'll never notice once I add the onions. And the mustard. And the vinegar." She pointed to a *Woman's Day* open on the table. "See. A new recipe for German Potato Salad."

Pressing her lips together, she grabbed the barely-warm bottle and bolted up the back steps. Upstairs she lay on the bed while she fed Jamie, then let him roll around and grab her hair and stick his fingers in her mouth. Surely, she told herself, she couldn't love another child as dearly as she loved this one. Yet she hadn't expected to love him like this either, with a depth that reached every cell of her being and touched the extremities of her soul. But poets proclaimed that mother love was as broad and timeless as the universe, so perhaps she'd soon find out.

When Kate was about to leave, she called up the steps, "Anna, you might want to look at your mail before Jim gets home. In case you don't want him to see the letter from that friend of yours in the Navy. You know. The one in Virginia?"

Stunned at the housekeeper's implication, Anna barely managed to say, "Thanks."

When Kate's car was safely up the street, she changed the baby's diaper and brought him downstairs again. The airmail envelope lay atop the pile on the hall table. Mark's return address in Portsmouth blazed at her from the upper left corner. She grabbed it, then took Jamie to the playpen in the breakfast room before she ripped into the letter with shaking fingers. To her surprise, it wasn't Mark's bold blue handwriting on the onion skin inside, rather a small, flowery script. So decorative and precise, the writer had obviously taken the Palmer method more seriously than she ever had.

Dear Mrs. Millett, [or perhaps I should call you Anna, because Mark has told me so much about you, I feel I already know you!]

I hope this won't seem forward, but Mark and the kiddies and I are planning a road trip this summer to as many historic spots as we can find in New England, including Boston. On the map it looks so close to Maine, we were wondering if we could stop off there for a few days—in a hotel or guest house, of course, since there are four of us [and another on the way, but not due till January!] We just got a new car and have to break it in before we undertake such a long trip, so Mark's put in for leave the first two weeks of August. I hope this will be convenient for you and your husband. And of course, Mark wants to see the other chaplain from the ship, so we'll find plenty to do without your having to entertain us. If it's not convenient, however, please let me know soon so we can make other plans.

Sincerely yours, Lynette [Mrs. Mark] Whitmore.

Oh my God, she thought, folding the letter back into the envelope. First a new pregnancy to contend with, now a visit from Mark? And his kids and pregnant wife? Her heart hammered as if she'd just discovered the house was floored with quicksand. It was all she could do to force her thoughts back to what she needed to do for the baby. A simple matter, actually—just opening a jar of Gerber's strained vegetables and spooning them into him.

As she fed him, she rehearsed how she'd tell Jim about her new pregnancy, since he'd assumed she'd faithfully used the diaphragm. Did that count as spousal deception? Maybe, but compared to her other big secret, it was nothing more than a sparkler in a sky full of fireworks.

It was after six when he drove in. She met him in the kitchen; he looked disheveled and hot, shoulders slumped, face weary. He sniffed the air warily. "Good God, Anna, what's that awful smell? Like Chester Philbrick's hog pen. Not supper, I hope."

She took his medical bag, helped him out of his coat, draped his tie over her arm. "Kate says we won't even notice when we eat it."

"Damned right we won't. Was thinking about going out for supper anyway. See, on the way home just now, I noticed that old hamburger stand at the inlet's open again. Except now it's a Drive In. Waitresses come out to the car and take your order, then deliver it so you can eat right there. Be perfect with the baby. What do you think?"

"Anything'd be better than the stuff Kate's made."

As she wiped Jamie's face, she realized that neither going to town nor coming back that afternoon had she noticed anything different along the familiar stretch of road. Of course not; she'd been blind to everything but the new concern that Simon had predicted would trouble Jim. Now here was the letter from Mark's wife; more trouble if she let Jim know how much she wanted them to come. Well, not all of them; Mark would be enough, but she had to take the others too. Damn. Lately so much of her life was in the underground tunnels of her mind. Was that standard in marriage? Did even Jim have his private concerns? Or was she the odd one?

In the car heading toward the drive-in, she read Lynette's letter aloud. As he listened, his eyes narrowed and the muscles of his jaw tightened almost imperceptibly. Anxious, she asked, "Well, what do you think?"

His smile was constricted, not the usual broad one. "Certainly, dear. I'd love to meet them. Uh…how old are the children?"

"Oh, about eight and ten, I think. A girl and a boy."

He nodded. "Then write and tell them they're more than welcome. We have plenty of room to put them up."

No, no, no, her mind screamed at her. Not Mark sleeping just across the hall and sharing the bathroom. "I think the hotel on the island might suit them better."

"Whatever you say. Anyway, something to look forward to later this summer. Thought by now more of your service friends would've come for a visit."

"Guess they're all caught up in their own lives. And let's face it: it's a damned long trip."

As they approached the inlet she noticed small, colorful billboards spaced along the road like Burma-Shave signs. On each was a cartoon of foods served at The Lobster Hut—Fried Clams, Hamburgers, Hot Dogs, Lobster Rolls, Fries, Shakes and Cones. The final one read Curb Service above a silhouette of a girl bearing a tray aloft. The place itself was little more than a shanty on pilings, but its steep orange roof suggested an affiliation with Howard Johnson's.

The spot where Jim parked overlooked a summery panorama of moored lobster boats, a few sailboats skittering in the wind, power boats at nearby piers. Within minutes, a bright-faced waitress in a short red skirt and bobby sox brought plastic-encased menus. She looked so familiar Anna wondered if she was the nurse from Simon's office. No; more likely the sister close enough to be her twin.

Tapping her pencil on the order book, the girl waited while they debated their choices, took their orders, and bustled off to another car. "Well now," Jim said, glancing around the nearly-full lot. "This is nice. Makes it easier to eat out with the little guy." He grinned at the baby in the car seat between them. Anna gave him a Zweiback because Dr. Patrick thought he was teething and needed hard but wholesome snacks to gnaw on.

A wave of nausea rose at the hot grease smell wafting from the restaurant. "Not a lot of choices, though."

"More than the Clam Bake."

She swallowed. "Did I ever tell you, in Hawaii they put pineapple on hamburgers?"

He grimaced. "Sounds awful. Ever have one?"

She nodded, recalling the first—on the beach at Kailua, after Mark and she had had unprotected intercourse and she was too wound up to notice something as minor as pineapple on hamburger. And the second, in the O Club at Pearl the afternoon they'd drunk rum and cokes while they read the suicidal Marine's diary. "Actually, I took the pineapple out before I ate it."

He laughed. "Sounds like something Kate'd make."

"Better not tell her."

Extending his arm across the back of the seat behind the baby, he squeezed her shoulder. "You know, sweetheart, aside from Kate's minor peculiarities, I really love our life. Hope you do too."

Her eyes stung. She reached up and touched his hand, nodded. "Of course. Except...."

When his face constricted, she read the sudden anxiety in his eyes. "Except what?"

The tears came on despite her efforts to squelch them. "Oh Jim. I went to see Art Simon today." She paused; when he didn't ask why, she wondered if he suspected her news. Perhaps, because his expression didn't change, except to intensify. "I couldn't believe it, but he told me...well, I'm pregnant again. Six to eight weeks. He predicted you'd be upset. Because it's so soon."

She felt rather than heard the breath go out of him. After what seemed a long while, and as if it hurt him to speak, he muttered, "I thought we were being careful."

"I thought so too. But maybe...well, maybe I didn't use the diaphragm right." Telling this self-serving lie seemed a lesser evil than blurting out the truth that she often hadn't used it at all. And risking a more intense reaction.

"Damn. Simon was right. I am upset. He explain why?"

"Yes. It's risky. He also said you might want to talk about a therapeutic abortion. I said No. Not if there's even a chance I could carry to term without mishap. He said there is. So...that's all I have to say about it, Jim."

He pushed his glasses up on his head, rubbed his eyes and sighed heavily. This man who only a few minutes before had loved every part of their life now resembled someone man regarding the ruins of his earthquake-ravaged home. Unable to comprehend his sudden abjection, she said, "Why do you look like this is the end of the world?"

He shook his head in that sorrowful way people do when the explanation is too grave to verbalize. "Because if anything happens to you, it will be."

"Oh, Jim, don't be silly. Nothing's going to happen to me." Beyond him, she saw the waitress bobbing toward them, tray borne overhead in a personification of the eatery's sign. Her cheerful freckled face smiled in the window as she handed him two bags. Jim set them in his lap, reached for his wallet, gave her a five and told her to keep the change. She said, "Oh, Dr. Millett, that's way too much," and passed back three singles.

He waved them away brusquely. "Keep it, please." When she'd bounced away, he passed Anna a burger and a shake. The smell of fried onions turned her stomach, so she only sucked on the milkshake. And tried not to notice his withdrawn silence. Even as he ate—faster than usual—his gaze remained focused out the windshield, on other cars, waitresses, boats, the cobalt inlet threading through the rock-studded shoreline. She knew, however, he wasn't absorbing this natural beauty but concentrating on the sudden dilemma that seemed about to devour the happiness he'd never expected to have: that wonderful, too-good-to-be-true state of marital bliss.

When he'd finished his burger, she passed him hers, untouched. "Here. I don't feel like eating right now."

"Come to think of it, you've been off your feed a while

now, haven't you? Should've realized what's going on." He took a cautious bite. "Then there was that business of weaning Jamie because your milk dried up. Why didn't I put two and two together?"

Because you trusted me to use the diaphragm. Because you can't see the guile and deception in me, she thought, but said, "I was just as shocked when Simon told me." This lie came easier than the first, both whitewashed by the noble intention of minimizing his distress.

"But you're not as shocked as I am. To you, it's another child, a brother or sister for Jamie. To me, it's the possibility I might have to raise him without you."

She wasn't prepared for this explanation. "But aren't there ways to mitigate the risks? Like wearing one of those corsets. Staying off my feet. And strict bed rest, if necessary. Listen, Jim, I'll do anything. Except have an AB."

He went back to shaking his head, slowly, in silent lamentation of a situation he evidently saw as absolute and intransigent. All the while, their son gummed Zwieback and drooled mess down his chin, smearing it with his fingers until his cheeks were covered. When he gagged, she fished out a slimy chunk with one finger and wiped him with the diaper she kept handy. And when he whined and held out his arms, she lifted him from the car seat onto her lap, then sucked more of the icy sweetness of the chocolate shake into her unsettled stomach.

Still silent, still staring everywhere but at her, Jim finished the second burger and stuffed the wrappings into the bag they'd come in. "Well now. Anything else before we leave? Maybe an ice cream cone?"

She shook her head. "Let's just go home."

He nodded. "Of course."

Scowling faintly, he took the long way, cutting across the peninsula to the Bayside Road. The narrow blacktop followed the Penobscot Bay shoreline through a smattering of quaint villages beside tidal inlets or miniscule beaches. At the lighthouse, it veered south along the Sound, winding over low hills back toward East Point.

She didn't ask why he'd opted for this circuitous route until she saw they were approaching Margie and Tom's cottage. Then it made sense, especially when he slowed and stopped at their mailbox. Even more so when she saw Margie snipping roses from a pink mass cascading along the white picket fence. In a blue checked chambray shirt and slacks, she looked like a *Better Homes and Gardens* illustration in some fiction about domestic bliss.

Anna rolled down the window as her friend walked toward them, ducking her head to wave in at Jim. "Well, this is a nice surprise. What brings you out this way so late in the day?"

"Just a ride," Jim said. "We ate at that new place on the road to town. The Lobster Hut."

"Oh? How was it?"

Anna said, "So-so," at the same time Jim said, "Tasty. And they serve you in the car. Makes it handy with Jamie."

The baby was drowsy now, heavy, warm and sweating in her arms. "Well, come on in and see what I've done with the place. Tom's still at the hospital and I'd love the company."

"Wish I could," Anna said. "But I need to put Jamie down for the night."

"I'll take him, if you want to stay," Jim said. "And Margie can bring you home later."

"Sure." She clapped her hands, childlike. "Come on, Anna. It's been ages since we had time for girl talk."

So that was it: he knew Tom was at the hospital, knew too Anna might benefit from the counsel of a friend who often expressed belief in the virtues of childlessness. She studied his face. "Well, if you're sure…"

"Go on, sweetheart. The boy and I'll be fine."

When he'd driven away, Margie gathered up a basket with the roses and led her along a flagged pathway to the back door. In the damp evening air, the perfume was almost unbearably sweet, tempting Anna to bury her face in the flowers until she was drunk with it. Margie set them on the kitchen drain board and dusted off her hands. "Want a glass of wine or anything?"

The thought of adding more acid to her digestive system brought on a new wave of nausea. "No, let's just talk. And can we sit in the front room and watch the light house?"

Curiosity flitted across Margie's face, but she said only, "Sure. But you don't want something else? Coffee? Or iced tea?"

"Nothing, thanks. Told you, we just had supper."

The living room was full of chintz—curtains, slip-covered chairs, sofa, ottoman. The tables were painted apple green and the lamps were wrought iron, and the bookshelves held more family photographs than books. Margie's contentment hung in the air like the scent of roses.

Anna sank onto an overstuffed chair facing the Boston rocker where Margie had taken a seat and now sat regarding her with narrowed eyelids. "Something's wrong, isn't it, Anna? What's going on?"

She fluttered her hands, aware of the onrush of tears. "Nothing much, It's just that... well, I'm PG again." She tried to smile. "Guess we got careless. Jim's really upset."

Margie's eyes went wide, brows shot up. "Upset? But why? Because it's so soon after Jamie? Or is he against having more kids?"

"It's the risk. You know. Because it's too soon after the last section. He and Ben Simon are trying to talk me into a therapeutic AB." Her eyes filled; she pulled a hanky from her skirt pocket and blew her nose.

"And you're against it."

Anna nodded, moving her hand involuntarily to her belly. "Makes me sick to think about it. Sure, I know the risks. But it's not a hundred percent certain I'd have trouble. Jim acts like it is, though. As if he's going to lose me. And have to raise Jamie alone."

Margie stared, compressing her lips before she said, "Sure you don't want wine? Cause I need some to help make sense of this."

"Go ahead. I'll just sit here and watch the lighthouse revolve."

She laughed and patted Anna's shoulder as she went to the kitchen. In the gathering dusk over the sound, the whirling light was a thin beam orbiting the squat white structure. Round and round, like her thoughts. Going nowhere, just spinning endlessly.

Margie was back almost immediately with a goblet of something golden. She sat again, sipped and nodded. "Now. Want to know what I think, Anna?"

She shrugged. "I probably already do. You think I should abort."

Margie sipped again. "Well, I certainly would in your situation. I mean, even if I wanted kids, I wouldn't risk my life like you're doing. Then again, I haven't been through what you have. I mean, losing your first baby. And the things you saw in the war, well… I really can't tell you what to do."

"Thanks. I'm glad you understand."

"Well, sure. But something else just occurred to me."

"Oh?" Sensing the mood was about to change, she asked warily, "What's that?"

"Kate," she said.

"Kate? What's she got to do with it?"

Margie shrugged. "Remember when I was thinking of breaking off with Tom, you told me she'd set her cap for him if I did? Well, I'll tell you the same thing now. Suppose the worst happened. Suppose you died. Then Jim'd be the poor grieving widower, trying to raise a little boy alone. And she'd be right there, so helpful, so caring. So convenient." Margie sipped more. "Now I don't think she was really after Tom, just any man who wasn't a bum. Jim'd do just as well. Maybe even better, because she could raise your son."

Disgust and denial surged through her like a rogue wave.

"Oh Margie, that's absurd. I knew Tom wouldn't fall for her; I only said that to wake you up. But Jim never would."

"Don't be too sure. Maybe that's something you should ask yourself: how would you feel if he did? Would you want Kate to raise your child?"

Anna shivered and shifted her gaze back to the lighthouse's reassuring constancy.

"How soon do you need to decide?"

"In the next four weeks."

"Well, you've plenty of time to sort it out."

Having no answers, she was relieved when Margie asked no more, but showed her around the cottage. She'd seen it all before, but there were new touches—hooked rugs, pillows, candle-holders, vases, small paintings. No surprise the end tables were stacked with home decorating magazines. The main surprise was that Margie had taken to this domesticity as if she'd been born for nothing else.

They were in the guest room when Tom drove in. He was whistling as he ambled toward the house with a paper bag in hand. Anna trailed behind as Margie rushed to meet him in the kitchen. Their kiss was passionate; well, of course: they'd been apart the entire day.

"Look, Anna. Tom's brought some nice fresh flounder to fry for supper." She cuddled against him. "He's the most marvelous cook."

His craggy face turned pink. "Says I'm even better than Kate O'Neill."

Anna thought of saying "It wouldn't take much," but didn't want to undercut the compliment.

Margie kissed him again. "Going to run Anna home now, darling; be right back."

Still, she drove slowly, at least for her. As they came into East Point, she said, "I know this is really hard. But it's not like it'd be a hyssie, just a D & C. You could still have another baby in a couple years, couldn't you?"

"I guess. But it just...oh, I don't know. It just feels so

wrong to terminate."

In front of the house, Margie pulled up behind Anna's Cadillac and patted her hand. "You'll do the right thing, Anna. You always do."

She gave her a wry grin. "Not always. Or I wouldn't be PG again."

Clearly anxious to get home to her flounder-frying husband, Margie gave a little wave as Anna stepped out and closed the door, then roared off up the street.

Watching her turn the corner, she dragged herself up the porch steps toward the welcoming lights in the hall. And the big question she didn't want to answer.

Jim was in the office talking on the phone when she came in. He pointed up the stairs and mouthed, "Baby's in bed." The rancid bacon smell still hung in the air, so she went to the kitchen, dumped the German Potato Salad into the garbage and ate some dry Saltines with a glass of ginger ale. With Jamie, the nausea had been minimal; she wondered if hormones would be stronger with a female fetus. Quickly, she shoved the thought aside; if she were convinced she was carrying a girl, how could she even think of terminating?

After the snack, she went back to the office and sat in the patient's chair until Jim finished talking. He swiveled around with one of his glad-to-see-you smiles. "Tell Margie about our dilemma?"

She nodded. "But she wouldn't advise me. Says she has no idea how I feel about this."

"Well, neither do I," he said slowly. "At least, psychologically. All I can do is provide a medical perspective. Probably no help."

She decided not to tell him Margie's theory about Kate. Instead, she said cautiously, "Suppose…just suppose I spent the last month or two in the hospital. So at the first sign of trouble, I'd be right there."

"Huh. But suppose you were on the island earlier, like at six months. And you started hemorrhaging. Then what?

You're a nurse, Anna, you know what can happen. Hell, look how your first pregnancy ended. You were working in the hospital then, weren't you? And they took care of you right away, didn't they? Yet your baby died anyway. You could've too. And this is a more serious condition." He sighed again. "Don't make me spell it out."

As she listened, she felt his logic pushing her toward the dark shadows of the unthinkable. Her face crumpled in tears.

He reached across the desk and clasped her hand. His voice was softer. "Sweetheart, we can still have another child, you know. Just not right now."

She nodded vaguely. All she could say was, "I have to think about it. Still four weeks before we have to decide."

"Sooner the better, though. Not just physically, but emotionally."

She got to her feet, slid her hand from his. "Look, let's not talk about it anymore. I know the risks. I know how you feel. Now, just let me think, okay?"

"Of course dear. Sorry I'm so insistent. It's just that I'm scared of losing you. Like I was when you left for the Navy. Except now it's worse. Because I know how good marriage can be."

Even before he said the words, she was making the same comparison. When she'd left, his level of fear had baffled her. It still did, even after a year and a half as his wife.

Unless, of course, it wasn't just fear twisting his emotions now. Maybe it was prescience. Lord knew, he'd been right predicting she'd fall for another man while she was in the service. Maybe his instincts were on target about this unthinkable possibility too.

CHAPTER TWELVE

He was late coming to bed, after eleven. Even so, she was still wide awake when he went through the usual nightly rituals. As soon as he'd put out the light, she moved toward him, kissing his cheek, then laying her head on his shoulder, one arm around his waist. When he didn't move to meet her lips, she knew the mood was still heavy on him.

For a long while, there was no sound but his breathing, wind in the trees, the occasional car passing. Before long, his silence made her uneasy. She gave him a few more minutes, but when he'd said nothing nor made even the slightest move toward her, she murmured, "I hate this, Jim. I mean, being disconnected like this. I want to make you happy. But there's something in me I can't reason with. I'm pulled in two directions—wanting to do what you want, and this feeling I just can't. I mean, I can't agree to an ΛB. Yeah, I know we can try again later, but I still can't shake it off. It's not rational at all."

Only then did she feel him loosen up. "Sweetheart, it's not your fault. It's a primitive instinct, old as time. Without it, the world wouldn't go on. Especially after a war like we've been through. It's all tied up with the sex drive. And that's not rational either. As we know too well."

She kissed his lips; for a moment they opened to hers and his breath quickened. Then abruptly he pulled away. "Sorry, dear. I'm scared to love you. Scared to even touch you for fear something'll happen. That's probably how it's going to be the next seven or eight months. And every time you leave the house, I mean, every time we say goodbye, even if it's just for an hour, I'll wonder if it's the last time."

Tears flooded eyes, nose, throat. She pressed closer. "Now you really are exaggerating. Don't you have any faith?"

His chest rose as he inhaled. "Of course I do. I have faith the Lord's always going to give me strength to deal with whatever I have to. But not that he's going to make things come out the way I want. Huh. If he did, I'd be able to walk like everybody else."

That jolted her. Only after a few minutes was she able to respond. "Well, maybe he didn't answer your prayers the way you wanted, but you didn't die. You can get around. You're certainly better off than poor Roosevelt was. And yes, you lost your sister, and your wife, and Jean. And your parents aren't in your life. But mine are. And I am. And our son. You've had a lot of restoration."

But even as they volleyed the ball of logic back and forth, she felt that dark glass still between them. Polio had crippled his body, but fear had warped his emotions far more drastically. Perhaps beyond repair. At least beyond her comprehension.

Finally, feeling the impotence in her words, she said, "Sorry, Jim. I love you more than anyone in the world. But that...even that doesn't seem to matter right now."

He chuckled, surprising her. "Of course not. Because love's a relatively recent construction of the human psyche." Now he sounded more like a visiting professor than her husband. "So it usually comes in second to these other basic urges." He sighed. "You're in the grip of the survival instinct. While fear's got me. Just plain old-fashioned fear. You can't reason me out of it any more than I can reason you out of yours."

"Well, at least you understand. You don't think I'm just

obstinate."

He reached for her hand. "Yes, I certainly do understand. That's the hell of it."

With that, she realized there was nothing more to say: they loved each other, they understood each other's reasoning. Yet there was no compromise. One or the other would have to yield, for there was no middle ground. Nothing but the black and white wasteland of either/or. They were talking about it, true. They even had the medical background in common. But their feelings and fears were still in charge.

When she felt his muscles go slack and he began to snore, she lay a long while before it came to her to pray. For a while this took the form of a conversation with the Lord, though she was the only one who spoke. Then all the words dwindled to merely "Thy will be done." Just as they had on the ship when she'd confronted those situations she could neither change nor accept. When men died despite the best work of those who cared for them. When even situations she understood made no sense. When the Marine had thrown himself overboard, when Indy had gone down and no one had looked for survivors till most had perished in the sea.

And when, time after time, she'd yielded to the temptation to love Mark despite all the moral and spiritual reasons not to.

She awoke as the night sky faded from gray to pink. Mist veiled the outside world, muting the bleat of foghorns on the Sound. On the way to the bathroom, she looked in on the baby, still peacefully asleep in the new maple crib in the other front bedroom. It seemed out of place amongst the ivory French Provincial furniture Jim's first wife had bought to complement the yellow-blossomed wall paper and creamy curtains. Now, regarding the spacious area, she wondered if they could accommodate Mark's family after all. If they moved Jamie into their room, they'd free up this one for Mark and Lynette, with the children in Jim's sister's old room.

Outside the bathroom, she pictured meeting him in this same hallway, in darkness, both of them in pajamas. What then? The quick, forbidden embrace, the remembered smell and feel of him, the flare of desire?

Shoving the notion aside, she went back to the bed, where Jim huddled on his side, facing away from her, afraid to love her, leaving her to remember desire with Mark. Innocent and unaware, he'd give her whatever she wanted, whether it be hosting her former lover and his family here in their own house, or letting her proceed with the pregnancy. He might object, but it was in his nature to give her whatever she wanted, even if he thought it might kill her.

Aching with new compassion, she snuggled him from behind, from her side of the divide the new pregnancy had created. And knew with sudden clarity that her choice was not simply whether to terminate, but whether to put his needs above her own.

Suddenly the equivocation was gone. And Margie's argument about Kate snaring him afterward hadn't even figured into her change of heart.

"Jim," she whispered against his neck. "You awake?"

He stirred. "Mmm." Then, apparently energized by the habitual alertness developed in years of medical practice, turned over quickly. "What is it, dear? What's the matter?"

"Nothing. Except I want you to know, you're right. About terminating, I mean. I still hate to think about it. But... well, if you think I should, then okay."

He stared at her through the pink dimness. "You sure, Anna?"

She nodded. "But soon. Before I change my mind."

"All right. I'll talk to Simon today. See what he can arrange." He blinked a couple times. "My goodness, dear. I know this is the right decision. But I want you to be sure too."

"Look, all I'm really sure of is, I can't disregard your feelings."

He sighed, lay back against the pillow and stared at the ceiling. "Have you told anyone besides Margie?"

"No. I only found out yesterday. But Kate...well, you know she's always on the lookout for problems people don't know they have. So she probably suspects. No one else has any idea."

"Good. Then no one needs to know the real reason for your...surgery. Maybe Simon can suggest some less controversial procedure for a cover story." He smiled over at her. "Oh sweetheart. This is such a load off my mind. You have no idea."

"I think I do." She nestled closer. "And now you don't have to be afraid to love me, do you?"

And he wasn't. It took a little persuasion, but eventually, he overcame his fear.

Afterward, her cramping belly was a reminder of what she'd face if the pregnancy continued—prohibitions on lifting, enforced bed rest, abstinence from sexual relations, perhaps even the hated support garment.

Worst of all, though, would be the perpetual glaze of fear in Jim's eyes as he waited for another loss to hit. She wasn't happy with the choice they'd made, but the relief that filled her was so unexpectedly sweet, she barely noticed the sour rise of morning sickness in her throat.

CHAPTER THIRTEEN

After three days' confinement, Art Simon released her from the hospital on Fourth of July afternoon. At home, she was to have a week of bed rest before resuming normal routines. The story he and Jim had concocted was that she'd needed minor surgery to repair a prolapsed uterus. Her mother didn't want to know what a prolapsed uterus was or why it needed repair, but agreed to keep the baby while Anna was away. Kate had only nodded wisely, as if she knew the real reason, even made a locking motion over her lips, as if promising to keep the secret. Her troubling clincher was, "At least you can have others."

"I hate that," Anna said as Jim drove them home. "I mean, the way she insinuates herself into things that are none of her business. She's always spying on us."

He gave a nervous little laugh. "Don't let it bother you, sweetheart. She only wants to make people think she's wiser than she is."

"Well, if she ever says anything like that again, I'll fire her. I really will. I won't have her meddling in our personal life, Jim. I just won't!"

He reached across the seat and patted her hand. "Now dear, you're just extra sensitive right now. I'd hate to try to get along without her."

"We could if we had to. I mean, there's plenty of other housekeepers who'd be just as good. And stay out of our personal lives."

He didn't answer, but his pinched expression told her he was under pressure. She'd had the abortion, so that wasn't the cause. What then? Surely not the fact she'd told the Whitmores to come for a visit. He'd concurred, had even helped her plan their two-night stay. If she was to have any time alone with Mark, so far she couldn't foresee when it might be. Or even decide whether she wanted it.

At this moment, however, she was focused only on getting home to Jamie, resuming her life and putting this ugly contretemps behind her. Most of all, on forgetting the brief pregnancy that had been doomed to come to nothing. Forget that she'd wanted it nonetheless. Forget the martyred sense she'd agreed only to appease Jim.

And why? Because she owed him atonement? Because she wanted to balance the record sheet? Or because she was genuinely concerned with his happiness?

Her mind was whirling when they pulled into the drive beside the house. Out front, Kate's Ford was parked behind her parents' Packard, Margie's red MG behind that. On the porch, Old Glory fluttered from every pillar. Pots of crimson geraniums stood on the steps; new oak rockers on the freshly-painted blue flooring nodded in the breeze from the harbor. Once this quintessential Norman Rockwell scene would have filled her with pleasure; now it repelled her with its ironic implication that a perfectly happy family lived here. That their life exemplified the American dream for which so many had given their lives on distant beaches and jungles.

All an illusion, she thought as he parked by the back door. From inside came the murmur of voices–the baby's sudden sharp wail, Kate's answering croon, Margie's musical laugh, then the deep rumble of her father's. Jim hoisted her bag up the steps and held open the screen door.

Suddenly she didn't want to see these good people who loved her, who trusted her to return their love in ways they could recognize and approve of. Without lies or the deception that she was purer than she was. With the understanding that there was nothing about her they didn't know, and wouldn't want to know.

"What is it, dear?" Jim asked, still holding the door.

She shook her head, compressing her lips to still their trembling.

"Feel okay?"

"Kind of faint," she lied.

"Come on," he urged. "We'll sneak you up the back steps for a nap. You can visit with everyone later."

And that was how they left it––that she was feeling shaky, perhaps from blood loss after this mysterious surgical procedure that only medical people understood. Meanwhile, she was home again, back with her beautiful little boy and her good husband. All she needed was rest and quiet. And time to heal, with lots of good, wholesome food, of course. Between Kate and her mother, they'd see that she ate well and took care of herself and was soon back to her old self. Everyone concurred there was virtually no condition that could resist such mothering.

Once she was in bed, one by one they came up to see her. Her mother brought the baby; Kate and Jim promised to take full care of him until Anna was on her feet again. Her father just sat quietly and held her hand, promising that anytime she wanted to talk, he was ready to listen. Just as he'd said after she'd come home from the war. But in all the time since, they never had, except in small, innocuous segments that barely hinted at feelings that haunted her. For a while he'd seemed so distracted by his coming retirement, she hadn't wanted to add concern for her to his other burdens. Nor would she now, especially with this new loss she'd conspired to bring upon herself, for reasons she could tell no one.

Last to come upstairs was Margie, with a cup of tea Kate had insisted would perk her up. "That bitch," she said as she set it on the night stand. "Acts like she knows what you were really in the hospital for. She doesn't, does she?"

"Not unless Jim told her. Or she guessed."

Margie sniffed. "Then there's this other thing she keeps mentioning. As if she and I are the only ones who know the whole story."

"Oh?" Dread chilled her like a sudden icy wind. "What's that?"

"Oh, that chaplain you knew on the ship. The one who tempted you. She said he and his family are coming for a visit, then gave me a sort of wink. As if there's something more to it. God, she pisses me off! How do you stand her?"

To her dismay, Anna felt tears ascending. "I'd love to fire her, but Jim doesn't think we can get by without her."

Margie's eyes narrowed. "Sounds like she's trying to blackmail you. At least acting like she has something on you. So if you fired her, she'd tell what she knows. Or thinks she knows. There's nothing, is there? I mean, he hasn't written any incriminating letters, has he?"

With trembling hands, Anna picked up the cup and sipped the odd-tasting liquid, then said, "No" so firmly her own voice surprised her.

"Good. Then what about a diary? Do you still keep one?"

"Yes. But I know better than to write anything I don't want anyone to read."

"Well, then. Maybe she just assumes there was something between you and this guy. After all, all you ever told me was he tempted you. Was there more?"

Anna closed her eyes, face flaming. She nodded.

"What, an affair?"

"I guess you could call it that."

Margie reared backward, shock on her face. "Really?"

"I told you before, there were lots of romances on the ship."

"Oh, so it was a romance? I mean, did you love the guy?"

"If I did, it wasn't the way I love Jim. But it wasn't just sex either. Oh Margie, you'd have to have been there to understand what it was like. On the ship, I mean."

Margie took a deep breath and let it out slowly, gaze focused on Anna's face. "But you want to see him again now."

"Well, I guess I do. And I shouldn't, should I? I mean, I love Jim. I love our life."

"Sounds like you're feeling guilty."

"Of course I am."

"Oh Anna. That's terrible."

"I know." Eyes flooding, she wiped her cheeks with her fingertips.

"I don't mean what you did." Margie handed her a box of tissues from the nightstand. "But the guilt. That's terrible."

"Don't you think I should feel guilty? After all, I was engaged to Jim. And I betrayed him."

"But you came back and married him, didn't you? You didn't throw him over for this guy—what was his name?"

"Mark. Mark Whitmore."

"Okay, then. Regardless of what you did while you were away, you honored your commitment. That's what counts."

"But I still think of him. Once in a while, I even dream about him. Sexually, I mean."

"Listen, Anna. You can't help what you dream. Hell, I have sex dreams of other men all the time, and not just dreamboats. Sometimes I don't even know them. Once it was even President Truman. I certainly don't feel guilty about that."

Anna smiled in spite of herself. "You never feel guilty about anything."

Margie's casual wave dismissed the statement. "Well, my father wasn't a priest, so I wasn't raised with sin and salvation and all that gobbledygook. Besides, I've never done anything to feel guilty about."

"Oh, you mean like killing a baby you were going to have?"

Margie clapped one hand over her mouth. "Anna, you had no choice. Unless you wanted to risk dying yourself."

"I did it for Jim, you know. I don't deserve him. I owe him so much."

"Oh Anna," she sighed again. "I had no idea." She reached across the covers and clasped her hands. "I've always admired you because you're so good. So dutiful. So pure. I had no idea you had so much guilt in you."

"It's just worse right now because...you know. The abortion. And Mark coming."

"Are you going to do anything about it? Feeling that way, I mean."

"What can I do?"

"I don't know. Talk to somebody? You know. Somebody neutral; somebody who can forgive you, if you think you need forgiving. Like a psychiatrist. Or a priest. Maybe even Luke. He was with you on the ship; he knows Mark, doesn't he? Maybe he can help."

She laughed at the irony of the suggestion. "He stood in judgment of us the whole time. He's the last person I'd ever talk to."

"Well, then, maybe the rector at All Saints', Father Bigelow. He seems compassionate. I bet he'd understand."

She nodded vaguely. "Maybe. If I don't feel better soon, I'll talk to him. I've been meaning to anyway. To compare our war experiences. See, he was in Europe with the Army. I imagine he's seen a few things he'd like to forget."

Margie nodded but her expression was speculative, as if she'd accept no easy, dismissive evasions. "Look, Anna. Don't just don't brush it off and expect to get over everything. Especially with ex-lover-boy and his family coming. I sure hope I'll get to meet them."

"Well, we're all going to the Clam Bake the evening they arrive. You and Tom can come too. And my parents, of course."

Margie studied her for what felt like a long while. "How long will they be here?"

"Just two nights. Jim thought they could stay with us, but

I told him the hotel on the island would be better all around."

Margie rolled her eyes. "My God, of course! Who knows what'd happen if they stayed here? You know. You and him. Mark. For old time's sake."

She shuddered, feeling more exposed than she ever had with this old friend. "No," she said firmly. "No, I could never do that."

"That's funny, Anna. Because you've already done so many things I never thought you could do. What's one more?"

Her first inclination was to let sudden anger fire her emotions, but she said, "One more would put me right over the edge." She had no idea where the unexpected statement had originated or what it portended, sure only that it was Gospel. Consenting to the abortion had brought her close, but going to bed with Mark again would generate more new darkness than her soul could contain. "It'd be the straw that broke the camel's back," she added, more for herself than Margie.

"Oh my dear," her friend said in a quiet, tender tone. "I'm so sorry."

"Don't be. I'll be fine. I promise."

Margie got to her feet, smoothing out creases in the skirt of her red, white and blue sundress. "I know you will. And you'll let me help, won't you, if you need me?"

"Oh yes." Her eyes flooded again. Hormones, she thought. Or the absence of those she'd grown accustomed to for the eight weeks the pregnancy had lasted.

Margie bent to the night table, picked up the tea cup and drained it. She wrinkled her nose in a look of disgust. "There now. That bitch'll never know you didn't finish her therapeutic tea. Tastes kind of weird though. Like she put something in it. So if I die, be sure she gets the electric chair." She wiggled Anna's toes under the sheet. "Now, don't you worry about a thing. Just try to rest and come back to yourself, okay?"

Anna nodded, forced a smile. But when Margie had gone downstairs, she turned her face into the pillow and let tears carry away her disappointment and grief, like glacial melt carrying flakes of pulverized rocks in its slow march to the sea.

She was still weeping when Jim came into the room a few minutes later. Without speaking, he held her to him; his silence told her he recognized the futility of further conversation. As if even without identifying the convoluted emotions tormenting her, he realized she was presently unable—or perhaps just reluctant–to put them into words.

So if his heart ached for her, she might never know, except in the small gestures that so often sufficed for the outpouring of emotions that might more fully connect them.

CHAPTER FOURTEEN

On a sultry August afternoon five weeks later, a dusty green torpedo-style Pontiac with Virginia plates shuddered to a stop in front of the house. Having just put Jamie down for his nap, Anna stood at an upstairs window watching the family emerge from the car, then straggle up the walk with the hesitant air of travelers who aren't sure they've arrived at the intended destination. Except for the children, who bounced along like wild creatures recently released from cages. The girl was pudgy, with a headful of golden Shirley Temple curls; squarish and squat, the boy was scowling down at the bricks. Behind them was a plump woman whose short brown hair was a mass of spit curls; she limped a little, as if her feet hurt. Her green plaid maternity smock was of the same fabric as Mark's sport shirt.

Trailing the others, he studied the house, almost as if aware that Anna was observing from behind the sheer curtain. From her second-floor vantage point, he seemed thinner and older. Maybe it was his clothing: except for a bathing suit or naked, she'd never seen him in anything but a uniform. Perhaps today's rumpled wash khaki trousers were remnants. Perhaps, two years before, he'd even shed them in her presence.

Blushing with the unbidden notion, she waited till they pressed the doorbell before she hurried down the front steps. And there they were outside the screen, staring in hopefully.

At least the kids and Lynette were; behind them, Mark was grinning in a way that touched off a flash of memories. This close, his face was leaner and more lined, and his hair, though still in a short military cut, was less sandy now than gray, thinning on top.

She opened the door, making her smile wide and welcoming. Mark introduced her to everyone; he seemed breathless, as if the others were irrelevancies, shadow figures in the more pervasive reality of their reunion. She tried to focus on the kids' names–Buddy and Alice—and absorb Lynette's rambling account of having gotten lost on Route One and ending up in Camden before Mark admitted he'd made a wrong turn. "I tried to tell him, but he just never asks for directions," she said in the most Southern accent Anna had heard since *Gone with the Wind.* "So we're a whole hour behind schedule."

"Come in," Anna said, standing aside with the smile still fixed on her face. "My husband's out on house calls and I just put the baby down for his nap, but the housekeeper's made lemonade and ginger snaps. If anybody's thirsty."

She led them down the hall through the kitchen and into the breakfast room where Kate served them, chattering the whole time in an accent thick as clotted cream. As she rambled on, Buddy and Alice glanced around and stuffed their mouths with cookies. Mark stared out the window, one foot tapping under the table. Lynette began to yawn.

"Don't mind me," she said after a dainty sip of lemonade, "but I get so tired this time of day. My condition, you know. In fact…" she glanced at Mark, nodding as if to cue him to his next line.

"My wife needs to rest a while," he explained. "Hope y'all don't mind."

"Of course not," Anna purred. "There's two guest rooms upstairs; take your pick. Sleep as long as you like." By her watch it was quarter to two. "We're not due at the restaurant till five-thirty."

"I hate to be such a drag," the wife went on. "But maybe y'all—you and my husband, that is—can show the kiddies around town. And they're just dying to go swimming if there's a beach somewhere close...."

"Sure. A couple over on the bay, where there's no surf to worry about."

"Oh, they're real comfortable with surf. We take them out to Virginia Beach most every weekend. It's a real nice officers' beach. So we don't have to associate with any riff-raff."

Anna gulped, but quickly said, "Well then, Kate, why don't you show Mrs. Whitmore to the guest rooms while I take the others sight-seeing."

Before they could start, the kids needed bathing suits from their suitcases in the car, and Lynette wanted her bag too so she could change into "something more suitable" after her nap. As he carried in luggage, Mark seemed weary, not surprising for someone who'd been driving for the past nine days, undoubtedly fetching things in and out of hotels and tourist cabins all the way from Portsmouth, Virginia. "Over nine hundred miles, counting the wrong turns," he added with a grin that didn't touch his eyes.

When he and the children were bundled into Anna's car, he twisted to regard the kids in the back seat. "As much as they've been in and out on this trip, seems silly we bought a two-door car. But Lyn wanted a Torpedo, so...well...." That grin again, this time conveying not so much good humor as resignation to the inevitable. Perhaps to the entrenched guilt that would forever guarantee his acceding to her wishes. Maybe the new baby was even part of it.

After a quick tour of East Point, Anna parked at the town pier. Spotting the snack bar, the kids began whining for hot dogs and sodas. Mark reminded them they'd already had lunch and cookies, but counted out a handful of change and passed it to the boy. As they spilled out of the car and ran toward the smell of hot grease, he muttered, "I swear, they're bottomless pits."

"Just healthy, growing kids," Anna said in her cheery nurse's voice.

While the children chowed down at a picnic table, Anna pointed out the hazy silhouettes of the islands and the hotel where they'd be staying. They barely listened, seemed bored and impatient. Until she added, "And right out there, a German U-boat hit some mines and sank. Later the Navy found saboteurs trying to get ashore, and some bodies in the wreck. But the most exciting part was, one of the German sailors hid out on that little island beside the big one where the hotel is. Until the Navy got him."

Buddy's eyes widened. "Gee. Then what happened?"

"They took him to a prison camp. He tried to escape, so they shot him. They were real tough on saboteurs during the war."

His mouth dropped open, exposing half-chewed hot dog. "Golly, Auntie Anna. Were you here then?"

She nodded, "In fact, I even saw the sub blow up. And I helped care for the German before they took him away. See, he'd been hiding for two weeks in the cold, so he was really sick."

The boy studied her with gray eyes like his father's but set in a round, milky face like his mother's. "Couldn't you just let him die? I mean, since he died anyway. That way you wouldn't have had to bother. "

Mark's gaze caught hers. "Buddy, that's a terrible thing to say," he said, shaking his finger. "We're Christians. We don't let sick people die."

"But you turned him in, didn't you, Auntie Anna? And he got shot, so it was the same thing as letting him die."

Mark shook his head, morose, almost bitter. "Okay now. That's enough. Back in the car so's we can find a beach."

Shaken by the boy's assessment of Wil's fate, she steered them through the village to the road that looped across the peninsula toward the bay. In the back seat, the kids were whispering between themselves, but Mark's mouth was tight. His left hand lay palm up on the seat between them, as if unconsciously seeking something from her. But what? An answering touch? A clasp? Or affirmation that they still shared a connection?

He cleared his throat as she turned out of the village. "Funny. I was just thinking about that Marine. What was his name? You know, the one on H-13?"

"Armistead," she said.

"You told him that story too, didn't you?"

"Uh-huh. But I'm not going to mention him now. For obvious reasons."

A long, pensive silence before he asked, "You think about those days often?"

"No. Too much going on right now. What about you?"

He nodded with a wry smile. "Of course I do. That was the best year of my life." His voice was low against the kids' background chatter.

"Well, it may have been so far," she said in her best Pollyanna tone. "But you don't know what the Lord still has in store for you. Maybe something even better."

His only answer was a sigh, heavy with disbelief. Or an absence of hope?

"I have to admit, though, sometimes I read the journal I kept on the ship. A lot of it was awful, yet it was such important work."

"I know. We were so...so needed. Now...well, it's just not the same."

She drove on, pointing out the rocky cove where the sheriff had found the two German saboteurs, and the lighthouse that had been turned off during the war, and the rugged cliff where an inter-island freighter had foundered two winters before. Then, suddenly curious, she gave him a sidelong glance. "Tell me something, Mark. Whose idea was it to come up here?"

He seemed startled, or perhaps reluctant to answer.

"Well...actually Lyn's. She's been dying to meet you and Luke. And of course I was all for it, since we were going to Boston anyway. Next year we'll have the new baby. So it had to be now or never."

She nodded as if this made sense, but didn't answer, concentrating on the road twisting between clumps of pines and outcroppings of rocks. Down the slope to the right, the Sound sparkled in the sunlight, while ahead Penobscot Bay shimmered like a mirage in the hazy mid-afternoon heat.

She parked at the first little beach, a curving strip of rocks and sand where a few other children were wading in the shallows. As soon as Mark got out and folded back the seat, the kids exploded from the car and rocketed across a low dune toward the water. Midway, however, Buddy paused at an overturned dory and began rocking it back and forth.

"Oh no," Mark groaned. "That's not an abandoned boat, is it, Anna?"

"Probably not. They really shouldn't disturb it."

Sighing again, he strode toward them across the uneven sand. With slumping shoulders, he looked almost as abject as he had when they'd learned of Indy's sinking. As she watched him scold the boy, she was conscious of unwanted emotions rising–pity and guilt and admiration and regret, and that curious tie she hadn't been able to sever while they were on the ship. Since then it had been frayed by time and distance and the circumstances of their separate lives. But not severed. No, definitely not severed.

Shaking his head, Mark plodded back. By then the children had abandoned the dory and were running toward the miniature breakers moving in from the broad expanse of the bay. On the horizon, banks of pink-tinged cumulus clouds were mirrored in the satin ripples along the shore. Swatting a horsefly, he got in again, but left the door open so a fitful breeze could waft through. It smelled faintly of seaweed and hot sand and salt water, and when he was inside, of his warm nearness. She was startled at how familiar it was even a year and a half since she'd last noticed it.

"Well, they seem safe enough here," he said. "I can trust Alice, but Buddy's a handful. Never know what he's going to get into."

Like father, like son? she wondered, but said, "They ought to be fine."

He turned toward her, shifting his body in such a way as to remind her they were alone together, certainly not in seclusion, but more intimately than before. "Now. Tell me how things are with you. I mean, how they really are."

She inhaled deeply, smiled her pleasant professional smile. "They're fine, Mark. You haven't seen my baby yet, but he's as perfect as they come. Jim's practice is flourishing and my parents are nearby. And I don't see Luke often enough to worry about him telling Jim any naval secrets. You know."

He chuckled. "Ah yes, those damning naval secrets. Well, good. Can't tell you how often I've wondered if all your dreams were coming true."

She averted her eyes from the probing intensity of his gaze. "Oh yes."

"Not that I could do anything about it if they weren't. Except wonder what life would be like if we'd ended up together. Or if you'd gotten pregnant that time at Kailua."

She'd been watching Alice shake her finger at Buddy, but now she turned with dismayed shock. "Really, Mark, I wish you'd forget that. I don't like sneaking around talking about our secrets. Then pretending we're just old friends with everyone else. It's hard enough being with your wife as it is. Talk like this only makes it worse."

"Sorry. But seeing you again– well, maybe coming here was a mistake. It stirs up so much...you know, old feelings. Makes me realize my life isn't what I expected it'd be. Certainly not what I'd like it to be."

"No," she said sternly. "That can't be true. After all, you

went back to her after the war."

He shrugged. "Seemed like the only thing I could do at the time. See, I thought it'd help me get over you. Plus the kids need me. Didn't plan on having another, but, well, I felt I owed her."

"Why? Because you feel so guilty?"

He nodded, staring at the beach with sad eyes. "Don't you, with Jim?"

"Oh, now and then. In fact..."

"What?"

"Well, it makes me give in to him when we disagree. For instance, I wanted to get pregnant as soon as we married, but he thought we should wait three months. For medical reasons. So we did. Then there's the housekeeper. She's not a good cook and she meddles in our private affairs, but I keep her on because he likes her." Tempted to cite the abortion, in the next heartbeat she knew she couldn't. Because if Mark perceived even a slight wrinkle in the fabric of her life, he might take hope that one day it would totally unravel, giving him a chance to rescue her. And the abortion was anything but a slight wrinkle. She clamped her lips shut.

"But you're basically happy?"

"Oh yes." Even as she said it, she realized her tone lacked conviction, credibility. "And there's really nothing I'd change, except the housekeeper. So sure, I'm happy. When you meet Jim, you'll understand better."

"Oh Anna," he said slowly, with the same wistfulness that had salted the phrase during their last weeks on the ship. Before she could respond, he reached over and clasped her hand on the seat, so tightly his wedding ring bit into her fingers. "I wish things had ended differently for us."

She pulled away, said, "They ended the only way they could," with more certainty than she felt. "And it's time you accepted it. Maybe that's why your wife's been so eager to come here–she senses she doesn't have your whole heart. And wants you to close the books on our...our little fairy-tale romance."

"Is that all it was?" he said with patent disbelief. "A little fairy tale romance? "

"It doesn't matter what it was, Mark," she said crisply, like a New England schoolmarm. Or a Puritan preacher. "It's what it is now. What it has to be now. You have to make up your mind to accept the way things are."

He inhaled sharply, with a minimal shake of his head. "You make it sound so easy. So simple. As if all you have to do is decide on a thing and voila, that's what it is."

"I'm a New Englander. We don't waste time worrying about things we can't change. Otherwise, we'd never make it through a winter."

"So...." he said, drawing the word out. "That's how things stand, is it?"

She looked over without smiling. "What did you expect?"

A casual shrug, his gaze fixed on the distant kids, splashing and jumping in the water. "Well, I hoped you'd say the things you said at the train. And in your letter. Tell me you still loved me. Still missed me. And wish we could be together."

"But even if I did, how would that change your situation?"

He turned back to her, eyes intense and deep. "It'd give me hope."

"For what? A happy ending?"

He nodded. "Not right now. Certainly not now. But someday...if we were both free."

She armed herself with a deep breath. "Oh Mark. This is too silly to talk about. Don't look to me to make you feel better about things. I have my own life to deal with. I couldn't make the promises you want to hear even if I wanted to."

His face turned hard, but he didn't answer. Before long he said he was going to check on the kids and left the car, striding across the sand, lurching over rocks until he reached the water. There, he appeared to be arguing with them, the boy gesturing widely, the girl pouting and stamping her foot. When Mark turned back, they followed raggedly, dragging their feet and towels, poking at each other and yelling things Anna couldn't hear.

Back in the car, he waited till they were inside before he climbed into the front seat and slammed his door. She sensed rising tension even before he said, "Is there another beach nearby?" His tone was impatient. "Maybe one with deeper water?"

"This one's for babies," Alice whined. "We can swim, you know."

She started the engine, backed out onto the road. "There's another about a mile north. With a regular swimming area and a lifeguard. But it's usually crowded this time of year."

"We don't care," said Buddy. "Unless it has a lot of rocks."

"We're not used to rocks," said Alice in a whiny tone that recalled her mother. "We don't have rocks in Virginia."

"So I've heard." Anna glanced at Mark, but his face was still a hard mask. "That's because the ice age didn't extend that far south."

"No, it's because the Navy cleared them away. At least from the officers' beach."

Even this repartee didn't get a response except to tighten his expression further.

With a so-what shrug, she drove on to a waterside collection of ramshackle summer cottages, fishing shanties and a general store with an Esso pump. The parking lot was full, so she let the children out, then pulled up on the shoulder further along the road.

"Damned kids, putting you to all this bother," Mark said. "Never happy with anything."

"Oh, they're just being kids. Cooped up too long in a car."

They sat without speaking for a few minutes, swatting the occasional horsefly that rode in the window on a breeze so sweet it was like a cake baking. Certainly it was hot enough to bake something; the car soon became an oven even with both doors open.

Trying to dissipate the tension, she finally thought to say, "Okay, Mark. Now tell me what you're doing in the Navy these days."

He shrugged, gazing toward the crowded beach. "Oh, pretty much what I did on the ship. Except without funerals on the fantail. You know. Prayer meetings and Sunday services, and visiting the sick and comforting the bereaved, even working with NP patients. Most of the long-term mental cases are in VA hospitals, so I don't see many. And by the way, starting the first of next month, I'll have another half-stripe on my sleeve."

"Oh, you made lieutenant commander! Congratulations. Guess that means you're going to stay in then. Maybe go for twenty?"

"Yeah, I guess. And sometime next year I'm due for transfer. I'm thinking of Philadelphia or Boston, but Lyn wants me to ask for Charleston or Jacksonville, Florida. So we're closer to family. So I guess that's where we'll end up."

She noted an overtone of blame in his voice. As if he had no complicity in the guilt that now seemed to trap him in this marriage. As if he were the victim of his own good intentions, an innocent man, ever-striving to do right by wife and kids, his only reward the prospect that at the end of his trials, Anna would be waiting to make him a happy man.

She took a deep breath and pressed on. "And what about your faith? Are you still troubled with doubts like you had at the end of the war?"

His smile was wry. "Funny you ask. I rarely even think about them anymore. Just do my job. After ten years as a minister, it's all rote. Plus the Navy has policies about everything, so I don't have to make many decisions based on personal faith."

"Must make your work easier."

"I guess." Another half-hearted shrug. "But more and more, I feel like a sham. Between the good husband act and the devout chaplain façade, I'm play-acting."

She wanted to comment in some neutral, impersonal way that discouraged interpretation. But when she said, "We all have to do that from time to time," the slight change in his expression suggested she'd opened a crack in her defenses. And possibly restored his hope that her marriage was as miserable as his, so bad that one day, she'd have had enough of it and would turn to him. Instead, she forced an optimistic lift into her voice. "But they say if you do something often enough, even if you're just pretending, eventually it becomes part of you."

"Is that right?" His look was skeptical. "Well then, I'll just have to keep trying."

As he said the words, she realized he was placating her, possibly to keep her from any further preachments. As if he'd either given up or was biding his time, hoping to win her over another day. Well, that was what she'd taught him on the ship, wasn't it? Because even after she'd learned he'd played fast and loose with other nurses, she'd soon returned to his bed, as if his carnal weakness was just another human foible. Like snoring, or eating too fast, or leaving the toilet seat up. Nothing of consequence, nothing that affected her feelings. In that sense, that he now expected more than she had to give was entirely understandable.

There would be no logic to sway him from this assumption, then, no fine arguments, speeches or sermons. Only time and her continuing resolve would convince him. Or maybe not. Maybe the man would go to his grave believing his personal happiness was in the hands of others. If so, she pitied him. Not for the dismal marriage or the disintegrating faith, but for living in the clutch of a delusion she hadn't recognized before. Odd, she thought, that for all the months of intimacies both physical and spiritual, she hadn't noticed this about him before.

And now that she did, pity, faintly etched with contempt, was all she had to offer.

The supper party gathered at the Clam Bake on the Rockhampton waterfront at 5:30 that evening. The ten of them filled their reserved table, the Whitmores along one side, Anna, her parents and Margie opposite, the baby in a high chair next to Jim at one end. Tom was at the other. "We have to keep Jim and Tom apart," Margie explained to Lynette, "so they can't talk shop. Otherwise, they're in their own world."

Mark's wife stared a moment before she turned on a tight, condescending smile.

After the waitress explained the service was buffet-style, Lynette asked Mark to fetch hers so she didn't have to stand in line. "I've been having a terrible time with my feet lately," she said to Mrs. Moss. "They swell so bad, I can hardly walk till I've had a good lie-down."

Margie's knee nudged Anna's under the table. And standing in line, she murmured, "Well, he's certainly cute, but hen-pecked as hell. Poor guy needs a good roll in the hay."

"Not with me, he doesn't," Anna whispered.

"What's the matter? Not tempted anymore?"

She shook her head and picked up a warm plate from the stainless steel serving table as the line crept toward steamed clams, cole slaw, baked potatoes, cobs of yellow corn and a red tangle of lobsters, all served this year with real butter, according to a hand-lettered sign.

Back at the table, Lynette shuddered at the lobster on her plate and said if anyone wanted it, they were welcome to it. Alice and Buddy were picking at kids' platters with corn dogs. Instantly, Buddy said he'd take it, if someone picked it apart for him. Sighing, Mark took over.

Sitting beside her, Anna realized her mother was trying to engage Lyn in a discussion of the joys and challenges of being a clergy wife. But evidently Lyn was free of all the duties Mrs. Moss had faced: she and the children even attended a civilian church rather than Mark's services in base chapels. "And I never go to any of those tedious ladies' guild meetings. Of course, once I find a good nanny for the new baby, why, then I'll do some charity work. Navy Relief, or the Red Cross. Some agency that helps our boys in blue."

Margie's knee bumped Anna's again.

Across the table, the boy was dripping butter from a large chunk of lobster tail he'd lifted to his mouth. "You know, Buddy," Anna said, "I forgot to ask where you folks stopped on the way up here. I think your mother mentioned historical sites. Is that right?"

He nodded, eyes wide, then chewed faster, bolted iced tea and swallowed hard. "We've seen everything, Auntie Anna. The Liberty Bell, and Betsy Ross's house, and Valley Forge, and the place where George Washington crossed the Delaware River, and the Empire State Building, and the Statue of Liberty, and Lexington and Concord and Old North Church, and that old ship they have there. What is it, Dad?"

"*Constitution,*" Mark murmured from behind an ear of corn.

"Old Ironsides, they call it," Buddy added breathlessly, then to the others, "And Auntie Anna showed us where that Nazi U-boat blew up here. Right here in Maine! She even took care of the sailor who escaped from it. But then the Navy took him away and shot him because he was a spy."

Lynette gasped, set down her fork and glared at Anna. "You took care of an enemy sailor?"

"We both did," Jim said calmly. "He was critically ill when he surrendered."

"Oh my goodness. And you told my children that awful story?"

Anna and Jim exchanged glances; Margie's next nudge

was almost painful. "Well, they heard a lot about the Revolution. I saw no reason not to tell them what happened here only four years ago."

"But we don't talk to the kiddies about this war," she said, pronouncing it *wo-wah*. "Didn't you and my husband have enough of it out there in the Pacific? I mean, to think there was killing right here...." She shook her head. "I declare, children don't need to hear these things."

"Sorry. I had no idea you felt that way," Anna said primly.

"Indeed I do. Let what's past stay in the past, I always say. I just hope you and Mark haven't been telling them the awful things y'all saw on that ship."

She glanced at him, but he didn't meet her gaze, just went on chewing. "Never thought about it. But if I had, I might have. Of course, now that I know you're against it, I'll certainly never mention any war again."

In the glare Lynette shot her across the table, Anna suddenly saw the confirmation of her suspicions: this woman knew full well what she and Mark had been to each other. Maybe not the total, damning extent of it, but at least that she'd been one of his women, one of several nurses he'd enjoyed carnally. Perhaps even the most significant of those dalliances, the one who still sparked fireworks in his memory. All this considered, Anna would be a woman she had to see for herself.

Why? To take her measure as an adversary? Or torment herself with images of them together, thus fueling the animosity that goaded her to punish him?

Good Lord, she thought; what mental perversity might drive such an instinct?

Then a new alternative suggested itself: maybe in Lynette's mind, coming here was also a way to rub Anna's nose in the apparent happiness of their marriage. To show off the fine, dutiful husband, not merely obedient and domesticated, but still passionate enough to get his wife pregnant. To draw a fence around him for once and for all. And get Anna to close the books on him, even if she still lingered in his mind.

As the group at the table worked through the food, the conversation shifted to ordinary matters–the kids' schooling, Mark's promotion, their choice of a new duty station. And their itinerary when they left here; Thursday morning: before heading south, they'd cross New Hampshire and Vermont, then soak up more Revolutionary War history at Fort Ticonderoga in New York. "Because next year, we'll have the new baby," Lynette concluded, "So we're not likely to get this far north anytime soon. If we ever do again."

No one else seemed to sense it, but for Anna the mood had shifted, swung into a cold region where the divide between the Maine people and the visiting Virginians was as ominous as the mood at Gettysburg might have been before the first shot was fired. These hostilities, however, weren't about territory, unless it was Mark's soul and which of these women possessed it—the good wife by virtue of her legal and moral rights? Or the wanton nurse whose unmentionable history with him had bonded them in forbidden pleasures?

Ironic, Anna thought, increasingly aware of Lynette's calculated moves; because just that day, her perception of him had shifted. No longer was he a might-have-been, one of the lost loves of her life, like Dan Donovan or the high-school football player she'd admired in tenth grade. Now, the net of pity and contempt she felt for Mark stretched to cover his wife too.

The meal seemed to last at least six months. By actual time it was less than two hours, ending just in time for the Whitmores to catch the last Hope Island car ferry from the pier near the restaurant. Watching it churn into the bay, Anna cuddled the drowsy baby and nestled against Jim. "You know," she sighed, "I've just realized I don't care much for Southerners."

He laughed. "All of them? Or just your friend's wife?"

She shuddered. "Now that I've met her, it's hard to understand why he was upset when he got a Dear John letter on the ship. Now…well, there's no accounting for tastes."

"Be glad we only have to see them again for lunch tomorrow. Glad they're not staying longer."

"I just hope if Willi and Floyd ever come to visit, they won't seem so awful. Now. Let's get back to our life."

Our life, she thought as they drove through the quiet town toward East Point. For the first time since she'd returned from the Navy, the dark remnant of her illicit passion no longer colored it. She expected guilt to cling to her a while even as time leached its intensity and wore down its sharp edges. But no longer would it torment her or goad her to give in to Jim against her will for any reason.

Except loving him, of course.

CHAPTER FIFTEEN

S ince Jamie had been born, Anna had stopped going to the island with the doctors on Wednesdays, but that morning she'd risen early enough to catch Fletcher's 8 AM run. Today only Jim was along, Tom being tied up at the hospital with the complicated delivery of twins.

As they came up the gangway, Jim said, "Where's Father Luke taking you on the church boat today?"

She stepped down to the afterdeck. "Not sure. I guess to one of the closer islands. Don't really know. See, I've decided not to go with them."

"Oh?" He followed her to the folding chairs under the canvas awning Fletch had rigged for passengers' shade. "How come? You've never been out with him, so I thought you'd want to see what he's doing . And have more time with your friends."

The notion of being part of the unholy trinity of Mark, Luke and herself–on such a small craft, with Mark's wife alert to every veiled hint, every nuanced threat—made her cringe internally. At times the tension between the two chaplains, even on a ship as large as *Compassion*, had been unbearable.

"Not today," she said, "I need to work on the dead files in the clinic. I'm four years behind."

Jim's tone was one of feigned shock. "Four years? Good Lord, I had no idea."

"Well, I did start on them when I first got to the island,

but it's so tedious, I can't even get Beth to do it. Besides, I'll hear all about the boat trip at lunch. Lorraine's coming too."

He squeezed her hand on the chair arm between them. "You're a good woman."

May you always think so, she prayed.

When *Molly B* glided into Hope Island harbor, *Evangel* was tied up across the town pier, the green Pontiac pulled up nearby. Mark was talking with Luke and Timmie, while Lynette in a large sun hat clustered with Lorraine and Cleve. When Anna and Jim came down the gangway, Buddy rushed over. "Hey, Auntie Anna. Better hurry. Uncle Luke's ready to cast off soon as you board."

"Oh, I'm so sorry." And she was, at least for disappointing the boy. "I have to work in the clinic this morning. But you remember everything you see and tell me about it at lunch, okay?"

His face drooped. Pouting, he shuffled back toward the group. Anna waved at them, then joined Jim in the short walk across the square and up the hill to the clinic building. When she glanced back and saw the others boarding the church boat, she told Jim, "You know, I like that boy. At first I thought he was a spoiled brat, but he's really bright. And interested in everything."

"Seems to like you too. The little girl, though, she strikes me as the spoiled one."

"Yeah. I suspect her mother's given her a Shirley Temple complex. Probably told her she's cute enough to be a movie star."

"You say she sent Mark a Dear John letter on the ship?"

"He got it the day the Kamikaze buzzed us. Said she'd met someone else. Another minister. Older. Who understood how lonely she was."

"And Mark was distressed?"

"Hard to imagine, isn't it? Now that I've met her, I mean. I was surprised when they reconciled after he got home. But I guess they realized it was best for the kids."

Jim didn't answer, slogging along beside her on his cane. Wondering what the real story was? Trying to imagine what force kept a man and woman of such disparate temperaments together? Maybe he was even including Anna in the equation as the unknown factor.

One day, years from now when time had given her the ability to speak calmly of that sordid episode, she intended to level with Jim and ask his forgiveness for having yielded to loneliness and the need for comfort. One day, when she more fully understood her own behavior, all those long-postponed good intentions would finally lead her to speak those hard truths. And accept whatever consequences they might ignite. Even if they blew up in her face.

Working in the front office with Grace and Beth, Anna culled through stacks of file folders undisturbed for almost ten years. A task more tedious than any she'd faced on this job or any other. Even worse than the reports the Navy demanded for every shift every nurse worked. The point of this chore was to remove deadwood— charts of patients who'd died or become inactive for two years for other reasons, like leaving the island. The deceased charts went into a large storage box, the others into smaller containers destined for the dusty shelves in the cellar.

Among the first she found was that of Jean's father, dead of appendicitis complicated by peritonitis in 1937. On her mother's, though the death in 1939 had occurred elsewhere, someone had written: "Apparent suicide in St. John's harbor, Newfoundland." Even Jean's medical history was recorded, and that of the old man Anna had found dead early in 1944, and an elderly woman with congestive heart failure a few weeks later. There was even one for Wilhelm Himmelreich, because they'd treated him for a few days before the Navy hauled him off to West Virginia.

Reading these old patient notes stirred involuntary memories and slowed the process of separating them from the active ones. She wasn't surprised the morning dragged. At noon when the fire house siren blew, she was startled to find she'd accomplished so little in three hours. At least, she rationalized, it was three hours she hadn't had to spend with Luke. Or Lynette.

But lunch loomed. At twelve-thirty, *Evangel* churned into the harbor in the wake of the car ferry. Later, the green Pontiac went by, heading up the hill to the hotel. When Anna reminded Jim it was time for lunch, his expression turned apologetic. "Oh sweetie, I'm sorry. With Tom gone, I have to make all the house calls. So I'll only have time to drive you up to the hotel and grab a sandwich from the Lunch Box."

She gave him a look that was half disappointment, half disbelief. "Wish I had such a good excuse. But somebody's got to show up."

He brushed a quick kiss on her cheek, patted her arm. "You'll do better than I would, dear. If all else fails, you can always talk about the war."

"No, I can't. You heard that woman last night. The wo-wah's not a fit topic for kiddies."

He chuckled. "All the more reason to talk about it."

He let her out in front of the hotel, then backed around and headed back to the village faster than he usually drove. Almost as if he didn't want to see any of the Whitmores. From the number of cars in the parking lot, business was booming. Sure enough: the lobby was full of guests heading into the dining room or checking in. Alex's wife was working the desk; she looked harried, her little girl whining in a play pen behind her. Anna smiled, but Pam's nod was curt and brusque, as if she were full of regrets for having ever poked pinholes in Alex's condoms.

The dining room was buzzing with chatter and full of enticing food smells. Mark and his family were already seated at a window table overlooking the cemetery. The scent of wild roses in a cut-glass pitcher stirred nostalgia in Anna for a time in her life she couldn't remember except in pale, wispy images evoked by the fragrance. But even without a specific memory, she sensed it was a simpler time than the present. At least this particular day.

Buddy patted the chair beside his. When she'd been seated, he leaned over and whispered, "Guess what? I found the graves of some German sailors, but Dad said not to let on to Mom. How come they're buried here?"

"We'll talk about it later, when we go to the beach."

"Isn't Jim joining us, Anna?" Lynette asked in a faintly accusing tone.

"Oh, I'm sorry. His associate couldn't come to the island today, so he has to make all the house calls himself. He sends his apologies." She glanced around at the table set for seven, with only five occupying it. "I thought Lorraine was coming too. Did she change her mind?"

Lynette's face turned hard. "Well, she was supposed to join us, but then she was seasick on the boat. So she went home to lie down. Ah have no idea why anyone would be seasick on a day like this. Not a ripple anywhere. Well, maybe it was the heat."

Or you, she thought. The waitress approached, a skinny island girl in a white seersucker uniform. When Anna ordered the lobster salad cold plate, Lyncttc said she'd had enough lobster for the rest of her life and just wanted something simple, like the chicken pot pie.

With neither Jim nor Lorraine to provide conversation, all Anna could think to ask was, "Where did you go this morning? On Luke's boat, I mean."

Lynette sniffed. "I think he called it Silversides Island. A dreadful little place with only a general store and maybe fifty houses. But the population's a hundred-percent Catholic, so they're going to build a church. For all the christenings, you know."

Mark passed a basket of rolls. Anna took one and immediately bit into it. "Sorry I missed it."

"I was surprised," Lynette went on, "that Lorraine and Luke never knew they were mother and son till you put two and two together out there in the South Pacific. How clever of you to figure it out, Anna."

Anna shrugged. "Pure coincidence. Though Lorraine claims it's a miracle."

"What about his daddy? Does she know who he was? Or was it just one of those unfortunate situations ?"

"She knows," Anna said through tight lips.

"And the little boy she's raising. Whose child is he?"

"Cleve's niece's, Jean. Her husband was on a tanker that was torpedoed in the North Atlantic." The distortion of truth came easily in such desperate circumstances. "If you'll excuse my mentioning the war again."

Lynette's rosebud mouth twisted in a look of unspeakable disdain. "And she died in childbirth? In this day and age?"

"It was an infection. Probably from a blood transfusion. Antibiotics could've saved her, but in 1944, there were none for civilians."

"Well, I declare. So now a woman of questionable morals is raising the child."

"Lorraine's the mother of a priest," Mark said sternly. "And according to Luke, a real help with his mission here."

In the heavy silence that followed, Anna asked the children what they thought of the boat trip. Their responses were reined in, constrained no doubt by what their mother had identified as her high standards about seeing, hearing and speaking no evil. Regardless of what their parents might be saying.

As the wait for their meals stretched on and on, Anna wished she'd stayed with the clinic files. The job had been boring, but not nearly as maddening as trying to remain sweet with this insufferable woman. After the food came, however, she reminded herself that the enforced association would soon end. A couple hours at the beach with Mark and the kids, then the trawler back to East Point with Jim. And in the morning, the Whitmores would leave, first on the ferry to Rockhampton then to points west, hopefully never to be seen or heard from again.

By the end of the meal, the kids were jumping jacks, ready to bounce upstairs to their room and change for the beach. After Mark excused himself to go with them, Lynette yawned and proclaimed the need for her afternoon nap. "That's the worst part of traveling. You can't stop to rest when you need to. Just have to keep going. And the trip home will be even worse because we're going so far out of our way. But, well, my husband wants the kiddies to see Fort Ticonderoga and Lake Champlain. You know. Because we'll probably never get up this way again. At least not before he retires. And after that, why, there's so much else to see, the western states and the national parks, and all."

"I think it's important for people to see as much of America as they can," Anna said in an artificially hearty tone, as if reciting a line in a play. "So they appreciate what a wonderful country it is."

"Oh, I couldn't agree more. Except it's so tiring."

"Well, I'm glad you folks made the effort to get here. I've really enjoyed meeting your children. They're delightful."

The other woman nodded and smiled, but a hardness about her features suggested she had something to say that she wouldn't in Mark's presence. Anna tensed as she added, "They're quite taken with you too, you know. Especially Buddy. Mark's talked so much about you, the boy thinks you walk on water."

The comment left her speechless. Until it came to her to rejoin with, "Sorry to disappoint him." Feeling increasingly trapped, she kept glancing toward the lobby. Relief swept her when Mark and the kids came down the stairs, now in bathing suits, towels over their shoulders and sand buckets in hand.

Lynette rose heavily to her feet, led the way toward the lobby, then set foot on the first step of the wide staircase. "Now, if y'all will excuse me, I'm going to retire for a few hours. And if I don't see you again, Anna, be sure and thank that sweet hubby of yours for treating us to that taste of Maine last night."

"I certainly will." Anna forced herself to smile until the woman had turned at the first landing and hobbled out of sight. "Now," she said to the others, "Why don't you go down to the beach while I get ready? I'll be right there."

Buddy urged her not to be long. When they'd left, she went into the ladies' room in the lobby and changed into shorts and a halter top that made her breasts look fuller than they really were. She hoped Mark would notice, and want her, and suffer that discomfort men got from unfulfilled passion. Because by damn, he was not going to have her again. And if afterward he was still full of lust, why, he could just take his wife to bed and pretend she was someone he really wanted. Except that Lynette probably used her pregnancy as an excuse to abstain from all forms of sex. If so, it served him right.

By the time she came down the steps to the beach, Mark had spread a blanket on the demi-lune patch of sand below the dunes. She hadn't been down here since the new pavilion had taken shape on the south side of the hotel; a hexagonal structure with glass sides, its conical red roof suggested a carousel. The addition was scheduled to open for Labor Day weekend, was now in the final stages of construction. A bevy of hired hands was augmenting Cleve and Alex's efforts to finish it for the grand opening, when a Tommy Dorsey sound-alike band was slated to play for a dance. Cleve had said they were already booked solid, but would save a table for her and Jim. Trying not to sound wry, she'd said, "I can hardly wait."

When she reached the blanket, the kids were digging holes in the sand, dredging up small stones for a protective wall on the surf side. The first thing Buddy wanted to know was why the Germans were buried in the hotel cemetery.

Anna looked at Mark. "Okay if I tell him?"

"Sure. I've told him lots of stuff about the ship too, unbeknownst to his mother. Don't worry; he can keep a secret."

This pleased her. "Okay then. Well, see Buddy, when the U-boat hit the mines, the Navy sent a salvage ship, and divers went down to look for secret equipment. But first they found these bodies in the part that was blown open. Usually they leave the dead on sunken ships, but this wreck was in such shallow water they were afraid they'd wash out and float to shore. So they built caskets and brought them up here, because the people that own the hotel had given permission to bury them here. There were a lot of other bodies that they couldn't get to, so they're still on board. It's a war graves site. There's hundreds of them all over the world."

"Auntie Anna's first husband was on an American sub that never came back from a patrol in the Sea of Japan," Mark said. "That'd be a war graves site too. Except no one knows exactly where it is."

The boy's eyes widened. "Gee. Not even the Navy?"

"No," she said, willing emotion from her voice. "See, there were lots of subs that never came back. But most of them sank in such deep water they'd never find them even if they knew where to look." For a moment she was tempted to tell the child about having seen the ghost of Dan Donovan in this cemetery, but knew that might be a secret too good to keep from his mother.

"Like Indy," Mark said almost inaudibly. "You remember that story, don't you, Buddy?"

The boy nodded, his gaze gone distant and solemn. Just then Alice returned from the water's edge, her bucket full of shells. "We don't talk about this stuff in front of her," the boy whispered. "She'd tell Mom. She loves getting me in trouble. So she doesn't know half what I know about the war. Especially things y'all saw on that hospital ship. I don't think Mom knows either, does she, Dad?"

He shrugged. "I only tell her what she asks about." His face was bleak in the harsh sunlight slanting across it, accenting lines he hadn't had two years before.

For the next few minutes, the kids went on digging, occasionally splashing into the low surf, but they claimed it was too cold and the footing too rocky for serious bathing. Alice compared it with Virginia Beach which, of course, was far superior.

Anna said, "On the ship, your dad showed us pictures of you two on a beach somewhere. I think it was Myrtle Beach."

Mark's glance on the girl was fleeting but tender. "They were a lot younger then."

"So were we," she said quietly.

Sitting beside her on the blanket, he sighed deeply. Aware of the warmth of his body, she was tempted to glance at his bare chest, arms, legs, letting her thoughts drift to Kailua. There, they'd lain side by side on a white woolen blanket with US NAVY on it, had gazed across the opalescent sea to an outbound carrier, touched each other possessively, talked about the possible consequences of having had unprotected intercourse, then hurried back to their rented room to love each other again and again. And though she saw him now through a sharper lens, something in her connected to the man he'd been then, or the man she'd needed him to be. Wishing she could embrace him once more, if only as a farewell gesture to those old illusions, she felt herself soften and warm.

As the thought whispered through her mind, she turned to look up at the hotel on the dune; who would see them if she did? Mark and Lynette's room was on the other side, but from what she knew of his wife, it wouldn't be out of character for her to find a way to spy in hopes of catching them in sin, even the minor sin of a merely-fond embrace.

Of course, even if she wasn't spying, one of the kids might mention it. Probably Alice the snitch.

Turning her gaze to the sea, Anna was filled with a sweet sadness that the relationship with Mark had run its course, the only one it could have, like a train on a track it had no choice but to follow. From now on, the secret corner of her mind where she'd stored his memory would be empty. At long last, after today she would be free of him. Free of the inescapably sweet torment he'd stirred in her for so long.

As she was smoothing out her thoughts, Buddy came running up, sand bucket in hand. "Auntie Anna," he said, pointing toward the southern limits of the beach, "What's on the other side of those rocks?"

"Cliffs, clear to the end of the island where the channel cuts between this one and Little Hope. Maybe after supper tonight you and your dad can walk out the road and look at it from the top of the cliff. That's where I saw the U-boat blew up, so I had a good view."

Next, he gestured toward a rocky spill at the northern end of the beach. "What's up that way?"

"Mostly rocks and little sand patches for, oh, a mile or so. There's even a spot where a ship went aground and broke up. It happened about seventy years ago, but would you believe they still find things from it?"

"You mean, it was a shipwreck?"

She nodded. When his eyes widened, Anna knew his next question would be, "Dad, can we go look? Me and Alice, I mean."

Mark's glance searched hers. "Think it's safe?"

"If they don't go in the water. Or climb the rocks."

"Well, can we?" the boy implored.

"I guess. But no climbing, you hear?"

"Sure, Dad. We'll be real careful. We'll just look for stuff from the shipwreck. Is it treasure, Auntie Anna, like gold doubloons?"

"I've never heard of any. See, the ship was carrying Norwegian immigrants, so mostly they just find dishes. Or chunks of dishes. Sometimes, though, a piece of jewelry."

"Can we keep anything we find?" asked Alice. "Even if it's real treasure?"

Anna assured her they could. When they'd taken off with their buckets, she told Mark, "If there is anything, it'll probably only be shards of chamber pots."

The grin with which he watched them recede restored him to the man she'd known before, not the shadowed stranger worn thin by guilt that he'd seemed the previous day. "Whatever they pick up, it'll be treasure to them. Souvenirs of Maine."

Anna stared at the scrambling children till they were lost from sight beyond the rock pile at the end of the beach. "They're good kids, Mark. And they need you in their life. I'm glad you're there."

His expression went solemn. "Yeah, I know. Just wish they had a mother like you."

She drew a deep breath and pressed her lips together, more conscious than ever of their nearness, of the few empty inches between them, of the lines of his body close enough to touch. She was tempted to clasp his hand or lay fingertips on his arm, stealing a moment to indulge past emotions one last time before she closed that door forever. Instead she said, "I'm sure Lynette's a very good mother," in a grudging tone she hoped he couldn't discern.

Gazing at the sea, he appeared to be considering a reply when, in one swift, seamless motion, he suddenly slid his arms around her, pulling her against his body and pressing his lips to hers. Before she could even begin to react, he released her and wrapped his arms around his knees again.

"Good God, Mark," she breathed, wondering if she'd dreamed it, except that her lips were wet where his had touched them. "What in the world did you do that for?"

"Sorry," he murmured, "but I had to. One last time. For

goodbye. Because you've made it pretty damned clear how things are." He chuckled. "Not that it's all I'd like to do, mind you."

"Well, it's all you can do. More than you needed to do, actually."

He turned to regard her again, his face in shadow. "Yeah, I know. Still, I want you to promise me something. Don't worry, though. It's the last thing I'll ever ask."

"What's that?" she asked warily.

He hesitated, his gaze on the sea again. "Just that if anything ever happens to Jim—you know, in the normal course of things–will you let me know? See, I'll stay in touch. I mean, I'll send my address anytime I move, so you'll know where to reach me. But I'd just like to know, okay? Is that reasonable?"

"Well, I guess. Except it sounds...oh, silly. Far-fetched."

"Please, Anna? Yeah, I know what you said yesterday. And I can live with that, if there's even a possibility we'll meet again. Even if we're too old to care by then."

She hesitated, surprised that this request pleased her. But strangely reluctant to accede, she said, "Well, I guess."

"And if you don't hear from me, it'll be because I've died."

She sniffed. "Now you're really being silly. Please. Let's not talk about it anymore, okay?"

Before he spoke, he reached over for her hand, brought it to his mouth, kissed her sweaty, sandy palm, then quickly dropped it on the blanket between them. "Okay. Now let's see what the kids are up to."

"I'm sure they're fine."

"Yeah, I am too. But if we stay here..."

"What?"

He glanced back at the hotel. "I'm going to do something I regret. Especially if Lyn's got the binoculars on us."

Averse to hearing more, she got to her feet, brushed away sand stuck to her legs. She looked up just as Alice came running toward them. Her voice was loud and shrill. "Daddy, daddy. Come quick! Buddy's climbing the rocks! Like you told him not to!"

Mark jumped up. "Damn! Knew I couldn't trust that kid." He took off, sprinted to the edge of the sand, then more slowly picked his way around the rocks at the end of the beach.

Alice was still standing there, a stricken look on her face. Anna walked toward her, hand extended. "Can you show me where he is?"

The child nodded. "I told him not to, you know. But he never listens to anybody. Especially me." Grasping Anna's hand, she led her toward the rocky barrier. "He's always getting in trouble."

Skirting boulders at the surf line, they rounded the curve of the beach. From here, Anna could see Mark hurrying toward the boy about fifty feet ahead. Sure enough, Buddy was clambering hand over hand toward an outcropping near the top of the cliff, a knob that locals called the Devil's Fist because so many ships had wrecked beneath it. It was also a place where a kid might feel himself king of the world.

As he closed in on him, Mark shouted at the boy to come down. But without looking back, Buddy went on climbing as if determined to reach the pinnacle ten or twelve feet above. From Anna's angle, he seemed small and fragile, but nimble. And for a kid who wasn't used to rocks, he had a sure instinct for climbing.

But not sure enough: as she and Alice drew nearer, one hand slipped from a precarious hold. Anna held her breath as he tried to regain it, then lost his balance, toppling back and downwards along the face of the cliff. He seemed to fall in slow motion, arms cartwheeling as he came down, striking his head on a protruding rock. He crumpled, limply sliding the rest of the way until he landed in a heap on a small patch of sand, face down, arms above his head. Incoming surf surged around his feet, only one of which still wore a white sneaker.

Anna felt her heart stop, as if the universe had trembled. For a split second, she was acutely aware of the tropical warmth of sunlight on her skin, of the smell of tidal pools, of dead sea creatures, of salt spray in the air. Of the hiss of surf, of her own heart hammering, of Alice's small hot hand in hers. Of the pivotal quality of a moment in which all their lives abruptly changed directions. It was a time for fervent prayer, yet all she could think of was the last resort petition—Jesus, Jesus!–that had carried her through brutal times on the ship when she'd felt as helpless as she did now.

Mark's shout–"Jesus!"—as he closed the remaining distance to the inert boy, started the world turning again. Dropping to his knees, he cradled Buddy's head on his lap as an incoming wave surged around them. Before Anna could warn him not to, he dragged him to dry sand above its reach, turned him face up and wrapped his arms around him.

Dear God, she thought, had no one ever told him not to move an unconscious person until he'd been checked for damage, specifically a broken neck? Breathless, she knelt too, noticed the boy's eyelids flickering; otherwise he appeared unconscious. First she felt for the carotid pulse— rapid but strong—then probed his head with her fingertips, feeling under the hair for a bleeding gash. Head wounds usually bled profusely, but this bump hadn't opened the scalp, just left a dent in the thin layer of flesh that was already beginning to swell. Finally she pulled back the eyelids; when there was no sign of uneven dilation of the pupils, she nodded at Mark to indicate she'd gone as far as she could.

His voice was strangled with fear. "What do you think?"

What did she think? That nobody could fall that far and strike his head without serious, even tragic consequences. She swallowed hard. "I don't know. We need to get him down to the clinic so Jim can examine him." Her mind raced to implement this plan; small details fell into tentative place.

"Now. I'll go back to the hotel and call the clinic. Then I'll get Cleve and Alex to rig a stretcher. I'll take Alice, but you stay here with Buddy. Don't move him unless you have to. And keep talking so he'll know you're with him."

She got to her feet, held out her hand to the little girl, hanging back now with a thumb in her mouth. "Come on, Alice. We'll go get your mother."

Mark nodded, mouth grim. "Don't be too long. Please?"

"Okay. Meanwhile, pray for him. Pray hard as you've ever prayed for anything."

He nodded again, eyes wide, mouth tight. She'd never seen him frightened before, even when a Kamikaze had buzzed their ship.

Clutching Alice's hand again, she hurried through the rocks and back to the beach, past the blanket with the imprints of hers and Mark's bodies, across the sand to the switchback steps up the cliff, and the path across the dune to the hotel porch. As she hurried, she was conscious of nothing but the imperative to get help, not of being winded, nor of the girl's anxious questions, nor a dark mountain of clouds rising over the mainland. But after they'd come in to the hotel, she was so breathless, she could barely tell Alice to sit on a bench while she phoned the clinic.

Grace Foye answered on the second ring. Trying to sound calm, Anna outlined what had happened, asked her to find Jim wherever he was on house calls, and have him meet them in the clinic. Grace assured her not to worry; Jim would know what to do. "He always does, you know."

Resisting the urge to come back with, "At least that's how he seems," she took Alice's hand again and led her over a temporary board path to the new pavilion. Inside, Alex, Cleve and three young men from the village were painting trim around the windows. When she blurted out news of the accident, Cleve volunteered to improvise a stretcher with 2 x 4s from the site, with an old quilt being used as a drop cloth nailed to the frame. Next, slowly and clearly in her nurse's voice, she told them where to find Mark and Buddy, adding, "He may have internal injuries, so be as careful as you can carrying him out." Last, she asked Alice to take her to her mother's room.

She knocked sharply on the second floor door the child pointed out. "Lynette? It's Anna. Something's happened. I need to talk to you."

It felt like five minutes before Mark's wife peered out through a minimal opening. She was in a pink satin housecoat, hair tousled, eyes bleary. "What's the matter? What's going on?"

Anna gulped a deep, steadying breath. "It's Buddy's. He's had an accident. On the beach."

"He was showing off, Mommy," Alice piped up. "Climbing rocks. Daddy told him not to, but he did anyway. And he fell. And now he's just lying there. Sleeping."

"He was knocked out," Anna added. "But he may have come to by now. I've called Jim, and the men here are going to take him to the clinic so he can examine him. I thought you'd want to be there."

Lynette's hand flew to her mouth. "He was climbing rocks?"

Anna nodded. "He wasn't very high, but he lost his hold."

The woman's expression instantly morphed from fear to anger. "Why weren't y'all watching him? Mark knows he's a daredevil."

"We were right there. Mark ordered him to come down, but he ignored him."

The other woman's eyes flashed. "And he was knocked out?"

"He's probably awake now. I'm going back to the beach and direct the men with the stretcher, if you want to come along."

"No. I'll wait here." She shuddered visibly. "I shouldn't walk that far in my condition."

"Well, you'll see him when they take him to a car.

Meantime, Alice should stay with you."

"Oh my yes." She pulled the child against her. "Poor little thing, seeing something so awful happen to her own brother."

By the time Anna reached the steps to the beach, the stretcher bearers had already crossed the sand and were rounding the rocks. She caught up with them at the accident site, then directed Alex and Cleve on placing Buddy on the litter and wrapping their belts around him to keep him steady. When neither quipped that his trousers might fall down, she knew they regarded the situation seriously enough to follow her orders without question.

As they set off toward the hotel, the unconscious boy seemed so insubstantial and his face so white a new presentiment of tragedy gripped her. Subsumed in it, she barely noticed when Mark took her hand as they followed the others across the beach. And almost forgot to ask, "Did he wake up while I was gone?"

"Well, he looked at me a couple times. At least his eyes opened. But I couldn't tell if he saw me or not."

She nodded. "Might be a while till he regains full consciousness."

His steps slowed. "How'd Lynette take it?"

"She was shocked, of course. Then she asked if we were watching him. I said we were right there, but he wouldn't come down, even when you ordered him to."

He groaned. "God. This is so awful."

She squeezed his hand. "It'll be okay, Mark. I promise."

But even as she spoke, she knew this was another promise she had no right to make. One didn't have to be a pediatric nurse to realize that terrible things happened to the innocents of the world–suddenly, undeservedly, and out of the natural scheme of things. Even her father, despite his stubborn faith that God ruled the world, conceded that some tragedies were beyond all human understanding.

Unless, of course, this child hadn't been supervised as

closely as he should have been. If his father and a former
lover had been too caught up in echoes of old lust, then what
had happened to Buddy might at least be explainable and
understandable. Ah yes. Understandable indeed.

Jim and Grace Foye were waiting at the clinic when Cleve
backed his pickup to the entrance. Anna was first out, having
crouched beside the boy in the back on the ride from the
hotel. As they followed Grace, Alex and Cleve to an
examining room, she filled Jim in on details of the accident.
He listened with the serious mien with which he attended all
emergencies.

"The only thing that worries me," she added in a low
voice, "Mark moved him before I could tell him not to.
Turned him over. Held him in his arms."

He shook his head with noticeable gravitas. "Well, we'll
hope for the best. Now, you sit out here with the family
while Grace and l check him over. As much as we can here.
Oh by the way, I called for an ambulance at East Point when
we get back. I'd feel better if he were in the hospital, at least
overnight."

She resisted the urge to salute, nodded instead.

"And since they're leaving in the morning, how about
booking thcm a room at the Mansion House so they can be
near him tonight?"

She nodded again.

When he'd gone down the hall, Anna joined the other
men in the waiting room. Spruced up minimally since her
early days here, it was still a dismal institutional space with
the same shredded magazines, the same faded posters and
sagging blinds. Outside, the sky was bruise-blue, the Sound
wind-whipped, a wall of rain moving towards them. Distant
thunder reminded her, as it always did, of the shelling of Iwo
Jima. She thought about mentioning it to Mark, decided this

was hardly the time to speak of their previous liaison.

He and Lynette came in, Alice between them clutching a Shirley Temple doll in a costume of the same green plaid fabric as her mother's smock and father's shirt. Its hair was sticking up in rude tufts, as if cut by an amateur barber. Anna waved them into seats. "Jim's with Buddy now. He'll talk to you after he's examined him."

Pulling a chair from the desk, she sat facing them to outline Jim's plan for the next stage of the boy's care. As she talked, she realized they were obviously too distracted by the big question—would he be okay?—to listen to answers to any lesser ones. Still, she kept talking, nervously filling time with words.

When Jim returned, his expression was the grave one she recognized as the harbinger of dire news. He'd just begun to talk when a crack of thunder exploded overhead and sharp pummels of rain hit the front windows. The lights dimmed; everyone jumped.

"Now then," he began again, "most of Buddy's injuries are minor. A greenstick fracture of the forearm, some abrasions on his back and extremities. Fortunately, the spleen doesn't seem to have ruptured, as it often does in falls like this." He paused. "I am concerned, though, about a head wound. It didn't break the scalp or there'd have been blood everywhere. Instead, the force of the blow went inward, resulting in a concussion. Which is why he hasn't come to yet. The brain may be bleeding internally too, but I can't be sure without x-rays."

The others sat quietly absorbing these ifs and maybes, until Jim asked if they had any questions. Mark and Lynette turned to each other, but only shook their heads. Jim waited a moment before he glanced at his watch, then announced Fletcher Hood would cast off as soon as the storm front passed. "And there's room on the boat for all of you." His gaze slid briefly to Anna's. "Meanwhile, it might help if Anna stays here and packs up your things at the hotel, then brings your car over later on the ferry. Is that agreeable?"

Mark got to his feet. "No need for her to do that. I'll take care of it myself."

Jim laid one hand on the other man's forearm. "No, your place is with your family. Anna will be happy to do it."

She rose too and turned on the professional smile. "Of course. All I need's your car keys. "

Eyes downcast, Mark nodded and handed them over.

"Now," Jim went on. "You folks can go in and sit with Buddy till we're ready to leave. He's in the second room down the hall. Back this way."

Sighing, Anna replaced her chair and began neatening magazines on the tables to keep her hands busy. Alex and Cleve were pacing around the waiting room now, smoking and reminiscing about other mishaps at the Devil's Fist, long the site of adolescent hi-jinks. One had resulted in a drowning, another in a broken neck, the victim confined to a wheelchair ever since. Suddenly Lorraine burst into the waiting room. In a yellow rain slicker and without makeup, she looked older than Anna had ever seen her.

With a minimal nod in Cleve's direction, she said, "Oh Anna, this is so awful. What happened to that child, I mean. I left Johann with the neighbors so's I could come help. Now. Tell me what I can do."

Anna could only stare as her mind attempted to make sense of the offer. "Oh, I don't know, Lorraine. Except maybe...well, you could help me pack up the Whitmores' things at the hotel. See, they're going to the hospital with the boy. Jim asked me to bring their car on the ferry so they can spend the night over there."

"Sure. Sure. Be glad to." She lit a cigarette with shaking fingers. "I know Luke'd be here too, but he left an hour ago for one of the other islands. I'll get word to him so's he can pray for the boy. Must be serious if they're taking him to the hospital."

Anna nodded. "Head injury. He's still unconscious."

"Oh my. Poor kid. But I'm not surprised. See, he struck me as one of them boys that's always in trouble. Too bright for his own good. Or his mother's. Hope my Johann don't turn out like that."

Anna was about to say that he wouldn't because Lorraine was a different sort of mother, when the phone rang: Fletch announced he planned to leave in fifteen minutes. "Rain's letting up, but it'll be a slow trip on account of headwinds. Tell Jim they'll need to get the boy aboard soon as possible."

By the time *Molly B* was ready to sail, Buddy was on a proper stretcher in the mate's bunk, while Mark, Lynette and Alice huddled on the other bunk in the cramped space behind the pilot house. By then the rain had settled into a cold, steady drizzle; the skies were still murky, the far shore veiled in mist. At the pier, Anna came aboard, kissed Jim, spoke clichéd words of comfort and reassurance to the visitors, and promised to see them in a couple of hours before she hurried back to the pier. The mate swung the gangway aboard and cast off the lines. The engine roared as Fletch backed out of the slip and headed into the harbor. No one was on deck to return Anna's wave, so no one noticed the sorrow in her eyes except Lorraine, waiting with her in Mark's car. And all she said was, "You're worried he won't make it, ain't you?"

Anna nodded as the boat was swallowed by a gust of rain. She wrestled the gearshift into reverse, backed around and headed up the hill toward the hotel. Suddenly averse to discussing the boy's condition, she asked Lorraine why she hadn't joined them for lunch earlier. "Lynette said you were seasick. But I didn't buy that, not for one minute."

The older woman sniffed, brushed a graying curl from her forehead. "Sick of her is what I was. Phony southern accent. Phony good mother. Phony perfect wife." She snorted. "My ass! You ask me, she's nothing but a troublemaker. Down home we call women like that beyitches."

Anna laughed in spite of herself. "My father'd kill me if he heard it, but I have to agree."

"And if I was you, I'd watch out for that one. Anything happens to that kid, I reckon she'll blame you. See. Luke's told me things about you and Mark. Not that I put any stock in them, mind you. But he says there was talk on the ship."

The breath caught in her throat, but she managed to say, "Yes, I know. But heck, there was talk about every nurse who was friendly with the officers. Still, I think Lynette wants to believe the worst. See, Mark told her about another nurse he was involved with. She thinks it was me."

"Well, like I said, I know there was nothing to it. Because after all, you came home and married Jim. You wouldn't have done that if you was in love with another man. Not that I'd blame you. I bet in uniform, that Mark's one handsome devil."

"They all were. Especially your Luke. My word. When I first met him, I blushed every time we talked, he reminded me so much of my first husband. All the nurses had crushes on him. But he was never even tempted. He's a good priest."

Lorraine's expression turned thoughtful. She nodded but didn't answer.

"By the way, have you ever told him about his father?"

She shook her head so emphatically more curls tumbled around her face. "No. I'll take that to my grave."

"But suppose he wanted to find him."

"No need of him to do that."

So many unspoken truths, she thought, went to the grave when they needed to be brought into the light of day. Like her actual relationship with Mark; why hadn't she told Jim yet? Lord knew, she firmly believed husbands and wives couldn't live with ugly secrets. Nor could mothers and sons, for that matter. But as long as life proceeded uneventfully, no one wanted to inject unpleasant truths into the status quo. Too well she understood Lorraine's reluctance; it mirrored her own.

Back at the hotel, they went through the two rooms the Whitmores had occupied. To her surprise, Buddy's things were with Mark's, while Alice's were in Lynette's. Why? Did the mother not want the children to see each other unclothed? Or was one of them subject to nightmares that required parental comforting in the night? Or, even more ominous, was this part of her punitive designs for Mark?

"Look," Lorraine said, pointing to the evidence, "she don't even sleep with him."

"Obviously she does now and then. Or she wouldn't be pregnant."

Lorraine sneered. "Bet she's one of them beyitches uses it as a weapon."

Anna grimaced and snapped the latches on the last suitcase. A bellboy carried them down the stairs and out to the car. Following, they passed through the hotel lobby, filled now with guests gussied up for dinner. Some were sipping cocktails, while in the dining room a tuxedoed young man with a thin moustache and a pasted-on smile was playing the grand piano; *Stairway to the Stars* gave the big space an urbane, sophisticated elegance. Even the aromas from the kitchen had become grander since the days of Mrs. Leech's mainstay Down East dishes; tonight's specialty du jour was Rack of Spring Lamb.

And if it had been any ordinary day, Mark and his family would be waiting to eat now too—the kids sunburnt, tired from the beach, everyone eager to get started on the long trip home in the morning. Instead…she shuddered and stepped outside, into the fresh, rain-smelling cold.

On the way to the ferry, she dropped Lorraine off at home. After the other woman got out, she had a sudden sense of her own isolation. Why, she wondered, had Jim volunteered her for this duty without so much as consulting her? Because he knew her capacity for doing what needed to be done? Because he wanted to keep her busy? Surely not to keep her away from Mark. Surely not. The very notion set her heart racing with new dread.

All things considered, the situation was fraught with dire possibilities, and likely to get worse if the child's head injury was what Jim suspected. Eventually, too numb to analyze further, she piloted the Pontiac up the ramp onto the big double-ended ferry, then sat staring beyond other vehicles to the wind-whipped gray Sound. She wished now that she and Mark had been able to make this final voyage together, silently sharing the memory of the awful moment on the beach. Perhaps even holding hands in prayer for his son. A symbolic trip, with an air of finality even stronger than their last deployment on *Compassion*. One final journey, she thought, watching lights bloom along Penobscot Bay as the ship slowed for the Rockhampton terminal.

But after she drove down the ramp onto the rain-glazed streets of the town, she reminded herself that every journey had to end somewhere, sometime. As this one would have even if Mark had been with her. And nothing would have changed about Buddy's circumstances. Nothing at all.

CHAPTER SIXTEEN

She left the Pontiac in the hospital lot next to Jim's car. Having no umbrella against the cold rain, she shivered as she splashed through puddles toward the main entrance. The clerk at the desk told her Buddy was in Post-op, a ward where unconscious patients were supervised from a central nurses' station. She herself had spent the first few hours there after the C-section that had delivered Jamie in January, and more recently, after the abortion. Already a place too crowded with memories.

Leaving word for Jim that she'd arrived, she rode the groaning elevator up to Two and followed the long corridor past the scrub and operating rooms to a waiting area furnished in wooden benches, overflowing stand ashtrays and No Smoking signs. A poster had been tacked up advertising a "A Modern New Wing to Serve You Better", currently in the skeletal stages of construction. The only light was the dim yellow glow of globes suspended from the ceiling.

She noticed the young girl—nineteen or twenty, heavy makeup smudged around the eyes, long stringy brown hair, and a slouch—before she realized the older man huddled with her was her own father. He was wearing clericals, pipe visible above the shirt pocket. When he glanced up, his gentle smile was like sunrise; it filled Anna with relief and the sense that all would be well. No matter what came to pass, all would be well.

Getting to his feet, he told the girl, "Excuse me, miss. But my daughter's here." Then introduced them, explaining that, "Jill's waiting to see her sweetheart. He was in a motorcycle wreck. I was just praying with her."

A motorcycle wreck? Memories of her first encounter with Dan Donovan flashed through her, but she said only, "Oh, I'm sorry. I hope he'll be all right." Then to her father, "Are you here for her? Or the Whitmore boy?"

"Jim phoned me about the lad, but I haven't seen him yet. I only just met Jill." He led her to another bench; they sat side by side, holding hands. "He thought I might be of comfort to your friends. Oh my. Such a sad thing to happen on a vacation. And he doesn't sound hopeful."

"I'm not either. But it's in the Lord's hands, isn't it?"

"Oh indeed. Which reminds me. I brought Ted Bigelow along too. Being he was a chaplain himself, he'll know better what to say than I do."

"Is he in with the child now?"

"And Mark."

"How's his wife doing?"

"Only saw her a minute when she took the little girl over to the Mansion House. Poor tyke's scared to death for her brother. Said he was showing off, but the mother kept shushing her and telling her nobody wanted to hear such sad stories."

"We saw it, you know. Mark and I saw him fall, I mean. Awful to watch something terrible while it's happening, without being able to stop it. A nightmare for both of us."

His hand tightened around hers, bony but firm. "Sorry, sweetheart. To think what you and he went thru in the war, and now this."

"This is worse, Dad. More personal. See, I was just getting to know Buddy. He was so bright and interested in everything, and full of questions. I was really starting to like him." Aware she'd reverted to past tense, she pulled a hanky from her purse and blotted her cheeks. Before she could say

more, Ted Bigelow pushed through the swinging doors from
the ward. She thanked him for coming, asked how Buddy
was.

"Still unconscious." His expression turned grave. "Saw
enough head injuries in the war to know prolonged
unconsciousness isn't a good sign. But Mark's contacted the
Navy at Brunswick. They're going to take over the case. Fly
him and the family back to Virginia so he can be treated
there."

"Oh my. Well, nothing we can do here anyway. He needs
a neurologist. Possibly surgery too. We'd only have to send
him to Portland or Augusta. "

Ted nodded, glanced at his watch. "Well, if you'll excuse
me, Anna, my wife's holding supper. Ready to leave yet,
Cranmer?"

"Thanks, but I'll wait and catch a ride with Anna and
Jim."

Ted took her hand, looked into her eyes. "Anna, if you
need anything—anything at all—promise to call, okay?"

"At the moment, all I can think of is prayer."

"Of course."

After he left, she went in to see Buddy for herself. The
ward contained twenty beds, only three occupied, one by a
young man in traction with a bandaged head, the second by
an inert form so elderly she couldn't tell its gender. And in
the nearest, Buddy, head swathed in gauze, an IV dripping
into his arm. Mark was hunched in a chair beside him, head
in his hands, elbows on his knees. Rain streamed down the
windows, smearing lights outside like those seen through
tears. Anna caught the tang of fresh coffee, overlaid with
antiseptic. Reminiscent of wards on the ship where there was
always coffee at nurses' stations. And usually Mark on his
rounds to comfort patients. She sighed. So long ago, so far
away, yet right here now.

He didn't look up as she approached. Assuming he was
praying, she laid one hand on the boy's forehead, noted the

flickering eyelids, the pallid face. She made the sign of the cross over him, then pulled up a chair and sat facing his father across the bed. She waited a moment, then said, "Mark?"

At first his glance was blank, as if he'd just awakened from a doze. He blinked, sat up straighter, and said, "Oh. Anna. Any problems with the car?"

"No. I did fine. Now. How's Buddy?"

His shrug was one of reluctant resignation. "Same way he's been since it happened. Jim's the only person has any idea why. And of course, nothing he can do about it. " He sighed. "Didn't know civilian hospitals were so far behind the times."

Suddenly defensive, she said, "Of course they are. For five years they had to make do with what they had, while the new drugs and the best doctors went to the troops. In 1943, one of my friends died here from an infection that sulfonamide could've cured, but Jim could only get two units. And then, only because an officer at Brunswick comshawed it."

He stared, looking puzzled, then rubbed his eyes. "Speaking of Brunswick, the Navy's sending an ambulance tomorrow. Going to fly Buddy—all of us, they'll put us on a plane for Norfolk. He'll get real medical attention at Portsmouth."

"Oh, good. We'll all feel better when they take over. Meantime, I hope you realize Jim's doing everything he can as a GP."

"Of course, Anna. You don't need to defend him. Or this hospital."

Tightening her lips against a further outburst, she drew a deep breath. "What time is the ambulance coming?"

"Noon. I'll follow it back to the air station. They'll arrange to get my car back to Virginia later."

She nodded, feeling as if someone had just pulled a plug that let all her energy drain, leaving her none with which to fight off this new onslaught of despair. Then the ward doors opened and Jim entered, leaning on the cane more heavily than usual. The sight of him energized her to rise from the chair and walk to meet him. And even though it was unprofessional, throw her arms around him.

"Ready to go home, dear?" He pulled away from the embrace and continued toward Mark.

"Unless he wants us to stay."

"No," he said in his resolute voice. "Even if there was something you could do here, you should be home with Jamie. Now. Mark, anything you need before we leave?"

Mark rose, shook his head. "No, I'm fine," he said, then chuckled. "Though I could use a good stiff drink. Can't remember last time I felt like that. Usually I'm a teetotaler."

"After Indy went down," she said. "Remember? When we all went to the O Club at Apra?"

"Oh yeah. The night of FUBAR."

Jim eased into the chair Anna had vacated, pulled a prescription pad from his jacket pocket, scribbled a moment and handed the scrip to Mark. "Here. Give this to the desk clerk at the hotel and he'll send a bottle to your room. For medicinal purposes. To help you sleep."

Mark frowned at the paper, then extended his right hand to Jim. They shook, an awkwardly formal gesture in the circumstances. "Thanks. This'll fix me up. Now, all I need's the car keys, Anna."

As she handed them over, she considered hugging him, decided not to. "Well, I'll see you in the morning then. Meanwhile, we'll keep praying."

He nodded but his look was skeptical, even cynical.

In the car, she huddled against Jim and watched the wipers rise and fall against the rain, while they talked about the baby and the fact Margie had taken over his care when Kate had left for home earlier. They stopped at the Lobster Hut; the waitresses were in yellow rain slickers, but it was too cold to eat in the car, so they took the bags home and sat at the kitchen table with Jamie in his high chair gumming French fries and slobbering, a pleasant distraction from the eventful twelve hours since she'd last seen him. Then, grateful for some simple motherly chore, she took him upstairs and got him ready for the night.

After he was asleep, she climbed into bed and tried to pray. But this situation resonated with other hopeless situations—the year when Dan was merely missing, and Jean's final days, when her prayers had felt useless even as she whispered them. Even as she'd tried to picture Jean whole and sound and healed, as she did for Buddy now. All in vain, as if the gates of heaven were not to be stormed, and every prayer only bounced off and fell at the feet of the angels. Like so many dead birds. Or so many lifeless hopes.

CHAPTER SEVENTEEN

She woke before first light when the baby wailed from his room, a half-hearted experimental whine that was more about summoning her than expressing distress. He usually woke this early, sucked down a bottle, then drifted off again for another hour or two. Rain continued to trickle at the windows and Jim's snore told her he was still asleep, so she felt her way into the chenille robe and to the baby's room. In the glow from the hall light, his smile sent joy racing through her. True to form, he was soaked from the skin out, so she wrestled him into a clean diaper and nightie, then lugged him down to the kitchen. While the bottle heated, she walked him around, all the while talking about the ordinary things his eyes lit upon. Then she took him back upstairs, sat in the Boston rocker Margie had decorated, and gave him the bottle.

As he sucked, his fingers curled around the lapels of her robe and he hummed as they rocked. She wondered if Lynette had ever had moments like this with Buddy. Of course; every mother did, every mother thought such times would never end, as she waited for her child to develop, to sit, stand, walk, talk, run, play, read, and grow into an independent human being who no longer needed her.

Jamie was asleep again before the bottle was empty, so she placed him in the crib and tip-toed back to her own bed. Jim didn't move as she slipped under the covers and snuggled closer to his familiar morning-smelling warmth.

She tried to pray for Lynette and Mark and the little girl, aware that beyond the quiet comfort of her world was the private horror of theirs. But even as she prayed, the new movie in her head–the boy toppling down the rocks—played and replayed, just as the Kamikaze attack sometimes still did, often in dreams that terrified her awake. Trying to stave off the horror of this one, she pictured the coming day, Mark following the Navy ambulance down Route One, the same road he'd driven two days before to get here. He'd be grim and numb, and whether his wife and Alice were with him or not, feeling cut off from the world, isolated by his own terror and helplessness. And probably guilt. Oh yes, definitely guilt.

And she knew then that however Jim or Lynette or even Mark might interpret her actions, she had to go with him those last miles, had to go as far as she could. She hoped Jim wouldn't press for an explanation, for there was none she could share with him, at least none he'd want to hear. Even imagining his possible reaction chilled her and undermined her resolve..

She hadn't expected to, but she fell asleep for a while, awakening to the gurgle of rain in the downspouts and the gray light of a cloudy morning, with the baby half-talking, half-wailing again. Jim was gone; from downstairs came the low rumble of his voice and the heartiness of Kate's, undoubtedly pouring forth torrents of sympathy for the Whitmores in the most maudlin phrases known to mankind.

Still in robe and slippers and with the baby over her shoulder, Anna came downstairs. Jim was in the office, the phone pulled across the desk as if he'd recently used it. He looked up when she came to the doorway. "Just talked to the post-op nurse. From the sound of the child's vitals, the coma's deepening. Thank God the Navy's coming today."

Bad news, just as she'd feared. She barely managed to say, "Will you see him before they leave?"

He nodded. "Have to make rounds anyway. Want to ride

along?"

"If you can wait half an hour or so."

"Of course, dear."

But it was more like an hour before she'd given Jamie breakfast, had a bowl of Wheaties herself, and thrown on the first skirt and blouse she came to in the closet. With no time for a shower, she felt grungy and ill-groomed, but even so, it was almost eleven when they got there. Mark and Alice were in the waiting area, the girl on his lap, thumb in her mouth again. She was so tall her feet rested on the floor; the same ill-used doll was held close to her chest. Mark looked as if he'd slept in his clothes and hadn't shaved. His eyes were bleary, a trace of sour mash on his breath.

He barely nodded as they came in. "Sorry I can't get up. My legs are numb."

"Is Lynette in with Buddy?" Anna asked.

"Of course. Been there since we got here this morning. Going to ride in the ambulance with him. Take Alice too. See, she doesn't trust me to care for our children anymore."

Jim's glance barely brushed hers, but Anna felt its significance. "If you want to ride in the ambulance with them," she said, "I could drive your car to the air station."

Mark shook his head. "No room. Lyn doesn't want me there anyway. But I wouldn't mind if you drove. Be glad of the company, in fact."

"That settles it, then." She sat in a facing chair. "Ted Bigelow's offered to help, so maybe he could follow and bring me back after you leave."

Jim cleared his throat. "I'll call and ask. Still expect the Navy at noon?"

"Right." Mark's gaze followed his hobbled walk up the corridor, then turned to her with disconcerting intensity. "Sure you want to do this, Anna?"

"Yes. See, I want to go with you today. As far as I can."

His eyes filled. "Thanks. But you know how my wife's going to feel about that, don't you?"

"Will it make things worse?"

He shrugged, gave a rueful chuckle. "Right now they seem as bad as they can get. But who knows? Thing is, I don't care anymore. I just want Buddy to wake up and be Buddy again."

She drew a deep breath to quiet the fluttering in her chest: Hope beating its wings against the headwinds of probability? She smiled at the little girl. "I bet Alice does too, don't you?"

The girl nodded. "Even if he is a dumb show-off."

When Jim came back he reported things were set with Ted. "Now I'll go inside and see the boy."

"While you're in there," Mark said hesitantly, "would you mind telling my wife about the new travel plans? She's less likely to give you a hard time about it."

Jim blinked, his expression neutral, unreadable as usual. "I'll do what I can," he said as he pushed open the swinging doors.

Anna leaned back in the unyielding chair. "So that's how it is, is it? Well, I'm not really surprised. Maybe blaming us takes her mind off Buddy's condition."

"Sure. Blame's powerful. Look how it helped us get thru the war. Having an enemy to hate fueled America's defense effort."

Avoiding his stare, Anna focused on floor tiles, ceiling tiles, the sagging leather of her purse, the scuffed toes of her shoes and her ragged fingernails. She was glad of the distraction, until a young couple came down the hall with the diffident air of those who aren't sure they should be there. The young man asked if this was the post-op waiting area, then urged the girl onto the bench beside him. "My pa's just come in with a stroke. Doc told us to meet him here," he added in a strong Down-East blue-collar accent. "Anybody asked for us?"

"Doctor Millett's in there now," Anna said. "Is he your doctor?"

"Ay-yuh. Ain't never met him myself, but he sounds good on the phone."

"The best there is," Mark said.

"Well, I sure hope he can get Pa back on his feet before we run out of summer." The girl whispered something in his ear, which prompted him to ask Anna where the ladies' room was.

"Come on, I'll show you."

When they got back, Jim was talking to fat, pink-faced Father Oleski from Our Lady Star of the Sea Catholic Church, who was waiting to give the old man last rites. When the others had gone inside, Jim leaned over, speaking quietly so Mark and Alice couldn't hear. "Just so you know, Lynette Whitmore says she doesn't give a damn how Mark gets to the air station. So long as she doesn't have to see you again. Blames you for distracting him so he didn't watch the kids. So try to stay out of her way. And if you can't, don't take anything she says personally. It's just the pain talking."

She regarded him with more questions than she could, or would, ask. "Whatever you say, dear. So long as you understand."

He picked up her hand, held it a minute. His smile was reassuring if not joy-filled. "Of course. Now I need to talk to the stroke patient's family and make rounds, then get back to the office for afternoon hours." A quick kiss just missed her lips. "Come home when you can."

After he returned to the ward, she realized she had no energy for making conversation with Mark for the hour before the ambulance came, so she asked Alice if she wanted to take a walk. "Just down the street. To my mother and father's. They'd like to see you. And they probably have cookies. Maybe even gingerbread men. I mean, if it's all right with your father."

Alice's face lit, but Mark only frowned. "Sorry, dear. Your mama wouldn't like it. I think Auntie Anna understands. Don't you, Anna?"

"Oh yes. Yes indeed. Well, then...." she bent to Alice. "Maybe I'll bring some back for you. Okay?" The child stared up with wide eyes, then nodded and resumed sucking her thumb.

Trying to ignore the tension rising within her was like trying to ignore hurricane warnings in a beachside cottage. Still, Anna smiled at father and daughter, said, "I'll see you at noon at the loading dock behind the hospital," and walked determinedly away.

When she got back later, Ted Bigelow's '47 Ford coupe was parked behind the Pontiac in the alley between the hospital and the hotel. A gray Cadillac ambulance was backed up to the loading dock; two sailors leaned against it, smoking in brilliant midday sunlight that had begun poking through the clouds. By her watch, it was just twelve. A distant siren confirmed the time.

She leaned in the window of Ted's car. "Thanks for helping with this. Even if you think I'm crazy."

As usual, his smile was gentle, reserved. "Not at all. Glad to be of service. Your friend's waiting in his car, by the way."

"Okay. Then I'll see you at the air station."

In the Pontiac, Mark was folded over the steering wheel, eyelids drooping. When she spoke his name, he blinked up at her with the bleary air of a man who's had at least one stiff drink recently. Even if she hadn't smelled it on him, she'd have known. "Better slide over," she said in her authoritative nurse's voice, "so I can drive."

He seemed about to argue, but edged himself across the plastic-covered seat, hoisting his legs over the gear shift. "This sure is nice of you Anna. But I shouldn't be surprised. That's how you are. How you've always been. Nice."

She nodded, watching the sailors come alert as an orderly

rolled a gurney toward the open rear door, then wheeled it into the ambulance. Behind them, Jim escorted Lynette and Alice. One sailor ushered them inside, closed the doors, came around to the front and climbed in next to the driver. As she observed, Anna remembered the black hearse that had brought Jean's body to East Point pier three years before. And wondered idly if General Motors used the same basic chassis for both ambulances and hearses.

When the ambulance had turned into the alley, Jim waved, so she tooted the horn, put the car in gear and drove out behind the gray vehicle. At the next cross street, she followed as it turned left toward the town square, and around the north end past the Congregational church, then onto Route One south. Now midday sunlight danced and dazzled through dispersing clouds, so she groped in her purse for sunglasses against the glare.

The road arrowed through Rockhampton's burgeoning industrial outskirts, past a newly-opened pink and green stucco Italian restaurant, then a billboard advertising a development of new houses you could buy for only $7990, with no down payment for GIs. So far the site was only raw mud, but the full-color illustration of Seaside Acres depicted a Cape Cod with a new car in the driveway, a smiling man getting out, a smiling wife at the front door and smiling children throwing a ball to a dog in the front yard. Even the dog appeared to be smiling.

Finally, with no more visible distractions to occupy her mind, she said, "I can't tell you how relieved Jim and I are that the Navy's taken over Buddy's case. Things will look at lot better when you get him back to the hospital in Virginia."

"No," he said with no trace of doubt. "They won't, Anna. They never will again. No matter how this turns out—I mean with Buddy—it's the end of everything."

Stunned, she managed to say, "If you mean your marriage, why, don't you know anything Lynette says now is just her fear talking?"

"Doesn't matter why she says it, things have gone too far. Not that they were great before, but at least they were tolerable. Now—"he shook his head morosely. "Now it's open warfare. I'm the enemy. You too. See, she thinks we've robbed her of everything she ever had. Except Alice, of course, and the new baby. And she's not going to give us a chance to take them from her."

Anna winced, trying to find a sliver of good cheer for him, like a peppermint Life Saver for a starving child. But all she could manage was inane chatter about her first trip here and the Bath shipyard worker who'd harassed her on the bus. Finally she said, "Thank God I'm riding home with Ted. I don't know him very well, but he strikes me as someone I can tell anything and he'll understand."

"I used to be that kind of chaplain," Mark said in a shaky voice.

Touched, she patted his hand on the seat between them. "And you will be again. The Lord's not done with you yet."

His smile was bitter. "Funny. I was just thinking. If Buddy doesn't make it, at least that'll be the end of my doubts. It'll be all the proof I need."

The disbelief that hit her was like a cold wave. "Proof? Of what? That God doesn't care?"

"Yep. At least not enough to override 'the sins of the father' clause. "

Now what could she say? Nothing except, "Well, that'd be the easiest way to go, wouldn't it? I mean, just give up?"

"Not easy, Anna. Nothing about this is easy. But I'm not going to keep trying to believe He gives a damn if I get solid proof he really doesn't. That's what's bothered me all along: if God's really a loving father like the church wants us to believe, how can he let people suffer? So maybe he isn't. And it's all bullshit."

Realizing he was presently beyond convincing, she said, "But if Buddy lives? If he comes out of this good as new? What'll you believe then?"

He sighed, took a long while to say, "Well, I guess that'd be my sign. Like the Lord staying Abraham's hand when he was about to slit Isaac's throat. Then I'd know."

She clutched the steering wheel tighter. "Oh my. I hope Ted can explain that to me, because I don't know what to tell you. Except...."

"What?"

"Maybe...well, maybe what you're really looking for is a sign the Lord forgives you. Forgives us. For everything. Most of all, for yesterday. I mean, for being more interested in each other than watching the kids. Maybe that's your real 'sins of the father'."

She felt him sit straighter, half-turn toward her.

"Because if he forgives us, then he forgives everyone and cares about them, and watches over them, and grieves with them, and gives them strength to go on. But if not, we're all doomed."

"Jesus. I hadn't thought of it that way."

"So it all hangs on whether that sweet child lives or dies, doesn't it? Your marriage. Your ministry. Your whole future."

"God. I don't know."

She patted his hand again. "No, I don't either."

Ahead, the high chain link fencing around the air station stretched along the highway into the distance. As they neared the main gate, the ambulance pulled into the center lane for the left turn. In the rearview mirror, she saw Ted follow. When oncoming traffic cleared, the small caravan swung up to the sentry; he waved the ambulance thru, but Mark had to show his leave papers and explain about the car behind them before they could pass.

Inside, they followed a long road toward a cluster of buildings, checkerboard-painted water tower, control tower, parked planes—PBYs and transports and some she couldn't identify, even a few spindly helicopters. She considered mentioning an article in the *New England Journal of*

Medicine about how useful the new whirlybirds were in medical emergencies, able to land and take off anywhere, even on hospital roofs and the decks of ships, dramatically life-saving, especially in wartime. But she knew he wouldn't hear, wouldn't respond. Well, maybe Ted would be interested on the way home.

When the ambulance slowed at the Operations building, a sailor directed it toward a loading area where a line of Navy officers was straggling toward a four-engine R-5-D. Beside it a smaller two-engine Lockheed Electra was parked. Anna braked, waiting for directions as the ambulance pulled around to the far side of the Electra. When the sailor walked over to the car, Mark showed his leave papers again and explained the situation. The red-haired swabbie saluted and told them they could board anytime; he'd find someone to unload the luggage and take the car away. Anna didn't correct his impression she was his wife. Soon another sailor pushing a dolly came along and stacked all the bags from the trunk, then wheeled them toward the Electra. A third man had Mark sign some papers, then took the car keys. They were still standing there when he drove off, taking the green Pontiac to some storage area from whence it would one day be delivered to Mark in Virginia.

Willing herself not to get teary, Anna turned on the professional smile, laid one hand on his arm, made her tone upbeat. "Well, Mark, I guess this is it. Another goodbye. Like Oakland, only worse."

He nodded. "Much worse." His voice was gruff, solemn.

"Let me know what happens, will you? See, I want to be able to pray, knowing what to ask for. If that makes any sense."

Another nod, brusque and strangely indifferent. He held out his hand and they shook, stiffly, like proper shipmates. Or former lovers being spied on by someone inside a nearby plane. "Will do. Now. Be sure and thank Jim for everything. He's a good guy." He glanced back at Ted's car and gave a quasi-salute. "Okay then. Anna. Now is the hour, I guess. Again."

"Take care of yourself," she said through the tightness in her throat.

Flashing her a last grin, he turned toward the plane. He walked with surprising energy, more like the man he'd been two years before than the beaten and depressed person she'd met on this visit. The ambulance emerged from behind the smaller plane and drove away. A sailor with a yellow flag beckoned Mark to hurry.

He stepped up his pace and almost sprinted around the wings, where he was hidden by the fuselage. Arming herself with a deep breath, she walked back to Ted's car and stood beside his window. At the loading area, the bigger transport swung around, spewing prop wash and a great roaring noise as it taxied toward the runway. When it was gone, the Electra's engines sputtered and caught, coughing out bluish smoke until they smoothed out. A sailor ducked under the wing to pull chocks, and the man with the flag led it into a tight turn toward the taxiway. Prop wash scattered dust across the tarmac before the plane bounced out of sight behind a grassy hummock.

"That's like the aircraft Amelia Earhart flew on her last trip," Anna said to Ted. "Navy uses them for small transports. Three years ago I flew on one like it from Quonset Point to Norfolk. The first leg out to join my ship. After that we were on R-4-Ds the rest of the way to Alameda. Two engines. The Army calls them C-47s. Best of all was the Clipper, San Francisco to Pearl Harbor. Then an R-5-D, like that big one that just left. You'd know it as a C-54, I guess. All the way from Oahu to Brisbane. I think it took 16 hours. You lose track of time on long flights like that."

She stopped talking after the four-engine had roared past on the runway and she'd realized Ted was staring at her as if she was babbling nonsense. As the larger plane lifted off and gained altitude, the Electra came into view from behind low trees, tail rising as it became airborne. Anna waved as it soared upward. Slowly, it wheeled around toward the east while the R-5-D curved slowly westward.

"I guess they'll follow the ocean," she said. "All the way to Virginia. That's what we did when we left Quonset Point."

Ted smiled up and patted her hand on the door frame, a quietly reassuring gesture her father had used with parishioners when words failed him. His voice was calm and steady. "Well now, Anna, shall we be getting back to Rockhampton?"

"Oh yes. Sure. Sorry to keep you waiting." She came around and got in the passenger seat, but when he began to back away, she laid her hand on his arm. "Wait a minute, Ted. I want to watch a little longer."

He tapped the brake. "Of course."

Through the windshield, her gaze followed the fragile speck that was the Electra carrying Mark and his family as it receded against the massed clouds over the ocean. When it disappeared into one puffy purple mass, she shuddered in a wave of something heavy and sorrowful and inevitable, like the culmination of all the lesser emotions preceding it during the whole time she'd known Mark. As if the plane hadn't merely been swallowed by a weather phenomenon, but had exploded into oblivion, forever removing him from her life in one swift stroke. And whatever had existed between them—passion or love, heat or light, obsession or genuine concern—these too were gone, leaving her suddenly spent and empty. Drained of anger and guilt as surely as if Mark and everyone aboard had just been uplifted into heaven.

She inhaled deeply as the wave receded and the new reality engulfed her. With profound relief, she realized she no longer either needed or wanted to talk to Ted about what had just happened. Because it was over. Whatever happened to Buddy now, her part in the drama was over. This matter too ugly, too sordid to think about further had ended. And thanks be to God that it had.

"Okay. We can go now."

He nodded and resumed driving away from the landing area. At the main gate, as he waited for a break in traffic on Route One, she said, "If you're not in a hurry to get home, maybe we could stop for lunch on the way back. And talk about what you did in the war. See, I'm interested in hearing someone else's war story. If you don't mind telling it."

"Be happy to, Anna. Glad you want to talk about it. Not many do, you know."

She smiled and sat back, relaxing for the first time since Mark and his family had come for their ill-starred visit. Even this close to the subject, her mind recoiled, craving instead the sweet relief that a part of her life had ended that day. The shadowed, secret, ugly part.

Now, finally, she could live without Mark's memory darkening every waking moment. And often, even her sleep.

CHAPTER EIGHTEEN

Two weeks later, on a Friday night toward the end of August, she and Margie went to the Roxy in town to watch a silly new Dick Haymes musical, then suck up ice cream sodas at the Rexall. When the MG stopped in front of the house, she got out, waving as her friend sped off in the usual cloud of exhaust.

Though it was after ten, Jim was still at his desk shuffling a scattered mess of patient charts. A mosquito hummed in the warm stillness of the office. As she brushed a kiss on his cheek, she noticed his grim expression. She tensed, hands clenched, breathing slowed.

"Hope you enjoyed the movie, dear," he said, "because I've had some bad news. From your friend down south."

"Oh no…about Buddy?"

He nodded. "Expired this morning. After a third surgery to stop the brain bleed."

The breath went out of her as she dropped into a chair. For a moment all she could feel was the sudden pounding of her heart, the trembling of her lips. And the cold sense she'd been swept back into Mark's orbit again. He hadn't really left her the day he'd flown out of Brunswick after all; here he was again, more needy than ever, and here she was, watching Buddy fall with the certainty she'd always be haunted by the consequences of the passion she and Mark had shared. Those tragic, irreversible wages of sin.

Still she managed, "Oh, the poor kid. That poor little boy.

After hanging on so long...."

"Never regained consciousness, though."

She made herself keep talking. "You know, I had a feeling he wouldn't make it. Sometimes when you pray for something, you get a feeling one way or the other. Like it happened with Jean. Oh, poor Mark. Poor Lynette. Did you talk to her too?"

"No, just him. He sounded...well, to be blunt, like he'd been drinking. Not surprising, I guess. But maybe it's more of a problem than we know. He said Lynette's left him, taken Alice with her, doesn't even want him at the funeral. Blames him for everything."

"And me too, I guess," she had to say.

"Didn't mention that. Anyway, I was wondering. Did he drink a lot when you knew him before?"

"There was no booze on the ship. Officially. Though he had a bottle in his stateroom. A lot of officers did. He gave me some bourbon once, to calm my nerves after that Kamikaze buzzed us. But I only saw him drunk once, after Indy went down. We all drank a lot that night."

Jim shook his head; weariness beyond that which usually beset him in late evening etched his features like a fine net. "So unspeakably sad, all of it. If only they'd never come."

She nodded, hoping he couldn't discern the intensity of her regret. Or old guilt given new energy by the child's death. Hiding it, she knew intuitively, would demand more of her than ever. How long could she mask it with this façade of simple, friendly concern?

"Wonder why they did," he went on. "I mean, why go out of their way to visit us? To see you and Luke? Ironic, since none of your other friends from the ship has ever been here."

"We may never know," she said as casually as she could, then got up, said she was going to bed. She made her tone suggestive when she added, "I hope you'll be right along." The last thing she felt like now was having intercourse, but if it convinced Jim that Mark's visit had been only an innocent coincidence, she'd try to make it happen. Tomorrow was time enough to deal with this awful new connection to that part of her past.

For the next ten days, the incident receded like waters after a flood, leaving her with not just this new haunting but a muddy residue of regret and sorrow that polluted every waking thought. Trying to work it into her consciousness, she made herself talk about it with everyone who seemed inclined to hear, and even a few who weren't. Kate was strongly inclined, of course; her lust for the morbid demanded every colorful detail Anna could remember or even invent. Predictably, she listened with clucks of sympathy interspersed with Irish tales of little people carried off too soon. But with no surprise; she claimed to have observed a fey quality in Buddy just in the half hour or so she'd served cookies and lemonade. "He was an old soul," she added sadly. "One who'd been around before and couldn't wait to get back to the other side."

"He was also a daredevil," Anna said drily. "That's what carried him off."

"Well, they do that, you know. Tempt fate every way they can. Sure, and didn't it work for him this time!"

Anna squelched the urge to roll her eyes, and took the baby to visit her parents. Their reaction was less dramatic, though her mother's comment was surprising: "That boy had a wild streak. Reckless. Some are like that. A wonder they ever make it to manhood. Of course, that mother of his had a lot to do with it. Spoiled him rotten, I bet. Same with the little girl. Chickens come home to roost, I'd say."

On the other hand, her father mused that Mark might well view the tragedy as confirmation of his previous doubts. "Every clergyman worth his salt goes through a doubting time," he said, "But most of us come out of it with renewed faith. I expect he will too. Eventually. Though the loss of a child would be the worst trial a man could face." He blinked slowly, averting his gaze from Anna's. "Or a woman too, for that matter."

"But losing a newborn," Anna made herself say in a normal tone, "wouldn't be nearly as bad as losing a half-grown child."

He shrugged and cleared his throat. "I can only take your word for that, dear."

She turned away quickly, unwilling for him to see the tears that had jumped into her eyes So quickly she hadn't felt them coming. As if a river of them flowed just below the surface of consciousness, ready to flood when she least expected it.

When she got home, she called Father Bigelow with the news; Ted invited her to stop by the church office and talk, if she felt the need. "Thanks. Maybe I will next time I'm in town. Right now, I'm almost relieved it's over. Even this way. Wish you could talk to Mark, though. It probably confirms all his previous doubts about the Lord's benevolence."

"If you give me his address, I'll write and share my own experiences with apostasy. Of course, mine stemmed from vicarious events, not personal tragedies."

"Well, you could try, but I doubt right now anything can help him." Even as she spoke, she realized she was talking about herself as well.

On Wednesday that week she went to Hope Island with Jim and Tom. She hadn't been back since the accident, but sensed if she didn't go soon, she might develop an obsessive aversion to the place where Buddy had crashed on the rocks. Maybe even the whole island. Still, for most of the morning, she hid out in the office, forcing herself to work on the dead files before she phoned Lorraine to invite herself to lunch.

"Sure," said the older woman. "Bring Tom and Jim along. Got plenty for everybody. Luke and Timmy'll be here too."

Anna stiffened, dreading the priest's reaction to Buddy's death. "No, it'll just be me," she said, wishing now she could back out. But no; like the island, she'd have to face him some day too. Better today than another time, when Jim might be present.

All of them had already heard the news, so initially, no one said anything Anna hadn't heard before. Except for Luke: "Mark should never have brought his family here." He spoke with the same dogmatic assurance that had annoyed her on the ship. "You know why he did, don't you?"

Oh God, there it was: the opening salvo of his attack. "Actually, it was his wife's idea," she said more calmly than she felt.

"But she wrote and asked first, didn't she? You could've told her it wasn't convenient. Then they wouldn't have come. And the accident wouldn't have happened. But you didn't, did you? You had to see him again."

Anna dropped her fork. Lorraine and Timmy continued to eat, eyes downcast, faces blank and innocent. As if Luke had discussed this before and left no doubt about his views.

"That's absurd," she finally managed.

"Is it?"

Her heart continued to jump as she picked up the fork and began eating again, now without tasting. "Look," she said between bites, "I only came to talk to your mother about Buddy's death, not for one of your judgmental homilies."

Shrugging, he left the table to pour coffee from an enameled pot on the stove into thick china mugs. He carried them back and set them at his place and Timmie's. "Okay, Anna. Then I won't remind you that if Lynette Whitmore hadn't been curious about you, they wouldn't have come. The accident wouldn't have happened and the boy would still be alive." She read the rest of the judgment in a hard stare that resonated with her own guilt and sent it spiraling even higher.

Desperate to dispel it, she was tempted to remind him of his own secret sins, perhaps even hurt him further by revealing his father' identity. But no. Not in front of Lorraine. Never in front of this good friend; all she could do was scream inwardly and try not to show it. Until it came to her to say, "Next time we talk about this, let's do it in private, okay? At the moment you have the advantage of me. See, I can't speak of personal matters as freely as you do." There; the momentary blink, the averted glance that told her the dart had hit home.

Still, for the rest of the day, the incident clung to her like sickroom odor clings to a nurse's uniform. Even as she slogged through more dead files, it kept replaying in her mind. Over and over, like a stuck record she wanted to stop hearing but couldn't. Dear God, was she losing her mind?

It was still playing when she met Margie for lunch the next day. She didn't mention Luke's judgment, nor did she recount what had happened on the beach after the kids had gone to look for shipwreck artifacts. She began, however, with candor about the reasons Mark and family had come to Maine in the first place–his wife had insisted, and he still harbored a passion for her. "And if I hadn't seen him again," she went on, "I might still feel the same way. You know. As if he'd been the love of my life. But when they were here, I saw a different side of him. And I didn't like it. In fact, after the night we all had dinner, I couldn't wait for them to leave. If only they had."

Margie studied her with disconcerting intensity. "Does Jim know any of this?"

"I've always planned to tell him about me and Mark, but later. Right now I'm just trying to put all of it out of my mind. Finally."

"But if Mark's marriage is over, suppose he comes after you again?"

She hadn't thought of that. Shuddering, she shook her head vehemently. "No. Even if he did….no! Just no! I can't bear to think about it."

Margie smiled one of her I-know-better smiles. "You know, Anna, for somebody I used to consider dull, you lead a wild life. Ever since you came home from the war, you've been walking the razor's edge between romance and disaster."

"Don't be ridiculous. Besides, even if I did, from now on I'm only a happily married woman with a child, and hopes for another. And that's all I'll ever want, believe me. Children and Jim."

Margie regarded her with a quizzical squint, but her only comment was a quasi-cynical, "Uh-huh."

The eleventh day after Mark's call was a Monday, normally when Anna worked mornings with Kate on domestic chores like changing bed linens and planning the week's meals. After lunch she drove up to town, had a quick visit with her parents and took Jamie for a routine checkup with Margie's pediatrician. Home again, she was feeding him some strained vegetables when Kate's heavy steps pounded down the hall, causing the floor to tremble. Pausing in the doorway, she produced an envelope from her apron pocket. "Anna, just look at this." Her widened eyes accented the tone of high drama. "Good thing I got the mail before Jim did."

At first all she noticed was that it was addressed to him. Then her gaze fell on the return address, some town she hadn't heard of in South Carolina. And "Mrs. L. Whitmore" above it. Her heart thumped and the breath caught in her throat.

"Why would Mark's wife be writing Jim?" Kate whispered.

Her voice quivered. "I have no idea."

"Anyways, I knew you'd want to see it before he does."

"Is he out on house calls?"

The maid nodded. "So maybe you should see what she wants. Now that the poor boy's dead and gone, she'll be after making trouble for some poor soul. Might just be you, Anna. Here. Just let me just steam it open so's he won't know you read it."

Anna debated a moment; Kate's logic was all too sensible. Yet something in her rebelled at the idea of colluding with the housekeeper to deceive Jim. Maybe he'd never find out. But on the other hand, such a deception might well feed the awful guilt she was trying, so far without success, to leave behind. She handed the envelope to Kate. "Very well. I'll read it, but then we'll reseal it and give it to him."

Though she knew Kate wanted to share the contents, when she'd opened the envelope, Anna carried the baby upstairs and read the letter as she gave him a bottle.

Dear Jim:

As you may have heard, my dear Buddy passed away on August 30th after a third brain operation. Poor brave little fellow never even woke up since he took that terrible fall. Now he's at rest in a cemetery behind the church here, where so many of my family are also sleeping. I find this of considerable comfort.

You may also know that I have left Mark. Alice and I have moved in with my parents. He has resigned from the Navy, left the ministry and taken to drink. The last I heard he was driving a city bus in Norfolk. How the mighty have fallen! I haven't seen him since the day Buddy died. He didn't even come to the funeral. If I have anything to say about it legally, he will never see Alice again. I hope never to lay eyes on him again either. As for the baby I was expecting, unfortunately I lost it due to the extreme sorrow Mark has caused me.

I tell you these things, Jim, because the illicit attraction between him and your wife has ruined my life, and may well ruin yours. Because after we are divorced, Mark may well return to Maine and try to win her from you. Perhaps she's confessed the carnal affair they shared on the ship and convinced you it was all in the past. But the passion between them was as strong as ever during our visit. So strong, in fact, that they sent the children up the beach so they could be alone together. Alice said she even saw them kiss. What a terrible thing for a child to witness!

I'm sorry to tell you such things about your wife. But perhaps this letter will save you future pain and prevent her from destroying your happiness the way she has mine. I wish you well.

Your friend, Lynette Whitmore.

"Dear God," Anna whispered, shaking her head as new shock closed around her like a vise choking off rational thought. So she'd been right: it wasn't over. Far from it; and regardless of how she tried to stifle it, it only became more suffocating. What was she to do to keep it at bay until she felt more capable of admitting the whole truth to Jim?

After a few minutes, she put Jamie into the crib, stuffed the letter back into the envelope and hurried down to the kitchen. "You're right, Kate. She's trying to make trouble."

"Then let's burn this poison letter right now. No need for him to ever see it."

She didn't have to ponder the suggestion to realize that destroying it would provide Kate with a secret, to hold over her forever to use as needed. Perhaps for a pay raise, or time off, or some other favor Anna wouldn't otherwise bestow. However she used it, it would give her power Anna couldn't risk letting her have. "I think not. I have to let him see it. He probably won't believe her, but he needs to know what it says."

Kate shook her head in that doomsday way of hers. "Mark my words, you'll be sorry."

Even as she said, "I have to risk it," she wondered if Kate

had opened it earlier, read, then resealed it. No way of knowing, nor any other way of dealing with it. The world seemed about to fall in again, and no matter how she tried to convince herself otherwise, there it was. The doomsday feeling had begun to bloom in her now too, taking a shape for all the world like the mushroom clouds over Hiroshima and Nagasaki. These clouds, however, portended not the destruction of distant foreign cities but of her marriage. Perhaps even her sanity.

She decided to wait till after supper, when she'd put the baby down for the night and Jim had finished his evening calls. Even so, he was late coming in from the hospital, then Tom rang and talked a long while before she could put the meal on the table. Afterward he had more calls than usual, so it was ten-thirty before he finally pushed the phone across the desk, switched off the light and rose unsteadily on his cane. Before he could make another move, she said, "I'll lock the house if you want to go up and get ready for bed."

He regarded her curiously. Usually by this time of evening, she was already in bed herself, reading or listening to the radio. He nodded with a minimal smile. "That'd be a help, dear. Been another damned long day. Thought having Tom in the practice'd give me more free time. But so far, hasn't worked out that way. Patient base must be expanding."

So he went up while she roamed the house checking locks she knew were already secured and trying not to imagine his reaction to the letter. Of all times to share bad news, this was the worst, because he wouldn't have time to make sense of it before sleep. And his mornings began earlier than hers, with Kate serving breakfast on the dot of eight. Tom and the nurse were usually there by eight-thirty, often with a few patients right behind them. Only on weekends could she count on his having free time, but she couldn't possibly contain this secret till then.

With feet dragging, she came up the stairs, waited till he'd finished in the bathroom, then got into her nightgown and returned to the bedroom. Already under the covers, he gave her a weary smile as she climbed in beside him.

But when he reached to turn off his lamp, she said, "Wait, Jim. Something you need to read." Without noting his expression, she withdrew Lynette's letter from her nightstand drawer and handed it over. "Here. This was addressed to you. But I had to see what it said. So I opened it first. Kate read it too, and said we should just burn it. But I couldn't do that."

Looking perplexed, he pulled the monogrammed sheet from the envelope, scanned it hurriedly, then read it again with a deepening frown. And she waited those few seconds, fear sent her heart into a wild gallop. With no change of expression, however, he stuffed it back into the envelope and set it on his nightstand. "Kate's right, dear. You should've burned it. This is nonsense, nothing but nonsense. I didn't need to read it."

She allowed herself to exhale slowly, with incredulous, hesitant relief. "You mean, you don't believe it?"

"Well, I believe you and Whitmore might've had a fling on the ship. I mean, I've wondered about that all along. But the rest as I said, it's nonsense. From a deeply troubled woman smothered by grief."

"Well," she sighed, not sure whether to comment on the suspected fling. "I hoped you wouldn't believe it, but I couldn't keep it from you."

He nodded, leaned over to kiss her with dry lips. "Now, let's get to sleep, shall we? This'll keep till another day." He switched off the light and turned on his side facing away. She snuggled up from behind, hoping he'd want to make love, thus tacitly expressing forgiveness for anything he suspected she might have done two years before. But he lay stiffly, unsleeping, she was sure, possibly even having second thoughts about what a few moments before he'd declared nonsense.

She kissed the back of his neck and murmured, "Good night." When he didn't answer, she turned away and stared into the darkness. And tried to pray that if he did reconsider, it would not be the end of his trust. Or his love. Or their marriage. Surely not.

Yet the question hung over her all night, and if she slept, it was only in short, restless segments peppered with dreams of Buddy's fall. It seemed a long while till Jim began to snore, and then he tossed off the covers, more restless than usual. As if Lynette's words had begun to ferment in his brain, like some malignant tropical fever getting ready to take over his body. And set them both afire.

When she came back to the bedroom after Jamie's early morning feeding, she was startled to see Jim already awake and sitting on the edge of the bed. Lynette's letter was in his hand. By the alarm clock, it was ten past five. Terror spiked in her when he said, "Now then, let's talk about this some more."

She crawled under the covers and pulled the pillow closer, huddling into it as if for refuge. "What about it? I thought you didn't believe it."

"Last night I didn't. But now I want to know more. For instance: Is it all nonsense? Or is some of it true? Particularly the part about you and Mark on the beach. Did you really send the kids to look for shipwreck artifacts so you could be alone?"

Appalled by the question, she gasped out, "No. Of course not. The boy wanted to know what was beyond the rocks. So I told him and they went off to look for treasure. But we didn't send them there. And they were only gone five minutes before Alice came back and told us he was climbing."

He nodded. "She says the little girl saw you and Mark kissing and touching each other. Is that a lie too?"

Her face began to burn and her throat tightened as if to choke off any words she might speak. "Well, she may have seen something. See, we were talking about the past, and all of a sudden he grabbed me and kissed me, so fast it was over before I knew it. Maybe she saw us. I don't know. But the kiss wasn't mutual."

He stared a moment. "Talking about the past? What about it? What you were to each other on the ship? "

She willed herself not to react visibly. "Mainly we were remembering other beaches in the South Pacific. Where they held ship's picnics. Guam and Ulithi. Oh, and Hawaii too."

"Uh-huh. Is that all? You were never lovers?"

Shock piled on shock. How long could she hide it? "Last night you said you wondered about that. Why? I mean, what made you think that?"

"Actually, lots of things. Oh nothing major. Just little things. Like how often you mentioned him in your letters. And the way you wrote about him. With such high regard. With, oh... affection. You know I was worried about another man even before you left. But I wasn't really suspicious till our honeymoon, when you were so sick. The night you were delirious, you called me by his name. And now this, these nasty accusations."

It took all her energy to answer this diatribe. "Why didn't you mention all this before? I mean, your suspicions?"

"Because you came home to me. You married me. I thought if it happened at all, it was just one of those wartime things. Ancient history. Then they came to visit. And I saw you together. Saw the way he looked at you. And knew it wasn't over. Not for him, Maybe not for you either."

She squeezed her eyes closed, picturing the images writhing under his perpetually calm façade. How long had he suffered before this eruption? "No, Jim. It was over. For me, at least. The day they got here, when I drove him and the kids around, I saw qualities in him I hadn't noticed before. Qualities I didn't admire. Still, the next day on the beach, I started feeling…oh, I don't know. Emotional, I guess. And sad. Disillusioned and sad."

"Uh-huh," he said quietly. "That's when he kissed you, right?"

She nodded, dreading the battleground to which this intense cross-examination seemed to be leading.

"And after that," he went on in the same determined tone, "did you wish you could make love with him one last time? I mean, if it'd been possible? Would that have been a good way to end things?"

Suddenly she had the sense of being cornered by a vicious adversary, a snarling wolf or ravening lion. Was this a new strain in him, or an old one reanimated by events? It took a moment before she was able to say, "Don't be silly, Jim. Nothing like that entered my mind."

His gaze bored into her, unrelenting and harsh. "So there was no lust in you that day."

Truth was burning closer now; she could only pray he couldn't read it in her eyes. "No. There hadn't been any of that since we left the ship."

"So, in all that time since you came home, you never wanted him and had to settle for me?"

This gasp was deeper, from within her whole body. "What are you doing, Jim? Why are you asking such questions? Haven't I proven myself? Haven't I been a good wife in every sense of the word? Didn't I respect your wishes when you wanted to wait to start a family? Didn't I have an abortion because you thought I should? What more do I have to do to prove my love?"

"Tell me about Mark," he said quickly, as if he'd been waiting a long while to say those particular words. "About your affair. And all the rest of it. Tell me everything the two of you did together. And be honest, Anna. Don't leave anything out. Or sugar-coat it."

Drawing on unknown reserves of energy, she made her voice strong. "No, Jim. I will not. I will not tell you what you want to hear. Because it's all in the past. Over and done with."

His laugh was cold and cynical, almost that of a menacing stranger. "So you say. And maybe for you it is. But for me it's just beginning. See, all this time the notion of you and him was abstract, far off as the war. Now it's right here, in my own bed. Do you have any idea how that feels, Anna?"

She closed her eyes again and huddled in the darkness. "Of course I do. But if I tell you what you want to know, it'll be even worse."

"I still need to know."

"No," she said again, voice thinning and rising. "It'd be the end of us."

"It'll be the end of us if you don't tell me. Oh, not outwardly. I'm not going to leave you or anything like that. But it'll be the end of my trust. The end of my faith in you."

She shook her head. "You're asking too much."

"Why? Is the truth so awful you can't speak of it? Or is what you felt for him, is that too sacred to discuss with your husband?"

Overcome, she flung herself from the bed and grabbed her robe from the chair. "Listen, I'm not going to talk about this anymore. I can't make sense of it. Can't make sense of you. Maybe later. But this—my God, you're a stranger to me right now."

Without giving him time to answer, she hurried from the room and across the hall, closing the baby's room door behind her as she groped her way toward the bed. The one Jim's first wife had bought, the one where he'd slept with her and spent his passion and talked about feelings she'd never wanted to learn. They'd both had past loves; why was hers so vital to him that without hearing its truths, he could no longer trust her? It made no sense, none at all. At least at the moment. Maybe in the course of the coming day, she could decipher its coded messages and find a way to restore his trust. To move beyond the guilt that was eating her alive.

If not, only one course seemed open—to leave this house for a while. Perhaps only until sense returned to their marriage. Or if it never did, for the foreseeable future. For with that one act of showing him the letter, she'd destroyed their proverbial happily-ever-after.

Oh God. This was worse than she'd ever imagined it would be.

And something in her gut warned it was going to get still worse before it got better.

If it ever did.

CHAPTER NINETEEN

As the day unfolded, a plan took form, generating a peculiar calm and new resolve within her. After Jim had settled in to morning office hours, she called her parents and asked if they could keep the baby for a few days. Her mother didn't buy the story that she wanted to get away by herself, but she stuck to her guns. With Kate, she also refused to offer more than the same brief explanation. Finally, late that morning, she drove to town, withdrew $500 from her personal savings account at the Penobscot Trust, then met Margie for lunch at the new Villa Romano.

Her friend–her oldest friend and confidante–was skeptical that she actually intended to do what she said she did. Still, Anna refused to explain beyond adding, "I'll tell you more when I get back, okay?"

"Oh. You're coming back, are you?"

Her mouth dropped open. "Of course I am. I'd never leave Jamie."

"Not even to go to Mark? Now that his wife's left him?"

"For God's sake, how can you think I'd ever do that? You and Jim both?"

"Maybe because I saw the two of you together."

"Oh God," she sighed. "Listen, I saw you with plenty of guys you were crazy about. But I know you'd never leave Tom."

Margie's look went distant, her smile enigmatic, but she said quickly, "Sorry. Only kidding."

Was she? Anna wondered afterwards as she walked the aisles of the new A&P super-market, where she picked up a baking hen, a package of Birdseye Frosted Peas and Carrots, and ingredients for the lemon meringue pie she'd asked Kate to make.

Back at the house, after the pie had come out of the oven, she put the chicken in to roast, then peeled and cut up potatoes to mash. The fact she was cooking the entire meal seemed to baffle Kate, who wheedled and cajoled and fairly twitched with curiosity to know what was really going on. And why Anna was going away. Or, in Kate's terminology, "Why you're running off some place all by your lonesome."

She was tempted to embroider a more elaborate story, but didn't want to undermine her resolve with even a small concession to the other woman's curiosity. In the end, no one else's understanding or approval mattered. Not even Jim's.

The festive dinner clearly took him by surprise, especially after their contretemps that morning. His pleased reaction suggested he assumed she'd do whatever he demanded in order to maintain the marriage. Well, of course; why would he think otherwise after all her previous concessions?

After she'd put the baby down for the night, they dined by candlelight on the good china in the breakfast room. She served coffee with the pie–his favorite–and was gratified to watch him enjoying it. After he had a second piece and more coffee, he began to regard her warmly, apparently with relief that the crisis had ended. Possibly with desire as well.

He drained his cup and got to his feet. "Now, dear, I'll help you clear the table. Leave the dishes for Kate, though, so we can make an early night of it."

"Oh, that'd be good," she said cheerily, gathering soiled plates in front of her. "I want to get an early start in the morning."

His expression became intent. "Oh? Why? Coming to the island with us?"

She shook her head. "Not sure where I'm going. Just

somewhere away from here. So I can think. You know, about what we talked about this morning."

His eyes widened and he dropped heavily into the chair he'd just vacated. "What do you mean, away? Where?"

She sat again too, absently brushing crumbs from the tablecloth into her hand. "Don't know exactly. Maybe an old hotel on Lake Winnepesaukee. Or Bar Harbor. My parents are going to keep the baby, so I'll call every night and tell them where I am. If you need to get in touch with me, they'll relay the message. See, I can't make sense of things when I'm around you. I realized that this morning. I need to be alone for a while."

He stared, studying her face as if he'd never seen her before. Then his eyes changed; the softness of bewilderment hardened into cold suspicion. "You're going to him, aren't you?"

She could barely inhale for the clutch in her chest, like some medieval iron torture device. "Is that what you think of me, Jim? That I'd throw all this away—my home and my husband and my child–and run off with a man like Mark?"

His eyes narrowed. "That's the thing, Anna. Yes, I've known you for four years. But maybe I don't really know you. Not the real you."

She rose and picked up the platter with the sagging, demolished chicken carcass. To her surprise, this drastic statement didn't ruffle her. "Then you probably won't even notice I'm gone." When she returned, he was still sitting there staring at the windows, but he said nothing more. So she carried away leftovers from that perfect meal—dried-up peas and carrots, stiff mashed potatoes, gravy with grease congealed on the top, and remains of the pie, its meringue wilting now and oozing moisture into the crust.

In the kitchen she covered the bowls with Cut-Rite and stuffed them haphazardly into the fridge, ran hot water into the dishpan, sprinkled Lux flakes, and stared past her reflection in the dark window as she washed the few plates they'd used. She wasn't aware Jim had come to the door until he said, "Very well. If this is how you want things, I won't try to change your mind."

She nodded and waited, but he said no more. As she heard his cane bumping up the hall to the office, she supposed he'd find refuge in the reassuring routines of calls to patients. All those flawed and weary souls he ministered to without the judgmental streak he was now bringing to bear on his wife. Acknowledging this inflexibility in him, she sensed a light dimming within her. Jim, her lighthouse from the day they'd met, had stopped beaming his love on her. Even at ten thousand miles, deep in the war and her passion for Mark, she'd felt that light brighten her soul with his every letter. To live without it now—to even contemplate that darkness again—felt like learning she was going blind.

Could she go on living without that beacon? Or would she turn herself inside out in an effort to keep it shining? Placate him, tell him everything he asked, despite her certainty it would eventually undo them? Plead for forgiveness? Give in again, and again and again, for the rest of their life together? Offer peace at any price? Or was there no peace under any circumstances?

She had no idea where this would take them. She knew only that she had to leave before real hostilities could erupt.

She slept in the baby's room, fitfully, wishing the night over, the partings and anxious questions behind her. Packing a suitcase for herself, assembling the baby's clothing into another, she lingered upstairs till Jim had gone down. She'd hoped to avoid another scene, but he came up again before he left for the island. For a moment, he stood in the doorway, regarding the bags on the bed. His face was lined and weary, but his eyes were bitter, colder than she'd ever seen them.

"I have no idea where you intend to go, Anna," he said

stiffly, formally. "But please be careful. And remember, I love you."

She nodded. "And I love you too. But right now, love's not enough, is it?"

The shrug was minimal. "That's up to you."

Like two inimical strangers, they stared at each other until the baby called from the crib. Jim bent to kiss the top of his head, then hurried from the room, his cane thumping down the steps and into his office where, she knew, he'd pick up his medical bag and go out the kitchen door to his car. Hoping he wouldn't return, she was relieved to see him back out the drive and turn down the street toward the harbor where Tom and Fletcher Hood would be waiting on *Molly B*. She stood at the window until she was sure he was gone, then sighed with the relief of not having to deal with his sudden obdurate notions for a while. Given his ability to compartment emotions, he wouldn't give the issue another thought, at least until he returned to her absence that evening. And perhaps not even then.

When she brought the bags downstairs, Kate greeted her with a plate of bacon and eggs and a tearful expression. "Don't you be gone too long now," she urged. "Jim's too good a man to leave alone like this."

Anna sat at the cluttered kitchen table and picked at the breakfast; her stomach craved resolution, not food. To placate Kate, though, she nibbled at a strip of overcooked bacon. "I won't stay a moment longer than I have to."

"And promise me you're not going to That One. You do something like that, that wife of his'd kill you for sure. And you'd lose the finest man ever lived."

For an instant she was so disgusted with the housekeeper's latest meddling, she could barely speak. She took a clean glass from the dish drainer, ran water and sipped before she was able to say, "You needn't worry about me. Just take care of Jim. And see he takes care of himself."

The older woman's sad eyes filled. "Oh I will, I will! But

how can you do this, Anna? How can you walk out like this
is nothing? How can you leave a man like that?"

She pushed the plate away and got to her feet. "This is a
private matter, Kate. That's all I'm going to say. And it's
certainly all you need to know."

"But didn't I warn you not to show him that hateful letter?
Didn't I myself warn you no good'd come of it?"

Turning her back, she returned to the vestibule, hefted her
bags out to the car, then went upstairs for the baby. When
she came down, Kate was at the foot of the stairs, her face
frozen with gloom. Before she could say more, Anna told
her, "If you need to get a message to me, call my parents.
They'll know where I am. "

Kate enveloped her in a massive hug that smelled of
Rinso, sweat and mildew. "Oh, Anna. I only pray this isn't
going to come to grief. But I have such a bad feeling...."

Stiffening, Anna carried the baby to the car and wiggled
him into the little seat beside hers. Kate followed, wringing
her hands, sniffling and begging her to reconsider. While she
was driving way, she saw Kate in the rear view mirror
watching from the curb. Only after the turned the corner did
she take a deep breath and begin to relax. At least slightly,
now that two leave-takings were behind her. She still had the
final gauntlet to run before she could be on her way; parting
from her parents and Jamie would be the worst hurdle yet.
But if she got through that without losing her resolve, she
could weather whatever else the journey threw at her. Even
the unspeakable collapse of her private world.

An hour later, she was on Route One heading south from
Rockhampton, the last tearful scene behind her, explanations
glossed over, her parents sad and perplexed but relieved she
wasn't taking the baby. By now a destination had taken
shape in her mind: Portsmouth, which she still thought of as

home, having lived there from the age of five till she'd gone to Hope Island twenty years later. Now, to surround herself with that segment of her past seemed a logical way to address the future. If there was any logic to what she was doing.

Beyond the Villa Romano, the new housing development showed signs of progress, streets curving over the low hills, sewage pipes being laid in the trenches in the raw earth, lots being graded, bulldozers churning up mounds of dirt, and construction crews banging nails into houses being framed up behind a sign: *Model Homes Opening Soon!* Farther on, coming into Bath, she thought of the trip with Mark the month before, and smiled wryly at her naiveté in assuming life had returned to normal. Later, passing the air station, she wished she'd talked to Ted on the way home that day. But her choice then had been to convince herself everything would be well. Her usual style, she reckoned–stuff the past into a closet and let it sleep. Then smile and charge into the future, ignoring anything about the present that caused discomfort. And quote Dame Julian of Norwich as often as necessary: *All will be well, and all will be well, and all manner of things will be well.* Never mind how or why: after all, wasn't it a Biblical promise that all things worked together for those who loved the Lord?

Well, she still loved the Lord, but what good could possibly come from this sordid mess? And even if she couldn't discern it now, was her faith strong enough to see her through until it all made sense?

Below Portland, threading her way through the little seaside towns of Southern Maine, she planned the next steps in this hiatus. First, she'd check into the Wentworth. And remember her honeymoon? Or try not to? Either way, her main goal was to give Jim what he wanted—as detailed an account of her affair as memory could provide. Chapter and verse, sparing nothing, sanitizing nothing, including every memory regardless of how much it pained her.

When she'd packed, she'd included her journal from the ship, mainly because she didn't want Kate to find it. Besides, it would provide the framework for her narrative, details and dates she might have forgotten; and between the lines, the what, when, where and why. Writing it originally, she'd been scrupulous about including no sordid details, but in her memory they were still fresh and vivid.

And Jim had asked for all of them. Therefore, despite her certainty they'd be a blockbuster blasting what was left of her marriage to smithereens, she'd let him have them. After he'd digested everything, the final decision would be his, of course, though she could hardly conceive of his reacting with anything other than revulsion, and the sense their marriage had been a sham from the start.

It took her miles to get beyond the closed-door feeling these thoughts evoked, to the unthinkable struggle to create a new identity—that of a divorcee with a child. What then? Return to her career, find a job and a place where she and the baby could live, with someone to keep him while she worked? Ideally, this would be at the Rockhampton hospital, with her parents just down the street. But there she'd run into Jim, would be known as his ex-wife and likely to find public opinion in his corner, not hers. So maybe Camden or Bath would be better alternatives; if not a hospital, some doctor's office.

By the time she reached Kittery, she'd come up with more questions than answers. Panicked but not surprised, she told herself she couldn't possibly plan the rest of her life in one three-hour drive, or likely even in the next few days. All she could do was write the letter detailing the fall from grace that had culminated in the death of an innocent child. Composing it would require a monumental effort of will: by putting words on paper, she'd also be forced to acknowledge her own culpability, her weakness, her shortcomings. It would take all her energy to force herself to admit everything, but if she came up short, Jim would sense it. And feel doubly cheated.

No; she owed him a complete accounting–every grain of truth she could sweep from the dusty corners of her past. Including details she found painful to admit even to herself.

CHAPTER TWENTY

Late that afternoon, in a narrow third-floor ocean-view room at the Wentworth, she pored through her diaries, reviewing what she planned to write. At first the notion of exposing the affair in all its naked glory seemed commendable, an act of courage. But as she read on, even the version she'd encoded seemed too odious to put on paper. She was tempted to sanitize it, omitting the sordid stuff and reducing it to a Hollywood production that would have no trouble passing Hays office scrutiny. Until she reminded herself he'd asked for the unexpurgated version. Well then, if that was what he wanted…

After two false starts, she crumpled the scribbled pages of hotel stationery and went for a walk on the beach. Alone in the twilight haze, she felt like the last person on earth. Later, the solitary dinner in the hotel dining room triggered a new sense of isolation so acute that she phoned her parents, not just so they'd know where she was but for the reassurance of their voices. Afterward she glanced through a *Collier's* she'd bought at a lunch stop in York Beach and told herself she'd see her way more clearly after a good night's sleep.

But the sleep was anything but good, more a series of restless naps interrupted by troubling dreams, not just the usual Buddy nightmare, but a terrifying new one– that Jamie was running a fever, crying for her, inconsolable. By four AM she was so agitated, she considered calling to make sure he was all right. But aware that a ringing phone at that hour might shock her parents into apoplexy, she comforted herself with prayer book collects until daylight tinted the window.

Later, after a room-service breakfast of scrambled eggs and toast, she sat at the little desk and began again:

Dear Jim,
  You asked me to tell you the details about the affair I had with Mark Whitmore. So the following is everything I remember.
  To begin with, he joined the ship in mid-December, 1944. Ironically, he replaced the previous Protestant chaplain who'd been implicated when my cabin-mate had a botched abortion. But I didn't really notice him until Christmas night. That afternoon Willi and I were in the duty section when we rendezvoused with a destroyer to pick up casualties from a boiler explosion. Later we went down to the wardroom for some chow. Luke and Mark had given the patients last rites, so when they came in, the four of us sat together and talked about what we'd done the previous Christmas. [That was when I first got the idea Luke might be Lorraine's son.] Mark had only been stationed at Navy hospitals, so he wasn't used to fresh casualties, especially those so horribly burned. He seemed sad and weary, until he showed us pictures of his children. A few days later all the patients had died. He and Luke did the funerals. Everyone was sad that day. We had a lot of days like that.
  The next time we met—other than casually at chow—was after Luke was stabbed. I wanted to find out if he thought I should tell Luke about Lorraine, so I asked Mark if we could talk privately some time. I didn't tell you at the time because I thought it might worry you. Anyway, the next time we put into Guam, he took me along in a Jeep when he carried donated food to a native church. After he advised me to tell Luke what I knew, he showed me the officers' beach and wreckage left from the invasion, and we walked in the sand. By then I felt so close to him, I even told him about losing the

baby, which no one else on the ship knew. The crux of it was, that day for the first time I was more conscious of him as a man than as a chaplain.

The next time we were together privately—meaning just the two of us– was on deck the night before we invaded Iwo Jima. The battlewagons were still shelling the island and we were offshore, so we talked about the casualties we'd be getting. He mentioned a prayer service he was about to have, and asked me if I'd pray. So I paraphrased a prayer from FORWARD DAY BY DAY. At this time I admired him because he was so spiritual. But afterward, lying in my bunk and thinking about the invasion, I realized I was becoming more and more physically attracted. Still, I rationalized that this was harmless, like reading a novel or watching a movie, just something to take my mind off the war.

A few weeks later, while we were steaming back to Iwo for more casualties, the Kamikaze buzzed us. That was the worst day of the war for me, not just because it was terrifying to think we were going to die, but because afterward we worked for 7 hours picking up men in the water from a sunken destroyer and the oiler that had been replenishing us. After evening chow Mark asked me to come topside so he could tell me about a Dear John letter from his wife. I listened but couldn't stop shaking, so he offered me a drink in his cabin. Something told me I shouldn't, but I went anyway. We drank bourbon and he suggested we just lie on his bunk so neither of us would be alone that night. I kept my clothes on but he stripped down to skivvies. Maybe he expected after two drinks I might be available, but we only held each other and slept spoon fashion. Until close to morning, I knew he wanted me; I acted shocked and left the cabin. I was upset with him but more disgusted with myself because I should've known better.

As the hotel pen scratched, memories filled gaps in the narrative, the smells and sights and sounds engulfing them–a partial moon like an orange slice rising above the patched-up tanker they were following back to Saipan, the smell of bunker oil on the sea, and the leftover fear of death making her nerves twitch and her heart race. And the bite of the bourbon she'd drunk from an ordinary juice glass he kept in the head; and all night long, the knowledge she was in bed with a man who wasn't Jim as she clutched the engagement ring around her neck and let the pulse of the ship's engines lull her back to sleep.

Pausing, she relived all of it, every sensation, every emotion, every detail, both the pleasurable and the agonizing.

After that I was careful, and he was too, to maintain space between us. For a while I was relieved. But as we headed to Pearl Harbor for liberty, I asked if he could show me around, because he'd been at the hospital there. He had plans, though, so I didn't see him until a luau they held at the O Club right before we sailed. Luke seemed to be watching us, even tried to cut in when we danced, but I refused. By then most of us had had several Mai-Tais, so I wasn't surprised that Mark wanted me. This time I wasn't shocked; in fact, I enjoyed tempting him, but expected nothing to come of it. Later, when we found out we were transporting Marines back to Guam in defiance of the Geneva Convention, he admitted I was starting to be important to him, and not just in a lustful way. I was surprised and pleased, especially when he kissed me outside the wardroom. I admired him for speaking up to the captain about the Marines, but most of what I felt was desire.

When we reached Guam, other nurses and I organized the kissing mutiny. Afterward I would have happily gone back to his cabin with him, but Old Horseface ordered me to get my ass to the wardroom so the CMO could dress us down for what we'd done.

After that, Mark and I began talking about sightseeing on

*Oahu if we ever got back to Pearl again. When he joked
about spending the night somewhere, I told him separate
rooms, and we laughed, but I knew what I wanted to happen;
I just didn't want HIM to know. So when we put in there a
few weeks later, he borrowed a friend's car and drove us to
the North Shore outside Honolulu, a beautiful place called
Kailua. The room he got had twin beds, which he said was
almost as good as separate rooms. It wasn't, of course, as
we discovered right after we arrived. We were in such a
hurry, in fact, neither of us remembered to use protection.
He said I shouldn't worry—he'd marry me if I got pregnant.
Besides the fact he was still married, I didn't believe him, so
the possibility kept me on tenterhooks till I got my period.
Then he acted disappointed, as if fate had deprived him of
something he wanted. I was only relieved and grateful that I
didn't have to make any tough decisions.*

*Jim, I don't want you to think this was all physical,
because Mark and I shared spiritual concerns too, like the
Marine I told you about. He'd been in almost every invasion
since Guadalcanal, but couldn't remember how he ended up
on Okinawa. We both tried to help him remember, but he
became more and more depressed, and one night he went
overboard. Mark had given him a copybook to use as a
diary, so when we got to Pearl we went to the O club and
drank rum and cokes as we read it. We both concluded sadly
he'd seen too much fighting to be consoled by any human
efforts.*

*Then the ship went down to Ulithi atoll for 6 weeks to
serve as fleet hospital for a huge armada anchored in the
lagoon. We found out later it was forming up for the planned
invasion of Japan. Half our medical complement stayed at
the Guam hospital, including Luke, so it was nice not to have
him glowering at us all the time. Duty was light, and we had
picnics and USO shows, and plenty of chances to go to his
cabin. Some captains wouldn't have tolerated that sort of
thing, but our CO didn't run a tight ship. His philosophy*

was, as long as everyone did their jobs and didn't embarrass him, he didn't worry about what we did off duty. Quite a few other couples found each other on the ship too, like Willi and Floyd, but they were single, so for them it was serious. When we returned to Guam, there was a picnic at the officers' beach. After lunch, Luke asked me to walk with him so he could tell me something. It turned out he'd heard that Mark was a womanizer, both at Pearl and the Guam hospital. The hospital exec—a friend of Mark's—had told him, so he knew it was true. He thought I should know so I didn't get my heart broken. I told him I wouldn't because I really loved you. Then he asked how I could do what I did with Mark if I loved you? I didn't know, except maybe it was the war, and seeing all those young American boys with shattered bodies and broken minds made me need someone close to share it with. That's still the only answer I can come up with.

The next day after we left Guam I went to Mark's cabin to confront him about his other women. But we ran into a sudden squall, and for a while it was so rough, I was sure we were going to capsize. I didn't intend to, but I let him make love to me again out of sheer terror. Afterward I told him we were through, because I knew he'd had a few affairs before me. He didn't deny it, but explained it on the basis of his unhappy marriage. He said I was different from the others, and he really cared for me, and wanted to give me a ring to prove it. I told him it was too late and we were over, and then I went back to my own cabin, hating him and resolved to cut off our affair.

I might have kept feeling that way too, except soon afterward, we heard that Indy had been sunk, with only 300 survivors from a crew of 1200. Everyone wondered what had happened, so Mark and Floyd went over to the Guam hospital and found out the Navy hadn't even noticed they hadn't arrived in the Philippines, so hadn't searched for them. And that's the night we went to the club and drank too much. *After that I got together with him again, because by then it didn't matter if he'd had other women, I just needed him. Especially after we went to Japan to pick up American prisoners from camps near Nagasaki, and we started hearing the awful stories of how they'd been treated.*

After that, on the way to San Francisco, Mark & Floyd & Willi and I made a point of talking to these men and taking notes, so over and over we heard about cruelty and starvation and abuse, of the Bataan death march and hell ships and slave labor camps. Day after day I listened and was horrified because it was so much worse than I'd imagined, and if I hadn't had Mark for comfort, it would have been unbearable. Or so I tell myself.

When we got to Frisco, the four of us went to the Fairmont. So when my call to you went thru that Sunday morning, he was right there in the bed with me. He seemed embarrassed and went into the bathroom. But afterward he asked me how I could act as if nothing had changed between you and me. It was almost as if that lie was a worse sin in his book than our fornication.

As you know, after that we went back to the Pacific for one last load of convalescents. We were so over capacity, the male officers doubled up and we couldn't go to his cabin anymore, so he began sneaking into Nurses' Country to mine, until we got back and debarked the patients and could go to his cabin again. By then, the last cruise was over, the ship scheduled to go into a shipyard, so we all left and stayed in the BOQ on Treasure Island till we could get trains back east. I was in a room with 3 other nurses and everything was so crowded, we never had a chance to be alone together again. Then Willi & Floyd & Luke & I got a train to Chicago and Mark saw us off before he left for LA. It was very sad saying goodbye, because I knew that in some way I really loved him, just not enough to change my plans with you.

After I got home and you went back to Maine, that's when

I wrote and told him we were being married, which is why he called the morning of our wedding. He told me he still loved me but had decided to reconcile with Lynette because the children needed him. I was pleased to know he still had feelings for me, but relieved it had ended as it had. And that was how we left it, until she wrote and said they were coming for the visit. From time to time of course I'd thought of him and wondered how he was doing. And once I even had a sex dream of him, and then I woke up and you were there, and we made love. But I didn't pretend you were him, in case you're wondering.

As for what happened during their visit, I've told you everything there is to tell about that. It seemed important for you to know whether I'd have made love with him one last time if it were possible. Now, being totally honest about everything, I have to say I might have, but that's a long reach since there was no way it could have happened short of doing it on the beach in broad daylight and in full view of the hotel– during the 5 minutes the kids were looking for shipwreck artifacts! Sometimes sex is just an idea in the brain and sometimes it gets into the bloodstream and pushes you to rash actions, but with me the circumstances have to be right before I'm really tempted. I'd like to think this isn't news to you, but who knows what you really think of me now?

In conclusion, while I admit that having an affair with Mark was a mistake in your eyes and certainly in Lynette's, reading this over, I remember that it never seemed like a mistake at the time. Forbidden, wrong, but not a mistake, though it would have, of course, if I'd gotten pregnant at Kailua! Lord knows how that would have ended. And thanks be to God I never had to find out.

But I have had to learn something equally horrific—that Buddy's death was the final consequence of my illicit relationship with his father. Because, as Luke reminded me and my own instincts confirm, without it that family wouldn't

Joan La Blanc

have visited us, and the rest wouldn't have happened. So, while that affair seemed innocent at the time, so many of us have been hurt that I must accept responsibility for my part in —in plain words—that SIN. That outright SIN.

Jim, I pray you can accept these facts. I've spelled them out in such detail only because you asked; I never wanted to cause you pain. I'm aware I don't deserve you, so if you can't, or won't accept me after knowing them, I'm prepared to live the rest of my life without you. I certainly don't want to, but I will, if that's how you want things.

All my love always,
Anna.

CHAPTER TWENTY-ONE

It had taken her all day Thursday to write the letter. Only when she finished did she get dressed and walk on the beach to stretch her stiff muscles. Otherwise, she was enveloped in a peculiar numbness, as if writing had finally purged the detritus of Mark from her soul. Almost as if he'd never crossed her path at all. The sense of his absence was so peaceful she slept deeply and without dreams all that night.

The next morning, trying to read her own hurried scrawl, she realized she needed to rewrite it. So she drove into town, bought a legal pad and business envelopes at a stationer's, then copied everything more carefully onto the lined yellow sheets.

She finished early Friday afternoon. Afterward, she drove out to Kittery Beach and sat in the car re-reading and making small additions in the margins and between the lines. It was much longer than she'd expected it to be, and as painful to read as it had been to write. When she finished, she sat on a rock overlooking the surf with a strange sensation of having come to the end of a long journey, yet without having arrived where she wanted to be. But relieved, at least, that she didn't have to keep going.

For a while, she tried to imagine Jim's reactions to the two parts that might impact him most strongly—that she and Mark had forgotten to use protection, and that he'd been in bed with her in San Francisco when she'd phoned him. But what the hell? They were all fragments of the same story, neither no more nor no less damning than the others, except as he might interpret them. When he'd asked—no, demanded—that she tell him, she'd thought his intentions were to forgive her and move on. Maybe he'd still see it that way: that she'd sinned against him, therefore it was up to him to either forgive or retain those sins.

But he hadn't been the real victim of her transgressions. So it no longer seemed an issue of forgiveness, rather acceptance. *Yes, this is my story*; not *Do you forgive me?* But *Can you live with it, with me, who felt these things for another man while I was engaged to you? After all, at the time we were united only by promises, not vows. Or is understanding all this too much to expect of any man?*

She had no idea. The questions were academic anyway. Nothing to do now but mail the letter, then wait and see. No, not with such passivity. Wait and make plans was more like it. So she got in the car again, but instead of driving back to the hotel, made a tour through Kittery, past her old apartment, then around the Navy base, past the hospital where she'd worked and met Dan, and the fitting out pier where Dan's boat had been until just after Pearl Harbor when she'd watched it sail out the Piscatagua en route to New London, and eventually, to Pearl Harbor, and war patrols in the Pacific. Everywhere she looked, memories of Dan took her back to an innocent time of her life, a time when she'd still believed in happy endings. A time before the losses had begun and convinced her happy endings were only myths.

Back in Portsmouth, she cruised past St. Stephen's and the rectory and the grammar school where she'd gone through eighth grade, then the high school where she'd met Margie and Bob Hallowell. And on the outskirts of town, the hardscrabble farm where Margie had grown up. Some of the fields were staked out now for a new housing project, but closing her eyes, she could visualize it as it had been when dairy cows roamed the rocky pastures, and she and Margie had walked for miles sharing adolescent dreams.

Remembering gave her an unexpected pang, not just for the past, but for her own naiveté, her conviction that marrying Bob would lead to eternal happiness. Where had that simplistic notion come from? Probably her down-to-earth mother, and all those personal advice columns in The *Ladies' Home Journal* or *McCall's*. Certainly romance had nothing to do with it. Maybe it was just that Bob offered the path of least resistance. At least until Dan had come along and lured her in a totally different direction. And now, six years later, she'd reached the end of that road too. The road to romance. And heartache more agonizing than she could have imagined.

Back at the hotel, she lay staring at patterns of reflected light on the ceiling for an hour before she changed clothes and went down to dinner. Dining alone, she forced herself to picture life as a single woman again. No longer a widow, but a divorcee with a small child and a notorious past. As part of the image, maybe she'd bleach her hair, wear too much makeup, take up smoking and flirting with lonely men, even those with wedding rings. If she was going to be regarded as a Jezebel, she might as well look the part.

But in her room again, she acknowledged that life without Jim wouldn't be easy, or filled with fun. Even if he gave her enough alimony and child support that she never had to work, his absence would echo in the rooms she occupied, wherever she lived. As much as any malignant presence might, his absence would constitute a haunting. When the lights were out and the radio silenced, the darkness would be heavy with ghosts. And even if she chose to fill her life with another man and more children, Jim Millett would occupy a lightless, lifeless region of her soul for as long as she lived.

After breakfast the next morning, she checked out and carried her bag down to the car. She wasn't ready to go back

to Maine yet, and wouldn't be until she'd given Jim a chance
to read and digest the letter. And possibly try to contact her.
So allotting herself a few more days to wait, she got a state
map from the Atlantic Station where she gassed up, then
traced the route to Lake Winnepesaukee, to an old resort
hotel where she'd spent childhood summers with her parents.
This was a sweet memory, filled with watercolor visages of a
magical place where rocking chairs lined a long porch, and
the steamer Mount Washington took on excursionists at a
pier out front. Where women carried parasols against the
sun, and guests dressed for dinner in the big dining room,
then stayed to dance to the orchestra, five men in tuxedoes
who played till midnight on weekends. The last time she'd
been there, she'd been eleven, and her parents had let her
stay up late to watch the dancers. On the cusp of
adolescence, she'd found it all achingly romantic. If she went
back now, would the future still extend the same promise it
had then? And if so, would she ever feel herself on the
exciting threshold of life again? Or had she learned too much
about the world to regard it with even a tinge of optimism?

It was almost noon when she parked at the big Portsmouth
post office and took the fat envelope inside to mail. It was
too heavy to get by with one stamp, so she pasted on the two
the clerk at the window sold her, then dropped it in the OUT
OF TOWN slot. For a moment, panic mushroomed as the
weight of what she'd just done hit her. As she pictured it
falling into a bin, being sorted into a big sack, thrown into a
truck and driven to Dover, there to be tossed into the mail car
on the Boston and Maine train for Augusta. On board, a clerk
would sort through the contents, then place her envelope in
another bag for Brunswick, where it would go into the belly
of the Rockhampton bus. Eventually, Monday afternoon or
Tuesday morning, it would find its way into Jim's mail slot
at the hospital.

Maybe he'd read it with a cup of coffee in the Doctors'
Lounge, a small windowless area near the operating rooms.

Or would he only scan first, then take it out to the car to peruse more thoroughly? More likely; in that private setting, he'd study it intently, poring through all those verbal images of her and Mark's passion, and the war, and intimate situations he'd have previously been hard put to imagine.

Yes, he'd wanted to know. But surely not this much, not all these nasty little details, just the broad scope of things. Maybe he'd merely wanted confirmation that they'd been lovers, hoping she'd explain what she had with Mark had been just physical attraction, a palliative against the unrelenting stress of that duty. But in the letter she'd given him everything—everything but anatomical comparisons. She'd been tempted a few times, but her intent was to enlighten rather than hurt. So she'd let Jim's imagination take care of the rest.

When she left the post office, the sky was pewter, a sea-smelling wind blowing from the east. So cool that she pulled a sweater from her suitcase, slipped into it, then locked the car and began walking in search of lunch. Just up the block a new chrome-and-neon greasy spoon caught her interest. But the door opened onto such a miasma of thumping jazz, cigarette smoke and hot grease fumes, she quickly backed away and continued wandering downtown streets. Though they felt familiar, she could no longer place them precisely in her Portsmouth memories. Until, a block from the courthouse, she spotted a tea room she recognized. Of course; here her mother had often met ladies of the Churchwomen's Literary Society for lunch and genteel discussions of the great classics. Relieved, she hurried toward it.

Inside, a wave of chattering female voices confirmed it was still a gathering spot for gentlewomen. The aromas here were subtle, of toast and chicken broth and hot tea. From a menu of crustless sandwiches, bland soups, salad platters and dainty sweets, she ordered an egg salad sandwich and a cup of cream of mushroom. A waitress brought a pot of Orange

Pekoe tea; sipping, Anna stared beyond the chintz-curtained window at passersby and traffic on a busy street in a town she no longer called home. Like a movie set, it suddenly seemed nothing more than an impersonal collection of thoroughfares and buildings where strangers lived and worked and loved, as she once had. Now her home was the tiny seaside village of East Point, Maine.

But for how much longer? If she moved out of Jim's house, then where would she call home? The notion set panic stewing within her, until she made herself switch off the speculation and focus on the pretty lunch now set before her. Pretty, but basically tasteless. Or was she was too distracted to notice something as irrelevant as flavors?

The courthouse clock was striking one when she finished and left the tea room. Disoriented again, she tried to remember where the post office was, where her car was parked. Nothing came, not a recollection of the route she'd taken to the restaurant, nor of the steps she needed to retrace. Panic began again. Until she told herself that though she hadn't lived here for the past four years, twenty years of prior memories were deeply imprinted in her unconscious. All she had to do was walk until something switched one on. She turned and headed into the wind.

Sure enough; at a nearby intersection, she recognized the steeple looming in the middle of the next block. Vastly relieved, she hurried toward the church that had been the nexus of her life for all those years. At St. Stephen's she'd certainly get her bearings and be able to find her way back to the post office. She could also reaffirm her identity and be assured of its continuity, whether Jim were in her life or not.

As she approached, cars were pulling up out front, discharging women in hats and gloves and Sunday dresses, men in shirts and ties and dark suits. Watching them walk toward the church, she wondered what was going on—a funeral or a wedding? Until moving closer, she heard the organ rendering *O Perfect Love*, one of the hymns played at her wedding to Jim. Of course; another Saturday afternoon wedding. Ironic, given the letter she'd just mailed.

Flashing through her consciousness, the memory of her own joyous day sparked a sudden urge to turn and run. And hide somewhere. But where? Until four years before, the rectory across the lawn had been her refuge from the world. Now the only trace of her old life was a little tombstone in the rear of the cemetery where her stillborn baby was buried.

Tears jumped into her eyes as memories of that loss abruptly overrode her concern for what might next happen with Jim. Intent on seeing the marker again, she followed the brick path alongside the church to the newer graves close to the rear wall. To the simple marble square engraved with "Baby Boy Donovan, 4 August 1943." Before she'd left for the war, she'd considered adding an Agnus Dei icon to the words, But with all that had happened since, she hadn't thought of it again until now.

Four years and one month, she remembered, kneeling on the grass beside it. As she brushed her fingertips across the chiseled words, a new truth dawned in her, slow as sunrise but with the same intense coloration: If this child had lived, her life would now be altogether different. Without any of the dilemmas she faced now. His presence in her life might even help fill the emptiness of Dan's absence.

Oh, If only he'd lived. If only he'd lived!

Strangely enough, at no time in those forty-nine months had she had a definitive answer to why he hadn't survived. The attending physician had had a theory about some hormonal imbalance caused by the stress of Dan's boat having gone missing. Otherwise, it had all seemed too obvious, at least to a nurse: for some reason no one had determined, at twenty-seven weeks the placenta had detached from the uterine wall, severing his lifeline to her body and causing fatal oxygen deprivation.

Now, however, as she reviewed the event again, new questions began to undermine her previous assumption that it had been inevitable. After all, she'd been working in the maternity clinic when the hemorrhage began. And as fast as humanly possible, she'd been taken to surgery for an emergency C-section. At that stage of gestation, the infant would have been dangerously premature. Still, she'd heard of other infants who had survived with intensive care. But for some element of chance no one had ever definitely identified, he might have been born alive. And if he'd survived his prematurity, she'd now have a four-year old son. What had made the difference? If she'd noticed the bleeding ten or even five minutes earlier, would the surgeon have found a heartbeat and started oxygen support in time to insure his survival?

She groaned at the notion and got to her feet, casting her gaze at the lowering skies as if seeking an answer. Lord knew, she'd come closer than she'd ever realized, not just to having Dan's child to raise, but to the probability that none of her present distress would have come to pass. To begin with, she wouldn't have left her parents' home to take the job on Hope Island. Wouldn't have met the doomed Jean Cropper, or Jim, with whom she'd fallen in love. Nor joined the Nurse Corps or served on the hospital ship in the Pacific, therefore, never met Luke Salaunas or Mark Whitmore, never known either existed, certainly never had a wild carnal affair with a chaplain, for God's sake. And never come back to marry Jim, have Jamie, later an abortion, be reunited with Mark. And eventually, watch his son fall to his doom, then feel the accusation in her husband's expression as his illusions shattered like stained glass windows in an earthquake. And finally, she wouldn't be standing now in a cemetery that felt like the end of the long, last road.

Instead, she'd have lived at home with Daniel Robert Donovan, Jr., just another of the world's myriad war widows with a child. Perhaps in time she might have met some suitable man, married him and had more children. Above all, she would never have endured this string of losses—that first

baby, and Jean, and all the casualties on the ship, and the
Marine who'd gone overboard, and Buddy Whitmore. And
now the new loss that had begun to loom over her, onerous
as the clouds of war.

Why—oh God, why hadn't that baby lived and spared her
so much pain? Had it really been some hormonal anomaly?
Or had it been part of the Lord's plan for her? If so it
seemed a cruel way to teach her some supernal truth. Maybe
Mark was right after all; maybe the Lord didn't give a damn
how much his people suffered. Whether to punish or teach
them, all that pain was just the Lord's will.

Lost in speculation, she barely noticed a mist blowing on
the wind. Eventually chilled, she took shelter on the bench
under the big oak in the church yard. For a while, she
huddled into her sweater and tried further to make sense of
the twist of the fate that had changed her life and those of so
many others. Even her parents'; without her presence in
Maine, they'd never have retired to Rockhampton, would
likely still be here in Portsmouth. So many irreversible
changes and choices had led her to this lonely place from
which there seemed nowhere else to go. And no one who
could help. For God's sake, she was so lost she couldn't even
find her own damned car.

The rain grew heavier. Finally too damp and cold to stay
where she was, she decided to take refuge in the church, use
the rest room, wash her face, comb her hair. And when the
wedding ended, ask for directions to the post office. Maybe
some kindly soul would even volunteer to drive her there.
Okay, that was the first step. But after she was reunited with
her car, what then? A couple hours' drive on rain-slick roads
to a hotel that might no longer be open for business? Or
should she head back to Rockhampton and hide out with her
parents until Jim got the letter? Telling them exactly what?
she wondered with rising panic.

Summoning all her resolve, she clutched her purse and
began to get to her feet. But as she rose, a sudden darkness

swelled in her head. Roaring like Niagara, it descended through her body, numbing her limbs, rendering her limp and darkening the light in her soul. With the last glimmer of consciousness, she toppled onto the bench behind the church that had been her rock for all the years before she'd learned the many forms human loss could take.

CHAPTER TWENTY-THREE

With no idea how she'd gotten there, she regained consciousness in an empty pew under the balcony at the rear of the sanctuary. For a few moments, her mind was foggy; when it began to clear, she realized a wedding was in progress. Then she noticed the priest was not her father, rather a large, florid man whose hearty voice fairly boomed out the words of the ceremony. Confusion gripped her again, until she remembered that now and then her father gave some other priest permission to officiate here. After all, it was wartime, and servicemen at the Navy base couldn't always get leave to travel to the bride's home for the wedding. Thus it was that often girls and their pastors would come to Portsmouth for a ceremony at St. Stephen's. So elegant, so classically magnificent it could have been the diocesan cathedral, it was a popular venue for wartime weddings.

This bridal party was clustered at the communion rail, so all she could see were clouds of white satin on the bride, six bridesmaids in jade green, and the groom in the dress uniform of chief petty officer, but no facial details she could recognize. She hoped she didn't know anyone, couldn't imagine socializing while her heart was so heavy, her consciousness so filled with fear. All too familiar, this sense that a storm was about to break over her. And not just because Dan was still missing in action. After all, it had been only two months now since the telegram had come, so it was still easy to heed her father's counsel not to give up hope. Many subs on patrol in the Pacific had gone missing for far longer. Dan would be the first to reassure her there was no cause for concern.

No, this premonition had to do with the baby's precarious condition. As if it had deteriorated and no one at the hospital had told her. Troubles were a given anyway with an infant nine weeks premature and less than two pounds in weight; he still had months in the incubator before he'd be able to survive on his own. She couldn't remember exactly how long he'd been there, only that he'd been born on August 4. Today's date, however, was veiled in the mental fog that had surrounded her since the birth. At the time, they'd told her the preceding hemorrhage had so depleted her red cell count that she'd needed a transfusion, except that there was no B-positive blood available. Fortunately, she was living with her parents, so she could rest as often as needed. Still this peculiar inability to focus, to plan, to keep track of small details continued to plague her.

Maybe this anxiety was part of a mother's mysterious instincts. In fact, maybe it was this particular need that had brought her to the church this afternoon, not for the wedding of strangers, but to pray for her infant in a place that for her was the dwelling of the Holy Spirit. Even as a child, even before parents or Sunday School teachers had suggested it, she'd been certain that this was indeed the Lord's house. From here, petitions and pleas went directly to the throne of the Almighty, where they were the first to be heard. And the most likely to be granted.

Lowering herself to the kneeler, she made the sign of the cross over her heart. And as the communion service proceeded and the wedding party received the Body and the Blood, she bowed her head and pictured her son's small, wrinkled body breathing steadily, turning pink, tiny hands and feet moving as he took nourishment and gained weight and strength. Until she would finally be able to hold him close to her heart. Until he would no longer need the incubator or oxygen. Until she could take him home, and learn to be his mother.

Her wordless prayer continued and her heart grew lighter; it always did when she'd released her fears to heaven. By now the service had ended, the priest had pronounced the benediction and the bridal party had turned from the altar to parade down the aisle. Relieved, she recognized no one, not the newly-wed couple nor a single bridesmaid or groomsman, so they were likely from out of town after all.

As they approached, she resumed her seat and smiled her good wishes until they passed into the vestibule, exclaiming with dismay about the rain. Other guests had also begun leaving. One, a pretty blonde in a top-heavy satin pillbox, paused, smiled, and greeted her by name. Anna groped for a name too, came up empty, but managed, "Nice to see you again."

"And how are your parents these days?"

"They're fine, thanks."

"Well, please give them my regards. And tell your father we still miss him." She dimpled and joined the surge toward the entrance.

Still miss him? Shrugging, she concluded maybe the woman no longer lived in the area. Or maybe she hadn't heard right in the hubbub from the vestibule and the blare of car horns as the bridal party drove away.

But the priest's greeting was even more confusing. Recessing down the aisle behind the others, he stared at her with a broadening smile. He paused at her pew, right hand extended. "Well, Mrs. Millett, this is a nice surprise. Visiting in the area?" His shake was warm and firm, his hand plumper than her father's had ever been.

Taken aback by a name she didn't recognize, she could only smile and nod.

"And how's your dad enjoying retirement?"

Retirement? "Uh, I'm sorry, father. I think you have me

confused with someone else. I'm Anna Donovan not...uh, the other name you called me."

His focus grew more intense; his eyes narrowed in a frown. "Sorry. I thought you were Father Moss's daughter. We met last year around the time he retired. Right after Easter, I think it was. But forgive me. My memory must be playing tricks."

"Don't worry about it," she said.

He stared a moment longer, smiled vaguely, then retreated toward the vestibule.

Finally the only people left in the sanctuary were two women changing altar hangings from the festive white of the wedding to the green of the season between Pentecost and Advent, then setting up communion for the next day's services. After a while the sexton came by with the vacuum. She nodded at him but he didn't speak; he was a deaf-mute with a cast in one eye, and he'd never communicated verbally with anyone that she knew of, except her father.

As she stared at the brass cross on the altar, the rector's confusion touched off a new strain of anxiety. All very strange, and so alarming she was able to ignore the chill touch of her damp blouse and shoes. And the camphor and damp wool smell of her sweater, the burnt residue of extinguished candles, the funereal sweetness of massed floral arrangements, the mustiness of the old church. Yet at the time he'd spoken to her, she'd been certain he'd mistaken her for someone else. Of course, she was indeed Father Moss's daughter; but what made this man think her father had retired? And why had he called her by a name she'd never heard?

Increasingly mystified, she tried to imagine logical reasons for the mistake. But her mind had gone numb, the way it did when she was confused and needed to sleep. Lately this had been happening frequently, with too much urgency to ignore. She'd been faithfully following the doctor's orders about an iron-rich diet of eggs and spinach and even liver, so that by the time the baby was ready to go home, she'd be strong enough to care for him. But so far she was still only half herself.

By now barely able to hold up her head, she forced herself to stay awake until the sexton had pushed the vacuum into the entry and the ladies had finished the altar. As they started down the aisle, she took off her sweater, folded it into a thin pillow and placed it on the pew beside her. If they spoke, she intended to tell them not to mind her; she'd just have a quick nap, then walk back to the rectory and let her mother heat some beef tea for her.

But when they paused at her pew, the tall skinny one with a headful of frizzy curls said, "Anna Moss, is that you?"

"Why yes, yes it is."

"Well, I declare. Thought so. Lovely wedding, wasn't it?"

She nodded, wishing them gone. "But it's worn me out. See, ever since I had the baby, I've been terribly anemic, so now I just want to stretch out here and have a quick nap before I go home. But please, don't say anything to Mother, okay? I don't want her to worry."

The woman—Anna thought her name was Clarice Etheridge—gave her a look that was half puzzlement, half astonishment. "Your mother? Why, I haven't seen her or your father since they moved up to Maine last year. To be near you and that nice new husband of yours. And now a new baby too."

"Nice new husband" jolted her awake. Verging on panic, she shook her head. "No. No. That's not how it is."

The other, a little dumpling of a woman, leaned toward Mrs. Etheridge and whispered, "You sure that's her, Clarice?"

"Oh my yes. Knew her since she was a child." Then to Anna, "Don't you remember me, dear? I was friends with your mother all those years. Even helped with the reception when you married that nice Down East doctor. Right after you came back from the war, remember?"

"No," she whispered. "No. You're thinking of someone else."

Clarice hesitated a moment, then murmured to her friend, "Something's wrong here. Can't think what to do about it, though, except call the rector. Ought to be at the country club by now. Hate to disturb him, but he should know about this." She bent toward Anna. "Now dear, why don't you just rest yourself a while? We'll take care of everything, don't you worry. All right?"

Anna nodded.

"Just stretch out on the pew, if you want. Nobody'll disturb you."

"Thank you," she said, but waited to recline until their footsteps had padded down the carpeted aisle to the stone-floored entry and around a corner to the church office. So these kindly women were going to call the rector, evidently the red-haired, big-bellied priest who'd performed the wedding. Because it seemed her father had retired, moved up to Maine to be near her and her husband and the baby. Or so they said.

Even folded, the sweater offered little padding on the wooden seat. No matter; she had other more pressing concerns, mainly, to draw some logical conclusion from these incidents. Perhaps it would only be that she needed to hurry home so her parents could reassure her that these peculiar happenings had been only dreams. That the baby was well and the world continued to turn predictably. And that what she believed to be true actually was.

But her brain refused to produce a usable thought, like a radio offering only static instead of music or speech. So she huddled on the pew, twisting her hanky and trying to pray again for the baby and her parents and Dan, wherever his boat was now.

As an autumnal rain spattered the stained glass windows and dripped from the eaves outside, a damp chill worked itself into her fingers and toes. By then, however, the fear in her had swollen so precipitously that it was all she could feel. A strange, dreadful terror unlike any other she could remember. Not just for Dan, or even the baby. But for what was happening to her, to her memory, to her mind. To what was left of the rest of her life.

And the only prayer she could manage was a hoarse, "Jesus, Jesus. Help me. Please."

CHAPTER TWENTY-FOUR

What woke her that morning was nothing more dramatic than the familiar discomfort of a full bladder. Without having to think about it, she found the blue-tiled bathroom, used it and returned to the bed with the sense that she hadn't finished sleeping yet. It was fully daylight, but she crawled under the covers anyway—white sheets with a white blanket and white chenille spread on a white iron single bed. Like a hospital's. Yet, except for the bed and bleached muslin curtains at the long windows, the room was anything but institutional. In fact, the rest of the furnishings–desk and chair, bureau with mirror, a leather wing chair and hassock, a wrought iron floor lamp, and the tan and blue oriental rug covering half the floor—could have been from some well-appointed private home.   The view from the windows reinforced the notion: regularly-spaced trees, naked of leaves except for those still clinging to the oaks, formed a neat line across a snow-patched lawn to a distant strip of dull blue water under a milky sky.

All of it was vaguely familiar, yet unidentifiable.

Puzzled but not alarmed, she noticed the gown she wore suggested a hospital too—white flannel, string-tied in front. Increasingly curious, she left the bed again and regarded her image in the mirror. Her own face returned her stare, but her hair was pulled back in a single braid. And on her left wrist was a bracelet with letters on pink beads spelling out MILLETT. After Jamie had been born, the Rockhampton hospital had put one on him with the same name, only on blue beads. Her watch and rings were gone, but her hairbrush was on the bureau beside her old ticking Westclox. Its hands stood at ten-thirty-five.

Moving to the window, she was surprised that narrow metal bars covered the lower sashes, suggesting a mental institution. Yet nothing else seemed restrictive; on a paved path below, two bundled-up people, a man and a woman, were strolling hand in hand, breaths steaming in the cold air. And the door to her room was ajar.

She peered hesitantly into a hallway lined with windows overlooking a steep, snow-dusted slate roof and an ornate brick chimney. At one end was a closed door; at the other, a nurse sat at a desk talking on a phone. When she noticed Anna's scrutiny, she hung up, rose and came toward her with one of those professional smiles nurses kept ready for use at a moment's notice. "Well, Mrs. Millett," she chirped. "Are we ready to get up now?"

Anna winced at the odious *we*. Tempted to come back with, "Don't know about you, but I am," she said only, "I guess so."

"And how are we feeling today?"

"Fine. Except I can't remember where I am. And I feel like I should."

The nurse, a plain-faced thirty-something woman wearing a frilly Mass General cap, said, "Then why don't you get back in bed and I'll find Miss Visser. She'll explain everything."

When she left, Anna huddled on the bed, covering herself to the neck in an effort to overcome a nagging hunch that her life was in total disarray. Where was she? Why was the room familiar but unidentifiable? And why was it winter when she had no recollection of autumn?

A few minutes later, Miss Visser—she assumed that was who it was–knocked on the door frame and asked if she could come in. An older woman, thick-waisted, graying, wearing a lab coat over a green sweater and a Black Watch plaid skirt. Rimless glasses did nothing to mask the kindliness in her blue eyes, and her smile looked like the real thing. "Well, Anna, you've had a good long sleep. How do you feel now?" She pulled over the desk chair and sat facing the bed.

"Aside from having no idea where I am, I'm all right." She studied the other woman more closely. "Don't I know you from somewhere? Are you one of my husband's patients?"

"No, but I went to school with him. I'm Kathryn Visser. Does that help you remember our first meeting?"

Nothing came except a faint image of this same woman in a too-tight dress blue uniform with three gold stripes and the insignia of a Navy Nurse Corps commander on the sleeves. "In the Navy?"

"No, but we were both in uniform. Memorial Day last year, remember? The parade in Rockhampton?"

Anna closed her eyes to bring the image into focus. "Oh that's right. I fainted, didn't I? And you helped me. I was pregnant, so you called that afternoon to ask how I was doing. Told me you had a crush on Jim once. Oh, and you knew Old Horseface in the Navy."

Miss Visser laughed aloud. "You remember all that, do you? Remarkable. Now tell me who you are."

Why wouldn't she know her own name? "Anna. Anna Millett, and before that, Anna Donovan. Originally Anna Moss."

"Very good. And how did you get here?"

She shook her head. "No idea. The last thing I remember was being in St. Stephen's church in Portsmouth. Two women said they were going to call the rector, but after that...."

"We'll talk about what happened later. Meantime, any idea where you are now?"

"Some sort of institution. Maybe a mental hospital?"

The smile was almost too faint to notice. "We prefer to think of Rolling Hill as a rest home. For people like you–men who've had too much war, and women who've had too many losses. And children who were never allowed to be kids."

"People like me? Why? What happened to me?"

"Well, to put it simply, you lost your memory. Blocked out things you didn't want to think about. It's called Hysterical Amnesia."

"Oh, I know that term. On *Compassion* we had a Marine diagnosed with it. He'd been in so many invasions he couldn't remember any of them. The chaplain and I tried to help, but one night he just…well, he climbed the rail and jumped overboard."

"Battle fatigue?"

She nodded, frowning. "Is that what I have? I'm a nut job?"

Miss Visser's laugh was hearty. "Well, you do have a form of battle fatigue. But you're not a nut job. See, your husband's told us about all your losses the past four years. More than some folks have in a lifetime. And the mind can only take so much loss, so much grief. Then it shuts down."

So she was indeed a mental case. A spate of questions hurtled toward her, but at the moment, she was ready for only the simplest of answers–those that would let her see the logical order in what had happened to her. Beginning with, "How long have I been here?"

" Since September 14. Today's November 28. Almost eleven weeks."

She gasped. "Eleven weeks! Good Lord. And I can't remember any of it. Why?"

Miss Visser studied her. "You've been in a sort of fugue state that's blocked out losses too painful to remember. Ever since you were admitted, we've been helping you recover those memories. Like putting a puzzle together, But we've had to go at it slowly, so they wouldn't overwhelm you. It was only yesterday you put the last pieces in place. By that time you were so drained of energy you could barely keep your eyes open. So we got you into bed and let sleep heal you. Almost twenty-four hours of it."

Dazed, Anna shook her head and asked the next logical question. "I remembered everything? What does that mean?"

The older woman sighed. "Well, when they first brought you here, you thought it was September, 1943. And your husband was missing in action. You also believed you had a premature baby in an incubator at the naval hospital. Told us his name was Daniel Robert Donovan, Jr., and he had lots of weight to gain before you could take him home."

New shock made her gasp more deeply. "But that baby was stillborn."

She nodded. "We knew that. Jim and your father told us everything. But it was a month before you could come to grips with the infant's loss. When you finally did, your father held a memorial service right here in our chapel. And you let yourself feel the grief you hadn't felt at the time it happened."

Anna pondered this, remembering an event that gave credence to it. "That day–the last day I remember, I mean–before I went into the church, I went to his grave. And pictured how different my life would've been if he'd lived. So much simpler."

"Evidently that idea helped you construct the story you told us about the baby. After that, the next loss you had to face was your husband's death. To help with that, we arranged a memorial service at the chapel on the Brunswick base. Your family and lots of friends from Maine were there. Including Luke Salaunas. Dan was Catholic, so it was a requiem Mass, and Father Luke assisted."

"Oh my," Anna whispered. "Did they sing *Eternal Father, Strong to Save?"*

"The Navy Hymn; of course. And at the end, they presented you with a folded flag."

"I was there? I always wanted to hold a service like that for Dan. But for a year he was just missing in action. And when I finally learned the boat had been lost, so much else was happening, I never thought of it again. But why can't I remember it now?"

"You probably will, in time. See, you're still feeling your way back into your old identity. After all, you had eleven weeks in the new one, the one your mind built for you. One that felt safe and comfortable. So it may take a while. But getting back to the service for Dan, do you know who Luke Salaunas is?"

"He was the Catholic chaplain on my ship. USS *Compassion*."

"At the service you didn't recognize him. Then again, you didn't even know who Jim was for a long while. You thought he was a doctor friend of your father's."

Staring beyond the other woman toward the windows, Anna tried to grasp her explanations. Most incomprehensible was that she'd lost almost three months of her life, yet her memories of the years preceding it seemed intact.

Miss Visser studied her, then glanced at her watch and got to her feet. "Well, now. That's probably enough for the time being. Since it's almost lunch time, why don't you get dressed and come down to the dining room. We can talk again afterward. If you're up to it."

"Dressed? Do I have anything to wear?"

"Underwear's in the bureau, rest of it's in the closet. If you need help, Nurse Waterman's right down the hall." She moved toward the door. "Anna, I can't tell you how pleased I am at your progress today. It's been a long uphill road, but I think you've almost finished the journey. And you'll soon be ready to go home." She paused. "How do you feel about that?"

How did she feel about going home? "I think I need to know a little more first. There was something that last day in Portsmouth...."

"Any idea what it was?"

She shook her head as a nameless, formless fear bloomed in her consciousness. Something dark, something she couldn't bring herself to look at yet.

"Well, maybe it'll come out when we talk later. Now, can you find the dining room?"

"If not, I'll ask someone."

Following her nose and Nurse Waterman's directions, she wandered down the curving main staircase to a grand entrance hall, then along a corridor to a cavernous, vaulted-ceiling space where gilt cherubs frolicked around a crystal chandelier massive enough for an opera house. At one end of this huge area was a stage draped in maroon velvet; at the other, a pipe organ almost as impressive as the one at St. Stephen's occupied the wall. Between them a bank of Palladian windows overlooked a snow-coated terrace that overlooked a covered swimming pool that overlooked lawns sloping to the same body of water she'd glimpsed from her room.

Overwhelmed by the scene, she stood in the doorway debating whether to enter or flee. Until a portly middle-aged man who could have been a banker beckoned her to one of the large round tables where groups of what she presumed were other inmates were spooning up soup. Four men and five women of assorted ages watched her approach. Most smiled as she took the only empty chair. And when she picked up the soup spoon, the young woman to her right asked if her parents were coming this weekend, and if so, could she play with the baby? She was young and fresh-faced, with long dark hair, bangs and intense black eyes.

Anna had no idea how to respond. Evidently this was her assigned table; those seated around it said she was in their therapy group; they seemed to know more of her recent history than she did. Listening to them discussing her progress, she felt herself withdraw into the persona of an alien who has just wandered in from another planet. Panic swelled, stifling any inclination to speak beyond what was unavoidable, so she ate hurriedly, swallowing the food without tasting and aware the others had begun to regard her curiously.

As slices of pineapple upside down cake were served, she blotted her mouth with the napkin and asked to be excused. The man who'd beckoned her to the table asked if she was all right. Blurting out, "Sorry. I feel a headache coming on. Please excuse me," she rose from her chair so precipitously it toppled backward.

When she reached the stairs, she took them two at a time in order to reach her room before someone came after her, as if she might have violated some hospital protocol. Or done something symptomatic of mental instability that might alert the men with butterfly nets.

But no alarms went off, and at the nurse's station upstairs, Waterman only nodded as she passed. She didn't even glance up from the *McCall's* she was reading.

In her room, Anna closed the door, would have locked it except there was no lock. Then, without so much as brushing her teeth or taking off her shoes, she got back into the bed and covered herself again. Feeling lost, rudderless, without any compass to guide her back to reality, she wondered if she could she trust what Miss Visser had told her. Was she recovering? Or had she totally lost her mind, her sanity, even her identity?

Oh God, was this what the poor guys in the Nut Ward on the ship had had to bear?

When the fear subsided, she splashed cold water on her face, brushed her teeth and combed her hair, then began pawing through drawers in the bureau, nightstand and desk in search of something–a picture, letter, journal, some scrap indicating that her twenty-nine years of memories were more than dreams. But nowhere did she find anything to connect her to them. Apparently no one had given her a notebook in which to record memories as Mark had done with the young

Marine on H-12. Yet even so he'd thrown himself off the fantail. She was beginning to understand his state of mind.

But that had been two years before, maybe more. Why did the name Mark light up in her mind now? He'd been the Protestant chaplain on the ship, and they'd been lovers. But there was something more recent as well. Unnerved again, she returned to the bed to scour her mind for some clue.

She was so deep in it, she was startled when Miss Visser knocked. She swung her legs to the floor as the nurse entered. "Please," she began desperately. "Help me remember more."

"Of course, Anna," she said gently. She pulled the desk chair to the bed again. "How can I help?"

"You said I'd come back to reality soon. But I haven't. I'm still lost."

"Oh, my. I was afraid of that when you left the dining room in such a hurry. I should've known better. You've come so far and made peace with so many losses, I thought you'd covered them all. Obviously, you haven't. Now. What's troubling you specifically?"

"Mark. Something happened with him last summer. Something terrible. Something I thought I'd never forget. And now I have."

The older nurse drew a deep breath. "Well, let's see. Do you remember when his family came to visit you and Jim in East Point? Mark, and his wife, and two children. Alice and Buddy. We talked about them earlier this week, remember?"

"Buddy," she said, barely breathing. Closing her eyes, she flashed to the dream that had haunted her those weeks before she'd left home. A nightmare in which she saw the boy lose his grip and fall, cartwheeling down the face of a rocky cliff before he crash-landed at the edge of the surf. "Oh God. Buddy fell," she said, knowing there was more. "Oh…and he died." Tears came in a rush, stung her eyes, burned her throat. "Mark's wife said we weren't watching him. Said we were lusting after each other. So he died."

Miss Visser nodded, her expression unperturbed. "Anything else?"

"Yes. She wrote Jim a letter. I read it before he did. She blamed Mark and me for what happened. At first Jim didn't believe it, but then he wanted to know if it was true. And asked me to tell him everything Mark and I ever did together. I said no, it was in the past. But he kept insisting. He was so angry, he was like a stranger. I didn't know what to do. All I could think of was getting away and sorting it out. So I left the baby with my parents and drove down to Portsmouth and wrote him a long letter. Every detail of our affair, just as he'd asked. After I mailed it, I started walking around town. That's when I stopped at St. Stephen's. First the cemetery. Until it started to rain. Then I went into the church. And I couldn't...couldn't seem to remember things I should have."

Miss Visser nodded. "That was the day your mind finally shut down. Because you'd convinced yourself Jim wouldn't want you after he read that letter. That was the last straw. Another major loss, even as you were still dealing with Buddy's death. You felt responsible for what happened, though of course, you weren't." She took a deep breath, wiped her nose with a floral-embroidered hanky. "You were at the end of your rope."

Anna stared at her. The afternoon light was fading, the room growing cool. A radiator began to click as hot water surged through the pipes. "I guess so."

"See, that was the last loss in a long string, starting with your first baby and your husband, and your friend Jean. And, oh, so many young men you cared for on the ship, including the Marine you tried to help. And it didn't stop even after you and Jim married."

Suddenly more chilled than before, she whispered, "You mean the abortion?"

"You were against it, weren't you? But you agreed for Jim's sake."

She nodded. "To make him happy. Because I felt so guilty about Mark."

"It was right after that, that Mark visited with his family, and Buddy died, and his wife wrote to Jim. So in your letter to Jim, you bared your soul, even on the chance it would end your marriage." She shook her head, a tender gesture of wordless compassion. "And each of those losses felt heavier than the ones before. Because you never really grieved any of them. Just soldiered on and told yourself you were strong. Told yourself you'd forget and get over it. And ironically, you did. That day in the church when your mind refused to face another loss, that was a form of forgetting. But it was totally involuntary."

The words flowed through her, carrying logic and acceptance into the deepest regions of her mind. Even without grasping the whole, even without all the details, the truth in them reverberated with what she already believed. Cleansing, scouring her clean, but leaving areas of her soul still raw and bruised.

Miss Visser shifted in the chair, glanced covertly at her watch, then rose to switch on the bedside lamp. "I'm sure you still have a lot of questions, Anna, but I think we've talked enough for now. If you're up to it, we can get into again after supper." She smiled. "Why don't I have a tray brought up? I shouldn't have assumed you'd recognize everyone at lunch. They're your friends, but you must have been overwhelmed. Sorry I put you on the spot like that."

"It's okay. Something I had to go through, I guess. But tonight, yes, I'd prefer eating alone."

When the older woman had left, her mind seethed with new questions. Finding a note pad and pen in the desk, she began listing them. An odd mixture, some related to the specifics of her therapy, means and methods a nurse would be curious about, especially one who'd spent so much time with battle fatigue patients. Others were generic, concerning the hospital's history and range of patients.

But the overriding question had to do with Jim. And what she might expect now that he was fully aware of her previous...what? Sins? Or indiscretions? In the day's conversations, she'd intuited he'd somehow been part of her healing, making the forty-mile drive from East Point to Belfast as often as he could. Just like him to be loyal and supportive, regardless of his feelings.

But loving? Anxious to resume life with her? To trust her with his future? Or just loyal, committed to doing "the right thing" whether his heart was in it or not?

When the other woman came back after supper, while she was an open book about the therapy, about Jim she said only, "All I can tell you is, he's been here every Sunday since you were admitted. Told us everything he knows. And helped us plan the memorial services. But I don't know what's in his heart, Anna. That's up to you to find out. First, though, your parents and the baby will be here tomorrow. I know you're looking forward to seeing them again. Especially that precious little boy."

Anna's eyes filled. "My goodness. I wonder if he'll recognize me after three months."

Miss Visser patted her hand. "Well, he's been here before, so it hasn't been that long for him. And judging from his reaction, you have nothing to worry about. Now. Are you ready to sleep? Or do you need a pill?"

Something else came to her. "Wait a minute. Jamie knew who I was. But did I know who he was?"

"Actually, for the first month, you assumed he was your first baby. That he'd grown so much so fast didn't occur to you. But after you'd worked through that loss, yes, you knew who he really was. Now. About that pill."

"I think not, thanks. I'll be fine tonight. I'm not worried about seeing my parents. Might need one tomorrow night, though. Because I'll be much more anxious about Jim's visit Sunday."

"We'll deal with that tomorrow, then. For now, sleep

well. "

"Yes," she said firmly. "I think I will."

CHAPTER TWENTY-FIVE

Just before eleven Sunday morning, she went down to the lobby at the foot of the grand staircase. Visiting hours were about to begin, most of the ornate high-backed chairs along the walls occupied by other residents tensely awaiting guests. Still uncomfortable in their company, she shifted her gaze from the front door to the complex patterns of the Oriental rugs that covered most of the floor, then back to the door. Time dragged, but finally Jim's car approached up the drive. Her car, actually…the Caddy. With a sigh, she willed herself to be calm, to smile and not run as she hurried toward the great entrance. It seemed to take him a long while to park and walk up the path, hobbling along on the cane with what appeared to be more difficulty than before. Nearing, his gaze connected with hers and a grin lit his eyes. Even so she was struck by how much older he seemed than she remembered more stooped, face more lined, wearier than a man of forty-three should be. As if he'd been through hell, too. She smiled to conceal the sudden ache in her heart.

When she stood aside to admit him, his embrace took her by surprise. His cheek was cold against hers and his coat smelled of fresh air. Trembling, all she managed was, "Hi, Jim."

He leaned to her lips, clutched her against him. "Oh, Anna," he whispered into her ear, "It's so good to see you again. "

She nodded. "They tell me you've been here every week,

so apparently you've seen me before."

"I mean the real you. The one who remembers me."

"I can hardly believe there was a time I didn't. Except when I thought it was September, 1943. Because I didn't meet you till October that year."

He shook his head in one of those is-this-really-happening gestures, then studied her eyes at close range. "Well, you certainly look wonderful."

She smiled. "I should hope so. I've spent all morning dolling up. Just for you."

He took her elbow, led her toward a corridor opening under the staircase. "Then let's go to your room, and talk privately."

She frowned. "Is that allowed? I mean, do they let patients entertain gentlemen callers in their rooms?"

"They have before. That's where we've always visited."

"If you say so. But the stairs are out front."

"Let's use the elevator. Bum leg's been giving me a bad time lately."

"Oh, there's an elevator?"

"Back this way. We've used it before. Something else you've forgotten?"

"I must have. Oh, my. It's so strange. I can't even remember when you visited before. I mean…in my room, we didn't…you know…do anything, did we?"

He laughed aloud. "Not with the door open."

"There's still so much I don't know. Mainly what happened since I came here. The rest of my life, though – it's slowly coming back."

The elevator, a claustrophobic, self-service closet, was in the new section behind the main house. It rose so slowly it might not have been moving at all. When it finally clunked to a stop, they were in a corridor with classrooms like those on the lower level. She wasn't sure how to get to her room from here, but he led her back to the familiar hallway. A nurse she didn't recognize was at the desk; she beamed a brilliant smile and called him by his first name as they passed.

Anna opened the door to her room. "I really do need to come home. That girl's entirely too familiar to suit me."

"You'll get no argument on that." He shrugged out of his overcoat and tossed it to the bed, topping it with his hat. For a moment she stood stiffly, self-consciously unsure of her role in this odd meeting. Finally she pointed to the wing chair with the hassock, and pulled out the desk chair for herself. They sat, regarding each other as she mentally reviewed the contretemps that had pushed her over the edge. Still, she said only, "You look tired, Jim. Have you been well?"

"As well as I can be under the circumstances."

"The circumstances?"

He nodded soberly. "Living without you."

She took a deep breath, leaned back. "But do you want to live with me?"

"God, Anna, how can you ask?"

She shrugged. "Even after my letter?"

He closed his eyes, rubbed his chin, scratched his nose. "Well, I won't pretend that wasn't a jolt. I know I asked for it, but still…by the time I got it, you'd fallen apart and I had no idea if you'd ever come back. That made a difference. See, when the rector at St. Stephen's called your father that day, he said you were sitting in his office and didn't seem to know where you were going. So he called me to come down with him. I had no idea how bad things were, until you didn't recognize me. That was the worst day of my life."

Stricken by his abject tone, she leaned forward to clasp his hand. "Oh, Jim. I had no idea."

"And on the way back, you rode with your dad, and I drove your car, so I didn't know the full extent of it till we got to your parents' house. You recognized them, but you thought Jamie was your first baby. And had no idea who I was. Or why we were in Rockhampton. You were so confused, so…so lost, I knew you needed help we couldn't give you. So I made some calls and arranged to get you in here. We were lucky. It's the best sanitarium in Maine, maybe all New England. Still, I wondered if you'd ever come back to us. Or if too much had happened and you'd be stuck in that limbo for all time."

She regarded him in stunned silence until she was able to say, "That must have been dreadful."

His grin was ironic. "To put it mildly. Later though, when you began making progress, I realized I'd helped push you over the edge myself. That was worse yet."

"As I understand it," she said more calmly than she felt, "what happened with you was only the…well, the last straw. My troubles began long before I met you."

"True. But if I hadn't demanded to know all about you and Mark… If I'd just ignored that damned letter from his wife, you could probably have gotten over Buddy's death." He shook his head morosely. "But no. I had to be a jackass and keep pushing until you couldn't stand it any longer."

"Well, maybe," she said, slowly putting words to a belief she hadn't articulated before. "That's one way of looking at it. But now I feel it happened—everything happened–for a reason. I mean, as part of the plan. As if each of us had to go through that bad time so things would turn out right in the long run. Like Jesus and the crucifixion."

He sighed. "Well, maybe I'll come to that conclusion too. Eventually. Right now, though, I feel like hell about my part in your…your crucifixion. At least, your Gethsemane."

"Even after you read my letter?"

He nodded. "Thank God, by then, I realized how far gone you were. So it didn't affect me the way it would have before. See, I was facing life without you. Nothing else mattered a pinch of shit."

For a few moments, she let herself absorb and savor the message in his words. Dare she let herself hope? "But the truth was brutal. And I spared nothing."

"Just as I asked. Even though it didn't make it any easier to read. Writing it, well, that must've been even worse."

She pondered this. Had it been? "Actually, going back over it all, I realized that from your viewpoint, sure, it must've seemed like the worst infidelity. And I certainly felt guilty about it for a long while. But it had nothing to do with you. Not really. So I wasn't looking for you to forgive me. Just understand. And either accept or reject me, as you chose." She paused, mouth too dry to continue, so she got a glass of water from the bathroom, sipping after she sat down again.

"Now, I'm glad you know," she went on. "I'd planned to tell you all along. But I might never have if you hadn't insisted. And I'd have gone on being afraid Luke would tell you."

He laughed mirthlessly. "That prig! Oh, I'm sure he's a fine priest, and Lorraine adores him, but he's got too much sin of his own to point the finger at anyone else."

She didn't answer right away, unwilling to divert his attention from the matter at hand. "Well, anyway, is there anything about the...my past we need to talk about now? I mean, anything that might come between us in the future?"

He studied his fingernails with only the suggestion of a frown. "Just that holiday you and Mark had in Hawaii." He cleared his throat, loosened his tie, blue and red regimental stripes; a bright contrast to the white shirt under a salt-and-pepper tweed jacket she hadn't seen before. At least that she remembered.

"What about it?" she asked, knowing, but needing to hear his version.

"Well, I guess the worst of it was, neither of you thought about contraception." He blinked a couple times. "I hated that you were so carried away. With someone other than me."

She nodded, focused on her breathing so as to avoid being sucked into the familiar emotional vortex that might prompt her to apologize. "I'm sorry that hurt you. But I know what jealousy's like. I feel it every time I think about your first wife. And the heat you had with her."

He stared. "But I didn't know you then."

"Well, suppose you had. Would it have changed what you had with her?" She watched his face, imagining truth conflicting with his ingrained need to reassure her. She held up her hand. "Listen, I don't really need to know. Or have you tell me about it in a letter! I only said it so you'd realize there are things I struggle with too. Despite our own history of passion."

He nodded. "I know. It's just something that's bothered me a hell of a long while. I told you about it before. The night Jean died. And you wanted me to...you know. Have relations with you. The only thing that stopped me was this insecurity. Thinking about your husband and knowing it wouldn't be the same with me. Feeling inferior because of my leg. And no matter how much you say it doesn't matter, hell, for me it's always there. "

"And there's nothing I can do about it, is there? Except go on living with you."

"That's about it. And tolerate me when I go overboard."

She smiled. "Maybe that's the secret to marriage. Forgiveness when necessary and toleration for the other stuff. The overboard stuff."

His smile was relieved. He leaned forward, hands clasped on knees. "So...are you willing to try again?"

"If you mean, come home, yes, I'm ready. Well, almost. There's still so much I don't remember. Can you wait another week? Because I'd like to work on it a bit more."

"Hell, what's one more week when I've waited so long already? Oh, not just the past three months, but the year you were in the Pacific. And before that, when I'd resigned myself to living as a crusty old bachelor. So another week's only a few heartbeats."

She hadn't anticipated her reaction. But abruptly she was

overwhelmed with tears and the weight of events she couldn't recall, the sum of the last four years with, and without, this man. Getting to her feet, she wrapped her arms around him as he sat in the wing chair. Surprise and joy lighted his face. It wiped away the signs of aging she'd noticed earlier, and restored him to the man who'd captured her heart before either of them had realized it.

"Oh my goodness," she said, wiping her wet cheeks. "Goodness, Jim. Now I feel like shutting the door. And letting you have your way with me."

His laugh was surprised. "Well, we probably wouldn't be the first couple who ever did," he said drolly, as if the same notion might have been tickling him too. "Except look at the time. Nearly noon. Wouldn't want to miss the big meal, would we? Driving up here all these weeks, Sunday dinner's what I've looked forward to more than anything."

She grinned and glanced at the old Westclox. "But it's only five of. As I remember, five minutes is plenty of time."

His smile chased the remaining signs of fatigue, restored color to his cheeks, sparkle to his eyes. He got to his feet somewhat faster than usual. "Well, if you're sure...."

CHAPTER TWENTY-SIX

S o it was arranged: the coming week she'd continue to do the work—private therapy with Miss Visser, group therapy with the Neuro-Psych resident, and collateral creative therapies directed by staff members—painting and pottery, music and nature walks and poetry writing, with the nine other guests who shared her table. Barring any relapse, which Miss Visser said was unlikely, Jim would pick her up Saturday and take her home. From that time forward, she'd be an outpatient, and could come back for counseling, if and when necessary. Or even for more in-patient care, if she needed it.

So, with a bittersweet sense like she'd felt when she'd left the ship, she went through the week with determination to find the last pieces of the puzzle—what she'd learned about herself during the missing eleven weeks.

"Although I have had some recall," she said in group therapy. "The other day when I found the chapel, I remembered the memorial service for the baby . And when I saw a drawing I made of the boy who fell on the rocks, that awful day came back. But that's all."

"Those are good starting places, " Dr. Todd advised. "Meanwhile, don't be impatient with yourself. You can't remember the rest for the same reasons you believed it was 1943 when you were admitted."

"You went through a hell of a lot of pain those first few weeks," said Ben, a twice-wounded veteran of the Anzio campaign.

"You had so much to grieve for," said Miriam, the dark-haired young girl with the bangs. "It was like you'd just lost that baby the day before. It tore my heart out."

"It was almost as bad with your other losses," Ben added. "But back then, we were all in bad shape. Guess you don't remember how often I broke down and bawled like a baby myself."

"But you remember what happened to you. Why can't I?"

No one had a definitive answer to that, only the same theories she'd heard over and over. Most predicted that being at home again with husband and baby, family, friends and normal routines, it would either all come back, or she'd stop caring. One way or the other, life would soon feel normal again.

Wednesday afternoon she was in the library, trying to give substance to her emotions in a poem. Finally she asked the librarian for a rhyming dictionary. "Maybe Emily Dickinson didn't need one, but I do."

"Forget rhyming. Go for the rhythm, the meter, the feeling instead," the stick-thin elderly woman advised. "You don't have to compete with Miss Emily."

As she returned to her seat, one of the secretaries from the front office came in and whispered to the librarian, who murmured, "Anna, you have a visitor out front."

"On a weekday? I thought that was frowned on."

The secretary said, "It's a priest. Handsomest man I've seen in ten years." She blushed, tittered. "There's no rule about clergy visits. You can even take him to your room, if you want. I sure would!"

Except for the comment about being handsome, she'd expected Ted Bigelow to be waiting. Her father had told her he'd been here often. Now, in the lobby, she was shocked to see Luke Saluanas, in clericals, smoking and pacing the Oriental rug. For an instant, she didn't know whether to smile or scowl, but decided to be gracious no matter why he'd come. So far as she knew, he hadn't been there before.

When they shook, his clasp was loose, almost reluctant, his expression solemn to the point of being morose. Still, she said, "Luke. This is a nice surprise. What brings you here?"

He cleared his throat. "Heard you were coming home next weekend, and I wanted to see you first."

"Well," she said, baffled and uncomfortable as ever in his presence. "Shall we sit?" She gestured at the empty chairs. "It's private here."

"Mmm…could we walk instead? Nice day today. Warm for December."

"Give me a moment and I'll run up to my room for a coat."

When she came back, he was staring through the glass in the heavy oak door. "Pretty place," he said, holding it open. "Never been here before. Your father said it used to be a private mansion."

She nodded. "It was the estate of a man who made a fortune shipping Aroostock Valley potatoes to market. Now it's for nut jobs like me. Like H-13 on the ship. Except we're pretty tame here. Never heard of anybody getting stabbed."

She'd expected the remark to elicit at least a chuckle of remembrance. Instead, his glum scowl persisted as she steered them down the drive and onto one of the paved walkways that crossed the winter-browned lawn toward the water. All the snow had melted the past few days with the help of sunlight slanting low from a cloudless pastel sky and a warm southerly breeze.

"Who told you I was going home, Luke?"

"Your father. I called to find out about visiting hours. Thought about waiting till you were home, but didn't know when we could speak privately." He gave her a quick sideways look. "See, this is all strictly hush-hush. Can't risk anybody overhearing."

For no reason except her history with this man, anxiety stabbed her. "My goodness. Sounds interesting." She pointed to a slatted park bench under a leafless tree close to a stone retaining wall. "Why don't we just sit and look at the bay? Or do you see enough of it from your church boat?"

"Pretty much, yes. But let's sit anyway."

They settled as far apart as the bench allowed. Before she could ask what was on his mind, he extracted a pack of Luckies from his jacket pocket and lit one with his Navy lighter, inhaling with what seemed relief. "This reminds me of the picnic on Guam," she said. "When you warned me about Mark's....shall we say, proclivities?"

"A lot of good it did," he murmured with a remnant of the old judgmental streak. "But that's not why I'm here today. Not at all." He inhaled again, squinting off toward the water. His hair was still brush cut, but now traces of gray streaked the temples. She wondered if Dan Donovan would have gone gray this early too. Of course, he'd be older now, thirty-one. Luke wasn't even twenty-nine.

"Okay. I'm listening. Why are you here?"

He shook his head, eyes downcast. "I think I'd have to say, to beg your forgiveness, Anna."

Startled, she gave him a quick look. "For what?"

"Well mainly, for giving you such a hard time about Whitmore. For judging you. And shaming you."

"That's ironic. Though it's true, I always resented your attitude, maybe because I already had so much shame in me I didn't need yours. But…why apologize now?"

He pulled on the cigarette and squirmed on the seat. "Well, to put it simply, because Lorraine read me the riot act. When we heard what happened to you, and where you'd ended up, and when we saw how awful you looked during the memorial service for your first husband, she reminded me of things I said the last time you were on the island. After the Whitmore boy died. She said I had no right to talk to you that way. You, or anyone else. No right to throw stones." He smoked the cigarette down to a stub and quickly lit another from it. "She was really upset. I never saw her that angry before."

Hesitant to coach him, she said only, "Did she tell you why?"

He nodded, brows lowered. "Said she never intended to this side of her deathbed, but she had to tell me about my father. Who he really was."

"She said that? She told you?"

"Uh-huh. Just blurted it all out. Finally. Even showed me his picture."

"Oh yes. The one who looks so much like you. That must've been a shock."

"Well, not really. I always thought there was more to it than that cockamamie story she cooked up about the town banker. She was just too defensive. I didn't buy it."

"I never heard his name. Did she tell you?"

The smile that tilted his lips was surprising. "Finally. Funny part was, I knew him. Met him years ago, on a retreat when I was, oh, sixteen or so. I was thinking about going to seminary, so he and I talked about it one night. He was one of the spiritual leaders. Pastor of a church outside Baltimore."

"Oh, that's interesting. See, according to Lorraine, he helped arrange her trip there for your birth and adoption. I wonder if that's why he was in the area. In fact...I wonder if he had an inkling you were his son when the two of you talked."

His face went wistful. "Who knows? I never saw him again. Or heard from him either. He's in Chicago now. A monsignor. Lorraine keeps track of him in *The Catholic Times*. Anyway, her point was that I was the child of sinners myself. And as such, I had no right pointing a finger at you and Whitmore. She didn't threaten to disown me if I didn't ask your forgiveness, but I had to anyway." He closed his eyes a moment, tightly, as if trying to avoid saying the next words.

"Because, see, I truly am sorry. Not just for that day on the island, but for all of it, all those times on the ship. Everything. Looking back now, I understand exactly what you meant when you said 'Let him without sin cast the first stone.' Because you knew the circumstances of my conception." He frowned with a quick glance at her. "How come you never threw that at me? You could have, you know. It would've put me in my place for once and for all."

"Oh, I guess because Episcopalians don't do that. Don't hurt people for no reason." Seeing his consternation, she grinned. "Sorry. Couldn't resist that! No, Luke, the real reason is, Mark advised me not to. Right after you were stabbed, I asked him if I should tell you about Lorraine. He said that was okay, but the news about your father wasn't mine to tell. It might turn you against your mother too. At the very least, it would shake you to your foundations."

He stared hard across the bench. "Whitmore said that?"

"Uh-huh."

"Wow, that's a surprise. Guess I ought to write and thank him. Ask his forgiveness too. Is he still at the hospital in Virginia?"

"Last I heard, after his son died he began drinking heavily, so he resigned his commission, left the ministry and took a job driving a bus. I noticed that too. The drinking, I mean. See, the night after Buddy was hurt, he hinted around until Jim saw to it he got a bottle at the hotel."

Luke closed his eyes again and shook his head. "So that's on my conscience now too. God, I have a lot to atone for."

"You're not to blame for that. Or anything else Mark's done." He didn't answer, so she sat quietly, studying tidal patterns and wind-driven crosscurrents that made the water look like blue taffeta. The sun was lower behind them now, the air turning cool. "As for me, all I can say is, of course I forgive you. We're old shipmates, right? So don't let that trouble you anymore. And make sure your mother knows it too. I don't want anything to mar your relationship. She waited too long to find you."

Another slow nod, then a glance at his watch, an abrupt rise to his feet. "I agree. And thank you. Now, well, it's a long drive back. Better get started so I'm not late to supper. That always worries her."

Anna stood, buttoned her coat, stuck her hands into the pockets as they turned back to the mansion. "If I ever hear from Mark, I'll get an address so you can write him. Might help him to hear from you. If anything can. If he's not beyond hope."

Luke grinned. "Oh Anna. That remark's so typically Protestant. See, we Catholics know no one's ever beyond hope."

She smiled at the obvious but good-natured jab. "I'll try to remember that."

When they reached the driveway, she waited by his car while he picked a chunk of gravel out of one tire. Then, opening the door to get in, he said, "Would you let me hug you, Anna, so I know I'm really forgiven?"

All things considered, it wasn't a bad hug, just stiff, as if he were afraid of being tainted, in this case by a woman and a Protestant. Still she leaned up and kissed his cheek and told him she was glad he'd come, and if she hadn't mentioned it before, she appreciated his helping with the memorial service at Brunswick. After this, without looking at her again, he climbed in and started the engine. She knew this meeting, this admission of guilt, this plea for forgiveness had been unnerving for him, so she wasn't surprised when he didn't look back.

She stood watching his car as it diminished between the lines of cedars that led to the highway, then went up to her room. She wished she could phone Jim and tell him about the visit, but making long distance calls was a complicated procedure, so she abandoned the idea. Easy enough with the prospects of seeing him again in two more days. After that they'd have the rest of their lives to catch up on such conversations.

CHAPTER TWENTY-SEVEN

S aturday morning it was snowing, nothing major, just a
quiet fall predicted to leave about six inches before it
moved out to sea. A good omen, Anna thought as she
anticipated a leave-taking unalloyed with regret for anything,
except not having filled in every last empty space in her
memory. Not yet, anyway, though the professional
consensus was, she soon would.

The night before, her friends at Rolling Hill had surprised
her with a party at supper and impromptu gifts—an amateur
oil painting of a still life on a small square of canvas, a
lopsided clay pot, a hand-woven pot holder, and a dog-eared
Selected Poems of A.E. Housman wrapped in handmade
paper. There were a few tears, her own and others'; she was
the first of their group to leave. She promised to return to see
them, maybe at Christmas, of course with the baby. She also
promised to write and send pictures of herself and Jim and
Jamie, although she knew she might not. These were friends
by virtue of shared experiences rather than choice. Like
those on the ship, they'd been important in each other's lives
mainly because each was temporarily without other anchors–
family, friends, home.

Afterward she'd stayed up late, packing and trying to
imagine what home would feel like. She could barely sleep
for anticipation of the morning, her final meeting with
Kathryn Visser and most exciting of all, the resumption of
her old life.

They met just after ten; for the next few minutes Anna focused on signing release papers and filling out other forms for the records. After that, Miss Visser delivered her final words, the encouraging sort the older nurse probably offered to all those who left in promising circumstances:

"I'm sure you're going to have a good life, Anna. You've done a lot of hard work and come a long way. And if you ever want to go back to nursing, there'll always be a job for you here."

She smiled. "Maybe if you ever open a clinic in Rockhampton. This is just too far to drive every day."

An answering smile. "Of course. Meanwhile, feel free to call if you ever need to talk. Doesn't have to be anything serious. Maybe just lingering issues I can help with."

"Thanks for that too. Good to know I'm not totally on my own."

"And if I see Dr. Jim this morning, I'll tell him the same. It's gratifying to know he turned out such a fine man. Always thought he would, back in the old days. Back when he didn't know I existed. No wonder I never married. Never found anyone who could measure up to him."

At this point, Anna expected her to wrap up the conversation and resume her work. But when she got to her feet, Miss Visser asked if she could wait a minute. "I want to share an idea you might find interesting."

Nodding, she resumed the seat. "What's that?"

"Just something you can think about. Something that occurred to me when you told the group you'd encouraged your first husband to talk about the nightmares he had after his sub was almost sunk. You even referred to it the way Dr. Freud did—as the talking cure. That was so insightful, as were so many of your observations with others in the group, I believe you have a natural gift for counseling."

Anna laughed. "Insightful in Dan's case maybe. But it never occurred to me I needed the same thing myself."

"Of course not. That's why doctors don't treat

themselves. Anyway, I've been wondering if sometime in the not-too-distant future, you might consider studying psychology so you can qualify as a psychiatric nurse, or a counselor, or even a psychologist. With this new GI Bill, you could get a degree at very little cost."

Anna blinked at the sketchy concept. "Right now, I just want to go back to being a wife and mother. Working with my husband, having another baby. I can't think beyond that."

"Oh, I understand completely. Just thought I'd throw out the idea so you can think about it when the time's right. Even if it's a few years down the road. Because with your aptitude for this work, you could help so many needy people."

"Well, I won't promise anything, but I will think about it. When the time's right, as you said."

The older woman's smile was warmer than usual. "Good. I hope you do. Now, I'll let you get on with your packing." She rose, extended her hand across the desk. "Please give your father my best too. There's another prince of a fellow. All in all, you're in good hands, Anna."

Suddenly her eyes were full. "The best," she said, and left the office in the clutch of a nostalgia as strong as she'd felt leaving the ship for the last time.

She didn't know what time to expect Jim, but by ten she'd cleaned out her room, had the porter carry her bags downstairs, and was alternately sitting and pacing around the lobby. The snow was still sifting down, a gentle fall like the one in December, 1945, when she'd arrived in Boston after the train trip from Oakland. And had met Jim at South Station, and talked him into getting married the following week.

Now she knew she'd done that for the wrong reason–she'd expected marriage to loosen Mark's hold on her. Just like that, she'd expected to put him out of her mind without doing anything other than shifting affections from one love interest to another. She should have waited, given herself more time to recover from a year in a war zone on a ship full of broken bodies, and a romance with a man she'd never planned to spend her life with.

And that had been only one of the many ways she'd avoided facing loss. Time after time, she'd shrugged off pain and taken the easy road to some promising new situation. Where she'd found comfort for a while, and pleasure. Now, watching the handyman shoveling the walk, she thought of herself as having so often pushed pain aside as casually as this fellow flung flakes into piles. In her case, however, the feelings she'd piled up had accumulated into a mountain that had eventually avalanched down on her.

Finally, the next set of headlights that came up the drive were on the Cadillac. As Jim turned into the semi-circle, she stepped outside, motioning him to park close to the door. The handyman was quick to realize her bags needed to be carried out and seemed happy to lug them to the trunk, even happier when Jim pressed some coins into his hand.

"Well now," Jim said, closing the lid. "Is that it?"

She nodded. "All my worldly goods."

"Do I need to sign any papers?"

"No. Took care of everything earlier. Unless you want to go in and thank Miss Visser for treating me so well. She could've murdered me, you know, so she could get her hands on you."

"Really? In that case, I'll be sure and thank her. Want to use the men's room anyway. If you don't mind waiting another few minutes."

"No, go on." She followed him inside, and sat on the edge of a chair, tapping her foot as she watched the handyman's continuing efforts to clear the walk. And reviewed Miss Visser's suggestion that she study psychology. Initially the idea had taken her by surprise, coming as it did at a time when she was focused on finding domestic bliss in a normal life. Now, projecting a few years ahead, she realized one day it might tempt her more. As for having a gift, true, with nothing more than instinct to guide her, she'd made Dan talk about the war experience that had plagued him after the boat's close call with a Jap destroyer. She hadn't been with him long enough afterward to know if it had had any lasting effect, but he'd seemed better while they'd been together. And more recently, on the ship she'd observed the chaplains doing essentially the same thing with the battle fatigue patients.

When Jim came back, she filed the idea away for future reference, then hustled him outside quickly, in case he thought of anything else to delay them. Finally, he started the engine, shifted into low and eased around toward the main drive. She took a deep breath and let it out slowly, with a fond and lingering glance behind at the grand mansion where her health and sanity had been restored. It was only when then they reached the highway that she remembered Luke's visit.

They explored the matter all the way to Camden, until Jim stopped for lunch at a diner north of town. Parking alongside the stucco building, he gave her a casual smile. "This okay for your first civilian meal in months? Food's only mediocre, but I never heard of a case of ptomaine here."

She laughed and opened her door to spattering white flakes. "Oh, that's a great recommendation. How are they on clam chowder, though? Wouldn't that be appropriate for another winter homecoming?"

They ducked inside, stamping shoes in the entrance. Another ordinary eatery, she observed as the hostess led them to a window table with a view of the slushy parking lot and the busy highway. Not exactly like the diner outside Boston where they'd eaten two years before, but close enough to remind her of her conflicted feelings at being home from the war.

Jim wiped steam from his glasses with a paper napkin, then studied the menu. "Never had the chowder here. But you're right. Nothing could be more appropriate."

The waitress came, took their orders, hustled away. "You know," Anna said, staring at traffic kicking up slush on Route One; "it's the same weather and the same soup, but everything else is different. At least I am, thanks to my little vacation the last few months."

"Different how?"

"Well mainly, this time I'm fully with you. Two years ago I was here physically, but so much of me was still on the ship. With those people."

"With Mark," Jim said matter-of-factly.

Jolted by his acknowledgement of that old truth, she nodded. Despite her letter detailing all the odious facts, she was still uncomfortable with the admission. She cleared her throat. "But now he's gone. Oh, not from my memory, but from my heart. " Before she could go on, she had to sip ice water. "Anyway, I guess the biggest change in me is, now I don't feel compelled to do anything just so I'll stop hurting or feeling guilty. That was the big thing, the day I came home. I couldn't wait to get married. Because I thought it'd stop me from thinking of Mark."

He reached across the table, laid his hand on hers, gazed into her eyes. "I figured that out when I read the letter. Even at the time, though, I knew it wasn't just love for me pushing you into marriage so soon."

Funny how the truth could keep surprising her. "So you had misgivings. Then why did you agree?"

"If you remember, I did try to convince you to wait, but you wouldn't hear of it. So misgivings and all, I caved in. Because I suspected you'd had a romance on the ship. Besides, I was desperate too, to wrap you up in wedding vows. Make you mine before you had a chance to change your mind."

She sighed, was trying to come up with an answer, when the soup arrived. Another surprise; it wasn't the hearty white chowder of the State Line Diner, but the tomato-based Manhattan style. Jim surveyed it as the girl brought coffee and grilled cheese sandwiches. He waited until she'd left before he said, "Look at that, will you. Didn't think they were allowed to serve this stuff anywhere in New England. Especially Maine."

She laughed at his vehement reaction to such a minor disappointment. "Send it back, then. Actually I prefer this to the other."

He chuckled. "Gosh, Anna. Really is truth time, isn't it?"

"I expect it will be for a while to come," she said and lifted her spoon to dig in.

On the road again after lunch, Jim observed the snow was falling more heavily. "Now this is supposed to be a surprise, but your mother's making your favorite homecoming dinner tonight. Sauerkraut and pork roast. I'm thinking, though, it might be best if we picked up the baby and headed to East Point before the roads get worse. What do you think?"

"Fine with me. Maybe she could do it tomorrow instead." She grimaced. "Oh, God, what if Kate's planning something special too? Like boiled mutton and turnips. Or did you give her the weekend off?"

"Interesting you should mention her. That's another surprise, dear. See, Kate's gone. Out of the house. Out of our lives."

Blinking, it took her a moment to say, "What? She quit? No, she never would have. What happened?"

"Well, I've known for a long while she's not your favorite person. But after the incident with Lynette's letter, I began to watch her. And I saw what you meant. About her being intrusive. But there was nothing really major. Until one night, oh, three or four weeks ago. She made supper, then hung around while I ate, and asked a lot of questions about you, going on in that morose way of hers about how she wouldn't be surprised if you never came back to yourself. And how she pitied me, so faithful, so patient, so alone. And how it wasn't fair of any woman to expect a man to live like that... without his creature comforts."

"Oh, my, creature comforts! And she didn't mean just meat and potatoes, did she?"

He laughed. "You got that right. Still, I pretended I didn't know what she was talking about, so I told her I had no complaints. Then she said that was one of the things she admired about me, how I never complained, just kept going even when I was dead on my feet, with no one to comfort me."

"Comfort you? Oh Jim! She didn't! I can hardly believe it, even of her."

"Wait. It gets better. Or worse. By then I was curious to see what she was leading up to, so I asked what sort of comfort she had in mind. And she said that one place she worked, she used to give neck and back rubs to the man of the house. Said they really helped a chap relax after a long day."

"Tell me you didn't let her touch you!"

He grinned. "Are you kidding? Anyway, then she went on about how men had needs that most women can't begin to understand. And even though I was the most wonderful fella alive, she was sure even I occasionally needed the special comfort of a woman's touch. Then she gave me a look that I took to mean she wasn't talking about a neck massage."

Anna bristled, sat bolt upright. "Oh, the brazen hussy! But I'm not surprised. Margie always said, if anything happened to me, Kate would set her cap for you. But quick, tell me what happened next. Unless it's grounds for divorce."

"Good Lord, Anna. Don't you credit me with more sense than that?"

She patted his hand on the seat. "Of course I do, darling. Go on."

"Well, by then I was tired of playing the game, so I asked her point-blank if she was offering to come to my bed. And she batted her eyes and said, 'Only if you invite me, Jim.'"

"I'll kill that bitch," Anna said. "I swear I will kill her with my own hands."

"No need, darling. See, I fired her. Right there and then. Told her to get out and not come back. Told her I'd send her a month's pay. Of course she sputtered and said she hadn't meant it the way it sounded. But I didn't relent. Afterwards, though, I began to worry she might turn vengeful and sic the Irish Mafia on me. So when I heard the priest at Our Lady needed a housekeeper, I called and said she was a fine woman, a devoted Catholic, and I could give her a good reference." He shrugged, glanced over with what she recognized as a smug expression. "Last I heard she was working at the rectory. And presumably giving him all the creature comfort he wants."

"Thanks be to God," she sighed, more relieved at the news than she'd expected. "Having her gone is the finest homecoming present I could ever want."

"Wait. There's more. I know we need a housekeeper, so I talked one of my patients into taking the job. A plain woman, a no-nonsense Congregational widow, early sixties. Skinny as a rail, with a chest like a washboard—"

"Oh Jim. How do you know what her chest looks like?"

"Hell, I've been her doc for five years, I should know. She might not be the best cook, but she's agreed to live in and take care of Jamie, except weekends."

"She doesn't have to be good at all to be better than Kate. Besides, if she's taking care of the baby and the rest of the housework, I can do the cooking myself," Anna said. "Oh, this is so good. Not to have to face that evil bitch again! It makes me so happy."

"Will you promise me, though, if Mrs. Dunlop doesn't suit, you'll tell me? Still don't understand why you put up with Kate as long as you did."

"The same reason I agreed to the abortion," she said slowly. "To make you happy. I know now there were sound medical reasons for it, but the main thing was that you wanted it. That's why I agreed to wait three months before we conceived Jamie too. I wanted you to be so happy married to me that even if you had suspicions about Mark, they wouldn't matter."

For a long while he stared past the swiping wipers and the flying whiteness they were tunneling through. His face was sad, not with a present sadness, but as if pondering past events that hadn't happened the way he'd interpreted them. As if her various revisions of truth were as impossible to comprehend as they were to change.

Finally, he said softly, "Oh my dear. Is this how you've been feeling the whole time we've been married? As if you had to atone for Mark? Over and over?"

"Yes, pretty much," she admitted.

"God, if only I'd known."

"If only I'd told you sooner. But see, it was always easiest not to. Oh, originally I intended to clear the air. But well, after a while it stopped being so important. And if things hadn't happened the way they did with Buddy, I might never have told you. That's why when you demanded to know the whole story, it was the best thing that ever happened to us. Because it brought everything into the light where we had to look at it."

He shook his head a long while, slowly, as if emerging from a vivid and troubling dream. Finally he turned to regard her with the gentle smile she'd always found reassuring, no matter what. "Even better than firing Kate O'Neil?"

She laughed, pushed herself across the seat and rested her head on his shoulder. "Well no. That has to be Number One. From now on, nothing will ever be as bad as having her around."

But as he slid one arm around her, she knew of course there would be matters that seemed every bit as bad–misunderstandings, quarrels, family crises. And times when she slipped off the straight and narrow back onto the path of least resistance. Oh, never another Mark Whitmore, never another physical transgression. Instead a gradual reversion to the old, easy ways of thinking. And being human, both of them: that alone guaranteed there'd be enough rough patches to keep life interesting.

Just to start with, there was the question of another baby; she hadn't brought it up yet, but it was about time. Would he agree it was safe now? Or would he make some logical medical pitch for another six months, another year? Then, if she agreed, would it be willingly? Or grudgingly, with the same desperation of Alex Cropper's wife when she'd poked holes in his condoms?

It all remained to be seen. That was the beautiful mystery of the human condition, the enigma that had plagued even Saint Paul. And while she'd learned an encyclopedia about herself the past three months, there were still those unanswerable questions that would keep her humble. Keep her from pride, which her mother had always warned went before a fall.

Ah yes. The road ahead was blurry with snow, landmarks indistinguishable in the fine, flying flakes. Still, she knew they were approaching Rockhampton. And her parents, and the reclamation of Jamie. Then home to East Point, to settle into routines there again. Normality. Ordinary time. The great adventure of the rest of their lives.

Bring it on, she thought as she had the day she'd boarded the ship in Brisbane three years before. And whatever happens, dear Lord, let me count it all good.

EPILOGUE
East Point, Maine
Sunday, 30 September 2007

After church that day, she and Margie had treated themselves to the gut-busting buffet at the Penobscot Yacht and Country Club, napped the afternoon away, and munched only popcorn and apples with Chardonnay for supper. Then, in pajamas, robes and slippers, they settled onto their respective sofas facing the big flat screen TV. Beyond the bay window, the darkness outside was abloom with the usual lights—the village below, the occasional navigation light on the black swath of the Sound, the island on the far side, and, if you craned your neck, even a glimpse of the whirling beam from the lighthouse up the coast.

At five of eight, Margie tapped the remote to activate the TV, set her wine glass on the coffee table, and tucked an ornamental pillow under her head. "God, Anna. I can't believe I'm still watching this depressing stuff. I feel like bawling the whole time it's on. But it's so fascinating I can't stop."

Anna kicked off her slippers and tucked her legs under the frayed plaid robe. "Cheer up. Only two more episodes after tonight."

Five years before, when they'd decided to share Anna's house, they'd made a pact to watch nothing troubling, nothing dealing with issues beyond their control, which meant eschewing large portions of the nightly news. The moratorium had begun with the wars in Iraq and Afghanistan, though they made themselves look at the PBS coverage of casualties. Feeling a moral obligation to honor these dead, they'd watch in silence to the conclusion. Then one of them would mutter, "Sons of bitch warmongers," in reference to the Bush-Cheney-Rumsfeld triumvirate they regarded as architects of both conflicts.

Tonight, however their focus was on World War II, that "good" fight depicted in the PBS Ken Burns documentary, *The War.* Even now, sixty years after her brief encounter with Lynette Whitmore, Anna still pronounced it *wo-wah.* Because it was a collection of nasty truths Lynette would never have let her kids see, a gritty, graphic account not just of major campaigns but of monumental failures of leadership, the disgraceful treatment of Negroes and Japanese-Americans, and the disclosure of secrets long kept under wraps in the interest of "public morale." Margie's taste ran more to sitcoms and dance contests, but when the series had begun the week before, she'd announced, "You know I don't want to, but I feel like I owe it to you to see what it was really like."

Anna'd said, "What it was really like? Hell, even when we were out there, we had no idea. Except for the part we were involved with. It was so much worse than we realized. And the whole picture's only starting to come together."

Margie's well-seamed face had turned pensive. "So, if you'd known then how bad it was, would you have joined the Nurse Corps anyway?"

Anna had sighed, but with a tolerant smile. This was their style on evenings with wine—to pose large-denomination questions, invariably without answers except in the abstract. Maybe it was a mental exercise, like crossword puzzles to keep their brains firing on all cylinders, Or efficiently enough to keep them out of custodial care. A good game for an age when almost nothing happened except for endless manifestations of degenerative physical processes. Not unexpected; they were both eighty-nine, and had been nurses long enough to recognize the inevitability of the changes in their minds and bodies. "The long downhill slide," Margie called it. Which made it sound innocuous, like a ride in a water park.

Margie drained the last of her wine as the opening theme began to roll. "Tell me something, Anna. From your experience as a psych nurse, can you get PTSD from watching this stuff?"

"Oh, maybe if you had it to begin with, you'd get flashbacks."

"Think you ever did? Have it, I mean."

"Probably. Might've been part of my mental breakdown in '47. And Dan, when the boat was in San Francisco after that awful patrol, I'm sure that was his problem. See, he had nightmares, and was drinking a lot more than usual too. Poor guy. God knows how much worse it would've been if he'd survived. Especially if he'd been in that Jap prison camp where they sent submariners because they were used to narrow passageways. A copper mine with underground tunnels." With a deep breath, she shook herself out of that nightmare scenario. "He might have had problems adjusting to civilian life."

"You mean, like he had in Frisco?"

"Uh-huh. Or worse. He might have started using drugs, or having affairs with other women . People with PTSD will try almost anything to help them forget. And feel less dysphoric."

"Poor guy. So maybe you're better off things worked out like they did with him."

Stunned, reluctant to comment on the cynical observation, she said only, "God, Margie. That's a hell of a thing to say."

Her friend appeared not to hear; her gaze shifted to the screen. "Oh look, Anna. This episode's called FUBAR. What's that mean?"

Instantly, the term flashed her back to the Guam O Club the night In August, 1945 they'd learned why Indy casualties had been so high. And Floyd Einhorn's explanation: " It's like SNAFU. Only worse. FUBAR's 'Fucked Up Beyond All Recognition'."

"Jesus. You mean it's going to get worse? Then we need more wine." Wincing, Margie rose slowly, padded into the kitchen for another bottle, poured a couple inches into their glasses, then flopped again as the heartbreaking military blunders began to unfold.

First, at Anzio and Monte Cassino in Italy, then in a dense forest on the western German border; and in the Pacific, Peleliu. With surprising candor, the film named the top brass responsible for these debacles, including MacArthur. When he'd planned his return to the Philippines, he'd ordered the small island captured to prevent Japanese attacks from its airstrip, though it was 500 miles distant.

Anna sat bolt upright. "Peleliu! That was the first campaign after I joined the ship. By then the Marines were supposedly mopping up. That was bad enough, but apparently it was even worse before we got there. A real bloodbath. And for what? Later they decided we could've retaken the Philippines without ever going near that hell hole. Which didn't bring back a couple thousand Marines who died there."

Margie's sniff was disdainful. "I never did trust that MacArthur. Self-serving bastard."

"Yeah, in some ways. Except what he did in Japan after the war was brilliant." She looked away from the black and white images of death and dying long enough to drain her wine. When she glanced at the screen again, the view of the offshore flotilla included a familiar white ship. She pointed. "Margie, look! I think that's *Compassion*." The picture changed, with a voice-over about a wounded Black Marine evacuated to a hospital ship. When the ship's barber had refused to cut his hair, the skipper had ordered him to do it.

In the next scene, an officer seemed to be making sure he did.

"Was that your captain?" Margie asked.

The picture was too grainy and fleeting to see clearly. "No. Our skipper didn't have the balls to do that. Must've been *Solace,* then. She looked enough like ours to be our sister ship."

She lay back again, connected by this brief invasion footage to the rawness of her emotions those first months at sea. By the time she'd met Mark at Christmas, 1944, she'd become inured, at least most of the time. Until she'd realized there were some situations to which no amount of experience, wisdom or training could harden medical personnel. The seeds of PTSD had been planted deep, and often.

It was after ten before FUBAR concluded. When Margie switched to an ABC drama, Anna tried to watch for the sheer relief of dealing only with some fictional family's clichéd problems. But her thoughts were still locked in the past, on the sliver of war she'd known, that small chip of the mosaic of the global conflict. So long before, yet her feelings were still as fresh and vivid as in the moment. Had Mark watched it too, and had a similar reaction?

She'd just begun to wonder when Margie clicked off the TV, then regarded Anna with a frown. "Tell me something. That stuff about the hospital ship. If Mark was still alive, would you want to talk to him about it?"

Startled, Anna realized she'd forgotten he was gone. How could she? His death wasn't one of those pieces of trivia that so often disappeared in her brain, like the whereabouts of her car keys. "No, not really. He didn't join the ship till December, so he missed Peleliu. I could've talked to Luke, though; he was there for the whole thing. Oh well, maybe he and Mark can share it, wherever they are now. I mean if they're even in the same afterlife. And still speaking to each other."

Margie snickered, which was as close as she came to giggling these days. "Ironic, isn't it, considering Mark asked you to let him know when Jim died. Guess he expected to sweep back into your life. And comfort you with a little nookie."

Anna glanced over quickly with surprise she could still be shocked at anything Margie said. "Come on, now. You know I didn't want him sweeping back into my life. Especially not for that."

"But you heard from him again, didn't you? I mean, after you got out of Rolling Hill?"

"Just a Christmas card. One of those cheap ones you used to get a dozen for a dollar in Woolworth's. With a little note saying he hoped Jim and I were well. There was a return address in Norfolk, so Jim wrote back. Said he hoped Mark was finding his way through grief. I thought that was so...well, so Christian of him after everything I told him about Mark and me."

She reached for her empty glass, poured what was left in the bottle. "For the next few years there were other cards, always with different addresses, and always the same message, but no real news. Jim made a point to answer, but then the cards stopped coming." She shrugged. "Until– I think it was in the early sixties–he wrote from San Diego. By then he was clean and sober, chaplain in a rehab facility. He'd even married again. I answered that one myself. You know, with congratulations. On the new marriage, and reclaiming his life. Didn't last long, though. Ten years later his wife wrote that he'd died. A CA of some sort, very quick."

"I remember you told me. Didn't know how you felt about it, though."

Anna shrugged, turned up the collar of her robe against a damp, rain-smelling breeze from the window. "Just sad mainly. When he and the family came to visit, I got upset with myself for not having seen what sort of man he was before. Probably because the uniform reminded me of Dan. But when Buddy fell, it knocked all that out of me. Well, at least in the end, he got his life back. And I like to think he found love again. When she answered my condolence note, his new wife she sounded nice, nothing like that awful Lynette. So I guess he got it right the second time. I can only hope."

Margie yawned and rose unsteadily. "Do you ever wonder how things would've turned out if you hadn't come back to Jim after the war? If you'd run off with Mark instead?"

"No," Anna said without hesitation. "That was never an issue. I was really attracted to him, but not seriously tempted. To end up with anyone but Jim, I mean. I guess too many people were praying to keep me safe."

"Oh Anna. The Lord's always had his hand on you."

She sent her a startled glance. Not a characteristic Margie remark. But as the years piled up, even a confirmed hedonist might begin to view life through stained glass lenses. "The Lord has his hand on all of us. You just noticed me because Dad was a priest."

Margie yawned again, switched off the lamp beside the sofa. "Mmm, maybe. Well, anyway, I'm about to pee my pants. So I'll see you in the morning." Wobbling, she headed toward her door. "Good night, Anna. Sleep tight."

"Same to you, Margie."

But as she went to her own room, she wondered what morning would hold. Would they both rise and greet each other as usual? Or would one of them face a rerun of what had happened to Jim? At some point after she'd kissed him on Halloween night, 1982, and the dawn of All Saints' Day, he'd silently transitioned from his pain-wracked, barely-functioning body to the one of light promised in funeral liturgies. When she'd woken to find him lifeless and cool, she'd known instantly that he was gone. Bereft, weeping, she'd held him for an hour before she'd finally left the bed, covered him with the sheet, then made the calls that had brought the doctor, the undertaker, the priest at All Saints', and eventually, her distant children. At no point was she surprised, however, except that he'd left without warning or drama: at seventy-seven, he'd already lived longer than most post-polios. She liked to attribute that unusual longevity to her refusal to consign him to a nursing home.

Years before, when he'd finally surrendered to the wheelchair, he'd researched the local facilities, recommended one in Camden. Instead she'd hired a practical nurse to help with bathing, dressing and getting him in and out of the car when they went places he could still access, like church and the library.

By then, he'd been retired from practice for twenty years; they'd sold the house on the island and built this compact cottage atop a hill in East Point. The large central room was open to a big, bright kitchen, with bedrooms and baths on either side. Because of his condition, they'd designed it with ramps instead of steps, grab bars in the showers, high toilets and door frames wide enough for a wheelchair. Now, a perfect place for her and Margie to live out their golden years.

So far their handicaps were minor– arthritic joints, unpredictable digestive processes, occasional mental fogs, diminishing stamina. That was a huge one. Still, they'd agreed if they made it to ninety, they'd move to a new Continuing Care Retirement Community in Rockhampton. Mainly to spare each other the rigors of caregiving. Or even worse, the solitary life after the other had gone on.

When she'd turned out the bedside lamp, she drew the comforter up to her chin and whispered the usual prayers for Jim and everyone else she now regarded as angels: Dan and the baby. Her parents. Mark and Buddy. Jean, Lorraine and Cleve Cropper. Tom Mullen, and only the year before, Father Luke Salaunas. Next she named those still living, starting with Jamie, his wife and son; Grace, the daughter she and Jim had had in 1949, and her husband and children.

And dotty old Alex Cropper, still chasing skirts but in the dementia unit at the county nursing home. Finally, though she didn't know which category he belonged in, she remembered Johann Himmelreich, who'd settled with relatives in Germany after Lorraine died.

As she named them all, she wondered who Margie prayed for, if anyone. She and Tom hadn't had children, so after he died, she'd married the pediatrician she'd worked for since 1946. Nice while it lasted—until he died and his adult kids eased her out of the mini-mansion on the bay. She couldn't imagine Margie praying for them, except to invoke divine retribution.

It was then she'd approached Anna about living together. Her initial instinct had been to offer to share the cottage. First, though, she wanted her children's approval. "Now Mother," Grace had assured her, "why don't you move in with me and Frank? We have plenty of room. And we'd love to have you."

"Sweet of you, dear, but I couldn't have stood living with my mother. So I think I'll see how it works with Margie." The truth was, she wasn't terribly fond of Frank Foster or his kids from a previous marriage. Besides, Grace was in a family practice in a dreary upstate New Hampshire town, and as busy with her patients as Jim had been with his. Frank, a pharmacist, was so short on small talk she couldn't imagine spending more than an hour a month —certainly not the rest of her life–in his company. The one bright spot was their daughter, Jeannie, but she was in grad school at Berkeley studying some arcane form of physics Anna had never heard of.

Jamie and his wife had issued a similar invitation, which tempted her somewhat more, except that they lived in Delaware. Ruth was a gentle Quaker— poet, musician and psychotherapist —who'd married Jamie while he was teaching Philosophy at the University of Pennsylvania, then encouraged him when he heeded a call to the priesthood at forty-five. They had one son; though named for Anna's father, he chose to be called neither Thomas nor Cranmer, but Todd. A better name, he said, for an aspiring actor, though so far Hollywood recognized him only as a bit player. He was a diligent grandson, however, but his yearly visits left no Anna with no doubts that he was gay. Flamingly so.

Fortunately her mother had died before she caught on, and her father was long gone by then too. He'd lived long enough to see ten-year-old Jamie as an acolyte at All Saints', but missed the rest of his journey to the priesthood. Not a direct route, though; life got in his way–college, a tour of Navy duty, the academic world, then Ruth and Todd–before the Spirit finally caught him again. Now twelve years into the new vocation, he was gradually restoring a neglected country church outside Wilmington. That he was so joyously following in her father's steps was her greatest source of joy and pride, tinged only slightly with regret that he wasn't closer geographically.

But that was how the world worked, wasn't it? Children moved into your life, filled it to overflowing, then slowly drifted into their own orbits, leaving a pervasive silence where there'd previously been noise and energy and purpose. At times this truth saddened her, but only briefly and superficially. All part of the Big Plan, she reminded herself.

Caught up in contemplation, she felt sleep receding. Another bane of old age, these long nights of wakefulness and anxiety that exacerbated the minor discomforts of joints and muscles. When the red neon of the nightstand clock blinked 1:00, she went to the kitchen to make a soporific Jim had invented—a dollop of brandy in a cup of hot milk, with a little honey for sweetness.

Before she carried the mug to the bedroom, she swallowed two Advil PMs and grabbed her Book of Common Prayer from the desk. Under the comforter again, she turned to Daily Evening Prayer: Rite One. And heard her father's voice intoning the same words from the 1928 prayer book, a Sunday evening ritual for most of her childhood. Back then, as she'd sat fidgeting beside her mother on the parlor sofa, this liturgy had bored her. Now it was bread and wine for her soul.

When she came to the Collects, she read them in a low murmur guaranteed not to disturb Margie, though she slept through thunderstorms, hurricanes and even the occasional mild earthquake. Her favorites were "for Sundays", "for Aid against Perils," "for Protection", and finally one she loved to whisper when she stood on the shores of sleep– "for the Presence of Christ."

Lord Jesus, stay with us, for evening is at hand, and the day is past; be our companion in the way, kindle our hearts, and awaken hope, that we may know thee as thou art revealed in Scripture and the breaking of bread. Grant this for the sake of thy love. Amen.

When she'd finished reading, the mug was empty, and she was too drowsy to do more than switch off the lamp. Snuggling into the covers, she had a sense of wrapping herself in recollections of the saints she'd known while they were still merely human. As the *All Saints' Day Hymn* put it: *We feebly struggle, they in glory shine.*

So here she was, still continuing her own feeble struggle to stay alive. Not because she expected her circumstances to improve, but because that was what you did, no matter what. Just kept hanging on, trying to survive as long as you could. Like the men in the sea after Indy had gone down–surviving, hanging on, waiting for the PBY that had come too late for most of them. They'd expected to be rescued. What was she waiting for?

Darkness gradually stilled the useless speculation. Peaceful, silent darkness. Until the old nightmare coalesced again around the edges. It had begun while she was still on *Compassion*, just after *Indianapolis* had been sunk. Once she'd expected psychotherapy to chase it, yet here it was again. Always the same—she was looking down on all those men in the water, not from a plane, somehow flying on her own power, or maybe just floating. Those below were waving up, calling for help, paddling, splashing, some in small rafts, some in orange life vests. Among them, Bobby McWherter's desperate face always stood out. But there was nothing she could do for him or any of the others. Except tell them she was praying the Lord would soon raise them from this watery hell. This feeble promise was all she had to offer; its inadequacy always awoke her sobbing with ancient sorrow.

This time, something felt different. She saw Bobby right away, but not only was he smiling, nothing else was the same. For one thing, this was not the shark-infested midnight sea of the other dream, but a sun-spangled tropical lagoon, layered turquoise and lapis and aquamarine , like Ulithi atoll. And this time she wasn't above, but with them in the water, immersed yet buoyant and warm. And those with Bobby weren't nameless drowning sailors, but loved ones she'd just visualized–Dan Donovan, and Jean Cropper and Buddy Whitmore and Mark, her parents and Lorraine and Cleve and Luke and Kathryn Visser, and Jim, of course, along with patients and others she'd almost forgotten. Nor were their faces desperate, but peaceful, even joyous.

As she regarded this group, Jim came forward, approaching with strong, confident steps and outstretched arms that folded her to him as if they hadn't been apart for all those years. She wanted to ask what was happening, but then she noticed the others were heading toward a plane moored alongside a sand spit. A big silver Clipper, with four engines and top-mounted wings, just like the one she'd flown from San Francisco to Pearl Harbor in 1944, except shiny and glistening, as if fresh off the Boeing assembly line.

Jim's kiss was warm and sweet. "Come on, Anna. We need to board."

More curious than ever, she clasped his hand and let him lead her toward the others. Now the water was so shallow they could step through the big hatch into the hull without a ladder.

"But where are we going?"

His smile was the gentle, fond one she'd missed the past twenty-five years. "Wherever you want , dear. It's up to you."

She was about to ask more when she realized he was walking effortlessly, without cane or crutch, as she'd never seen him do in life. And he was young again, about the age she'd first met him. His face was smooth and unlined, his spine no longer stooped, and his voice had the old lilt.

By the time they reached the plane, everyone else had boarded. As soon as they were inside, someone slid the hatch closed. In the dimness, Jim led her toward a pair of empty seats, then motioned her to precede him so she could sit by the window. "Because I know you like to watch the takeoff."

As she settled herself into the seat, she remembered they'd never flown anywhere together. So how did he know? For a while when the children were young, they'd talked of flying down to Florida. But before they could make plans, his parents had died when their car spun out of control and landed upside down in an Everglades canal. So how did he know this about her?

She smiled. Of course, this was a dream, and anything was possible in dreams. Including the convenience and comfort of this aircraft: there were no seat belts to buckle, just wide luxurious chairs better than first class, and no tinny voice over the horn welcoming them to these friendly skies. Nor any perky flight attendants demonstrating oxygen masks or pointing out escape hatches. And no noise. In fact, before she ever felt the motion, they were skimming over the water, soundlessly, not at all like that other Clipper's takeoff from San Francisco Bay with all four engines screaming overhead. Smoothly, silently, this plane rose, circling over land as colorful as a patchwork quilt.

She stared down until she could no longer see it, but with no sense of having left anything behind. After all, she was with Jim again, and all those others she'd loved and lost. Release and peace crept into her, as if life was beginning to take shape after so many years when she'd merely endured it.

Until new curiosity began to chew at her. She turned to him again. "Now. Tell me where we're really going."

He chuckled. "Darling, it's going to be more amazing than you ever dreamed. Still, it'll feel more like home than any place you ever lived."

As she puzzled over his words, a tiny worm of fear tunneled into her consciousness. She took a deep breath and bit her lip. "But what about the others? Like Margie? And the kids? Aren't they coming?"

"Don't worry, dear. They'll be along soon enough. Meanwhile, you won't miss the kids. See, your other two will be there."

"My other two? What do you mean, *two?* I only lost one."

"Your son with Dan, of course." He closed his eyes, regret momentarily darkening his features. "The other…well, she's the daughter you and I would have had sixty years ago. If I hadn't insisted on termination."

Her eyes misted; it was all she could do to nod silently.

"I've never given her a name. I thought we should do that together."

Another nod; she swallowed hard. Old, old pain clutched her. But only briefly.

"So you see," Jim went on. "This is the start of a great adventure. You're going to love it."

A great adventure? With her two lost children? Lines from another hymn reverberated through her mind: *The night is gone;/ And with the morn, those angel faces smile / Which I have loved long since, and lost awhile. . . .*

And then she knew. Not precisely or specifically, but

generally where they were bound, almost as she'd known flying across the Pacific in 1944 that their destination was Brisbane, Australia, and the hospital ship, and that great adventure. Could this one be even greater?

Even without knowing more, she began to relax, to feel warm and light, and interested in whatever was happening. Younger, energized, animated. Even her hands were no longer bony and age-spotted, but silky, white and smooth. Like those in magazine ads from the old days, when suitors apparently noticed pampered hands before anything else about a potential wife.

"Oh my," she breathed as the certainty swelled and became more viable. "Both lost children. But whose wife will I be? Yours or Dan's?"

"Now dear. Don't think in terms of marriage as we knew it. Remember what Jesus told the Sadducees in Matthew 22?"

"Oh, you mean about the woman who'd been married to seven brothers?" He nodded and she went on. "That's right. He said there was no marriage in the resurrection. Because everyone would be like the angels in heaven. And she'd be married to none of them. So, is that what I'll be...nobody's wife?"

He clasped her hand between both of his. "Something like that."

More questions poked up from the part of her mind that hadn't yet been caught up in the flow of this dream, or whatever it was. "Oh my," she said again as the biggest question of all, yet the one of least consequence, swirled into her consciousness. She and Jim had even joked about it during his dried-up final years. Now, feeling somehow irreverent, she plunged into it anyway. "Does that mean there's no sex where we're going either, because spiritual bodies can't lust?"

He grinned, squeezed her hand. "I knew you'd ask that."

"You wondered yourself, remember? So is there?"

He laughed. "Let's just say you won't be disappointed with any aspect of the new life."

The ambiguity of the answer was frustrating. Sighing, she turned to the window again. The ground was no longer in sight, only clouds piled like whipped cream, reflecting golden light onto Jim's face. "Well, I don't understand anything that's going on," she said, glancing at the seats behind them, "but I'll take your word for it." And then, directly behind, she saw them– her mother and father, both so young she barely recognized them, and smiling with a joy she'd never seen before, even on her father. In fact, everyone was smiling, like members of a club on a charter flight to welcome her to their group.

As she took it all in, suddenly she realized that directly across the aisle, Dan Donovan was watching her with the same half-smile she'd observed on the first day–knowing, wise, vaguely impudent. As if he'd known even then what they'd eventually become to each other. Now, in dress blues with the Submarine Force dolphins on his chest, his skin was ruddy, touched with the shadow of beard, his eyes the same bright blue that had drawn her to him that spring day in 1941 when she'd met him as her patient.   And every bit as handsome as he was in the photo she'd carried around all these years. So real, so close, she could almost smell the diesel fumes that had always permeated his uniform.

As she returned his gaze, her heart went into a crazy gallop. Whispering, "Dear Lord," she slid her hand from Jim's clasp. Silly, she thought; If there was no marriage in this new life, there'd be no jealousy either, would there? So Jim would understand her visceral reaction to Dan's unexpected presence. After all, his was the only unfinished story from her life. The only one with potential still unexplored; the one amputated by telegrams announcing the cruel realities of World War II. And the only significant presence with whom she'd had just a beginning, a few promising months, then the sudden end. No middle years, no ordinary time, no exploration of what might have been. Even worse, no chance to know what had become of him.

The feeling that warmed her now was an old friend, nearly forgotten. But this longing was untarnished by the dark foreboding that had haunted her during their short life together. This felt pure. And fresh. And entirely possible.

Sitting straighter, she glanced around again. Dear to her, all those angel faces. Especially Jim's and her parents'. But none more so than Dan's, almost as she'd seen him from the train window in Oakland, in March, 1943. That day the anguish of their last parting had dulled his eyes, and filled hers with tears. Now, the separations were behind them. So, apparently, was all sorrow.

The smile that touched her lips arose from a startling new perception of possibilities. Had Jim noticed? She was about to look at him, when Dan turned on one of the eye-crinkling, deeply- dimpled grins that had sent warmth pulsing through her even when she couldn't stand his boorish behavior, his cocky self-assurance, his nasally Brooklyn accent, his rude manners.

Now the slow wink her gave her could have passed for suggestive, at least in an earthly setting.

Jolted anew, she took a deep breath and forced her gaze back to Jim's. "Gosh. This is all so interesting. I can hardly wait for the rest of it."

His fingertips were light on her hand. "Darling," he said, "you ain't seen nothing thing yet."

She smiled, murmured, "Yes, I'm sure of that," and glanced back at Dan. The familiar half- smile lingered, and he winked again. Then slowly nodded, as if answering a question she hadn't yet asked. As if agreeing to anything she wanted.

What would that be? For a start, to find out what had happened to *Wolf Fish* in June, 1943, that had caused the Navy to declare it "missing with all hands". After that, though,....what? She had no idea. But possibilities vibrated in every fiber of her being. Trembling with them, she stared out the window at the tall clouds sailing past, like a sky full of clipper ships. And wondered, if she fell asleep, would she awaken here in this plane, with Dan and Jim and the others? Or would she be back in her own bed, in the cottage in East Point, Maine, with only Margie nearby, and another tedious day in their worn-out bodies?

No matter; she already sensed what was coming, whenever it came. And that was all she needed to know. Some things you had to take on faith. In this case, the church's promise of an ultimate reunion with loved ones. She'd been a true believer from birth, yet it had never offered the comfort she needed when she'd lost the baby, and Dan, and in all the tragedies since–too vague, too flimsy, like a band-aid across the raw slash of loss. But here was proof, absolute, final proof.

Glancing covertly past Jim at Dan again, she returned his smile. And made a mental note to tell her father that he'd been right about the Lord being in charge of absolutely everything. Thanks be to God, he'd been right all along.

Why had she ever doubted?

–The End–

ABOUT JOAN LA BLANC

Born in 1929, Joan Hartzel La Blanc discovered the joy of fiction writing during her childhood in Philadelphia. While she set this addiction aside to raise four children, it later enabled her to survive marriages to two career Navy men and one with Alzheimer's Disease. Now, in her "golden years", it continues to offer romance, travel, and the adventures of an international spy without the associated dangers. After a "real" career as a PR and non-fiction writer, she crafts circumspect prose for church publications between visits to the various parallel universes that still provide inspiration and creative fulfillment.

THE ANNA DONOVAN NOVELS

ORDINARY ANGELS is the concluding work in a series of four World War II-era novels about young Anna Donovan. The first, INNOCENCE OF ANGELS, recounts her romance and short-lived marriage to submarine officer, Dan Donovan. The second, MINISTRY OF ANGELS follows a newly-widowed Anna to a Maine coastal island where she expects to be able to forget her losses. The third, ODYSSEY OF ANGELS, takes her deep into the hell of the Pacific War as an ensign nurse aboard USS *Compassion,* a Navy hospital ship in the final year of the conflict. ORDINARY ANGELS follows her return to civilian life, a new marriage, and eventually, a measure of peace. All are available from Northampton House Press in both ebook and paper formats.

Northampton House Press

Northampton House publishes carefully selected fiction, lifestyle nonfiction, memoir, and poetry. Our logo represents the muse Polyhymnia. Our mission is to discover great new writers and help them springboard into fame. See our list at www.northampton-house.com, or Like us on Facebook – "Northampton House Press" – for more innovative works from brilliant new writers.

www.ingramcontent.com/pod-product-compliance
Lightning Source LLC
Chambersburg PA
CBHW071053250626
47159CB00002B/458